ENOUGH

ENOUGH

KIMIA ESLAH

Roseway Publishing
an imprint of Fernwood Publishing
Halifax & Winnipeg

Development editing: Fazeela Jiwa
Copyediting: Amber Riaz
Text design: Brenda Conroy
Cover design: Zainab's Echo
Printed and bound in the UK

Published by Roseway Publishing
an imprint of Fernwood Publishing
2970 Oxford Street, Halifax, Nova Scotia, B3L 2W4
and 748 Broadway Avenue, Winnipeg, Manitoba, R3G 0X3
www.fernwoodpublishing.ca/roseway

Fernwood Publishing Company Limited gratefully acknowledges the financial support of the Government of Canada through the Canada Book Fund and the Canada Council for the Arts. We acknowledge the Province of Manitoba for support through the Manitoba Publishers Marketing Assistance Program and the Book Publishing Tax Credit. We acknowledge the Nova Scotia Department of Communities, Culture and Heritage for support through the Publishers Assistance Fund.

Library and Archives Canada Cataloguing in Publication

Title: Enough / Kimia Eslah.
Names: Eslah, Kimia, 1979- author.
Identifiers: Canadiana (print) 20230461085 | Canadiana (ebook) 20230461093 | ISBN 9781773636351
(softcover) | ISBN 9781773636504 (EPUB)
Subjects: LCGFT: Novels.
Classification: LCC PS8609.S45 E56 2023 | DDC C813/.6—dc23

To Andrew,

this is some first date. I'm impressed.

Chapter 1

Monday Morning, May 14, 2018

"Oh, so you're not the caterer?" the receptionist asked again, staring at Sameera reprovingly from under her long false eyelashes. "Are you sure?"

Seeing herself through the eyes of other people had always been a corrosive, unhealthy experience. She was not a courier, someone's nanny, or any other stereotype concocted to explain the presence of a Brown woman in a corporate setting. Despite the laptop bag slung over her right shoulder and the hipster couture she favoured, her colleagues never thought that she could be — was — their superior.

Sameera Jahani chose her own lens now — an avant-garde millennial, an Iranian Canadian, bold in speech and style. Her wild mane of black hair floated about her unadorned face. Her black eyes shone from under her bushy brows. Her muscular thighs filled out her red palazzos and her underarm hair peeked out from the capped sleeves of her black silk shirt. Sameera was an enterprising marketer, a creative genius, a trendsetter with an impressive number of online followers. But on this day, her first day as manager of the seven-person Web and Digital Communications team at Toronto City Hall, Sameera had reached a roadblock.

"Not the caterer," Sameera repeated tersely, losing the smile she had adopted during her first response. She looked over the young receptionist's head, through the glass security doors that divided the beige waiting room from the bustling administrative offices, and willed her liaison to appear. Seated at a beige desk that matched the carpet and the paint, the receptionist clicked on her keyboard importantly. To avoid grimacing at this gatekeeper, Sameera averted her gaze, examining the collection of home décor lined up on the desk. White-painted wood cutouts of inspirational words flanked portraits of the receptionist and a polished man, both dressed in matching white and blue outfits, in cinematic poses outdoors. *Ugh. How pedestrian*, Sameera decided.

The receptionist stopped typing and continued reproachfully, "Okay, see I expected the caterer to appear right about now and—"

"Not. The. Caterer. Really. Listen, Howard Crawley's assistant is supposed to meet me here …." Sameera paused to look at her watch, "… right now. Can you please message his assistant?"

As usual, Sameera's tactlessness slowed her progress. The receptionist leaned back slowly and narrowed her eyes, exuding resentment at being rushed. She seemed to be assessing Sameera's intentions, especially pertaining to Howard Crawley, city manager and overseer of all city employees — tens of thousands of civil servants.

Louder and more slowly than necessary, the receptionist said, "If you're applying for a job, you have to do it online. On the website. He doesn't meet with walk-ins."

Pursing her lips and stifling a groan, Sameera turned away from the receptionist and walked the couple of steps to reach a corner of her beige purgatory. She would message Diane Waverly, the human resources representative whose fifth-floor office she had left minutes earlier after a cumbersome briefing on corporate and personnel policies. Diane had assured her that Howard Crawley's assistant would receive Sameera at the reception desk on the tenth floor. Sameera kicked herself for not having requested the assistant's name or phone number. Now, she was at the mercy of the receptionist-cum-surly-gatekeeper, who first ignored her arrival at the desk, then confused her for a caterer, and was now questioning her motives for being there. *Where is the assistant? This is so unprofessional.*

Sameera composed a succinct but neutral message to Diane,

requesting contact information for Howard Crawley's assistant. There was no use complaining about the obstinate receptionist to Diane since most white people disregarded or denied the microaggressions Sameera recognized.

"Excuse me. This area is designated for ..." the receptionist started. When Sameera did not turn to face her, the woman continued in a jarring soprano, "Excuse me!"

Under the pretence of being on a call, Sameera held her phone to her ear, and then motioned to the phone with her forefinger to silence the receptionist. The woman's interjections subsided but Sameera sensed that she was being closely observed. She continued her charade by oscillating her gaze and nodding sombrely, hoping Diane would respond to her message before the receptionist called for a security escort. *First, the receptionist's an asshole, then the assistant's a no show, and now the HR rep's deserted me. This is not looking good.*

The room felt increasingly warm. Beads of sweat formed under her arms, and Sameera lifted her elbows to avoid causing stains on her silk shirt. She cursed the new organic deodorant she was wearing, having recently given up her antiperspirant in an attempt to accept her musk.

To dampen her worst fear — she'd made another dire career move — Sameera reminded herself that she had accepted a position under one of the most influential people in the public sector, Mr. Howard Crawley. A career bureaucrat at the City of Toronto who had held his current position as city manager for seventeen years, Howard Crawley had wealth, influence, and a trailblazer's reputation for modernizing public programs. This job was her opportunity to propel her marketing career in the public sector. After wasting all that precious time and energy on her last job — a dead-end pet project of a wealthy visionary — Sameera was dedicated to progress at full throttle. She'd learned the hard way that the leadership of an organization sets the tone and pace of its progress, and from her research on Howard Crawley, she was filled with hope for her professional future. A graduate of the prestigious Rotman School of Management and a member of the exclusive York Golf Club, Howard Crawley was an ambitious man who was well-connected to the cohort of powerful decision-makers in the city. Sameera daydreamed about becoming his indispensable associate.

A brown-clad courier arrived with a loaded dolly, occupying the receptionist momentarily.

Stay focused, Sameera coached herself as she composed another message to Diane Waverly, one tinged with greater urgency, all the while keeping her elbows up to dry out her underarms. *Things don't always go smoothly but they can work out all the same.*

Sameera recalled her uneasy job interview during which Mr. Crawley barely looked up from his phone, even when she mentioned his achievements. The human resource staffers ran the show. Given the city manager's disinterest, Sameera was surprised to receive the job offer. *They chose me. I belong here.*

"Ms. Jahani?" a voice asked.

Sameera turned toward the glass-door entrance of the administrative offices to face a remarkable middle-aged woman of colour, dressed in a flattering pantsuit and carrying a slim laptop.

"I am Faiza Hosseini," she said with a friendly smile and an outstretched hand, nails flawlessly manicured. "It is nice to meet you."

Sameera noted her caramel skin, botoxed lips, breezy blowout, and the hint of a Middle Eastern accent. Ms. Hosseini was the archetypical manifestation of the chic Iranian woman, one inspired by Iranian communities in Los Angeles and achieved through cosmetics and surgery.

"*Salaam, az didane shoma khoshhalam*. Hello, it is a pleasure to meet you," Sameera replied in Farsi and offered her hand with confidence. Since she had stopped biting her nails, she'd started to enjoy handshakes.

"*Eh! Irani ast-te.* Oh! You're Iranian," Faiza Hosseini said with genuine surprise, taking Sameera's hand and squeezing it gently, rather than shaking it.

Sameera had recently resolved to declare her ethnicity upon first contact with other Iranians to honour her roots. She was breaking another bad habit of whitewashing her identity. She tried to live authentically, leveraging her experience to connect with others — as an Iranian, a woman of colour, an urban queer, and a technophile.

"*Bale*, yes," Sameera said, holding herself erect, noticing she felt a tad diminished by Faiza Hosseini's conventional beauty.

Her collective of aunts and female cousins — cosmopolitan Iranians who had immigrated to Toronto in adulthood — had always been irked by Sameera's alternative style. The wiry hairs on her legs, the downy hairs above her upper lip, and the bushy hairs that framed her brow were an affront to their hairless sensibilities. These preened and polished women supported a woman's right to higher education, voting, and abortion, but feminism be damned if it meant Sameera Jahani was going to look like *yeh maimoon*, an ape.

"*Bah bah, khosh amadeed.* Wonderful, welcome," Faiza said with a radiant smile. "For transparency, let's use English."

Sameera noticed that the receptionist was unabashedly staring at them, her brows furrowed and her lips pursed with impatience.

Turning to the receptionist, Faiza said pleasingly, "Sheila, if Howard or Shirley ask, Ms. Jahani is with me."

Sameera watched from the corner of her eye as Sheila responded with a shrug and then returned to swiping on her phone. The disdainful gesture agitated Sameera, and she looked at the floor to avoid revealing her displeasure — and to allow Faiza Hosseini to save face. Faiza swiped her security badge at the glass doors, and held one open for Sameera. As Sameera stepped into a narrow grey hallway, devoid of decoration, she heard Faiza remind Sheila about a birthday celebration that afternoon.

"I bought cupcakes from Bébé," Faiza mentioned. "It'll be in conference room 4."

"Yeah, I'll be there," Sheila said, her icy tone warming a few degrees.

"Wouldn't be the same without you," Faiza added and let the glass door close behind her.

Sameera recognized the dicey exchange between Sheila and Faiza. It was as familiar as it was unavoidable and infuriating. Sheila's dismissiveness revealed her perception of power over Faiza despite their jobs. Resentful white people concerned Sameera, and she resolved to keep a distance from power-tripping Sheila.

With her trendy leather roll-top bag over one shoulder, Sameera followed Faiza through a maze of cooled hallways, narrow paths that wound around the core of the building. The conference rooms and storage spaces were nestled in the centre on her left, and every few metres, a gap on the right revealed a set of spacious cubicles pressed against the floor-to-ceiling windows of the modern structure.

"I didn't mean to cause confusion," Sameera explained, half a step behind Faiza to allow room for passersby. "I wanted to contact you when I got here but HR didn't give me your info."

"Oh, no need to worry about that," Faiza answered breezily over her shoulder. "Howard's in a last-minute meeting. His assistant messaged me because she had to attend, too."

"Sorry, I thought you were his assistant," Sameera said, confused. "So, which team do you work with?"

"I lead Program Support," Faiza said, and then paused to point out the location of the washrooms. "There are others but this one's the closest. Anyway, I've worked with nearly every team in City Hall."

Faiza Hosseini is a director. She reports directly to the CM. Why was the director of a core team onboarding a new manager? Was it related to their shared ethnicity? Whatever the reason for the match up, Sameera recognized the networking opportunity and hoped that Faiza did not judge her negatively for her bare face and natural hair, as did her mother and aunts.

"Wow, that's great. How long have you worked here?" Sameera asked, trying to sound more curious than calculating.

"Oh … coming on seven years, soon," Faiza said with a smile but Sameera thought she heard a hint of fatigue. *Or is that agitation?*

"Congratulations," Sameera replied. "I'm surprised you have the time to take me around like this."

"We all try to help out," Faiza said, stopping as a group approached.

The young quartet carried laptops and notebooks, and Sameera assumed they were heading to a meeting. They greeted Faiza with genuine smiles and she introduced Sameera as the new manager of the Web and Digital Communications team. The four business analysts welcomed her to City Hall, and then one asked Faiza about the birthday gathering.

"Yes, in conference room 4. At two o'clock," Faiza confirmed.

"I heard you ordered cupcakes," one colleague probed in a singsong voice.

"She did," replied his grinning coworker. "I saw the Bébé box in the fridge." To Faiza, he said, "You're such a good office mom."

"Thank you," Faiza said with a gracious smile. "It is my pleasure. I'll join the meeting in half an hour."

Sameera remained composed but she felt disgusted by the behaviour of the thirty-somethings who treated the senior bureaucrat like a matron. *Office mom? Who says that?!*

"And here is Howard's office," Faiza said as they approached the spacious glassed-in room in the corner. "His assistant, Shirley, won't be back for a bit, so we can tour the place."

"Okay, thank you," Sameera said amiably, though she would have happily set to work instead. The ordeal with the receptionist had drained her enthusiasm to meet anyone else that morning.

* * *

Staring out her tenth-floor office window on Monday morning, Faiza Hosseini acknowledged to herself that she was starving. It seemed to her she had spent her life starving. Her empty grumbling stomach, the accompanying headaches, and fatigue made her question her latest diet but she did not have an alternative way to shed the last ten pounds to reach her ideal weight.

All of the diets — the wheat-grass shots, the no-carb all-protein regime, drinking her meals, fasting all day, or eating only once before 8:00 — had worked to some extent. She'd even lengthened her daily hour-long exercise sessions. Still, the scale refused to budge and Faiza was growing desperate.

Whenever she was at home, her mother insisted that Faiza eat more at mealtime, infuriating her because her mother was also the first to bring attention to the slightest weight gain. Faiza's husband, Robert, insisted that she was as beautiful as the day they had met, eight years earlier in a dentist's office. *Nonsense. He's not the same. I'm not, either. No use pretending.*

She dampened her hunger with a series of deep inhalations, and then resumed working on an upcoming presentation to upper management; it was an equity, diversity, and inclusion — EDI — initiative she had authored on Howard's behalf. The afternoon sunshine across her cluttered desk reminded her of time lost touring the new hire that morning. *Howard owes me another one.* She counselled herself to think positively about her contributions to City Hall, even if an increasing number of her contributions were Howard Crawley's duties — tasks that he either did not want to or could not complete himself, including the presentation at hand.

City Council had tasked Howard to identify key marketing initiatives to improve engagement with marginalized communities in the City of Toronto. Howard had delegated the task to Faiza, claiming that public engagement was her forte. She had seen through his flattery, but she had also perceived an opportunity to demonstrate her prowess directly to upper management, a chance to step out of Howard's shadow. The presentation slides — hours of research and analysis — stared back at her. *Come on, just a few more changes. It's almost finished.*

She had arrived two hours earlier than usual in the hopes of completing the presentation, which was scheduled to be delivered at the end of the week. At dawn, when she emerged from her walk-in closet dressed immaculately, her hair straightened and her makeup perfected, Robert had woken briefly to kiss her goodbye. He wished her luck on her presentation, and then burrowed his bald head and long limbs under the duvet for another hour of sleep. Now in his late fifties, Robert had reached the top of the corporate ladder by becoming an executive at a plastics manufacturer, and he was content to reach work at nine o'clock and leave at five, counting down the years to retirement.

Faiza's 69-year-old mother had been sipping weak tea, watching the sunrise, perched on a kitchen stool by the window overlooking the Scarborough Bluffs and Lake Ontario. The two women closely resembled each other, especially in the controlled way they carried themselves. That morning, they had chatted briefly, in whispers. Her mother, called Bibi by her loved ones, had relayed news about Faiza's successful older brother — Firouz, who lived and worked in Boston — and about his two daughters, who were both promising engineering students at MIT — the Massachusetts Institute of Technology as her mother was so fond of saying. Faiza had not admonished her mother for aggrandizing Firouz's most recent accomplishments — a larger mansion and an extended holiday overseas — but she had refrained only to keep from prolonging their conversation, which would have negated her early morning start and made her reach work in a bad mood. Instead, she'd kissed Bibi goodbye and promised to arrive home in time to help with dinner, immediately chiding herself for making such a promise since she would most certainly be delayed at work.

A soft knock on her office door interrupted her ruminations, and she called for the person to enter. Voula Stavros, director of the Customer Services team, slid into Faiza's office, quietly closed the door, and leaned against it. *She always knows how to slim her waistline. I should get a skirt like that.* With a manicured thumbnail gently nested between her front teeth and a broad smile that clearly guarded some juicy secret, Voula eyed Faiza. Faiza smiled back, ignoring her anxiety and hunger pains.

"Hi, I know you're plugging away at that presentation but I ..." Voula said, inching forward, gripping her own elbows as if to keep from bursting. "Well, it seems that Howard has been up to something."

Oh, dear god. What now?! Like a disappointed parent, Faiza groaned and tilted her head back, and Voula burst out laughing. Over the years, Howard's unsavoury behaviour had been at the root of several personnel issues. His domineering and opinionated attitude, which upper management considered a strength, aggravated personnel and resulted in resignations and long-term leaves of absence.

"What has he done now?" Faiza asked tentatively, rolling her eyes and resting her arms in her lap.

"Well, it seems that Howard has been pressuring HR to create a new tier of management, a level between his and ours, like an assistant city manager," Voula divulged, tucking her skirt underneath as she settled into one of the two seats placed across the desk from Faiza.

Just then, there was another knock at the door. Faiza smiled apologetically at Voula, and then called out, "Come in."

Voula toyed with her phone while Faiza advised a harried manager on how to handle an uncooperative vendor. Grateful for Faiza's suggestions and supportive attitude, the manager left minutes later, looking considerably less overwhelmed.

"Another level?" Faiza asked, slipping back to their conversation. "Since when?"

"Apparently, it's been in the works for some time, all hush hush," Voula said, crossing and re-crossing her legs in excitement. "I'm surprised you didn't know about it. I figured you would have told me, if you knew."

In disbelief, Faiza shook her head and stared off blankly. She had heard rumours about organizational changes but in an enterprise as large as the City of Toronto, there were always some changes pending in the name of progress.

"Well, Howard probably thought … well, he probably wanted to surprise you with the position," Voula pondered, leaning over the desk to perch her chin on her palm. "He can be such a control freak. I mean, it's your job nearly to a tee … well, the job you do for him, not the one on paper."

Faiza would have never tolerated such frank comments from her juniors or other directors, even though she sensed that the entire corporation perceived her as Howard's lackey. But Voula understood the challenges of furthering her career while reporting to a chauvinist bigot.

"How do you know the details?" Faiza asked, blinking back into the conversation.

"It's posted. Check the site," Voula said, waving her manicured finger at the computer screen. "They posted it this morning. I can't believe Howard hasn't mentioned it to you yet."

"He's been in with the higher-ups all morning," Faiza said over her shoulder as she turned to her computer screen and navigated to the job portal, scrolling through the recent postings.

"Lousy bastard, probably waiting for you to mention it," said Voula, nodding to herself. "Probably trying to get you to admit you've been looking at postings."

Faiza found the posting and skimmed the job description, the pay grade, and the qualifications. It was an impressive position, offering nearly twice Faiza's salary, and composed of the same executive responsibilities that Faiza had been performing on Howard's behalf for three years. The hunger pangs disappeared, as did Faiza's awareness of Voula's running commentary. She blinked at the screen and leaned in to re-read the qualifications. *This is it. It's mine.* The qualifications matched the bulleted lists on her resume, nearly line for line. *Finally, they realized how much sense this makes. For everyone.* She had never stated her rationale aloud to her superiors. Instead, she made a point to present herself as the perfect candidate for promotion. *I'm a known commodity. Intelligent. Beautiful. Driven. I make them look good.* She smiled as she pictured the pale and white-haired higher-ups flanking her for photos at media junkets; her brown eyes, beige skin, and long dark tresses offered a pleasing progressive face to the bureaucracy.

"Oh, and I met up with Amihan …." Voula let that piece of information hang in the air, waiting for Faiza to look her way.

When it registered, Faiza spun toward her, looking shocked and delighted. "You did?"

Nodding devilishly, Voula whispered, "For coffee. Well, she had tea. She took me to the observation deck, upstairs. It was nice, really nice. The view was gorgeous, and there's no one up there, well, almost. And … she asked me out." Voula bit her thumb, careful not to muss up her lipstick or nick her polish. "This Saturday, lunch. At High Park."

"That's wonderful Vee," Faiza said, sending air kisses. She knew that Voula had been waiting months for the demure auditor to notice her, biding her time, going on disappointing one-off dates. *So exhausting. I hope I'm never single again.*

"Thanks. I'll tell you all about it," Voula said, and then rethinking her words, she added with a smile, "Or, just the PG parts. Anyway, I have to run." She rose and excused herself. "I'm still hunting down that damned infrastructure report."

"I know, right?" Faiza agreed, throwing up her hands. "You'd think their reports were hidden treasure, that's how deep they bury them. Folders nested in folders nested in more folders."

Voula sighed and shrugged, "Oh, well." Then, her kittenish smile returned and she nodded at the screen, "Go on, then. I know you're dying to get into that."

Faiza grinned back, "Thanks for the heads up. I owe you one."

"One?!" Voula joked as she disappeared out the office door.

Faiza bit the corner of her lip as she perused the posting for her dream job, her chin propped on her hand and her mind racing. *This is it. Howard's finally come through.*

* * *

The minutes were ticking toward nine o'clock on Monday morning and Goldie Sheer was mentally trash-talking the woman in line ahead of her at City Hall. Exhaling, Goldie consciously moved her tongue from one side of her mouth to the other, her teeth clamped. All the while, she spun her phone in one hand and shifted her weight from one gleaming pink sneaker to another. *Fuckin' bullshit.*

This was Goldie's first day at her first job since graduating university, and the woman bent over the counter conferencing with the desk clerk was ruining it. All Goldie needed was for the clerk to announce her arrival to her new manager, Patricia Addington, so someone could collect her from the rotunda. *Shit's fuckin' stupid. Who uses the fuckin' phone? Fuckin' boomers!*

Goldie grew certain that the entirety of her three-month contract as a database administrator would be spent staring at the backside of a woman with nothing better to do than to hang out at the Information Desk like she was at a country club. Forget her aspiration to secure a full-time, permanent position with benefits. Forget her plan to be the perfect employee with all the right answers. Forget her trotting to a meeting, decorating her cubicle, or seeing a deposit in her bank account. The next three months were going to be spent in line, in the rotunda of City Hall, and Goldie would never raise enough money to move out of her parents' apartment. *Arrgh! Move, bitch!*

With one hand, she examined the texture of her long hair, ensuring her locks remained smooth — the result of an hour-long straightening session. In her other hand, she spun her phone faster between two finger pads and chewed visibly on her tongue. All the while, she considered how her life seemed to be perpetually on standby. She was waiting to be turned on, put to use. All of her plans to live independently, to pay her own way, and establish a career were on hold until she could secure a job with prospects. This opportunity was supposed to be her chance to start life as an employed adult, a unit independent of her parents and mercifully distanced from her two brothers. Yet, here in line, she was again on standby. *Bitch, move!*

The woman in line ahead of her, dressed in a cardigan that reached her knees and in slippers clearly intended for indoor use only, could not see Goldie's narrowed eyes or hear her tapping foot. Neither the woman nor the clerk seemed to notice or even care about Goldie's presence. In the reflection of a glass wall, Goldie occupied herself by reexamining her athleisure outfit: oversized cream shirt, black jacket, navy wide-legged pants, and pink Converse creps. She'd straightened her hair and applied her favourite set of blue eyelashes, though her mother declared she did not need the enhancement. She posted a close-up photo of her sapphire lashes online, and within seconds her friends commented she looked like the gorgeous boy beauty influencer @luisandres. The comments went a long way to lightening her mood.

When listening to the clerk's chuckles became unbearable, Goldie pressed forward.

"Excuse me," said Goldie to the clerk, sounding friendly and apologetic, and leaning to one side as if to side-step a great wall that had been concealing her.

The clerk glanced in her direction briefly but returned to her conversation with the cardigan-clad woman, who did not turn even in the slightest to Goldie's prompt. Agitated by the likelihood that she would arrive late on her first day at work, Goldie pressed forward with a little more force.

"I'm sorry to interrupt your conversation," Goldie said, still smiling but stepping directly next to the hunched figure to ensure that she interrupted the conversation.

The clerk, who seemed accustomed to interruptions, stared blankly at Goldie and waited for her to continue with her inquiry. The cardigan-clad woman, who remained hunched over the counter, languidly turned her head toward Goldie. She was not frowning or glaring at Goldie. In fact, the woman's face seemed frozen in a dispassionate state. The cold reception from both women intimidated Goldie and she tried to smile warmly. But before she could ask the clerk to ring Patricia Addington, the woman with her apathetic expression pointed to the sign mounted behind the clerk. It was a display, a directory of the public offices in the building.

"Social assistance is on the third floor," the woman offered matter-of-factly and restarted her conversation with the clerk.

Goldie was confused. She had not slept well the night before, waking every couple of hours to check the time, and her commute had been a half-hour longer than expected because of an obstruction on the subway track. Her anxiety about starting a new job was worsening with each passing minute, and now she felt befuddled by the hunched woman's instructions.

"What do you mean?" Goldie asked chirpily, trying to mask her agitation but the woman and clerk ignored her.

It occurred to Goldie that she had been dismissed, an experience familiar from being young in her household. She had been ejected from many conversations and denied re-entry due to her youthful righteousness and her lack of life experience. Usually, she walked away because she was too hurt to fight back. This time though, she had to press on. She was desperate to prove herself in this position and finally claim her status as a working adult.

"I need to ..." Goldie said with a quavering voice, leaning over the counter to reinject herself into their space and conversation. "I mean, can you please call up Patricia Addington? She's expecting me."

The clerk continued to stare blankly at Goldie even as she lazily lifted the receiver to make the call. Goldie smiled and nodded encouragingly at the clerk in the hopes of speeding her up.

"Don't call," the woman instructed the clerk.

Complying, the clerk put down the receiver and stared at Goldie, who turned wide-eyed to face the cardigan-clad woman. The script in Goldie's mind had already run out. She had expected the rudeness of the experience but she had not expected overt obstruction. Disoriented, Goldie stepped back and momentarily squeezed her eyes shut.

"What's your name?" asked the woman, stepping forward and grimacing at Goldie.

"Pardon? Why?" Goldie staggered mentally to grasp the shift in events.

She rose to the balls of her feet to look over the woman's shoulder, and she spotted the clerk engrossed in a magazine and disinterested in all else.

"Your name?" insisted the hunched woman, crossing her arms and positioning herself to block Goldie's access to the counter.

"Goldie," she replied, hoping to assuage her interrogator long enough to side-step her.

"No, it's not," sneered the hunched woman as she appraised Goldie from under her drooping lids.

Goldie opened her mouth but could not think of a mature responsive. While she was accustomed to certain reactions to her Iranian name, Golnuz, such as the untoward compliments or questions about its origins that caused her to cringe self-consciously, she was irked at being questioned about her nickname. Goldie had been her lifelong moniker, and there were plenty of famous Goldies, so there should be nothing to discuss, nothing to pronounce or spell out.

The woman continued to stare at Goldie, expectantly. "Your actual name?"

Goldie felt like being insolent, pretending not to understand her meaning, but she reserved this tactic for her parents, two people who didn't presume that she was an idiot when she feigned ignorance. With others, Goldie answered the implied questions. There was no benefit to acting aloof or looking inept in the presence of people who had already assumed you were an idiot.

"Golnuz Sheer," Goldie offered, touching her smooth hair for reassurance. "Nice to meet you," she added out of habit. Goldie glanced at her phone. She was ten minutes late on her first day. She glanced at the counter to find it void of the clerk and her heart sank.

"So, why did you say your name was Goldie?" the woman asked in a perturbed voice.

"It is," said Goldie, embarrassed by the stranger's probing. "Goldie's short for Golnuz."

"That's not the same," the woman muttered to herself, pulling her cardigan close.

This conversation is bizarre. This woman is too much. When Goldie spotted the clerk returning to the Information Desk, she quickly sidestepped the woman and rushed to the counter.

"Can you please call Patricia Addington and let her know I am here?" Goldie blurted out, gripping the edge of the counter to maintain her spot in the non-existent line.

The clerk sighed in response but she began to dial again.

"No need, Mary," the cardigan-clad woman declared, and Mary the clerk began to hang up the phone. "I'll take her to Patricia."

Goldie glanced back and forth between the two women but

neither looked at her. She felt like a child trying to interject herself in a conversation between adults.

"Do you work with Patricia Addington?" Goldie asked.

"Yes," said the woman in a voice that implied Goldie was simple. "She sent me down here to get you. Come on, you're late."

With a bored expression, the woman wrapped the cardigan about herself, turned, and shuffled toward the elevators. Goldie rushed to catch up, weaving through a group of professionals with lanyards and clipboards. At the elevators, the woman stood with her eyes focused on the elevator floor indicator.

"I'm sorry about the time but I wasn't late. I was in line behind you," Goldie explained.

"Don't worry," the woman replied, still staring at the indicator. "I won't mention it."

Goldie didn't want to make a bad impression by pressing the topic but she was confused about what had taken place. She probed, "Why did you tell me to go to social assistance?"

Just then, the elevator door opened and it emptied of civil servants and city residents. The woman stepped in without answering, and Goldie followed. A few others boarded the elevator and when the doors had closed, Goldie repeated her question.

"I didn't know you were the new database admin," the woman answered, not looking away from the floor indicators in the elevator.

"Oh," Goldie replied, feeling brushed off by the vague answer. She touched her hair and found confidence in its smooth texture. Trying to gain some ground, she said, "Sorry, I didn't get your name."

"Beth," the woman answered disinterestedly.

Intentionally sarcastic, Goldie asked, "Is that Beth like Elizabeth, or like Bethany?"

"Elizabeth," Beth replied with a shrug.

Annoyed that Beth had not picked up on her cutting remark, Goldie added, "Oh, so Elizabeth is your real name."

"Beth," she stated coldly. "My name is Beth."

The elevator jerked to a stop and an electronic bell signalled the opening of the doors. Beth walked out, ungrasping and unfazed, and Goldie followed sulkily. They had arrived in an empty waiting room, carpeted, furnished, and decorated in pastel blue. The room was flanked at each end by a glass door and security console. Beth swiped her security card at the console, and walked through with nary a glance back to confirm whether Goldie was instep.

Goldie was impressed by the security measures and the implication that her work was important and confidential. She wondered when she would procure an access card, but she didn't attempt to ask Beth, who was navigating the hallways quickly, like she was trying to lose Goldie or had forgotten about her.

As Beth led them further into the office maze, Goldie caught glimpses of what could be her future, her life as an adult: a database administrator for the City of Toronto. Pastel blue cubicles personalized with potted plants and framed photos, copy centres with shelves of stationary supplies, and conference room tables covered with laptops and composition notebooks. She vacillated between feeling anxious about her ability to perform the job, her ability to function in a professional office among real adults, and feeling ecstatic about landing a job that required a lanyard, that provided a cubicle, and that supplied her with all the pens she could need.

"Here," Beth said, stopping in front of a glass-walled office with a closed door.

Inside, Patricia Addington's angular figure was leaning in a chair, a phone to her ear. Goldie could not guess her age. She looked to be somewhere in her fifties or sixties, but she recognized expensive taste in clothes and jewellery. When Patricia spotted Goldie, she waved her in with a smile and raised a finger to signal that her conversation would soon come to an end. Goldie waved back at Patricia, and then turned to Beth to thank her but she had disappeared.

* * *

At the end of her first day, Sameera walked the half-dozen blocks from work to her one-bedroom apartment in the Queer Village. It was an easy urban route that offered her an opportunity to unplug and appreciate the changing season, a mindfulness practice she had adopted. The wellness articles, which she devoured insatiably, encouraged her to observe the present moment, and she began the practice immediately after stepping out of the office. *Oh, there's a cluster of clouds blocking the sun. A flock of pigeons is flying in circles.*

Minutes later, once she had arrived in her own neighbourhood, she realized that her mindfulness had lasted less than a block. At some point, she had glanced at her screen to check for the time, and then continued to mindlessly consume media feeds for the remainder of the walk. *Fuck! This is hopeless. Maybe if I lived in the country …*

Sameera pocketed her phone begrudgingly as a stream of oncoming pedestrians continued to stare at theirs. The warmer weather had converted patios and perches into communal spaces, packing the sidewalks with plenty of people to observe. Probably appraising the posture and wardrobe choices of strangers was not in line with mindfulness, but it was at least remaining in the present moment, however superficially.

As she was judging nearby footwear while waiting for the lights to turn on Carlton Street, Sameera heard yoo-hooing from somewhere behind her and turned to see handsome Elewa waving as he cleared tables on her favourite patio, The Friendly Bean. During small talk that morning, Sameera had mentioned that it was her first day at her new job, and Elewa seemed to be checking in with her. Sameera smiled and gave a thumbs-up in response. Elewa flashed a toothy smile and returned the gesture before heading inside with a tray of dirty glassware.

She crossed eastwards toward home, away from the gleaming

condominiums and the haute couture shops, into the derelict outer edges of the Village. It was only at the raw edges of the Village where affordable housing, however dilapidated, was still available, and Sameera would rather live in a dive in the Village than in a palace anywhere else.

She had moved downtown to attend college, while her parents and older siblings remained rooted in suburban North York, the same borough to which they had immigrated in 1996. There, mature trees, cul-de-sacs, and shopping malls were ubiquitous. No one slept on grates or park benches, people drove to every destination, and walking was a leisure activity, not a mode of transportation. There, ethnic enclaves were fortified, and people fraternized based on their shared diaspora. But Sameera treasured her network of friends, people who shared her liberal worldview, not necessarily her ethnicity.

Heading south, she walked past the sprawling tent city in the public park, and at the edges, she spotted the scrawny band of queer teenagers who seemed to share one blue dome tent. Long bangs and hoods covered their familiar faces, and Sameera nodded as a sign of acknowledgement and respect. A slim trans girl smiled back shyly, and then joined the others in ogling a screen.

Sameera turned onto a smaller street, one recently gentrified by a boutique grocer, an overpriced dry cleaner, and slim, million-dollar townhouses. The second-floor apartment that she rented with her girlfriend was located in an eyesore of a brick house, a forgotten building on a noteworthy corner of real estate, owned by a landlord who was holding out for a ludicrous payday. The patchwork repairs on the house were visible from a block away: the drain pipe duct-taped to vertical telecom wires, the mismatched roof shingles, and a broken attic window covered with a sheet of plywood. Sameera tried to recall her excitement when they had moved in a year earlier, before she became aware of the faulty plumbing, idiosyncratic electrical system, and fickle heaters.

The sleek townhouses along her block taunted her, especially the prospect of a new bath tub or a reliable hot water heater. Sameera sneered at them like an angry, hurt child. She had lived in the Village for seven years and she was bitterly aware of the costs of gentrification. The modern real estate options were possible, in part, due to the increased police activity in the neighbourhood, measures that targeted street kids, sex workers, and the mentally ill. She was witnessing a neighbourhood cleansing that branded the Queer Village as the new place to raise a woke family, a place where everyone belongs as long as they have the means.

Groceries! You need eggs and avocados. Sheepishly, she turned back to the boutique grocer's, the same one she had judged as gratuitous moments earlier. It was better to shop at an independent grocer than the chain supermarket located a few blocks away. Though she knew that if she had been hired at a job without a salary increase, she would have trekked to the larger store for its lower prices. *Even hypocrites have to eat.*

The Organic Village was equal parts grocery store and pick-up joint. In addition to the three aisles of food products, the place buzzed with sexual energy that Sameera found difficult to ignore. Like in nightclubs, customers chatted up one another and the strikingly beautiful employees who described textures and flavours salaciously, peering over ripe produce into hungry eyes. Sameera often dressed her best to shop there, and today she checked her reflection in the front windows before stepping in. She only needed groceries but it didn't hurt to be admired.

Inside, the air — cooled by the open refrigeration units — and the scent of cucumbers enveloped her. For a few moments, the only sound in the shop was the industrial blender in the back where the juice bar was located. Sameera counted four people in the store: two chatting at the bulk bins, one bagging cilantro — or was that parsley? — and one at the juice bar mouthing words to the aproned employee. The friendly cashier, a glowing twenty-something, smiled courteously at Sameera and then returned to wiping the wooden counter.

Sameera smiled back but too late, and feeling self-conscious, she zoomed down the middle aisle to the refrigerators at the back of the store. A few minutes later, she was stacking three avocados on a wrapped cut of beef, a chunk of cheddar, and a container of yogurt, and privately cursing herself for not having picked up a basket and for being too self-conscious to get one at this juncture. As she gingerly walked past the juice bar, she saw a familiar attractive face behind the counter. *I definitely know this woman. She's a … she had a cat who liked pineapples! Why do I know that? Do I follow her online? Is she Shannon's friend?*

Sameera shook her head at this last thought about Shannon, her girlfriend. Shannon's few friends were mostly other electricians from work, and aside from the couple of women she had dated casually on moving to Toronto, Shannon had not made any other friends. She claimed that after her ten-hour shifts she was too tired to meet people, but Sameera suspected that it was culture shock since Shannon had grown up in a small and predominantly white community. Because of this, it was sometimes hard for her to interact with Sameera's diverse friend group. On their second date, for example, Shannon had remarked that she had assumed Sameera was white because of her lack of accent. Sameera had cringed but forgiven the slight. *Definitely not a friend of Shannon's.*

The face looked up from wiping the counter and smiled at her. "Hi!" The young woman said cheerily. "Surprise!"

She rested her bare forearms on the high counter. Her long, kinked bangs and rust-coloured hair reminded Sameera of a Korean pop star, as did her coquettish smile. *Stop objectifying her and say hi!*

"Hi!" Sameera replied with matching enthusiasm, trying to buy some time to recall her connection to the woman.

"Metromart. Salads and sandwiches," the woman said with a wink.

"Oh, yes! You work at Metromart. I'm sorry. I'm really bad with names," Sameera explained, recalling the server from the deli counter at the chain supermarket. Sameera had chatted with her several times over the last year. Before starting her keto diet, she would often stop by the supermarket to buy her favourite cold pasta for a takeaway lunch.

"No worries. I don't think we ever exchanged names," she said with an easygoing shrug. "I'm Tina."

"Nice to meet you, Tina. I'm Sameera," she said, shifting the load in her arms to keep the avocados from rolling off her pyramid of packages.

"Here, take this," said Tina as she ducked behind the counter and reappeared in the aisle with an empty basket.

"Aw, thanks. I must look really stupid," Sameera said, unloading her groceries into basket.

"Not at all. You look really nice. I like your new hair. Totally suits you," Tina replied and bit her lower lip in a way that made Sameera blush.

Sameera reflexively touched her bountiful mane of dark waves, and said, "Thanks. I'm trying to use less product."

"Yeah, for sure. More natural. It looks good," Tina added, leaning back against the glass display case of cubed fruits and vegetables.

"Thanks," Sameera replied, willing herself to accept the compliment.

"So, I stopped seeing you at the deli ...."

A pause followed and Sameera shyly admitted, "Yeah, it's a new diet."

"Oh, which one? Is it a charcoal cleanse? The Bible diet? Or is it the baby food diet?" Tina asked with great interest.

Sameera laughed out loud and shook her head, causing her hair to swish from side to side. "No, none of those. It's keto. No pasta salads," Sameera explained, pouting until she realized she was flirting with Tina.

"Ah, I see," Tina said, and then tipped her head to one side and added, "Well, for what it's worth, I think you look great as you are."

Sameera chortled and squeezed her eyes shut. Despite the effort she put into her appearance, it remained difficult to accept a compliment.

"Thanks," she managed with a shy smile. "It wasn't to lose weight, or anything. I just wanted to, you know, eat more healthy stuff."

Tina nodded in appreciation, her fringe of bronze hair bouncing.

"Hey, T," cooed an attractive white woman in short shorts who appeared from around a corner. Adorned with diamonds and dressed in white ankle boots that matched her Hermes bag, the woman was clearly moneyed. Ignoring Sameera altogether, she sashayed to Tina and presented herself, as if to be devoured. Sameera resented being overlooked but having lived the experience countless times in bars and clubs, she didn't dwell on the moment. Instead, she prepared to depart gracefully.

To her credit, Tina continued to look at Sameera, even as she said, "Hey, Jackie. I'm just talking to Sameera. I'll catch up with you later."

Jackie was gone before Tina finished her sentence, clearly perturbed at being brushed off. They heard the chime of the front door as Jackie walked through seconds later. Sameera felt giddy but she tried to hide her pleasure at being chosen over a very good looking white woman. Everyone knew the social hierarchy in the Village was topped by white women and men. People like Jackie who were also rich were accustomed to getting whomever they wanted, especially when it came to hot and young East Asian queers like Tina. *People are not trinkets, lady.*

"Sorry about that. So you said you're eating better," Tina reconnected, brushing aside her bangs.

"Uh, yeah, but that's enough about me. What about you?" Sameera segued. "Are you still at Metromart?"

Tina grimaced, thrusting her thumbs into the beltloops of her skinny jeans and shaking her head slowly. Sameera noticed the islands of chipped red polish on her jagged fingernails. On Tina, the neglected nails looked trendy and artistic, part of a creative package. *Probably doesn't even think about it. She's just being herself.*

"No, they don't deserve me. Assholes," Tina said with a shrug, tucking and re-tucking her bronze locks behind her ear.

"Oh, sorry. I mean, you're right. You were the best deli …" Sameera stumbled, trying to find the right term, "… deli … food … server … ."

Tina laughed at Sameera's attempt at a title before offering, "Prepared Foods Attendant."

"Right, best Prepared Foods Attendant ever in the whole city. No, the world," Sameera said, trying to make Tina laugh again.

"Thanks," Tina replied with a smirk. "They got theirs anyways. The last batch of creamy potato salad was over salted."

"Oh no!" Sameera said with feigned horror. "You're a monster!"

"Now you know the truth," Tina said with a smile and a slow blink.

"So, what happened?" Sameera asked, wondering whether she was being too forward, as usual. "I mean, if you don't want to talk about—"

"No, I don't mind. I'm telling everyone. Fucking assholes," Tina said from under the same dark cloud as earlier. "They're fucking racist. That's the bottom line. They give shifts based on race."

"Damn! I'm sorry," Sameera said.

"Why? You didn't do anything," Tina shot back, and then softened her tone. "It's okay. Well, not okay, but you know what I mean."

"Yeah," Sameera agreed. "Have you considered filing a complaint? Like with the union?"

Tina sighed and brushed her bangs to one side. "I did, and it was all bullshit. I thought the union was supposed to be on the worker's side but it was like the rep didn't even care. She acted like I was making a big deal about nothing."

Sameera responded with fervour, "Well, that's not fair. You deserve to be treated with respect. What about going public? I remember the story about two women who filed suit against the Ontario Public Service for anti-Black racism. One of them was treated so badly, she gave birth prematurely. Like, her son was just over a pound. Their unions did not stick up for them either. Wait …."

Sameera scrolled on her phone, slightly self-conscious about her filed and buffed nails, and then passed it to Tina. "That's them. You don't have to sue. You could spread the word online. There's probably a lot of other—"

"Thanks," Tina interrupted her, smiling appreciatively. "Honestly, I'm too bogged down with … like, a bunch of other shit that hit the fan at the same time. Anyway, I appreciate your support. It's kinda nice to hear someone get worked up about it, besides me."

Disheartened, Sameera paused and chewed her lower lip thinking of a thoughtful response. She wanted to appear detached and non-judgemental but inwardly, she believed that Tina was making a mistake. Had Shannon been present, she'd have suggested that Sameera was misconstruing events, interpreting the facts to support a political crusade. Grounded in her experience of growing up closeted in a queerphobic town, Shannon espoused the pitiless belief that people needed to adapt and persevere, to accept the flaws in a world that would never be perfect. To keep the peace in her year-long relationship, Sameera had started to keep her opinions to herself. *I should probably just do that now, too …*

"So, you wanna have coffee sometime?" Tina asked, terminating Sameera's train of thought.

"Uh, yeah, I mean, uh, like, I …." Sameera stammered, uncertain about what she wanted to add to her answer.

Tina's eyes widened and she smiled as Sameera continued to open her mouth without producing words.

"You're seeing someone?" Tina asked softly, again wiping her long, bronze fringe away from her eyes. "It's cool. We can still go for coffee, you know, like just to chat."

Relieved but also saddened that Tina had assumed correctly, Sameera nodded and accepted the invitation. They exchanged contact information, and after a subdued farewell, Sameera headed to the cashier. All the while, she felt guilt-ridden by her underlying desire to be mistaken for someone unattached. She was in a happy and monogamous relationship with her live-in girlfriend, an arrangement that she had insisted upon. On its own, flirting was unproblematic but Sameera had sensed a stronger current compelling her to go beyond harmless flirting. *Self-sabotage! For fuck's sake, I'm too old for this shit.*

Without looking back at the juice bar, Sameera completed her transaction and left The Organic Village with a large brown bag of groceries. The door closed behind her, and then she realized she had forgotten the eggs. But she strode ahead toward home. *And that's your punishment. No eggs for saboteurs!*

* * *

Faiza did not make it home in time to help with dinner on Monday evening after all. During a late-day conference call, upper management worked themselves into a frenzy with conjectures, and she spent the following hours on the phone assuaging their unfounded fears. By the time she drove up to her bungalow on the bluffs, all that remained of the springtime sunset were shadows cast by the pines bordering the western side of the house. The porch light was on but the rest of the house was dimly lit. Faiza assumed they had already eaten and washed up.

She parked her luxury sedan behind her husband's SUV and her mother's compact hatchback. Like every other day, she felt like she had lost a race, always arriving home last. Dejected, she slipped off her flat driving shoes, tucking them under the seat, and squeezed into her high heels. Crossing the cobblestoned walkway carefully, she carried her handbag, laptop bag, and attaché case to the front door. When she found the door locked, she cursed herself for dropping her keys into her overstuffed handbag and began rooting through her belongings while balancing the bag on her knee.

Once inside, she unloaded the bags in the front hall, slipped off her suit jacket and heels, and sighed at her reflection in the hall mirror. Her hair and makeup were immaculate — she touched them up every couple of hours — but the fatigue in her eyes wasn't anything cosmetics could fix.

Muffled music from the other side of the house suggested that 16-year-old Mina was holed up in her room. As much as Faiza had missed her elder daughter — who had spent the weekend at her father's house — she was not tempted to knock on Mina's door to touch base. Conversations with Mina required more patience and empathy than Faiza presently had in reserve, and from all the parenting books she had read, she knew that she could not be a good listener being as stressed out as she was at the moment.

A conversation with Mina at this point would most likely lead to an argument about her 9:00 p.m. curfew or her slipping grades, or the contentious topic of that month — an unsupervised weekend trip with her friends. As expected, Mina's father, Faiza's ex-husband, had assented to the trip without consulting Faiza. Now, Mina was furious with her mother for objecting and effectively ruining her social life. *Later, much later. After some food and a shower …*

She sought out 7-year-old Pari, instead, watching TV in the basement family room with Robert and Bibi.

"Hello," Faiza said as she descended the stairs into the dimly lit family room.

Her presence was masked by the darkness, the only light being the glow of the large television, and her voice was drowned out by the soundtrack of a mobster scene filled with gunshots. She saw everyone in their usual places. Bibi rested in an armchair, dressed in a stylish pant set, her dark tresses coiffed in an elaborate bun and her designer glasses perched high on her nose. In contrast, Robert and Pari wore matching Blue Jays tracksuits that had seen better days. Robert was sprawled along the length of the couch with his long limbs dangling over every edge, and Pari lay prone on him, with her head on his chest so her father could lightly stroke her back.

"What are you watching?" Faiza asked them, touching Robert's smooth scalp out of habit.

"Mama!" exclaimed Pari, lifting her head to receive Faiza's kiss, and then grunting at Robert to continue rubbing her back.

"Can I kiss my wife, first?" Robert joshed Pari.

The couple exchanged a quick kiss, and then Faiza moved on to greet her mother. Bibi was engrossed in the television program, her hands clutched at her chest in anticipation.

"Salaam, Bibi-*jaan. Chetori?* How are you?" Faiza asked, kneeling to kiss her mother's scented cheek. "I'm sorry about missing dinner."

"Khoob khoob, merci. Toh? Good, good, thanks. You?" Bibi replied distractedly, barely taking her eyes off the screen. "Your dinner is in the microwave. There's a salad in the fridge. *Khoob khoob*. Good good."

Relieved that she did not have to endure another lecture about the significance of family dinners together, Faiza kissed her mother's cheek again and slipped under Robert's legs to find a seat on the couch. On the screen, gangsters congregated and threatened reprisals. They spoke in Farsi, which was translated into English subtitles, and Faiza recognized the backdrop as Tehran, likely set in the 1950s. The cinematography was reminiscent of Scorsese's and Tarantino's new wave and neo-realism, so decidedly a modern series.

"What are you watching?" Faiza asked Robert, and then got shushed by Bibi.

Robert whispered, "*Shahrzad*, season one." Quieter still, he asked, "How are you? How'd it go with the presentation?"

With an eye roll and a tilt of her head, Faiza gestured that she was surviving. "It's done."

"That's great. I'm glad you're home," Robert cooed and extended his left arm to hold her hand.

Promptly, Pari prodded him to continue rubbing and he released his grip on Faiza's hand to return to the task. They smiled at each other and Faiza leaned in to rub Robert's arm as he drew circles on Pari's back. For a few minutes, they watched the drama on screen and Faiza felt herself drifting off, in spite of her hunger.

When another scene filled the room with gunshots and screaming, Faiza stirred and commented to no one in particular, "It seems really violent."

Pari shot up to sitting position, which caused Robert to wince in response to the pressure of sharp elbows and knees pressed into his torso.

She pleaded, "No, Mama. It's not. It's good, it's … My Farsi is getting better. Right, Bibi-*jaan*?"

Bibi responded by shushing the room, never lifting her eyes from the screen. Silently, Faiza settled Pari down again, which produced more yelps from Robert as Pari used his throat to position herself.

"*Bache-ha!* People! If you don't want to watch …." Bibi chided them, still staring ahead.

"Okay, Bibi-*jaan*," Robert replied respectfully. "Let's go kiddo. It's bedtime, anyway."

"No, no," Pari protested, laying herself flat against her father. "You said I could watch the whole thing."

Robert tucked his hands under Pari's armpits and rose to his feet, lifting her 60 pounds to standing.

"I'm sorry, kiddo. It happens sometimes," Robert said, stretching his limbs only partway to avoid hitting the ceiling tiles.

Pari stomped her feet in one spot, agitating Bibi, and Faiza was about to chasten her daughter when Robert intervened with the promise of a piggyback ride to her bath, which Pari accepted. Feeling exhausted and lacking in imagination, Faiza was grateful for Robert's drive and creative parenting. The same situation could have easily ended in Faiza admonishing Pari for her childishness and Bibi reproaching Faiza for being too hard on the young girl. *He's untethered, weightless in comparison to me.*

Without saying another word, Faiza followed father and daughter up the stairs, out of the darkness and into the soft warm glow of the first floor. At the top of the stairs, Faiza turned right toward the kitchen and they veered left, down the long hall of the bungalow, to the bathroom between the girls' rooms.

As her dinner heated in the microwave, Faiza poured herself a tall glass of red wine. After a quick glance about to make sure she was alone, she downed half the glass, and refilled it to the rim. She told herself that she deserved the drink, especially after her long day, but it was a waste of effort to lie to herself. She drank every night because every day was difficult. She had no further capacity to make excuses to herself about her drinking. *It takes too much effort to be a good mother, a dutiful daughter, and a successful director to have any resources for self-deception.*

Faiza carried her plate of koufteh ghelgheli, lamb meatballs in rich gravy spooned over steamed rice, and the glass of red wine to the formal dining table adorned with a lace tablecloth protected by clear plastic. She had curbed her appetite all day with glasses of water and the promise of a large green salad for dinner. The salad was prepared and readily available, but Faiza could not resist the rice and lamb alternative. She promised herself that she would resist the temptation of her mother's cooking the following day.

From down the hall, she heard Robert prompting Pari to brush her teeth and wash her face. Knowing that she had less than half an hour before Pari summoned her for bedtime kisses, Faiza quickly settled into her usual spot at the head of the table to eat her dinner.

Behind her were the glass doors leading to the backyard. Elegant lanterns hung over regal patio furniture, stone pathways circled the iridescent pool, and delicate lights called attention to the topiaries and flowerbeds designed by Bibi and maintained by their landscaper. Before her were the spacious open concept living room, dining room, and kitchen — all furnished with minimalist pieces and modern Persian art, all decorated by Bibi and Robert. Faiza wondered whether anything in the house had been selected by her since they had unpacked seven years earlier. *Let them do what they like. It's all the same to me.*

On the table, she placed her phone, screen side down, in an attempt to eat a meal without responding to late-night work messages from Howard. Just as she picked up a spoonful, the phone buzzed. *I should've left it in my bag.*

Faiza shoved the food into her mouth and picked up the phone. It was a message from Howard, as expected. The man did not seem to sleep, and Faiza did not understand why since it felt like she was doing all his work for him. He was responding to the EDI presentation that City Council had requested of him, which she had completed and sent to him that afternoon. She was proud of her work regarding public engagement with marginalized groups and excited to present her ideas to the Resident Engagement Committee.

Howard Crawley's message read, "That's it? Kinda dull. Jazz it up. Sending pics. Add them."

Faiza counselled herself to finish chewing her food, to remain calm, because any outburst would incite the attention of her entire family. Instead of clearing the table with her forearm, she swallowed her mouthful and drank heavily from her glass. Pedar sag, *asshole! Dull? That's what he thinks?!* Bisharaf, *wretch! Not even a fucking thank you. Piece of shit!*

The hour-long presentation — which she had produced single-handedly in addition to performing her regular directorial duties — had required dozens of hours of research and analysis. The slideshow consisted of thought-provoking slides which were intended to inspire visions of an inclusive approach to city building. Faiza had scoured their media resources and added stirring images of notable city-run initiatives. The accompanying report was substantial, and it detailed the strategies that had proven most effective in engaging and connecting with marginalized communities in other North American cities of a similar size and density to Toronto. *Dull? He's a fucking idiot. Probably didn't read a word. Aargh!*

Faiza was tempted to open the image files to examine Howard's contribution. She had been down this road several times, and she knew that the more sensible path was to put her phone down, finish her meal, and handle the issue in an hour. By then, she would feel more sated and less angry.

She opened the image files anyway, as she considered whether she was a glutton for punishment. The images were stock photos of people of colour in stereotypical scenarios: young Black men playing basketball, young Brown women in head coverings learning English, a Latin couple surrounded by eight children, and an East Asian family with one son in his graduation gown and cap. *Ugh. He can be so daft!*

She was rubbing the bridge of her nose and trying to think of a workaround when Pari called for her. Faiza put down her phone, downed the remainder of her wine, and shuffled down the hall.

Ten minutes later, after kissing Pari good night and leaving Robert to read bedtime stories, she returned to the dining table. Bibi was cleaning an already spotless kitchen, which meant that she wanted to talk with Faiza. Any alterations to the presentation would have to wait until everyone had gone to bed. Faiza braced herself for what was coming, expecting one of the usual topics: Mina's weight gain, Faiza's long hours at work, or some recent achievement of Firouz, Faiza's successful brother in Boston.

"Is your show finished?" Faiza said, reseating herself at the dining table and taking in a spoonful of the now cold rice and stew.

"Oh, I only watch one episode a day. You know, it's a very good show," Bibi answered earnestly. "It has won awards."

"Okay," Faiza mumbled through a mouthful and furtively watched her mother putter about the island in the kitchen. "The lamb is really good, Bibi. I'm sorry I wasn't here earlier. I tried to wrap things up but there's just a lot going on—"

"You know, Faiza," Bibi interrupted, acting as if Faiza hadn't been speaking.

Here it comes.

"Firouz called today," Bibi said.

Uh-huh. And he's won the Nobel Prize? Solved the crisis in the Middle East? Found the cure for AIDS?

Bibi took a seat at the other end of the dining table and busied her hands by smoothing out the delicate lace tablecloth underneath the plastic sheet.

As if speaking to herself, she said, "He's such a good son." Then, she continued, glancing once at Faiza to confirm that her daughter was paying attention, "He's bought a large house. Very big, and lots of space."

Unable to guess the trajectory of the conversation, Faiza replied less than enthusiastically, "Wonderful. Good for him. I'm sure it'll make him very happy." She scooped another spoonful into her mouth and eyed her empty wine glass longingly. *Wait until Bibi is gone. She'll just get on your case for drinking too much.*

"He's invited me to Boston. They have lots of space, you know," Bibi said, stealing glances at Faiza.

"Okay, that'll be nice," Faiza remarked, shovelling the last grains onto her spoon. "You haven't visited him in a year, or has it been longer?"

"Oh, about one year. Last spring," Bibi confirmed, and then she paused, clutched her hands, and said quickly, "Firouz wants me to live with them."

Faiza sat up and stared at her mother with mouth agape. There were so many comments she wanted to make, most of which would upset Bibi. *Firouz has never wanted you to live with him. He's told me time and again that he can only handle a month at a time together. His wife is a wretch of a woman who can't stand to share Firouz with anyone, including you. You are miserable at the end of every trip to Boston. None of you get along or like to spend time together. This is the stupidest idea I have heard all day, all year.*

For her mother's sake, Faiza simply nodded in response. Is it possible Firouz invited her for a visit and she'd misunderstood?

"I know you need me here," Bibi continued, bravely looking up from the tabletop. "I thought maybe I could help Firouz for a bit—"

Faiza jumped in, "Bibi, Firouz and Nasim don't need your help. They hire help. And what do you mean about me needing you here? Maman, I want you here. I can get someone in to do the housework. You don't have to do anything."

Bibi did not respond immediately, and Faiza wondered how many parenting books her mother had read to help her manage their relationship.

Bibi readjusted her seat and smoothed out her blouse, and then she replied softly, "*Meedoon-am, azziz-am*. I know, my dear."

Faiza sensed that the underlying reason for this conversation was surfacing. She had to be patient, to demonstrate her willingness to hear whatever unpleasantness her mother was about to reveal. Again, Faiza eyed the empty wine glass and contemplated whether this conversation warranted a refill with her mother watching. She pushed her plate aside and rested her elbows in its place. Then, perching her chin on her intertwined fingers, she offered her mother a sympathetic smile.

Bibi was a woman who was sensitive to subtle offerings of respect and compassion. She refused to be treated carelessly, and her relations knew better than to rush her or pressure her for explanations and decisions. Faiza admired this trait in her mother, and other women too, and she liked to think that she took after her mother in this respect but she suspected that her mother did not think so.

Mustering all the patience afforded to her by the glass and a half of red wine she had already drunk, Faiza asked in a concerned tone, "Bibi-*jaan, chee-ast?* What is it?" She paused for effect, and then added, "Do you want to live with Firouz?"

In a characteristic move, Bibi crossed her chest with her left arm and took hold of her chin with her right hand. With down cast eyes, she tilted her head to the right, then to the left, and back to the right. A heavy sigh followed, and then Bibi looked up.

"Faiza-*joon, jigaram-aste.* You're my life. *Doret megardam.* My world centres on you. And on Mina and Pari. You know that," Bibi said, stopping to look directly at Faiza.

"*Bale, hatman.* Yes, of course," Faiza answered reflexively since this exchange was routine dialogue for the mother-daughter pair. "And I understand that you want to be there for Firouz and Nasim and the girls. I don't expect—"

Bibi interrupted her, "Faiza-*jaan,* I think it is best for me to give you some space. Some room to come into your own."

Faiza was speechless. She had never heard her mother express such a foreign sentiment — to make space for her child to come into her own. *What does that even mean to Bibi, the woman who parents my daughters as if they were her own children?*

Seemingly uncomfortable with the topic, Bibi resettled in her seat and recrossed her arms, all the while not meeting Faiza's gaze.

"I don't understand," Faiza admitted. "You are trying to give me space? For what?"

Another pause followed as Bibi titled her head and cast her gaze from one side to the other, rubbing her chin in contemplation. Faiza was beginning to lose patience but she bit her lip and silently counted to twenty. Any sign of impertinence at this point would cause her mother to shut down the conversation and Faiza would have to work twice as hard to make amends.

Following an audible sigh, Bibi replied, "I think that my being here is … not allowing you to … be the mother you want to be."

The mother I want to be?! What is she talking about? Confused by this answer, Faiza splayed her arms across the table as she pleaded, "What does that mean? Bibi-*jaan,* can you just tell me what's going on? Did something happen with Mina?"

Faiza imagined some monumental row between Bibi and Mina, a culmination of cultural and generational clashes. Faiza and Robert had grown accustomed to Bibi crossing Mina's personal boundaries and the tantrums and hostility that ensued. Whether the upsetting comment was about Mina's weight or her wardrobe, or a disrespectful tone or gesture that offended Bibi, the household expected conflict between the grandmother and granddaughter.

"Well, that is some of it," Bibi explained, looking troubled.

"Pfft," Faiza interjected with relief, dropping her forearms to the table. "She's just being a teenager. It'll get easier in a few years. You don't have—"

Bibi interrupted her, "Faiza-*joon*, she needs you. She needs her mother, at home, here for her."

"She has me," Faiza said without conviction. "What do you mean? And what does that have to do with you living with Firouz?"

Bibi inhaled and exhaled, and this time her words were quavering, "I don't want to be a crutch, *azziz-am*, my dear … as long as I'm here … The girls need you, Faiza. I can't be their mother."

Faiza was shocked by what she was hearing. Her mother was

crying, however softly and with dignity, about not wanting to be a mother to her granddaughters.

"*Na-mefam-am.* I don't understand," Faiza said, suddenly very tired and unable to reach across the table to comfort her mother. "I am here. I am their mother. You don't have to worry about that."

"Yes, yes, I do," Bibi said, reaching for a tissue from a nearby box and composing herself. "Robert is a good man … a very good father … but he can't be both parents, and as long as I'm here … it is easier for you to … go on like this." Bibi gestured with a sweep of her hand that caused Faiza to wonder about which concern her mother was referring to, her drinking or her long hours at work.

"I heard my name," Robert said cheerily as he walked into the dining room and crossed the floor to plant a kiss on Faiza's temple. "Better be something good." He walked to the fridge and fetched a can of diet soda.

Faiza took a deep breath. *Is he pretending, or is he oblivious to tension?* She said to Bibi in Farsi, "*Badan harf bezaneem.* Let's talk later."

Bibi nodded and excused herself for the night. Faiza rose to kiss her mother goodnight but Bibi made haste.

"Goodnight, Bibi," Robert said, settling into the seat next to Faiza and flashing a smile. "So, you wanna cuddle on the couch? Watch some hotshots solve a crime in under an hour?"

"More wine, first," Faiza said, leaning back in her chair and dropping her arms to her sides.

"Got it," Robert replied, taking leave to return with the bottle.

He filled a quarter of the glass and began to recork the bottle when Faiza cleared her throat and smiled up at him pleadingly. He topped up the glass to a third-full and as he corked the bottle, he heard Faiza emit a whine.

"Finish that first," Robert negotiated, placing the bottle back in the fridge and returning to his seat at the table. "So, what was all that about? Is she okay?"

Faiza examined her glass of wine, talked herself out of downing it in one gulp, and sipped several times in a show of moderation. In response to Robert's query about Bibi, she shrugged and shook her head, finally resting her chin in her palm.

What could she say to Robert? She did not want to voice Bibi's concern that she was a negligent mother, an absent caregiver to her daughters. Already, Faiza felt ashamed for being called out on her absence for the past months, or possibly years. She feared that Robert might echo her mother's sentiments, and she was too vulnerable emotionally to face that kind of criticism from him. *What would make Bibi say those things?*

"Did something happen with Mina?" Faiza probed in a desperate attempt to find a catalyst elsewhere. "I mean, did Bibi and Mina get into an argument?"

Robert took a long drink of soda and contemplated the day's events. He shook his head and answered, "Not that I know of. You could ask Mina."

With her chin propped on her palm, Faiza shook her head emphatically.

"Have you talked to Mina?" Robert asked in a casual tone.

Again, Faiza shook her head and polished off the rest of her drink.

"Go, talk to Mina. She misses you," Robert reminded her. "I think she had a nice weekend with Ali."

He placed his hand on her forearm and squeezed lightly, prompting her to look up at him. Faiza lifted her gaze, and the hot tears that had filled her eyes rolled down her cheeks and pooled under her chin. *I love my job. I don't want to work less. I don't want to be home early. What am I supposed to do?!*

The love of her life, the man whose compassionate gaze greeted her every morning and evening, was the person who single-handedly chauffeured the girls, reviewed their homework assignments, and organized weekend outings. She had sidelined herself into the role of working mother, a woman preoccupied with budgets, mandates, and personnel, one who lived with but apart from her husband and children. *Is it supposed to be this hard?*

"I'm sorry about the weekend," Faiza said through her tears. "I know you wanted it to be special."

"Aw," Robert cooed, wiping her chin with his index finger.

The previous weekend, he had planned a romantic overnight trip to Niagara-on-the-Lake, taking advantage of Mina's being away at her father's and Bibi caring for Pari. They were packed and ready to go when Faiza had received a last-minute message from Howard to review and revise a report he had authored for City Council.

Initially, she was indignant, pacing her bedroom and cursing Howard's abuse of power while Robert nodded in agreement. She intended to inform Howard that she was unavailable, and she drafted several messages to that effect. After an hour of Faiza rewording her reply, Robert suggested they cancel their trip.

Faiza had tried to persuade Robert that she still wanted to go but her pleas were unconvincing. *We should have gone. But refusing Howard even once might have cost me dearly.* He had his pick of directors who would gladly do his work. Jeffery Stanton, the Director of Business Improvement Services, came to mind. He was a scheming man who often reminded Faiza that, like Crawley, his Canadian ancestry also dated back five generations. *What does that even mean?*

"Really, Robert. I'm sorry. We should have gone," Faiza said, and then cut her sentence short when she heard her words slurring.

"It's alright," Robert assured her, patting her forearm in a manner that revealed unresolved feelings, and then changed the subject. "Come on, let's do something just you and me now. Shall I make popcorn?" Sitting upright, he drummed the tabletop with his fingers and wiggled his eyebrows for comic relief.

She obliged with a chuckle and he rose to prepare a snack,

taking her dirty dish with him to the sink. All the while, Faiza calculated the amount of time she required to insert Howard's random images into the EDI presentation. She would go into work early the next day to get it done. Howard did not need the presentation until Friday, and it was only end of day Monday.

"Ooh, do you want to try that racy one?" Robert whispered, leaning on one foot to peer down the hall for the others. "The cops who solve crime in their underwear."

"Really? Sure, sounds good," Faiza replied with a sincere chuckle.

She picked up her phone to respond to Howard but answering his confrontational messages required her undivided attention. Howard was as obtuse as he was susceptible to being offended, which was to say very much so. Faiza struggled to produce a response that expressed her appreciation for his contribution while allowing her the flexibility to make minimal changes.

"Ready," Robert said a few minutes later, a bowl of popcorn in hand.

"I'll be down in a second, hon," Faiza answered, still seated at the dining table.

"Alright, I'll cue it up," Robert said as he descended to the family room.

A moment later, Faiza sent the message. Then, she retrieved the bottle of wine, filled her glass to the top, and drank half before heading downstairs.

* * *

In her bedroom on Monday night, Goldie turned up the volume on her headphones to drown out the explosive soundtrack coming from the adjacent living room. Her two adult brothers had commandeered the space to watch their favourite show, a mythical drama, and the battle cries of warriors reverberated through the apartment. While they jeered at the screen, Goldie wished for a power outage. *It's a magical medieval soap opera! Come on. It's fucking fantasy. Who cares?!*

After Goldie had finished dinner with her mother and brothers, during which she barely spoke, she had spent the evening holed up in her unlit bedroom on her unmade bed, catching Pokémon, messaging with friends, and sharing pictures of her work cubicle. There was so much to say about her first day at City Hall, but Goldie had no interest in discussing any of it in her brothers' presence. They seemed to perceive her successes as personal affronts — at least that's how her older brother behaved.

punk asses takeover, she messaged her friend, Issa.

blame trump, Issa quipped. *kuz man child wasnt entitled enuf?*

Goldie chuckled and typed, *enuf said. need own place already.*

The three-bedroom apartment she shared with her parents and younger brother, Hussain, had become even more cramped with the unexpected return of her older brother, 32-year-old Dariush. Two weeks had passed since Dariush had taken up residence on the living room couch, after the break-up of his last short-lived relationship, and Goldie had had enough of his bad habits and egotism.

Another thunderous whoop erupted from the living room and Goldie heard Dariush holler, "Take that, you cow!"

She gritted her teeth on hearing the sexist remark, one of the many he habitually hurled at the women onscreen. She wondered what attracted anyone to her brother. Dariush had spent the last decade moving from one relationship to another, often living with one girlfriend while seeing another at the same time.

Goldie had overheard him describe his strategy to Hussain like a wizened gambler mentoring a protégé, "The older they get, the more they expect. When they're young, they're so dumb. They're happy with any scrap you offer."

It was this very conversation — one of the many she overheard — that had hardened Goldie's heart toward her older brother. It hurt her more than she would ever admit that Dariush saw young women like herself as stooges, mere playthings for opportunistic men. There was no room in their relationship for Goldie to share her feelings with Dariush. She did not expect him to take her feelings or opinions seriously anyway, and if given the chance, he was bound to criticize her for making herself vulnerable.

hate living here, Goldie messaged Issa, sinking lower in her bed.

move out. u got a job, Issa replied.

gotta save $ first, Goldie texted back. She reflected on her living situation before Dariush moved back. Hussain's disposition was different from their older brother's, at least insomuch that his introverted personality kept him from voicing his small-minded opinions. They had tolerated each other and restrained from expressions of overt hostility.

With Dariush's arrival, Hussain had become equally insufferable, cheerleading his older brother's vile rhetoric about women. Over the past two weeks, the brothers had kept up a running commentary expressing their misogyny, and Goldie was now fed up.

The door to her bedroom opened, letting in a ray of light, and Goldie removed her headphones. Peeking through the gap was her mother, Fereshteh Sheer, dressed in a long silk dressing gown with her hair wrapped up for the night in a linen scarf.

"*Deh, beedar-aste*. Oh, you're awake," her mother said, pleasantly surprised.

She slipped into the unlit room, sat at the edge of Goldie's bed, and began rubbing the tops of her daughter's feet. Goldie checked her screen for the time — quarter past eleven — and tucked the phone under her pillow.

"*Azziz-am*, dearest, they say the blue light is bad for your sleep," her mother told her.

"Mama," Goldie whined like the little girl she turned into around her mother. "Stop. I sleep just fine."

"Okay, okay, as you like," her mother said, patting the tops of her feet. "So your first day was good?"

"Yeah, it was. I liked it," Goldie said with a shrug, laying her long hair over her chest to examine its ends.

"*Khoob khoob*, good good," her mother replied. "I'm glad. You deserve the best."

"Mama, when's Dariush moving out?" Goldie blurted out, withdrawing her feet to underscore her seriousness.

"Golnuz," her mother's tone was reproving initially but she continued in a more compassionate tone. "Dariush is your brother. He needs us to be supportive. He will stay as long as he needs."

Another round of hooting and hollering blasted from the living room. Goldie harrumphed and shook her head in frustration. Her mother inched closer to her and placed a hand on her knee, rubbing gently.

"I know it's a little cramped in the apartment but this is the right thing to do," her mother assured her. "It's what we would do for you or Hussain, should you ever return after moving out."

Goldie shot back, "I will never move back after I move out. No way."

When she felt her mother's hand stop rubbing her knee, she guessed that her words had landed badly.

"I mean, I'm happy here but I want to be independent once I move out. Grown-ups don't move back in with their parents," Goldie declared.

"Hmm, well, some do," her mother replied matter-of-factly. "Your father and I moved back in with your grandparents after we had Dariush. It made sense to be with our family, to receive and offer help."

"That's different," Goldie claimed. "You were in Iran, and it was like a million years ago."

Goldie had intentionally exaggerated to make her mother laugh, and she succeeded.

"Well, some things don't change. When family needs help, we help," her mother said, cuddling Goldie.

She rested her head on her mother's lap, careful to avoid crimping her hair which would add to her morning prep time. "Yeah, but I bet you weren't rude and messy like Dariush when you moved in with *maman-bozorg* and *baba-bozorg*, grandmother and grandfather."

Her mother chuckled and lightly stroked Goldie's hair, also attentive to its straightened condition. "No, we definitely weren't."

Goldie sensed an opening to air her grievances about Dariush and took it. "He's always picking on me, and telling me that I'm not really Iranian 'cuz I was born here. Hussain wasn't born in Iran and he never says that to him." Sitting up, she complained hurriedly. "And the other day, he was using my UofT sweater to mop up something he spilled. I told him to stop, and he said I was being uppity about going to university, that a sweater did not make me better than him. I never said it did."

She stopped to take a breath but did not pause long enough for her mother to respond. Tears streamed down her face and she was glad that the darkness offered some cover to balance how very exposed she felt. These miserable emotions had been simmering for two weeks, or two decades, and Goldie needed to say them out loud to a sympathetic ear before her emotions boiled over and her anguish was revealed in an angry outburst at Dariush.

"Sometimes, I think he hates me," Goldie continued, her voice quavering with distress. "He acts like I'm too stupid to understand his jabs, like I can't understand Farsi, or I don't know when someone is insulting me. What have I done to him? Why does he treat me like garbage?"

Goldie sighed, wiped her nose on her pyjama sleeve, and waited for her mother's response. From the living room, they heard the soundtrack of a sword fight and the two brothers cheering on the hero.

"*Dokhtar-am*, my daughter, you are a brilliant young woman," her mother said in a slow methodical voice.

"Uh-huh," Goldie replied dejectedly, intuiting that the remainder of her mother's response would leave her unsatisfied.

"You are going to come across your share of detractors," continued her mother. "They'll have their reasons for trying to bring you down."

"Hmm," Goldie said, unsure of the underlying message and frustrated by the cryptic manner of speech which her parents' generation adopted.

"Whatever their reason for targeting you, it doesn't matter. That's their burden to overcome. You need to focus on your goals," her mother advised.

Having had her fill of the sermon, Goldie protested, "That's not fair. You want me to ignore his abuse. How can I ignore him? He's here every morning. He calls me *farangi*, foreigner."

"Goldie, you need to understand that Dariush isn't like you," her mother pleaded. "You didn't have the problems he had—"

Cutting her off, Goldie said in a cynical tone, "I know. I know. He had to do ESL and figure stuff out on his own, but that's no reason to be a jerk."

"Goldie! He's your brother. Show some respect."

Goldie huffed and chewed her lip in frustration, tired of hearing her parents defend Dariush and attribute his failures and flaws to the challenges of settling in Canada as a youth. As far back as she could remember, her parents bragged to overseas relatives about Dariush's so-called excellence. Then, as a teenager, she realized that her brother wasn't the successful entrepreneur, hotelier, or realtor her parents talked about; their boasting had been embellishments of his daydreams.

"I don't understand why we treat him like he's a … like a …" Goldie said, stumbling on her words, unsure of how to describe Dariush without offending her mother. "Like, he's different from all of us."

"I know it's hard to understand but not everyone is as strong as you," her mother replied in a tone that sounded less compassionate and more perturbed.

Goldie had no response to this statement. She had heard it so many times before and it explained nothing about the state of her world or the difficulties faced by others. It seemed like a backhanded compliment that placed a greater burden on her to accommodate and tolerate her brother's hatefulness.

"When does Baba get back?" Goldie asked, trying to change the conversation and avoid another lecture.

"He messaged a couple of hours ago from Montreal. He's driving back a double trailer from Kirkland, so he'll probably get here mid-morning," her mother said, sounding relieved by the change of topic.

"Okay," Goldie replied, and a yawn escaped. "That's good."

"Okay, time for bed. Remember, the blue light isn't good for—" her mother started.

"Mama!" Goldie whined, slipping under her duvet.

"Okay, okay," her mother conceded, and then she kissed the top of Goldie's head. "*Shab-bekhair*, *azziz-am*. Good night, my dear."

"*Shab-bekhair*, Mama," Goldie said, kissing her mother's cheek.

After her mother left, Goldie retrieved her phone and messaged her apologies to Issa for dropping offline.

mom dont get it. always takes D side, Goldie typed, her anger returning to a boil.

Patriarchy = bs, Issa replied, along with emojis of a stiletto and excrement.

tru dat, agreed Goldie, adding emojis of prayer hands and a coffin, and signing off. *msg tmr.*

The commotion in the living room had died down, and through their shared wall, Goldie heard Hussain typing in his bedroom. Covertly, she snuck out of her bed, opened the door quietly and crossed the hallway to the unlit kitchen to spy on her older brother around the corner. Sprawled on the couch in his nest of crumpled chip bags, unwashed clothes, and video game gear, Dariush was eating ice cream from the tub and staring at the television his attention completely absorbed by two wrestlers dripping in sweat gambolling theatrically on screen. Goldie captured several photos and short videos of Dariush dripping ice cream on himself as he shovelled it into his gaping mouth.

Back in her room, she posted a sardonic how-to message and a looping three-second video which she titled *Pest Control: Man-child Infestation.* Within an hour, the message had been shared a few hundred times, and Goldie fell asleep feeling better than she had in two weeks.

Chapter 2

Friday Morning, June 8, 2018

Sameera stood to stretch her cramped muscles after an hour spent at her computer poring over quarterly reports. For the first time in weeks, she noticed the dazzling view from her cubicle window. The morning sun reflected off the rows of glass towers — a line of shimmering domino tiles. She sighed, daydreaming of a luxurious walk along the lake. She raised both arms to the ceiling, lowered her shoulder blades, and then bent at the hips to touch her toes. The forward bend sent a rush of tingling sensations through the backs of her legs. *There's always the Saturday morning class at the gym. I could drop in tomorrow. Start the weekend right ....*

Shortly after she'd stopped attending yoga class, she'd quit her keto diet and begun to leave her smartwatch on the dresser; after all, it only quantified her lack of activity and added to her anxiety. Her marketing blog — once updated daily with original articles and photos — was also suffering visibly from neglect. For the time being, Sameera had modified the site to allow subscribers to contribute pieces and to lead conversations. It was a makeshift solution that could tarnish her brand as a trendsetter but she tried not to dwell on that possibility. *It's temporary, just 'til I get it all under control.*

She rose to her full height and rolled her head from side to side, releasing the tension in her neck. Late last night, Shannon had offered her a massage — their precursor to sex — but Sameera had declined, determined to finish another hour of work before bed. Visibly disappointed, Shannon decided to run herself a bath. *She did make me tea first. Besides, I'm not ashamed of working hard.*

She had wasted years at GenhCor, working for a trust-fund visionary with big dreams and no substance, and now knew that those years would be recouped at City Hall. Every non-profit and municipal corporation would be at her doorstep, begging for her expertise and connections. But first, she had to revive her team from their creative slumber. She had to get out from behind her screen and find a way to engage her seven team members.

"Hey, Sameera," called Agatha Chavez, the team's search engine optimization (SEO) specialist, who seemingly appeared from nowhere, her tablet in hand. "Can you look at these linking strategies?"

"Sure thing." Sameera turned to peer at Agatha's screen.

Her team of twenty-somethings messaged her throughout the day and through several platforms, but they rarely stopped by her cubicle to discuss work. They were disinclined to in-person contact. Online, they held multiple concurrent conversations while working. Agatha's appearance piqued her curiosity.

"Nice work, Agatha," Sameera commented with enthusiasm, eager to acknowledge the creativity of her SEO specialist.

Having researched Agatha's qualifications and portfolio online, Sameera recognized her as a talented marketing tactician with a proven track record. She was someone who was most likely sought after by other firms. Yet, during Agatha's nine-month stint at City Hall, she had been tasked with performing minor updates to an antiquated online system. It was Sameera's good fortune that Agatha had not resigned. *Is she Filipina or Latina? Agatha … that's a Christian name, right?* Sameera wondered for a moment before she scolded herself, *Oh, and what the fuck does it matter?!*

"That's definitely going to get us more traffic through the hub," Sameera remarked, taking a seat and nodding approvingly at Agatha. "Wanna present it at the next quarterly … Wednesday, I think?"

Agatha beamed, and Sameera knew she had hit the mark.

"Yeah, I can do that," Agatha agreed. "Maybe a demo for the higher-ups?"

"Yes, even better. Good thinking," Sameera said, adding further praise.

Just then, Courtney Moore, a forty-something manager from Infrastructure Services, appeared at her cubicle entrance carrying her oversized travel mug, laptop, and customary disgruntled expression. She had offered to walk Sameera to her first ADM, an all managers and directors meeting held monthly in the West Tower. Sameera had accepted the offer, careful to avoid offending the queen bee of the managers and close friend of Sheila, the snarky front desk receptionist.

Now, Courtney stood rigidly beside Agatha, whom she ignored, and offered Sameera a tight smile. The small space grew quiet and tense. Something about the way Courtney did not acknowledge Agatha implied that she habitually ignored non-management staff, with the exception of gatekeeper Sheila.

"'kay, bye," Agatha said to Sameera, retrieving her tablet and bounding out of the cubicle.

"Good work, Agatha," Sameera said, loud enough for their team members in the adjacent cubicles to hear.

Courtney pulled a face to signal that Sameera's volume was disruptive.

"I like to compliment them publicly," Sameera explained, trying to give context to her volume.

"Why?" asked Courtney, her forehead knotted.

"Because, they need it," Sameera said dryly, then picked up her tablet and began to follow Courtney — who had started walking away — down the halway toward the elevators.

Courtney sneered, pounding the elevator button with barely repressed anger and then immediately checking her French manicure for scuffs. "They're not children. Why are millennials so desperate for approval?!"

I wonder if I could manage to wear polish. Maybe something clear, Sameera contemplated, not even remotely interested in outing herself as also a millennial. There was no benefit to being forthright with Courtney about her poor management style. *The woman's too burnt out and disillusioned to care.* Sameera had read about the midlife crises among Gen-X women — the cohort raised to believe they could have both a career and a family, only to realize that it was a figment of their mothers' imaginations. *At least she's white. And straight. She could have had it a lot worse.*

"So, any plans for the weekend?" Sameera tried to change the topic as they entered the empty elevator.

"Yeah, my in-laws are taking the kids," Courtney said, hitting the button for the main floor with gusto. "And I get to catch up on quarter-end reports. You?"

"Uh, my girlfriend Shannon really wants to bike down to Lakeshore but—" Sameera started.

Courtney's hand shot out and landed on Sameera's forearm, and an animated and hungry expression blossomed on her face.

Despite being alone in the elevator, Courtney leaned in to ask, "Girlfriend-girlfriend? Like Ellen DeGeneres and her … wife?"

"Portia de Rossi. Yes, but we're not married," Sameera answered plainly in the hopes that her uncomplicated answer would curtail the predictable line of personal questions.

She did not trust Courtney enough to confide in her about her romantic relationships. Sameera had learned to avoid oversharing with co-workers from past experiences, especially with the eager ones who were very curious about her life as a woman in a same-sex relationship. Casually, Sameera took half a step backwards, forcing Courtney to drop her hand.

Then, she continued, "Shannon really likes biking but I'm not as—"

Interrupting again, Courtney probed, "But, what about your family? Did they disown you?"

Sameera looked at her quizzically, trying to silently urge her to change the topic by delaying her response.

Instead, Courtney filled in the awkward gap, "I thought Muslims didn't accept gay people."

Sameera took a deep breath and glanced at the panel above the doors. *Another five floors to freedom.*

"Good thing I'm not Muslim," Sameera clarified without animus, "and I think Islam is like all the other religions. Some sects accept diversity and others—"

"You're not Muslim? But you said you're from Iraq," Courtney jumped in.

"Iran, and we're not all Muslim," Sameera explained, turning up the corners of her mouth to avoid coming across as dismissive as she felt. "Uh, yeah, so I'm probably sleeping in. Maybe catching up on shows."

Her curiosity dampened slightly, Courtney's shoulders drooped and she returned to her customary wistfulness, "Lucky you. I'd be happy to get even an hour to veg in front of the TV."

Mustering all the enthusiasm she could to continue the conversation, Sameera asked politely, "Oh, what're you watching these days?"

Predictably, Courtney shrugged and rolled her eyes. A distasteful habit from youth, Sameera presumed. Were she to roll her eyes or shrug in response to co-workers, she'd have a reputation as an ungrateful immigrant. Nevertheless, responding rudely was not conducive to her goals or even in her repertoire . *Maybe getting to be rude is a white thing … yes, definitely a white privilege.*

Courtney went on to describe the drama series she was binge watching, "It's about a woman, a lawyer, who kills her best friend's husband but she doesn't tell her and she has to hide the body … but it's okay because he was a womanizer and corrupt, too, stealing from the bank he worked at … anyways, she … the lawyer … finds out that her friend was planning to kill him anyway …"

The elevator doors opened, and Courtney continued jabbering

as she crossed the atrium to the elevators for the second tower. Sameera followed a step behind in the hopes that it might discourage Courtney from blathering on about an unlikely drama in which wealthy white people kill each other. *Everyone knows rich white people don't kill each other; they sue each other. They kill Black people, or they call the cops to kill Black people.*

At the elevators for the second tower, Courtney pressed the button, this time tenderly, and continued her monologue. By the time they stepped out onto the fourth floor, Sameera had grouped favourite TV shows with religion and politics as topics to never discuss with white co-workers.

When Courtney paused to look at her phone, Sameera took the opportunity to change topics, "I'm excited to meet Howard Crawley. I hear he's shaking up the old-school approach."

"Enh, I guess," Courtney shrugged, her eyes locked on her phone as they trod through the wide hallways between the multiple conference rooms on the fourth floor. "He's okay."

Sameera reminded herself that anyone as disengaged as Courtney was unlikely to look forward to new initiatives. The path of least resistance was paved with the same programs and services year after year, primarily because it required less creative input. *I don't blame her for being indifferent. They cut our hours and still expect us to churn out first-rate work.*

Nonetheless, she was excited by Howard Crawley's strategies to engage marginalized communities. His message about bridging the racial digital divide, by empowering businesses and non-profits in racialized communities with technical and social media support, had caused her to gasp. *I couldn't have asked for a better opportunity. This project is gonna skyrocket my career. There won't be a Steve or Jennifer who can top me.*

"Don't get your hopes up, though. These meetings are pretty mundane," Courtney remarked as they approached the forty-person conference room.

Mere steps before they walked through the open double doors, Courtney whispered in a sage tone, "And don't say a word, unless you want more work."

"Yeah, course not," Sameera mimicked Courtney's disaffected tone to amuse herself. *Enough white privilege to suffocate a Brown woman.*

* * *

Goldie was at a loss about how to react to Beth's criticisms but she knew enough to blink back her tears. It was Friday morning, and Patricia had called Goldie and Beth into her office for an impromptu meeting. For the past five minutes, Beth had been relaying to Patricia every error Goldie had committed over the course of three weeks, mistakes Goldie had made in the process of updating the regional transit database.

She forced herself to remain seated and listen attentively, though she wanted to run out the door, away from the humiliation of having her work labelled defective and inadequate. She thought she had performed well, and she felt foolish for assuming so.

"Here's an entry from three days ago, and there are several incorrect inputs," Beth said sternly as she handed another red-inked printout to Patricia to examine. "See fields HF6 and HF8 are in the completely wrong format. And then there's the EF fields, the whole row is ...."

Beth continued itemizing Goldie's errors, all the while ignoring her trainee and directing all her comments to Patricia. The embarrassment and shame of being reported to her manager, like an irredeemable delinquent, kept Goldie from facing Patricia. Her temptation was to resign on the spot and end the torture of having to listen to Beth's chronicles. *I'm so done. Might as well quit no cap. Why're we even meeting?!*

The previous weeks had jaundiced her hopes of establishing a career in the municipal corporation, and this meeting seemed to signal the death of her aspirations. She was not meeting job expectations, none of her team members engaged her, and there were only two months left before the end of her contract, at which point she'd lose her coveted status as an internal applicant for municipal job openings.

Already, the stress of being disregarded by her teammates had led to regular bouts of crying in the washroom stall. Now, she was also considered inadequate, a weak link in the team, and she had to bite her inner cheek to keep from crying during the meeting. She sought comfort in her hair, smoothing out the strands against her sweater.

"This one is riddled with errors, see on line 23, and there on … on the other side of the page," Beth continued her line of prosecution, momentarily leaning over Patricia's desk to jab at a printout.

The vehemence in Beth's demeanour shocked Goldie since they had not spent any time together following her first couple of days of training. Initially, Goldie had felt proud of her independence and what she perceived as Beth's confidence in her skills. When Goldie did need help, she went in search of Beth but often ended up requesting assistance from the other two database administrators in the team, Sandra and Holly, who sat around the corner from her cubicle.

Goldie assumed that Beth, who had served in the role for over a decade and who was the sole person responsible for generating database reports on behalf of the Transportation Services Division, was withdrawn because she was overwhelmed with work, or possibly a recluse by nature. As time passed, this proved to be wrong; Goldie observed that Beth chatted easily and often with Sandra and Holly. When Goldie tried to include herself in their conversations, it felt cumbersome and uncomfortable, and so she stopped trying. *Basic AF. Not like we have anything in common. Kids … mortgages, and shit.*

"I don't know how things are done elsewhere," Beth turned to sneer at Goldie, "but here we pay a lot of attention to our work."

Patricia did not address the personal attack. She seemed absorbed by the printouts on her desk, and Goldie wondered whether she had heard Beth's biting remark. When Goldie refused to meet Beth's gaze, she resumed itemizing Goldie's errors in gruelling detail to Patricia. *Elsewhere?! Where else is she talking about? She knows this is my first job.*

Goldie wanted to defend herself but she was bewildered by Beth's portrayal of her work. Her performance was the one thing about which she had felt confident. By the end of her first week, she had doubled the rate at which she updated records, and in her second week, she had memorized all the shortcuts and some of the common troubleshooting methods.

The previous week, Goldie had been inspired to produce a wiki page on the intranet, a resource that identified the procedural tasks, troubleshooting tactics, and various tips and tricks she had collected after considerable research and enquiries. Although Beth, and to a lesser extent Sandra and Holly, were proficient in managing the transit database, no one else in the division knew how to use the database to produce reports used most commonly, including Patricia Addington, the division manager.

Goldie had imagined that her contribution to the team in the form of a handy wiki that compiled their knowledge, truly a credit to their years of experience, would be welcomed. When she'd suggested her idea to Patricia, her manager had commended the undertaking and applauded Goldie for prioritizing team success.

Beth's reaction, on the other hand, had been severe. She'd dismissed the wiki as a threat to the integrity of the database and refused to discuss the idea any further. Goldie had tried to explain her intention, which was to empower other teams and to improve the flow of information, but Beth had accused her of insubordination. The term had terrified Goldie, so she had not broached the topic again with Beth.

That was the last conversation they had before Goldie was called into Patricia's office.

"Alright, I see what you mean," Patricia said plainly, interrupting Beth.

Unfazed, Beth continued pontificating, "The integrity of the database is very important, and these are the errors I noticed and fixed but I don't have time to keep reviewing hundreds of records to catch mistakes and what about the—"

"I agree, the database is very important," Patricia repeated. "Can I keep these printouts?"

Beth nodded, then leaned forward, and placed the remaining stack of papers on Patricia's desk. Shame had curdled Goldie's confidence and she kept her gaze low, staring at the pile that documented her failure. How had she lost sight of her main responsibility: to enter data accurately? *Yikes. Such an idiot! I shoulda stayed on task.*

"I will discuss this matter with Goldie. Thank you for your help, Beth," Patricia said, interweaving her slender, manicured fingers on her desk and pausing long enough for Beth to leave.

When Goldie heard the door latch behind Beth, the first tear escaped and ran the length of her cheek and down to her chin. She tried to stop the ensuing flood of tears but she failed, and soon she was accepting a box of tissues and weeping into her palms. A couple of minutes later, she accepted a glass of water and sat facing Patricia who had taken the seat vacated by Beth.

"I'm sorry, about the mistakes … and my crying. I shouldn't … I'm sorry," Goldie apologized, wiping her nose and smoothing out her hair.

"No need to apologize. It's not easy hearing criticism," Patricia reassured her, patting her knee.

"Hmm," Goldie managed, taking a moment to inhale deeply and look out the window at the cityscape.

Patricia leaned back in her chair and crossed her arms. It was difficult for Goldie to read the older woman's expression. She was definitely contemplating something but it was difficult to discern whether she was disappointed or amused. In the previous weeks, Goldie had not spent any significant amount of time with Patricia to be able to read her well. Her manager seemed unflappable but she also seemed sociable and supportive of others.

"How is the wiki coming along?" Patricia asked plainly, as if the meeting had not started with a verbal flogging.

"Uh, the wiki, I …" Goldie stammered as she tried to follow Patricia's lead and change topics. "It's … skeletal, I guess. I mean, I added the main pages, and some headings and subheadings but there's no content yet."

Patricia adjusted her seat, recrossed her arms, and gazed out the window. This time, she looked like she was pondering a delectable idea. Patricia stroked her own chin, and Goldie noticed that her manager was nodding to herself.

"Good," Patricia said, turning slightly to face Goldie. "Keep at it. If you arrive at a stumbling block, come to me."

"You want me to make the wiki?" Goldie asked, more perplexed than ever.

"Oh, yes. It's a brilliant idea," Patricia said smilingly. "Once you've got the basics filled in, we can present it to the other divisions."

Goldie felt her eyes widen and her jaw drop at Patricia's idea. She tried to formulate a question that was not insulting of her manager, or one that did not undermine Patricia's authority or her intelligence. *Deadass, lady? Beth thinks I'm a fuck-up. You're fucking mental!*

"I don't understand," Goldie said slowly, glancing in the direction of the stack of printouts to make her point.

"The wiki, it's ingenious. Encourages teams throughout City Hall to use our data," Patricia reasoned, tapping her knee.

"But, they already do. I mean, we already generate reports for them," Goldie said flatly, knowing that she was stating the obvious and certain that she had failed to grasp some underlying message. "Right?"

"Yes, that's true," Patricia said with a glimmer of pleasure. "Right now, we generate the reports. The wiki, if it's thorough, empowers teams to generate their own reports."

Goldie nodded in response but she did not understand the significance of empowering other teams. Based on Beth's arrogance, generating reports was the most important function performed by the team, followed by the work of updating the database with the barrage of incoming information from the various transit centres. *Dang, Goldie! What is she fucking talking about?! What am I supposed to be doing?*

"So, keep me updated as you make progress," Patricia said, uncrossing her legs and sitting up. "I know a couple of the information architects upstairs, if you need help with that."

What's an information architect? Is that a person or a machine? How do I know if I need one?

Patricia stood up and walked around her desk to her own chair. Goldie had many questions but she was also eager to leave the office. On Patricia's desk lay a stack of printouts documenting all of the errors Goldie had made in the past three weeks. Goldie must have stared at them a beat too long because they caught Patricia's attention as well.

"Take these with you. Look them over," Patricia said casually, collecting the pile.

Goldie accepted the papers with a shaking hand, and said reflexively, "Thank you."

"Yes, you're welcome. Good luck," Patricia added with a reassuring smile.

"Thank you," Goldie repeated as she left the office and closed the door behind her.

In her hand was a pile of papers, and in her head was a jumble of questions. Nothing about the meeting made any sense — not Beth's contempt for her mistakes or Patricia's exuberance about the wiki. It seemed that Goldie had attended two meetings, distinct and disparate from each other, and neither conversation offered Goldie any indication of her own standing within the team.

Am I doing shitty or not? Is Beth wrong, or am I really a total fuck-up? Does Patricia think I suck? Is she just being nice 'cuz I'm new? Are my mistakes normal? Is she just bad at her job and doesn't know that I suck too?

As Goldie walked toward her cubicle, tears began to form in her eyes. She could not imagine facing Beth, or Sandra and Holly, in whom Goldie was certain Beth had confided about the meeting. Instead, she turned down the hall toward the washrooms, tugging at her straight hair for comfort. *Stay chill. Just, stay chill.*

* * *

On Friday afternoon, Faiza listened inattentively as Howard presented a vision of inclusive city building to the fourth-floor conference room, packed with three dozen managers and directors. It was her vision, based on her research, but he neglected to mention that. Instead, he trumpeted her ideas as he strode about the front of the room, exuding confidence in his tailored suit and with his forceful gestures.

Seated upfront and facing the audience, Faiza meditatively sipped the black tea that served as her lunch. She was visible to every pair of eyes in that room, and she had no intention of revealing her disgust in the CM's thievery. As far as she was concerned, publicizing Howard's transgression would be adding insult to her injury.

The week prior, he had pulled the same stunt at the Inclusivity Advisory Committee meeting with elected officials and upper management. Minutes before its commencement, Howard declared that he was the better orator, more influential and commanding, and then tasked Faiza with running the slideshow. Toward the end of the meeting, when the committee agreed unanimously to pursue her strategies, she struggled to remain composed as they praised Howard. *I should've called him out.* Pedar sag, *asshole.*

She sat up taller, to accentuate her slim torso, and took another graceful sip. Faiza reassured herself that she was playing Howard's game according to his rules and he would reward her when it was time for promotions. She refused to jeopardize her career by challenging her highly influential superior — she was determined to bide her time and wait for him to reciprocate.

"... and it is time for City Hall to do its part. Inclusivity begins here!" Howard concluded the presentation with a flourish. "Of course, your feedback is also important."

Immediately, half the attendees raised their hands, as Faiza expected. The directors and managers were tasked with translating the strategies into practical tactics, and understandably, they were asking complex follow-up questions about resources and mandates. Theirs were questions which members of last week's committee could not have conceived given their lack of knowledge and exposure to the daily management of city programs and services. Theirs were also questions which Howard had not pondered, and his unease was apparent in the furrowing of his brow and the setting of his jaw.

Sitting across the immense conference table was Voula, Faiza's ally and director of the Customer Service team, who was coyly smiling at the CM's discomfort. Her large brown eyes sparkled as Howard stammered while trying to answer their questions, and, to avoid snickering herself, Faiza looked down and brushed invisible crumbs from her lap.

"All of that will get sorted out in time," Howard said impatiently to the room, now full of discontented whispers.

He slumped in his leather chair at the head of the table, glum at having his success sullied by mundane practical questions, and side-eyed Faiza who sat on his left. When another three hands rose,

Howard looked at Faiza accusingly, as if she had set him up for failure.

She leaned toward him and asked quietly, "Shall I take some of the questions?"

Howard gave her permission with a small nod, and then busied himself with his phone, not bothering to present Faiza to the room or look up as she stood and addressed her peers. *Ungrateful son of a bitch.*

For the next half-hour, Faiza fielded questions, offering answers where possible, accepting feedback, and suggesting network opportunities between teams that might face similar challenges. The cooperative tone of the audience was palpable, and Faiza recognized it as a function of their attributing her strategies to Howard. No one wanted to offend or contradict the CM, a well-connected bureaucrat who could bring their career successions to a halt. Had the audience known that she had been the one to develop the strategies, Faiza expected there would have been more pushback. *Maybe it is better that Howard leads this project. He's always taken more seriously. There'll be more buy-in and a better chance of follow-through.*

"It might be prudent to connect with Rosamie's team," Faiza suggested in response to another manager's scheduling concerns.

Presently, a chuckle came from her right, and Faiza glanced at Howard who was preoccupied with his phone. She recognized a popular messaging platform and a thread of messages with altered images of the American president. Howard was often distracted by his phone when they attended meetings, and Faiza dedicated an unreasonable amount of time reiterating conversations after the fact. *When did I turn into his assistant?!*

A hand rose from the outer circle of the conference room and attracted Faiza's attention. She nodded at the wild-haired woman whom she recognized from a couple of weeks ago — the new manager in the media group, Sameera.

Sameera stood and confidently introduced herself to the room, "Hello, I'm Sameera. I lead the Web and Digital Comm team. I have a question for Mr. Crawley, um Howard."

Everyone, including Faiza turned to the CM, who was still consumed by his screen, scrolling mindlessly.

"Mr. Crawley," Sameera started, and then paused for him to look up.

Howard did not register that his name was being called, so Faiza lightly tapped his leg with hers. He shot her a perturbed look before he realized that the room of managers and directors was gazing at him. Reluctantly, he rose and straightened his suit jacket and pants.

Faiza took her seat and turned to the CM with a pleasant, attentive expression, knowing that the audience studied her as carefully as they did Howard. After Faiza's promotion from manager of Customer Services to director of Program Support, Voula had informed her that those closest to the CM were characterizing her as duplicitous and cutthroat. Her seven years of exemplary public service and her dual master's degrees in business administration and public administration were seemingly irrelevant to the naysayers. They felt robbed of their opportunity to climb the corporate ladder, and Faiza was an easy target. In a show of solidarity, Voula had scoffed loudly enough for anyone to hear, "We're punished both ways. Either we're overeducated self-publicists or know-nothing outsiders."

She brushed more imaginary crumbs from her lap and smiled up at Howard, who disgusted her despite his fine clothes and perfect grooming. *They probably think I'm sleeping with him.* Bisharaf-ha, *wretches!*

"Mr. Crawley," Sameera restarted, "First, I want to say that this is a truly progressive approach to city building. I think it might be a real game-changer for marginalized communities."

Inwardly, Faiza rolled her eyes at the servile comment, and

wondered why managers ever tried to be recognized by Howard Crawley. She knew that he regarded managers as expensive babysitters and directors as a necessary evil; everyone else in City Hall was a nameless expenditure in the personnel budget. *Then again, flattery is the only frequency he hears.*

Yet, more than anyone else at City Hall, Howard Crawley loved to be admired. Pleased with the compliment, Howard smiled broadly and announced, "Yes, it is a game-changer. We need to be spearheading these kinds of initiatives. It's what our residents deserve."

Then, he made to sit down but Sameera interjected, "Yes, I agree. Mr. Crawley. That's really important. And from the recent public policy research coming out, there's evidence that increasing representation of marginalized groups in the public service is the long game to improving engagement."

The new manager paused expectantly, still smiling, and Faiza glanced up to find a familiar expression on Howard's face. He had never been comfortable handling unscripted questions, and at that moment, Faiza recognized the disguised look of contempt. It was his tight smile and narrowed eyes that willed the new hire to sit down and shut up, but she did not.

"I mean, if we want to promote inclusivity in city building, as your presentation laid out, then it makes sense that we hire greater numbers of people from the same marginalized groups," Sameera remarked earnestly.

At this point, Faiza realized that the new manager was not seeking Howard's approval. Sameera Jahani was attempting to engage Howard intellectually, to build on the ideas which she attributed to him, Faiza's ideas for inclusivity. *Fat chance of that!*

Howard exhaled from his nostrils, a scornful move only Faiza registered, and she knew that Sameera Jahani was about to be rebuked. Then, with a confident grin and in a casual, comedic tone, he replied, "There's always room for new talent. If you've got a cousin in mind, send them to HR."

Titters erupted throughout the conference room, and Sameer Jahani's face fell for a moment. She remained standing while Howard Crawley took his seat, quickly resuming his preoccupation with memes.

Faiza watched the managers seated on each side of Sameera pull away slightly, and she thought about the backlash the new hire would face from her peers. The snickering died down but the shuffling of papers signalled an agitated audience who was ready for the meeting to end. Faiza made to stand but the new manager continued.

"Yes, alright. I understand, Mr. Crawley," Sameera started shakily. "I mean that as city manager, someone obviously interested in inclusivity, I would think hiring from targeted groups to increase representation would—"

"We can't hire everyone off the boat," Howard scoffed, glancing at Sameera briefly and then turning to Faiza with a pointed look.

Faiza knew that she was expected to end the meeting and bring the question period to a close, but she delayed action for another moment. Sameera Jahani was standing resolutely, though obviously shaken by the exchange, and Faiza wanted to know what more she had to say. After all, witnessing Howard Crawley grow flustered by intelligent people was a perk of the job which Faiza rarely denied herself.

"Right, not everyone," Sameera agreed urgently over the murmurs of a restless audience. "But an outsider might question our inclusivity policies when a packed room of managers is overwhelmingly white."

Silence descended on the conference room, and the only movement was that of glances darting from Howard Crawley to the new manager and back.

Without rising or speaking directly to Sameera, Howard announced, "HR can address any concerns about diversity initiatives. Thank you all. End of meeting."

Instantly, bodies were in motion as the audience rushed to exit the conference room. Howard ignored the commotion, refocused on his screen, and leaned back in his chair to emphasize his untouched state. Faiza also remained seated as the room emptied. Astonished by the grittiness of the public exchange, she continued to stare in Sameera's direction, long after the crowd had absorbed her and all that remained was her vacant seat. Faiza wondered about the millennial's upbringing, whether she was born in Canada or grew up in Iran, and about her professional endgame, which would be severely impacted by this incident. *She might as well pack up her desk. There's no way anyone'll associate with her now.*

A twinge of pity pierced Faiza's heart as it occurred to her that Sameera's inquiry was rooted in her desire to address injustice, rather than an attempt to curry favour with the CM. The woman wanted to balance the inequities faced by marginalized persons, and she had thought that Howard wanted the same thing. All because of her presentation, which the CM had nearly nothing to do with. It was equally heroic and naïve to initiate a discussion about discrimination, especially racism, before an audience of fragile white people. *This kind of talk's too unpleasant for their white sensibilities.*

Given the chance, Faiza would have informed Sameera that change came incrementally, through covert actions. She would have advised Sameera to manipulate the powerful and work within her sphere of influence no matter how limited. Charging at the system with a rallying cry of racial equality was bound to trigger disbelief and defensiveness among white people. *Good things happen piecemeal, over time. That's a fact.*

"So, again next week, at the Community Development Committee," Howard announced, standing up and stretching his arms. "I'll have Shirley send you the invite."

"Another presentation?" Faiza asked, keeping her eyes on her laptop screen to avoid revealing her disappointment.

"Oh, send me the answers from today," Howard instructed her, tapping on his screen as he inched toward the exit.

Faiza was about to ask which answers he was referring to but she guessed it was the ones to every question he could not answer. This meant another hour of work typing up notes for Howard, for a presentation she produced, a report she authored, and on questions she could answer.

"Howard, wait a sec," Faiza said cheerily as she rose, straightened her tailored blouse and skirt, and assumed a jovial expression. "I had a question and—"

"I don't have much time," Howard interjected, eyes downcast, focused on his screen. "Meeting across town."

Uh-huh, on the green. "It won't take long," Faiza lied. She stepped into the edge of his personal space, forcing him to look up, and continued in a subdued tone, "It's about the deputy CM position, and—"

"Right," Howard interrupted her. "Listen, Faiza, our current setup works really well. I mean, we are a good team, right?"

"Oh, yes," Faiza replied with a wide smile. "I think so too, and that's why I was thinking about the Deputy—"

"So, why disrupt matters by shifting unnecessarily?" Howard asked with a grimace, shrugging to underscore his aversion to her idea.

Shifting unnecessarily?! Pedar sag, *asshole!* "You're right," Faiza said with a winsome smile. "I think we make a great team. I mean, this inclusivity and engagement initiative demonstrates how well our skills combine. We could continue in this partnership, even more successfully, if I were to serve as your deputy CM."

"Faiza, why do you even want this position?" Howard asked, disingenuously confounded. "It's more hours, more meetings, more headaches. I mean, you might as well kiss your family goodbye. God knows, I barely see my kids. Don't you have a couple?"

Faiza resisted the temptation to inform Howard that he had

met her two daughters, and she had met his whole family, on several occasions at company picnics and holiday parties. She tilted her head to appear contemplative. In the pause, she recalled the countless times when her parents required her to fulfill social obligations while her brother was permitted to abscond and study. It seemed that she had been managing work and life balance since childhood. She had never had the privilege to throw herself completely into her work.

"Certainly, it's a tough balance," Faiza replied solemnly. "These last three years working with you have taught me a lot about managing work and family life. Lessons that distinguish me as grounded, well-balanced … really the ideal candidate to serve as a Deputy CM."

"What do you want me to say, Faiza? I can't stop you from applying," Howard declared with a pout.

"I would like your endorsement," Faiza answered with a smile that pleaded for his approval. "I would like you to present me as your ideal candidate."

Howard exhaled loudly and rubbed the bridge of his nose. Another moment passed and he shrugged. "Let's see how things go," he said cagily. "I'm running late now."

"Yes, thank you, Howard," Faiza replied graciously as Howard rushed out of the room.

It'll happen. Piecemeal.

* * *

Goldie had a sliver of counter space at the hectic ramen eatery but her window seat overlooking Dundas Street West was worth it. People poured out from office towers, shops, and campuses onto the sidewalks and produced Friday evening rush hour traffic, a surge of human lives in motion. From a distance, the bustling sidewalk scene entertained her. She caught a handful of common Pokémon, more out of nervous energy than conquest.

Presently, a hunky waiter arrived with her large bowl of steaming noodle soup, the same server who had taken her payment upon ordering. She shifted on her barstool to give him access to the counter, and the closeness to his bare arms and sandalwood scent caused her groin to pulse and her thoughts to race.

I need to get out more, she thought with a sigh as he dashed back to the kitchen unaware of her response to him.

After she took a quick photo of the noodle soup, she adjusted her earphones, and started her chill playlist. With her chopsticks and flat bottom spoon at the ready, she remained leaned over the steaming bowl until she had devoured the mélange of noodles, beef slices, egg, and sprouts.

The patrons on each side of her were equally engrossed in their dishes and phones, and Goldie was grateful to be living in a city where she could be alone in a crowd. In addition to its five-dollar bowls, she had chosen the eatery based on its online ratings; in the spirit of paying forward, she posted a glowing review accompanied with the photo of her soup.

Goldie scanned her socials for more sympathetic comments from friends and acquaintances. Following the torturous meeting with Patricia and Beth, she had shut herself into a bathroom stall to cry but soon found herself posting at length about the experience. Her anger and frustration, once overshadowed by shame, surfaced as she typed feverishly in the stall, recounting the lack of training, Beth's long absences, and the cold shoulder treatment from the other staffers.

Even before she left the stall, several people had commented. People sympathized with her loneliness and expressed disgust at Beth's behaviour, and Goldie felt vindicated by their comments. The diner on her right made motions to leave, and Goldie leaned far left to give him room to squeeze past. With some breathing space, she stretched out and continued a deep dive into the newer posts. She noticed that her post had been reposted by @

tanyaassabeau, an online acquaintance and twenty-something Indigenous woman. Tanya had added her own thoughts about white women in power who closed ranks to avoid losing approval among their white peers.

Goldie grimaced as she scrolled the comments, envious of the hype Tanya had generated. Tanya's post had garnered dozens of comments from middle-aged professional women who described being scapegoated by white female co-workers. None of them mentioned her original post, and none of the experiences resonated with Goldie. While she did not dispute their claims, she did not understand how their experiences of scapegoating related to hers. *OK boomer, this isn't about colour. Beth's just a bitch.*

The pendulum swung and Goldie no longer felt validated by her peers. Once again, her search for sympathy had been appropriated by others, and she fumed as she scrolled responses to @tanyaassabeau's post. *What the fuck do they know?!* She packed her belongings and headed out the door. On Dundas Ave West, she allowed the throngs of pedestrians to carry her forward while she scoured previous posts by @tanyaassabeau. *Seriously, over two thousand followers?! Fucking hardo! She doesn't know shit.*

As she descended the stairs into the Dundas subway, she became engrossed in the disturbing stories of racialized women having their contributions overlooked or appropriated by their white co-workers. A couple of commenters described being excluded regularly from social events. They referred to microaggressions and unconscious bias so often that Goldie searched the terms for definitions. *That ain't it. Patricia likes me. She's not the problem.*

The northbound train arrived, prompting everyone on the platform to push forward. Feeling irritated, Goldie stayed back to avoid being pressed in by the commuters closing in on the open doors. She snuck in as the chimes sounded and the doors closed, and found a place to stand near the conductor's booth.

From years of taking transit, Goldie knew that the world was filled with white racists. The evidence was graffitied on bus seats and station walls. It was visible in the disrespectful way white bus drivers spoke to Black kids. Or the number of times a white person had glared at her unprovoked from across a train.

Racism exists, and she wouldn't deny that. Still, Goldie was certain that her experience in the office was ordinary, nonpolitical. The team's coolness, Beth's bad attitude, and Patricia's approach were unrelated to her ethnicity, and to believe otherwise seemed contrived, egotistical. *Beth's nasty personality is the problem. Patricia's on my side. Heck, she's trying to get me a permanent job! Isn't she?* Goldie looked up and blinked at the sudden realization that her manager might be set to make her position redundant — to make the team redundant — and her wiki would help move the process along. She slumped her shoulders back down. *Whatevs. If I hadn't done it, someone else would have.*

The train continued northbound, emptying along the way, and soon a nearby seat became available. Goldie hunkered down. For comfort, she smoothed out her hair and scrolled through photos of a friend's party, but in vain. Something about the meeting, something besides Beth's nastiness, pestered her. Beth's animosity did not completely shock Goldie. She was accustomed to boomers being rude and defensive. They seemed simultaneously envious and distrustful of her generation. It was the duality of Patricia's responses that perplexed Goldie. If Patricia approved of Goldie, why had she remained silent while Beth berated her? Was Patricia demonstrating how to handle Beth's tirade? *Fuck me, is that what Patricia's doing? Teaching me to put up with it?*

When the crackling speaker announced her stop, Goldie snapped out of her unpleasant preoccupation and rushed off the train. Suddenly, she felt very tired. She dragged her feet as she shuffled down the platform and up the stairs to the bus depot. There were two months left in her contract, and she felt exhausted thinking about the days to come.

* * *

Friday afternoon became evening, and Sameera remained buried under the covers, her pillow dampened by tears and her apartment consumed by darkness. The embarrassment of being dismissed outright, and publically, by Howard Crawley stung even hours after the ADM. She'd endured the pitying glances and patronizing head shakes as she had slunk out of the conference room, and she'd made it through the day by hiding in her cubicle, avoiding anyone who might mention the incident. Once home, she'd crawled into bed and cried until she'd fallen asleep.

She awoke to an aching head and intense hunger but she refused to rise, or even remove the covers. Fumbling between the sheets, she found her phone and checked the time. Shannon would be home soon, excited about their Friday night ritual of brewery hopping and street food, and Sameera was not in the mood to leave the apartment. She considered ordering takeout from the comfort of her hideaway; possibly burgers and poutine, Shannon's favourite.

The blue light of the screen lit up her blanket tent as Sameera browsed menus and added a copious amount of food to her cart. A notification popped up, indicating a text message from Agatha, her brightest team member.

It read, "Heard about ADM. Here if you want to talk."

Sameera dismissed the message, cringing at the vision of her coworkers sharing snippets about her mortifying exchange with the CM. Each time she reassured herself that the episode was minor, she recalled Courtney Moore, queen bee and self-appointed mentor, leaving the meeting without glancing her way, conveniently preoccupied by a conversation with another manager and too busy to offer a sympathetic smile. *He's the racist, and she treats me like a pariah. How does this even make sense? Who initiates an EDI project and then says they can't hire everyone "off the boat"? What the fuck is wrong with these people?*

The floor boards creaked and Sameera paused, hoping to hear Shannon climbing the stairs to their second-floor unit. The sounds that followed belonged to the downstairs neighbours, a trio of graduate students who travelled as a pack. Sameera's lower lip trembled in disappointment and tears escaped from the corners of her eyes. She wiped them away and tried to complete her takeout order.

Still, Crawley's quip tormented her, "If you've got a cousin … send them to HR."

More tears dripped onto the pillow, and Sameera returned to berating herself for speaking at the ADM. Courtney Moore was burnt out and uninspired but she was not a joke; she knew better than to broach a controversial topic before an undependable audience. Then again, Courtney was white and Sameera was Brown, and her being Brown was the basis of Crawley's joke. *Why was he … so offended, so hostile? I didn't say anything radical. It was all in line with that presentation.*

Keys jingled, and Sameera heard Shannon walk into their apartment. At that moment, there was no sound more welcoming than that of her girlfriend's steel-toed work boots as she clomped down the arms' length hallway, making a beeline to the kitchen. After her twelve-hour shifts at the hydro company, and having eaten every morsel in her travel cooler, Shannon still always returned home hungry. Her first destination was the fridge, where she grabbed a block of cheese and an apple.

"Babe?" Shannon called out, and Sameera could tell that her head was in the fridge.

"Hey," Sameera replied weakly from under the covers just as she submitted her takeout order.

"Where are you?" Shannon asked around a mouthful as she neared their unlit bedroom.

During their first months living together, they fell into bed as soon as Shannon returned home, and Sameera served as her lover's first course. Nowadays, they bonded at the kitchen table where they binged on snack foods and traded work stories.

"Sammy?" Shannon whispered playfully from the end of the bed.

Sameera felt her girlfriend lift the bottom edge of the blanket, and in a flash Shannon was tickling the soles of her feet.

"No, no," Sameera shrieked, kicking her legs to free them of Shannon's strong grip. "Watermelon! Watermelon!"

Upon hearing their safe word, Shannon stopped her tickling and dove under the sheets. Sameera nestled herself into Shannon's larger frame, breathing in her lover's musky fragrance and the lingering scent of solder and rubber.

"So, what're you wearing under here?" Shannon asked huskily, fondling Sameera in the dark and expecting to find her nude. "You're dressed! Well, I can fix that." Shannon's hands moved quickly to untuck Sameera's shirt.

"No, no," Sameera pleaded, pulling toward Shannon and closing the gap between their prone bodies.

"Aw, babe. What's wrong?" Shannon asked once she realized she had misinterpreted Sameera's intentions.

Grateful for the opener, Sameera sighed deeply and related her experience at the ADM. While she spoke, she kept her arms tucked in between their bodies and her nose pressed against Shannon's collarbone. It was childlike, she realized, but it met her need to be soothed, and Shannon, who was rubbing circles on Sameera's back, responded lovingly.

"I don't understand why he was being such a jerk," Sameera blubbered. "I mean, I was building on his ideas."

Shannon did not respond other than to stroke Sameera's back.

"I was basically saying the same thing. I don't understand," Sameera said shakily, remembering the side-eyes from her colleagues.

When Shannon continued to remain silent, Sameera pulled

back and pouted, though the gesture was fruitless in the dark. "What? What is it? Why are you being so quiet?" she asked, her voice quivering with concern.

Shannon shook her head and replied apathetically, "What do you want me to say?"

This expression triggered Sameera, who recognized it as disapproval and bolted upright. She snapped back at Shannon, "That I'm right. That he was being an asshole. That it doesn't make sense."

Shannon remained prone and silent. In the dark, Sameera could not make out her lover's expression but Shannon's shallow breaths signalled her annoyance.

Infuriated by the bitter turn in their conversation, Sameera exclaimed, "What?! You think I'm making this up?"

Unhurriedly, Shannon answered, "No, I don't think you're making it up. I see you're mad. I get that. It sounds really embarrassing."

Sameera waited for more to follow, something that substantiated Shannon's reproving tone and when nothing came, she shot back, "It was more than embarrassing, Shan. It was ..." *Racist!* The word refused to pass her lips. If she sounded that alarm, then all hopes for sympathy would be dashed. Instead, she settled on describing her feelings. "Insulting. Really fucking insulting."

She met more silence from her lover. Tired of being unable to read Shannon's expression in the dark, Sameera jumped out of bed and hit the switch, flooding the room with overhead light. Shannon sat up in bed, throwing her legs over the edge and leaning forward with her elbows on her knees and her fingers interlocked. Instantly, Sameera wished she had not left the bed and turned on the light. She did not know where to sit, and any distance away from Shannon seemed like an act of unkindness. Yet, she was too angry to sit next to Shannon. Compromising, Sameera sat on the same side of the bed but at the far corner.

In a muted tone, she asked, "You think I'm exaggerating?"

Matching Sameera's subdued tone, Shannon replied, "No, not

exactly. I mean, I think maybe it won't seem so bad tomorrow."

At face value, the statement seemed reasonable to Sameera. She knew that time would dampen her feelings, and if not tomorrow, then by Monday morning her distress would have dissipated. Shannon was speaking frankly about the effects of time but Sameera heard judgement in her tone, the accusation that Sameera was taking the matter too seriously in the present moment.

"What are you talking about?" Sameera growled, arms crossed in anger. "He embarrassed me in front of everyone in the room. He acted like I was hassling him."

Shannon did not respond but Sameera noticed that she rolled her eyes and puckered her lips into an expression which suggested that she sympathized with the city manager.

"You think I was hassling him?" Sameera scowled at her girlfriend who refused to look in her direction. "Seriously? That's who you think I am?"

Treating Sameera's questions as rhetorical, Shannon unclasped and clasped her hands, unresponsive. After a brief silence, she replied in a restrained tone, "Maybe, he didn't want to discuss that … the topic, at the meeting…."

Sameera jumped to her feet and barked, "So, he had to humiliate me in front of everyone? Tell me to shut up?"

Shannon remained still, pausing for a time before she responded, "I mean, did he say that? I thought you said he suggested talking to HR, or something. That's not the same as telling you to shut up."

"Why are you taking his side?" Sameera switched tracks, placing her hands on her hips and glaring at Shannon from above.

"I'm not," Shannon started, her eyes downcast and her tone flat. "I mean, you're probably not considering his perspective. Like, he was talking about one thing and probably didn't want to take attention away from it."

"I wasn't taking attention away from anything. That's bullshit," Sameera yelled and stomped her foot. "I was talking about—"

At that moment, Shannon rose and left the room, and Sameera yelled after her, "Where are you going?"

When Shannon didn't respond, Sameera followed her into the kitchen and declared, "You can't just walk away from a conversation."

Shannon rubbed her face with both her hands and after a pause, she replied evenly, "You're upset and I don't think we should keep talking about this. I'm just pointing out stuff that you don't want to hear, and it's gonna make you more upset."

"Bullshit!" Sameera exclaimed, hitting the doorjamb with her palm and causing Shannon to grimace. "I'm not upset 'cuz you're talking some truth, Shan. I'm fucking pissed off 'cuz you're taking that asshole's side."

This time, Shannon snapped back, "Right. Any side that's not yours is bullshit."

"What?!" Sameera yelled, balling up her hands into fists. "You don't even know this guy!"

"Yeah, but I know you," Shannon rebuked as she walked past Sameera and to the front door.

"What does that mean?" retorted Sameera as her girlfriend knelt to lace up her boots. "I'm the asshole?"

"Don't put words in my mouth, Sam," Shannon said through gritted teeth. "I'm trying to be civilized."

"And, I'm not?" Sameera barked. "I'm the savage, right?"

"You're laying it on thick," Shannon stated gruffly, changing position to tie up her other boot. "That's what you do. Everything is a personal attack against you. It's the world against Sam."

The character assassination hurt Sameera but it didn't stop her from yelling back, "This *was* against me!"

Shannon rose, and with her eyes squeezed shut, she shouted for the first time, "You didn't have to start the conversation!"

The conversation had gone from bad to worse and Sameera was at a loss for how to regain composure. She was always the one who grew heated in their arguments, the one who spoke loudly, stomped about, and cried in frustration, not Shannon. Her girlfriend preferred to make space. With Shannon yelling, Sameera realized that the argument had spiralled out of control. Still, she was determined to defend herself, to be heard and seen by her lover, so she continued barking at Shannon.

"It was the Q&A session and I complimented him!" Sameera said, leaning in with a scowl.

"So why did he put you off?" Shannon asked with a pointed look.

Sameera shook her head in disbelief and replied slowly, "I don't know, Shannon. And why does it matter? Do you need a reason to take my side?"

"Yes," Shannon retorted, "because you are always against something and—"

With an expression of disgust, Sameera interrupted her, "And did you wonder why? Doesn't it occur to you that people attack me, that they see me as an easy target?"

Just as quickly, Shannon rejoined, "Why? Why would people attack you? You're fucking paranoid."

Sameera was crying and angrily choked on her next words, "See! You don't understand. I have to deal with people's aggression every day."

The sight of tears dripping from Sameera's chin softened Shannon's tone. She stepped forward to place a hand on Sameera's arm but Sameera shrugged it off and stormed away, back into the bedroom.

"Why do you think everyone is against you?" Shannon called after her in a voice that expressed confusion, not anger.

"Because they are!" hollered Sameera, her anger as raw as before.

"Ugh! That's what I mean, paranoia," Shannon huffed in frustration, standing resolutely in the bedroom doorway.

At this repeated accusation, Sameera spun around and bared

her teeth. She felt like a wild animal, cornered and desperate to escape further attacks.

"You're white!" Sameera spat back, glaring at Shannon. "You're white and you have no fucking idea what you're talking about." *There, I said it! She was never gonna side with me anyway.*

Shannon grimaced in disgust as she asked, "What does that have to do with anything?"

"See, you don't even recognize your privilege!" Sameera exclaimed.

"My fucking privilege?! I grew up hiding myself to avoid getting the shit kicked out of me," said Shannon, baffled, pacing just outside the doorway. "Seriously, Sam. Not everything is about race. Where do you think we live, anyways? In the South?"

Sameera squeezed her temples as she sneered condescendingly, "Because racism only happens in the South."

Shannon, who had stopped pacing to sneer back, asked, "Why would they have hired you if they thought you were—"

Sameera completed the question with a snarl, "Inferior? Why would they hire me if they thought I was a stupid immigrant? Why'd they hire a Brown girl if they're racist?"

"Oh, come on!" Shannon whined, punching the air. "One guy doesn't answer your question, so they're all racist?"

Sameera leaped to her feet and faced her girlfriend. "What the fuck, Shannon?! What do you need to convince yourself — a lynching?"

"You're nuts!" Shannon said, throwing up her hands in surrender and stomping toward the front door.

Sameera did not form a reply quickly enough for Shannon to hear. Her girlfriend slammed their apartment door, and Sameera heard her heavy work boots clomping down the interior stairs and out the front door of the house. Immediately, Sameera dove into bed, covering herself with the blanket.

From under a pillow, a ringtone chimed. Desperate for contact with Shannon, Sameera scrabbled in the darkness to locate the phone, only to find an alert from the takeout app that her food parcel was on the porch. She pressed her face into the pillow and screamed until her throat ached.

* * *

That Friday night, Faiza arrived home in time to help Bibi with dinner. *This should make up for missing so many dinners. When everyone's sleeping, I'll work,* she thought as she stepped through the door.

The women worked side by side, discussing the children, the housework, and Bibi's heart medication. At times, they were silent, each woman preoccupied with her inner thoughts. They prepared vegetables and peanut noodles for a colourful stir fry, and Robert dropped in to exclaim about the alluring scent and their ability to cook without recipes.

"You can do it, too," Bibi addressed Robert. "Trust your intuition."

"Hmm," Robert smirked, swiping a red pepper from the frying pan. "I like instructions. I'm good with instructions."

Faiza smacked lightly at the back of Robert's hand, and pressed a stack of plates into his hands as she kissed his peanut smeared lips.

"You might like instructions but you don't follow them," Faiza quipped as she poured the cooked noodles and hot water into the colander positioned in the sink. "Remember Pari's bed? It took you three days to put it together."

Robert guffawed from the dining room, directly across the marble kitchen island, "Two line drawings do not constitute instructions."

"Robert is a good husband," Bibi said earnestly to no one in particular. "He cooks and cleans and takes care of the girls. Few husbands are helpful like Robert."

Bibi directed this last statement at her daughter, who rolled her eyes and shrugged at the sentiments she had heard before. Bibi frequently advised Faiza to demonstrate greater adoration for Robert. He deserved it for his ungrudging contribution to their family, she claimed.

When she felt diplomatic, Faiza would explain that Robert was intrinsically motivated to perform housework and parent their children; he valued equality and collaboration, and he was living his best life. Bibi would shake her head slowly and forewarn that a man who was not praised was bound to search for a woman who provided it readily.

I am not my husband's keeper, Faiza said to herself as she shook the colander over the sink, releasing steam.

Robert returned to the kitchen and swiped another sautéed red pepper from the wok while Faiza was occupied at the sink.

"Rob! There won't be anything left to eat," Faiza chided, sweeping a leg in his direction.

"It was quality control, I swear. That pepper was misshapen," Robert joked, approaching Faiza from behind and nuzzling her neck.

Aware that her mother was watching them covertly, Faiza softened her tone and asked Robert to finish setting the table.

Faiza's divorce had traumatized Bibi, who interpreted irreconcilable differences as her former son-in-law's unhappiness with her daughter's conduct. Faiza explained to Bibi with restrained bitterness how they had grown apart and become invested in different life goals. Unmoved, Bibi maintained that it was Faiza's demanding work schedule that had caused her divorce.

Faiza did not deny that she worked long hours or that she desired a prominent position at City Hall. Her parents had pressured both their children to complete graduate studies and seek prestigious positions in government. Bibi had been immensely proud during Faiza's convocation and boasted to their relations when Faiza landed her first position in Iran's Ministry of Economic Affairs and Finance.

She doesn't tell Firouz to work less, Faiza thought as she nudged the last strands of pasta out from the colander and into the wok.

She considered her older brother's work-life balance, or lack thereof. Firouz spent nearly every waking hour at his office, having had to be dragged away for the births of his daughters. He resented any task unrelated to his engineering enterprise, so he hired a housekeeper, a car service, and a nanny while he attended to his infrastructure projects.

Faiza empathized with her brother. As much as she enjoyed spending time with her daughters and Robert, it was her work that galvanized her most. She was a powerful executive in a prestigious organization and her work impacted over two million residents of the largest city in Canada. Being a mother and a wife were roles she cherished but being an executive at City Hall was central to her identity and sense of purpose. *And I'm supposed to worry about my husband deserting me, while Firouz lives at the office and our mother tells his wife to cope.*

"Mama!" Pari cried as she rushed into the kitchen to her mother's side. "Mina said I can't ride the tubes. She called me a baby."

Faiza's hands were wet from preparing the pasta, and she reached for a cloth before kneeling to soothe seven-year-old Pari. From the corner of her eye, she noticed Bibi discretely watching her as she tended to her young child.

Bibi had once analogized Faiza's style of parenting to cutting the grass when the neighbours complained. Faiza admitted that she preferred thinking her own thoughts to playing their games, and she'd rather wait out their arguments than become tangled. She believed that distance allowed Mina and Pari to learn about themselves but Bibi interfered often, negating the effect. *She acts like there's only one way to be a good mother. It's bad enough out there, with all the working-mom guilt. Does she have to shame me in my own house?*

As Faiza brushed away the hairs from Pari's brow, she said gently, "Pari-*jaan*, I'm sure you and Mina can work it out. Why don't you go back and talk to her?"

"No, she's not nice. She called me a baby," Pari insisted, crossing her arms and frowning at her mother. "I can go on the tube rides. Daddy said so."

Faiza did not know which rides Pari was referring to but she understood anxiety centred on missing out. The world seemed set on leaving Faiza out of every equation, and she had fought since childhood to be seen as a person worthy of consideration. Like herself, her daughters also demanded inclusion, and Faiza had made it her habit to validate their demands first and ask questions second.

Before Faiza could respond, Bibi chastised the young girl, "Pari, you need to respect your older sister."

With a jerk, Pari pulled out from her mother's tender embrace and stomped down the hall crying. Bibi tsk-tsked her grandchild and began tossing the noodles, vegetables, and peanut sauce in the wok. Faiza heard her mutter about insolent children and the predictable consequences of lax parenting.

The skin on the back of Faiza's neck grew hot as her temper rose. She considered several harsh rebukes to assert her own authority. Then, her gaze fell upon Robert, standing in the dining room, and from his wary expression, Faiza knew better than to berate Bibi, a strategy that had not paid off once during their six years living together. Admonishing Bibi only contributed to the compounding resentment that characterized their mother-daughter relationship.

Presently, Robert approached the kitchen island, cleared his throat, and called respectfully to his mother-in-law, "Bibi-*jaan*."

Her eyes sparkling with esteem, Bibi turned to Robert. He was her beloved son-in-law, the beautiful man who married her divorced daughter, accepted Mina as his own, and created a new family by fathering Pari. Her mother's enchantment with white skin and masculinity, a mindset rooted in her upbringing, made her imperious to Robert's shortcomings. While Faiza was leery of enabling Bibi's bigotry by having Robert speak for them, he never suffered consequences. As far as Bibi was concerned, Robert could do no wrong. With a modicum of shame, Faiza turned her gaze and busied her hands at the stovetop.

"Hmm, Robert-*jaan*?" Bibi asked sweetly. "You want me to add peanuts, too. I can sprinkle them on top. Or maybe a bowl of chopped peanuts for the table?"

"*Bale, merci.* Yes, thank you. Peanuts are good," Robert started courteously but continued with resolve, "Um, Bibi-*jaan*, you are a wonderful grandparent. The girls are lucky to have you."

"Ah, Robert!" exclaimed Bibi, swatting away at the compliments. She smiled at Faiza knowingly, and her daughter understood the message: *Even Robert understands the importance of praise.*

As Bibi crossed to the kitchen island to stand across from her son-in-law, she said in a honeyed tone, "I am even luckier to have them."

Faiza watched Robert offer Bibi a charitable smile, and she realized that he was mustering courage. The man who avoided teachers and mechanics because one-on-one exchanges unnerved him was about to address her mother's nasty habit of butting into their parenting.

At the sink, Faiza busied herself with cleaning pots and utensils as quietly as possible to overhear their talk. Over her left shoulder, she eyed Bibi's unconcerned demeanour and Robert's face, reddening from the neck up.

He cleared his throat again, and addressed the island countertop, "Yes, yes … Bibi-*jaan*, it's my uh … opinion that some … some jobs are best suited to grandparents. And some jobs that are … jobs for parents."

"Hmm?" Bibi said, stepping back and tilting her head with suspicion. "Okay."

"Okay," Robert said, still speaking to the countertop. "And, when we are doing parenting jobs, then we need space for that ...."

"*Bale*, yes," Bibi replied coolly, rubbing a spot on the counter with her thumb. "Okay."

"Okay," Robert repeated with relief, lifting his eyes to smile appreciatively at Bibi. "Okay. Thank you, Bibi. You're a wonderful *maman-bozorg*, grandmother."

"*Mo-chakeram*, thank you, Robert-*jaan*," Bibi replied politely.

Soon, he had turned away and absorbed himself with setting the napkins and utensils, seemingly content with the result of their conversation. Faiza remained uneasy because she had sensed the defensiveness and resentment in Bibi's reaction.

Presently, Bibi arrived at Faiza's elbow with an unenthused expression. Faiza focused on the sudsy dishwater in the sink now devoid of dishes, and began washing the sink itself to avoid her mother's gaze.

Speaking with reticence, Bibi said, "*Un ke nameetun-e beraqs-e, mig-e zameen kaj ast.* One who can't dance claims that the floor is uneven."

In one proverb, Bibi had recast the conversation with Robert and placed Faiza in the role of antagonist, and the message had changed from Bibi's lack of respect for boundaries to Faiza's refusal to adjust her parenting style. Faiza did not look up from the dishwater because she did not know how to respond. *Ugh, she blames me! Nothing sticks to him!*

A moment later, Bibi retired for the night, claiming fatigue and the need for an early bedtime. She exited swiftly, depriving Faiza or Robert the opportunity to plead for her to remain, at least through the dinner meal.

When they were alone, Robert asked guiltily, "Was it 'cuz of what I said?"

Faiza touched his arm, nodded slowly, and replied, "Don't worry. She's not mad at you."

"She looked mad," Robert said frowning and glancing at the empty doorway where Bibi last stood.

"Oh, yes, she's mad," Faiza agreed, swiping a bite-size broccoli floret from the large serving dish of steaming stir fry. "But she's not mad at you."

"Oh," Robert replied, seeming more disappointed than relieved. "Sorry."

"It's alright," Faiza reassured him, chewing on broccoli and plucking a snow pea. "You were trying to help."

Her words did not seem to comfort Robert, who continued to stare at the empty doorway. Faiza prepared a tray with a bowl of stir fry, complete with a small bowl of chopped peanuts, a tumbler of mango juice, and Bibi's nightly dose of heart medication.

"Here, take this to her," Faiza advised, pressing the tray into his arms.

"Why me?" Robert asked, puzzled but taking hold of the tray. "If she's mad at you, then you should—"

Faiza interrupted him, "She'll take it better if it comes from you."

"Oh," Robert said, staring at the tray and grasping at his wife's logic.

To discourage Robert from asking for an explanation, answers that would reveal the depth of inequality she suffered even in her own home, Faiza preoccupied herself with putting out the salad and filling juice glasses. Robert did not speak, nor did he rise. He remained holding the tray of food in his lap, needing more time to recover from difficult conversations than she did.

"On your way back, can you please call the girls to dinner?" Faiza requested, returning to the kitchen for salad tongs.

"Yeah, I will," Robert answered softly, slowly stirring from his unsettling thoughts.

To lighten the mood, Faiza asked, "What are the tube rides?"

"Hmm? The tube rides …" Robert started. "Oh, Pari and Mina wanted to go to the water park. We planned it for tomorrow."

"Oh," Faiza replied, instantly realizing that she had started a conversation that was sure to underscore her absence as a parent. She did not return to the dining table, though she had found the salad tongs. Instead, she filled a glass with wine and drank in the corner of the kitchen, pretending to wipe the spotless counters.

"Did you want to come tomorrow? I didn't ask. I didn't think it'd be … you know, something you would want to do," Robert said in a hurry. "Do you?"

"No, no," Faiza said without turning around. She could not face Robert or the truth about how she wanted to spend her time. "You all go. Have fun."

"You can always change your mind," Robert said encouragingly.

Faiza did not respond. She waited for Robert to leave with the tray, and then she refilled her wine glass. *Bibi's right. I'm terrible at this.*

Chapter 3

Wednesday Evening, June 20, 2018

Sameera listened from her cubicle as the last of her colleagues bid each other farewell. It was nearly six o'clock. The chitter chatter that punctuated the day's end had dissipated, signalling an empty floor. Two weeks had passed since the ADM but her work life had not returned to normal. While her co-workers weren't hostile or unfriendly, Sameera sensed discomfort in every interaction. *They think they know me. See if I care.*

She might have been less miserable about work if her home life was not even more disheartening. She stared at Shannon's framed portrait smiling at her from the corner of her cubicle, a smile Sameera had not seen in person since their heated argument. They had reconciled but their reunion lacked tenderness and generosity. Implicitly, they agreed to disagree on a profound issue, a matter of deepest principles. She assured herself that it was a natural part of long-term relationships. *This is normal. Couples argue.*

Sameera knew that Howard Crawley had insulted her readily and publically because she was a woman of colour, an easy target. *He knew he could get away with it.* She also knew that Shannon refused to believe this, and Sameera was determined to manage these truths to maintain her relationship. At home, she talked about her meetings and projects but she never mentioned her anger at the CM and her resentment of her co-workers. Censoring herself was a bad habit from the past she had mastered in her youth when she catered to the sensibilities of white friends. *It's no better at work. If it wasn't for Agatha, I'd barely say anything about myself. Whatever happened to celebrating my differences, being my best self? Suddenly, I'm acting like a backslider — all hype, no substance.*

"Hey." Agatha peeked around the cubicle wall, smiling.

"Hey." Sameera returned the smile, pushing away from her desk and shaking out her hands. "Come in."

Agatha popped into the cubicle and sat cross-legged in the extra chair, as had become her habit. Unlike the others, Agatha became friendlier and chattier with each passing day. At first, Sameera suspected that Agatha was currying favour, but as time passed, she accepted that Agatha was fostering a friendship. In all the months working at City Hall, Sameera was the first likeminded person she had met, and Agatha was overjoyed at the opportunity to connect.

"What's up, yo?" Sameera asked in a quirky voice, a new in-joke.

"WIT in Vancity, yo!" Agatha whispered as loudly as she could to show her excitement about the upcoming Women in Tech conference in Vancouver. "You in?"

Sameera leaned back and rubbed her chin to feign serious contemplation.

"Hmm? Women in Tech?" she asked skeptically. "Sounds shady, like unicorns in pantsuits. Are you sure it's not a scam?"

"Come on! Erica Baker might make an appearance. I know you love The Baker," Agatha teased, slapping her own knees giddily. "And on the company dime, yo! It's on the okayed conferences list. I checked."

"Of course you did," Sameera replied, smiling. She spun in her chair and grabbed her phone from off the desk. Opening her calendar app, she asked, "When is it?"

"I'm sending the deets right now," Agatha said, tapping her phone a couple of time before proclaiming, "There ya go."

Sameera read through the message briefly, noting that the WIT conference would be held in a month's time at the Marriott Pinnacle in downtown Vancouver. *It's too soon to ask for this. There's always next year.* Attending the WIT conference would improve her performance and benefit her team. Just the networking opportunities were worth the time away. Still, conferences geared to female professionals were considered niche, of relevance to the employee rather than the employer, and after that meeting fiasco Sameera needed to reshape her reputation from lone wolf to team player. In another two weeks, her probationary period would end, and then there would be room for these kinds of requests.

"I can approve your request when it comes in," Sameera offered plainly, returning her phone to the desk.

Agatha narrowed her eyes and pursed her lips at her manager. Sameera mimicked her for comic effect.

"You don't want to ask because you think you don't deserve it," Agatha said without breaking eye contact.

Sameera tilted her head at an imaginary third person and replied in a dopey tenor, "For a clown fish, she really isn't that funny."

Without missing a beat, Agatha named the altered movie quote, "*Finding Nemo*. And I *am* funny. And intuitive."

"Okay," Sameera said with a shrug, pivoting back to her desk.

"It's the ADM thing," Agatha pressed her. "Right?"

"Nothing you have to worry about, really," Sameera said as she pulled her chair toward the desk and signalled an end to the conversation. As much as she wanted to confide in Agatha about her anger and resentment, the fallout with Shannon had made her weary. *What if she tells me I'm imagining it? What if she takes Crawley's side?* Sameera feared Agatha's reaction, her take on events, so she coached herself to let go of past events and focus on the present.

Behind her, Agatha rose and quoted with uncharacteristic perkiness, "You must always have faith in people. And, most importantly, you must always have faith in yourself."

Sameera swivelled. Her thoughts were jumbled and she failed to identify the quote. Shaking her head, she admitted defeat.

Smirking, Agatha revealed, "Elle Woods, *Legally Blonde*." As she left the cubicle, she added, "See you tomorrow."

"Ditto," Sameera replied distractedly, looking at her screen.

"*Ghost*," Agatha called back from a couple of rows down.

Sameera smiled to herself, grateful for the friendship she had developed despite her turbulent start at City Hall. She glanced at the time displayed on the bottom corner of her screen and listened for the ambient sounds of the office. *When did I turn into such a wimp? Who am I hiding from?* Courtney Moore came immediately to mind, a conservative bureaucrat who toed the line and disparaged agitators. The ADM incident had visibly disturbed Courtney. It seemed very unlikely that Courtney had ever dialogued with the CM, much less disconcerted him with her ideas. *She probably thinks I'm an anarchist. Rogue manager. Antiestablishment public servant. How does that even work?*

To pass time, she browsed her media feed for entertainment, unconsciously biting her nails. A news headline caught her attention: "Anti-Black Racism Lawsuit Dismissed." The article described the Ontario Court of Appeal's decision to dismiss a lawsuit against the Ontario Public Service and two of its unions, stating it did not have jurisdiction. The plaintiffs planned to appeal to the Supreme Court, an arduous process that would deplete them emotionally and financially. *Why is it so hard to make things better? They preach equity while they deny existing inequities.*

Sameera leaned back, shook her arms out at her sides, and closed her eyes. The ambient sounds of the office had levelled off to distant typing and a hushed conversation in a far off corner. After turning off her laptop and pushing in her chair, she perched her sunglasses on her natural bouffant, hooked her oversized handbag on her arm, and headed to the kitchen to grab her half-eaten lunch from the fridge.

The tenth-floor kitchen was a spacious room with floor-to-ceiling windows, equipped with multiple fridges and microwaves, and a commercial coffeemaker. During her first couple of weeks, Sameera ate lunch daily at the lively communal tables, making an effort to introduce herself to unfamiliar faces. Since the incident, she had not joined the others at lunchtime, opting to eat at her desk or at the outdoor benches in the concrete plaza. She looked around at the now-empty chairs. *I should be eating in here with them. I shouldn't be hiding. I didn't do anything wrong.*

She sighed with longing for the happy times she'd enjoyed there. Her Pyrex container of creamy risotto was on the bottom shelf of the refrigerator, and seeing its contents instantly made her hungry. *Might as well eat while I'm here.* She set down her handbag on a table for four near the windows and waited for her meal to heat in the microwave. The sky was bright blue and cloudless, reminding her of the summer days when she and Shannon had fallen in love. She recalled that on just such a day last year they would have rushed home to change and spend the evening on a busy restaurant patio, blowing their pay checks on organic beer and farm-to-table entrees. Again, Sameera sighed.

"*Salaam*, hello," came a greeting from behind.

Sameera whipped around to see Faiza Hosseini at the kitchen counter, dressed in a flattering white pantsuit and carrying an empty glass mug in her perfectly manicured hand. Faiza was smiling at her amicably and not expectantly but Sameera felt encumbered by her presence, pressured to perform. *For fuck's sake! Seriously?! Of all people. Is Crawley next?*

"*Salaam, hal-e shoma chetore-e?* Hello, how are you doing?" Sameera replied, remembering to smile with her eyes.

Presently, the microwave let out a series of beeps that signalled the timer's end and attracted Faiza's attention. She glanced at the microwave and back at Sameera.

"*Mal-e shoma?* Yours?" Faiza asked politely.

"Uh …" Sameera stalled as she debated grabbing her handbag and abandoning the risotto.

As friendly and professional as Faiza Hosseini seemed, Sameera feared disclosing any personal information to the director, even her claim to the container. The director's close proximity to Howard Crawley, which had initially excited Sameera, now overwhelmed her. The last time the two women had been alone was on Sameera's first day at City Hall, when she still felt confident about making a good impression and overcoming gaffes. Since her public shaming at the ADM, every interaction seemed fraught with the possibility of going awry. *Keep cool. Be yourself.*

"*Bale,* yes," Sameera replied, quickly crossing the room to retrieve the container.

Absorbed by her fretting, Sameera did not register that the risotto had overheated. When the hot glass burned her fingertips, she instantly dropped the container onto the counter, spilling most of its contents. The skin on her fingertips stung and Sameera fought the urge to put them in her mouth.

"Oh, oh," Faiza remarked. Turning on the kitchen tap, she instructed, "*Be-ya enja*, come here."

Embarrassed by the mishap and desperate to make a good impression, Sameera followed the directions to place her fingers under the stream of running water.

"*Merci*, thank you," Sameera said abashedly, mortified doubly by the possibility that Faiza Hosseini had noticed her chewed-up fingernails.

"*Hatman*, of course," Faiza replied in a steady voice that reflected genuine compassion. "I'm sorry about your meal."

Sameera eyed the sticky mess she had caused. The glass container, nearly empty, sat in a puddle of creamy rice that had spread under the microwave and flowed over the counter, onto the linoleum floor. To her horror, she watched Faiza Hosseini produce a tidy bundle of paper towels to clean the mess.

"I can do that. It's my fault," Sameera said, turning off the tap and stepping in between Faiza and the spreading puddle of cheese sauce.

"I'd like to help," Faiza insisted, handing Sameera the paper towel roll, and then proceeding to scrape the puddle on the counter directly into a well-positioned waste bin.

After a couple of minutes of cooperative effort, there was no sign of the mess. Sameera recapped the container, wiped it off, and placed it in her handbag. She watched Faiza fill the electric kettle, and waited for the right moment to thank the director and bid farewell. Judging by Faiza Hosseini's sympathetic tone, it seemed possible that at least one person had not written her off.

"Thanks again for your help," Sameera said, making sure to smile directly at her.

"My pleasure, Sameera," Faiza replied. "I hope your fingers get better soon."

"Oh, yeah. They're better already," Sameera lied, nodding, eager to leave.

Just as Sameera began to say goodbye, Faiza Hosseini crossed her arms and said, "How are things going?"

The question stumped Sameera who opened and closed her mouth a couple of times without saying anything. She smiled and nodded, trying to appear casual and content as she formed a reply.

"My team is great. Really wonderful, hardworking bunch. Especially our SEO, Agatha Chavez," Sameera boasted. "I'm really excited about the inclusivity initiatives, and I think there're a lot of great opportunities there for the web developers and the marketers. Agatha is already making headway with online communities."

This much was all true, and since Sameera did not want to lie or complain about the difficulties she was experiencing, she stopped talking altogether. Instead, she smiled and nodded some more.

At that moment, the kettle switched off, and Sameera thought it was an opportune moment to depart. At the same time, Faiza Hosseini turned away to pour hot water into her glass mug, which caused Sameera to delay bidding farewell, to avoid rudely rushing out while the director's back was turned.

"And, your ideas about racial equity in City Hall? How is

that coming along?" Faiza Hosseini asked plainly, facing Sameera again.

Sameera was stunned by her casual reference to a topic that had agitated the CM.

"I … uh, I think that the CM's inclusivity initiatives are priority, right now. For me and my team," Sameera said straight-faced, uncomfortably aware of Faiza Hosseini's nearness to the CM.

"Yes, you're right," Faiza agreed, crossing her arms and leaning back but not making contact with the counter. "Spreading resources thin can be detrimental to progress."

Sameera nodded as a stop gap for lack of a diplomatic reply. *Yeah, detrimental to the progress of the white man. It's not progress unless everyone benefits.* She repulsed herself by not speaking her mind, especially to another woman of colour. They should be able to speak frankly about the bigotry prevalent in their organization. Instead, they made excuses for not pressuring higher-ups to address systemic racism. Worst of all, no one called attention to the CM's duplicity, peddling inclusivity but downplaying equity.

Overcome by frustration, Sameera cleared her throat and started, "I have been wondering about the initiatives … and, also how they … why is …" Sameera realized that her attempt to be tactful was causing her to blather. The director appeared unfazed by Sameera's false starts. Her posture remained relaxed and her expression was attentive.

"I mean, the idea of …" Sameera started again, "The idea of equity at City Hall, that's not so far from the inclusivity initiatives we're deploying. Is it?"

She maintained an easy smile and demeanour while the director took a moment to consider the question, "Some might argue that equity in government is the ultimate measure of inclusivity in civil society."

Sameera nodded energetically, grateful to hear her sentiments echoed. Warmth spread through her, and the tension in her back released for the first time in weeks.

"Exactly," Sameera agreed, a little too loudly.

Faiza Hosseini smiled and continued unhurriedly, "Inclusivity remains a controversial topic, one that requires championing. Once there's buy-in from prominent leaders, then it's palatable to others."

Entranced by Faiza Hosseini's charm and confidence, Sameera nodded while the director proselytized, "Without a long-term strategy to get buy-in, a good idea can remain unrealized. Worse yet, it might cause the downfall of its proponents."

Sameera wanted to shake her head to break the trance, or at least to stop nodding in agreement. The warmth, which had soothed her loneliness moments earlier, was slowly being replaced by a gripping chill. Frozen in place, she read the director's underlying message: lower your expectations and appreciate any strides toward racial justice.

Exasperated, Sameera lashed out, "But the CM already champions inclusivity! That's what all his initiatives are about. How is hiring more people of colour any different?"

Sameera's outburst did not seem to faze the director. Faiza Hosseini picked up her cup of hot water, which she held in both her palms, and contemplated her response. In that moment, Sameera grew embarrassed for her forceful tone and wished she shared the habit of pausing before speaking.

"You could focus on that question," the director answered, slightly raising her brows. "Or you can consider the long game. Invest in strategies to garner support, enlist prominent champions."

For the sake of decorum, Sameera nodded silently. Keeping her lips sealed was the only way she could avoid another outburst. A moment passed while both women stared in different directions.

"Well, I should get back at it," Faiza Hosseini remarked, seeming reluctant to take leave. "Drop by my office anytime, Sameera. *Khoda hafez*, goodbye."

"Yes, bye," Sameera replied through her clenched jaw.

Through the open doorway, she watched the director disappear around the corner. She waited a minute longer to ensure there was distance between them, and then Sameera released her handbag to the floor and punched the air with both fists. The dense icy layer, which had formed over Sameera's spirit as Faiza Hosseini advised her to kowtow to bigots, shattered violently and erupted in burning tears. All this time, she had remained tight-lipped about her experience to avoid being judged, and Faiza Hosseini had lured her into confiding her feelings and then lectured her about diplomacy. *Fuck! She played me!*

Sameera fled to a private corner of the kitchen where she doubled over, pressing her temples with the heels of her hands, and screamed without making a sound. She felt both ashamed for having dropped her guard and angry at Faiza Hosseini for taking the opening to deliver her deranged worldview. *How can she believe such nonsense? A series of deals with the devil, for what? Justice? Equality? Fuck that! Fuck her!*

Holding herself upright, she shook her head in disgust, wiped her cheeks with her palms, and resolved to steer clear of that director. She reminded herself that women like Faiza Hosseini would always make excuses for the powerful; they wanted to live in the master's house, not burn it to the ground. *And what the fuck am I doing?! I'm not setting fire to shit.* Her Sunday brunch friends — with their social venture startups, making tempeh, and repairing bicycles — had discouraged her from corporate work. "It's a trap! That's how capitalism gets you," they had warned. "There's no fixing anything in that system. It's all based on white supremacy. There's nothing to be gained." Sameera did not disagree, but she did not disregard the gains. In that inherently prejudiced system, there was money, connections, and esteem to be had. A decade earlier, she wouldn't have considered a desk job, and now she wanted it and all that came with it. She planned to buy a condo, go on holidays, and worry less about her bank balance.

Shrugging off the experience, Sameera coached herself. *Come on! You had expected to meet millions of Faizas. And this isn't a monastery. She wants power and money, and this is how she's doing it — and how I'm doing it.*

* * *

After work on Wednesday, Goldie waited for Issa on the upper level of Eglinton station. She stood near the general store kiosk, visible to emerging riders but distanced from the stream of commuters pouring out of the station and on to the street. To pass time, she played games on her phone and discreetly admired the huddle of beddable young men across the way. Hunched over their respective screens, they were fit, sporting stylish haircuts, designer clothes, and amazing Adidas sneakers without a crease, flagrant symbols of privilege.

This strip of Eglinton Avenue was an old-money neighbourhood in uptown Toronto, a gentrified extension of downtown, and a place she visited infrequently. Her hangouts were bubble tea shops and dessert boutiques that dotted the shopping plazas of Scarborough.

Pricey uptown cafés made hanging out with friends an expensive affair, so Goldie met her friends at thrifty haunts where servers were accustomed to refilling mugs with hot water for second-run tea bags. She was determined to save enough money to move out, which meant austere measures: bring her own, borrow when possible, and buy when half-priced.

This shopping trip to a trendy beauty store was Issa's idea, and Goldie had agreed to accompany her on one condition: they commit to a twenty-dollar spending limit, each. Goldie did not need any more makeup; her handbag and dresser drawers were filled with each kind and colour. What she needed was her own place, away from her annoying brothers.

"Slut!" Goldie heard Issa yell even before she spotted her friend emerging from the throng of bodies moving past.

"Hoe!" Goldie hollered back. When she caught the kiosk attendant sneering, she sucked her teeth. *Fuck off, posho!*

Issa threw both arms around Goldie and the friends double cheek–kissed, reviving Goldie who had had another hostile day at work. She squeezed her friend a moment longer than usual, burying her face in Issa's kinky-coiled hair and breathing deeply of her grapefruit scent, an aroma that she'd associated with Issa since primary school. Without warning, she was overcome by tears.

"G, what's wrong?" Issa asked softly, holding on to Goldie.

"Nothing, nothing," Goldie hiccupped. She stepped back to smooth her hair and wipe away tears, using the same ball of tissues from earlier that day — when despair had overwhelmed her and she'd run to the safety of the bathroom stalls.

"Doesn't look like nothing," Issa said, brushing a stray hair from Goldie's cheek. "You want me to buy you Pocky? They've got strawberry."

Issa nodded encouragingly at the row of biscuit sticks displayed in the kiosk. Goldie chuckled and shook her head, dabbing at the corners of her eyes, careful to not smear her eyeliner. She noticed the self-involved young men across the way, and worked to regain composure, in case they noticed her.

"Just work. Fucking drained," Goldie summed up her feelings as she turned her back to the guys and checked her hair and makeup in her compact.

"Forget those sad old bitches," Issa said, poking at Goldie's shoulder playfully. "This gonna be shitty right here."

"Fact!" Goldie agreed, powdering the bridge of her nose and gazing at the young men in the mirror's reflection.

"I see you eyeing them snacks," Issa teased, looking over Goldie's shoulder to size up the men.

"Who?" Goldie feigned ignorance, sucking her teeth and glancing dispassionately at the guys. "Whatever! You wild!"

She packed her mirror and, to emphasize her apathy, checked her phone at length.

"'Course, the tall 'un is swole," Issa added lustily, admiring the muscled arms of one guy.

"Right?!" Goldie swung instantly from disinterest to desire, biting her lower lip with yearning. She locked arms with Issa and purred, "Yum!"

At street level, Issa took charge and steered them toward the three-tier beauty store, a few blocks further north along historic Yonge Street. They walked leisurely, allowing the hurried office-types and the scheduled stroller-pushers to weave around them.

"Hashtag uptown so white," Issa quipped about the passersby.

"Several points made," Goldie agreed, albeit uncomfortably. *Can we just stop with the labels? We're all Canadian. That's enough. Why isn't that enough for her? Why do we have to be Brown, or Black, or anything? Why make it about race?*

"Here," Issa said, stopping at an elegant glass storefront, decorated with three-story tall banners draped from the top floor.

Goldie was struck by the larger-than-life portraits of women, specifically the spectrum of skin tones represented. One caramel toned model in a teal hijab smiled back with ruby red lips. An umber toned youth posed winking, revealing a pallet of dazzling violet and silver eye shadow while an androgynous model with a flourish of freckles and glossy, puckered lips dared Goldie to take a risk, to buy something new.

"Twenty bills," Goldie prompted Issa, halting their movement into the store.

"Yurrr," Issa affirmed as distracted as she was by the window display.

"Pinky swear?" Goldie insisted, equally unable to take her eyes off the display.

"Pinky swear," Issa echoed, pulling Goldie through the front door.

Once inside the lively store, curated with glass shelving and precise lighting, all financial concerns fell by the wayside. Goldie had the sensation of being in a candy shop and wanting to buy one of every delectable offering. They stood shoulder to shoulder at the end of the aisles, overwhelmed by the vast selection.

"This place's lit," Issa whispered her compliment with a giggle.

"I know, right. Monika's is good but this place hits different," Goldie agreed, referring to their regular beauty outlet store.

"What first? I needs me some leave-in conditioner," Issa said, rising to her tiptoes to survey the space while remaining at Goldie's side.

"Uh, yeah. I'll come with," Goldie replied.

To their astonishment, every aisle was meticulously arranged and lined with samples, unlike Monika's where products were piled in bins, row on row in a narrow windowless facility. Here, the ends of the aisles were fitted with touch screens, and profiling apps prescribed colour palates and skin care regimes. Women of all ages, pubescent through to postmenopausal, studied the on-screen results and received recommendations from the glamorous sales reps who fluttered about the store.

"I finna do this," Issa said excitedly, stepping up to a hair-care console promoting personalized tips.

Goldie joined her briefly, becoming distracted by a tutorial video playing on a small screen midway down the aisle. The attractive young model demonstrated how to create a winged look with eyeliner, and Goldie found herself lured to the screen. As the video played in a loop, she studied the technique and mustered the confidence to try her hand at it in public. Along with samples, cotton pads and bottles of makeup remover were conveniently placed nearby for customers to apply and remove makeup.

Self-consciously, Goldie wiped clean her eyelids. A furtive look about confirmed that no one was interested in her activities. She stepped up to a mirror, steadied her hand, and with one eye closed she copied the technique in the video using the sample eyeliner. As Goldie turned her face side to side to judge her reflection, she heard Issa, her tone indignant.

The rigidity of Issa's speech alarmed her, alerting her to imminent danger. Goldie collected her handbag and proceeded down the aisle toward Issa at the hair-care console. A white sales rep in stilettos towered over Issa, blocking Goldie's view of her friend.

"Why?" Issa questioned the rep.

"The kiosks are for customers," the rep answered acerbically, glancing over her shoulder at a pair of young white women nearby.

"I am a customer. See, here I am customer-ing," Issa rebuked, returning her gaze to the console.

"Right," the rep sneered, offering the pair of white women an apologetic look. "Well, it's the store's discretion—"

"Hi," Goldie interjected, her voice quavering from apprehension. She stepped around the sales rep and next to Issa, hooking her arm into her friend's. Issa squeezed her forearm, and Goldie felt her trembling. She recalled a time when 14-year-old Issa upset a high school senior, a girl with a mean streak who threatened to thrash her. Issa had hidden in the bathroom, crying and shaking, and Goldie had skipped class to comfort her. She had not known how to handle that problem and she did not know how to handle this one.

The sales rep shifted her posture from one heel to the other, sizing up Goldie with a menacing stare unconcealed by her extravagant lashes. Off to the side, the onlookers clutched their handbags and cringed at the scene, disdain evident in their puckered white faces. With her free arm, Goldie pulled her hair flat against her sweater, smoothing it repeatedly. She avoided their scornful gaze, embarrassed by the implication that she was unruly, difficult. Apart from the irksome qualities she exhibited among her family, Goldie presented as a composed, conscientious overachiever. Drama was messy and exposed, something that had never appealed to her or to Issa.

"You need to leave," the sales rep decreed, crossing her arms theatrically.

"Why?" Issa asked, her trembling body reverberating in her voice. "I'm a customer, just like them."

Jutting out her chin in their direction, Issa indicated the two white women. Instantly, both women clutched their handbags closer to their chest and returned a look of horror at having been implicated in the scene.

The sales rep did not budge as she insisted, "You are making the other customers uncomfortable. You have to leave."

"You're making me uncomfortable," Issa retorted, this time choking up on the last syllable.

Goldie saw tears roll down Issa's cheeks and collect at her quivering chin.

"Let's go," Goldie whispered to Issa, squeezing her arm.

Issa inhaled sharply but remained silent, glaring at the rep.

Emboldened by the pause, the rep asserted, "Leave now, or I will be forced to call the police."

"Relax," Goldie muttered angrily, afraid to provoke the rep any further but frustrated by the sudden escalation. Turning to Issa, she whispered her plea, "Come on, Iz. Let's go."

Issa continued to glare at the rep. Tears dripped off her chin but she did not move. With her arm in Issa's, Goldie tugged gently, covertly, to conceal any sign of discord.

"Forget you," Issa hissed at the rep, before she dropped Goldie's arm and marched out of the store.

Goldie hustled to catch up to Issa who had continued down

the sidewalk at a hurried pace. She dodged oncoming pedestrians and tried to gain ground without calling out for Issa to slow down. As the distance between them lengthened from one block to two, and Issa travelled at an unrelenting speed, Goldie acquiesced. She called out to Issa, and to Goldie's embarrassment several people looked at her.

"Issa!" Goldie called again, looking away from the passersby who gawked.

Issa had reached the busy intersection of Yonge Street and Eglinton Avenue, where the steady rush of vehicular traffic forced pedestrians to obey the red light and wait to cross. Goldie caught up to Issa just as the traffic light turned green.

"Issa, slow down," Goldie said, panting from the sprint.

Issa did not reply. She walked with her gaze fixed ahead. Goldie did not try to demand any more attention knowing that Issa was reeling from the upsetting episode in the beauty store. She walked alongside Issa as they crossed the street, descended the entrance to the subway, and paid their fare.

A train pulled out of the station just as the friends arrived on the emptying platform. The overhead monitor indicated that the next train would arrive in three minutes.

Issa walked to the far end of the platform and leaned against the tiles, waiting to board the first car. Goldie followed and stood silently beside her, trying to think of a conversation starter. The agitation that had consumed her during the exchange with the rep, causing her mind and body to quaver uncomfortably, had transformed into a mild hysteria, a mixture of incredulity and invincibility.

"That bitch was crazy, Iz," Goldie chuckled, shaking her head.

"Hmm," Issa replied without looking up from her phone.

"You're forcing me to call the police," Goldie mimicked the rep's voice. "Fucking classic."

"Hmm," Issa said impassively.

"What?!" Goldie prompted, prodding Issa by leaning into her space.

"What what?" Issa snapped back, stepping away from Goldie and returning to her screen.

"What did I do?" Goldie asked.

Issa gave her a knowing look, sucked her teeth, and returned to scrolling.

Flustered by this unexpected response, Goldie grew angry, "What? Just tell me. Why are you mad at me?"

Inhaling sharply, Issa raised her eyes but looked directly ahead, not at Goldie.

"I am not mad at you," she said through clenched teeth.

"Then what?" Goldie demanded, crossing her arms petulantly.

"I am disappointed," Issa said tersely.

"You look mad," Goldie argued, pulling on her strands. "And you're acting all . . . ."

Immediately, Issa turned to glare at Goldie, awaiting the end of her speech. When Goldie hesitated, unsure how to complete her thought, concerned that she was making matters worse, Issa pursed her lips and raised her eyebrows expectantly.

"Why didn't you say anything?" Issa probed.

"To the crazy lady? What are you talking about? I did." Goldie insisted.

"What? What did you say to her?" Issa asked, her tone changing gears from anger to determination.

"I told her . . ." Goldie started, paused, and realized she recollected nothing of the incident. "Why?"

"You think you said something, right? What did you say?" Issa persisted, her furrowed brow smoothing out.

Goldie tried to recall her words. She was certain that she had contributed to the showdown. It definitely felt like she had made a stand but she could not remember the details. She stroked her hair, to buy time, to jog her memory. At the other end of the platform, a cluster of riders descended the steps, their lively conversations echoing through the tunnel.

"Why does it matter?" Goldie asked defensively.

"It matters. You didn't say a thing to defend me," Issa explained.

Goldie's jaw dropped and she shook her head in disbelief. Indignant, she shot back, "That's fucking crazy. I was right next you."

"Yeah, you were," Issa agreed disappointedly. "And still, you said shit all."

"What was I supposed to say, Iz?" Goldie asked with a huff.

"Right," Issa confirmed with a small nod, turning back to her phone.

More conversations joined the cacophony as the platform filled with riders. Privacy and peace were fleeting, and Goldie considered whether to stop pursuing this conversation.

In her chest, she felt a tightness that only appeared during arguments, and the only people she ever argued with were her family and her best friend, Issa. Arguing with anyone else was not worthwhile since she could compartmentalize herself, hide her self or her pursuits from others. Her family and Issa knew her wholly, and it hurt to be at odds with them.

A train arrived at the station and riders began to move up to the edge of the platform. Issa pushed off the tiled wall and shuffled closer, too. Goldie followed her but she was not ready to leave their conversation behind.

"Please, Issa, tell me what's bothering you," Goldie pleaded, tugging on Issa's arm and pulling her back to the wall.

Issa allowed herself to be pulled back. They leaned against the wall and waited for the train to pull out of the station, creating a brief moment of peace.

Looking up but away, Issa explained, "You know how sometimes something is like … really bad but it's so bad that it's like hard to see it. Like, it's hard to believe it's that bad? So, like you only deal with a part of it because it's like … just too much for … for you to take all together?"

Goldie nodded but she didn't grasp the relevance of this speech, "Yeah."

Issa continued, "It's like that. Some things are so bad that it's just hard for you to see more than a little of it."

"Okay," Goldie said quietly.

Issa looked up with a kind expression that softened Goldie's own.

"I don't think you get how bad it is for me," Issa said slowly.

"Like … like, um," Goldie said, swallowing to find the words. "Like being Black?"

"So you noticed," Issa quipped, cracking a small smile.

"Har har. Yeah, I noticed," Goldie smiled back, however self-consciously.

"It's really hard, and it's like you don't wanna think about that," Issa admitted, pocketing her hands and chewing on her upper lip.

"What do you mean? I know you're Black," Goldie said confusedly. "I'm Brown. I'm not white."

"That's right. You're not white," Issa repeated with added stress. "But sometimes I think you forget."

Goldie exhaled loudly and decried, "That's so bullshit. I hear this crap from Dariush. I can't believe you'd say that. I don't think I'm white. I've never pretended to be white."

Matching Goldie's fervour, Issa defended her claim, "You don't think you're doing it but then you do. Like this whole thing at your job."

"What thing?" Goldie asked, flummoxed at the shift in topic.

"Those women at your job, they're racist," Issa said pointedly, locking eyes with Goldie.

"What women?" Goldie's voice cracked.

"All of them," Issa snapped, and then added with greater compassion, "even the nice one."

Goldie rolled her eyes and shook her head, "This's from hardo Tanya, right? Is that where you got this from? That's fucking bullshit."

"Why is it bullshit?" Issa asked earnestly, pushing off the wall and standing before Goldie.

"They don't even see me like that at work," Goldie responded, immediately hearing the implication in her statement.

"Like what? Brown? Not white?" Issa said, reading between the lines. "They know you're not white, Golnuz."

"Yeah, I know they know," Goldie rebuked hotly. "They're not that bad, and my boss is really nice to me. She's trying to get me hired on permanently."

"Right," Issa affirmed. "She needs you doing the grunt work. And she's letting those racists shitheads get away with … being racist. Don't you see that?"

"Oh, come on, Iz," Goldie said, flustered. "What is she supposed to do? Fire them for being mean?"

"It's not *being mean*. It's discrimination, and you're letting them get away with it," Issa persisted. "You pretend no one sees your colour so that you don't have to do anything about it."

"I am not!" Goldie argued.

Another train pulled into the station and the two friends watched as riders disembarked and the cars filled up. Neither woman spoke nor moved from their place against the wall. They waited for the train to disappear into the tunnel, taking with it the commotion.

"Why are you mad at me?" Goldie started with renewed vigour, leaning on her shoulder to face Issa's sombre profile. "What does it matter to you? You don't work there."

Issa sucked in her lips and stared upwards. To keep from answering her own question, Goldie bit her lip and examined the dirty tiles underfoot. The stop-start pace of their conversation agitated her. She wanted a speedy resolution, a peaceful end. She wanted a harmonious return home, away from this uppity neighbourhood and the people who had complicated her life.

"That's just one example," Issa said, shaking her head.

Sucking her teeth loudly, Goldie threw up her hands. "Seriously?! Everything's not about race."

"Everything is about race," Issa affirmed, crossing her arms and refusing to look at Goldie. "You just don't want to deal with it."

"Deal with it?" Goldie snapped, pacing in a small arc as she hurled rhetorical questions. "Is there a playbook? Am I doing it wrong? What the fuck, Iz? When'd you get militant?"

Issa did not respond but continued to stare upward and shake her head. Another train arrived, and the diversion of mechanical noises and human traffic allayed Goldie. Her mind flitted about, seeking a route toward reconciliation. She needed to know that they were okay, that their friendship was untarnished.

"Issa, I'm sorry about what happened in the store," Goldie tried, inching along the tiled wall until her shoulder met Issa's. "I should've cussed her out. I'm sorry."

"Shit like that happens all the time, Goldie," Issa said, her voice and chin quivering.

Goldie placed a hand on Issa's shoulder and replied softly, "I'm really sorr—"

Issa pulled away, just enough to be out of reach. "Your attitude is part of the problem."

"I'm not racist," Goldie said defensively.

"You're not racist but you've got a problem with race," Issa retorted with a knowing look.

Goldie scoffed, "What does that even mean?"

"It means, you don't want to admit that you're not white," Issa explained, "or that white people treat you badly because you're not white."

"What do I care what other people do?" Goldie cried, feeling her own eyes well up with tears. "Why do I have to define myself by colour?"

"You're already defined by colour," Issa shot back. "You're just ignoring reality."

A train pulled into the station and Goldie turned away from the disembarking riders, sheltering herself from prying eyes.

"Come on, let's go," Issa said, sounding tired and looking defeated.

She looped her arm into Goldie's and led them into the nearest subway car which held a handful of single riders. The friends sat side by side, looking at their respective phones. When Issa offered Goldie an earbud, one of her pair, Goldie accepted the peace offering with a heavy heart. As the train travelled eastbound toward home, they listened to Issa's playlist in silence, saying little when they parted ways at the end of the line.

Chapter 4

Friday Morning, June 22, 2018

Pacing her cubicle the following Friday morning, Goldie stopped to brush negligible dust off her black blazer and navy leggings. Then, with her fingertips hovering at her hairline, she confirmed that every strand was in place. She returned to pacing but stopped abruptly to survey her presentation equipment again: ancient laptop, power cord, and VGA cable to connect the laptop to the projector. She tried carrying the items in her arms, trying to look unencumbered. *Sheeeiiit, it's a brick.* She regarded the laptop.

The five-year-old laptop was on loan to Goldie for the purpose of presenting her wiki at a bi-weekly meeting of directors. There were programs installed on the computer that Goldie had only seen parodied in memes, and running more than two programs at once caused the operating system to crash. Thinking about Patricia and her shrouded mission to replace the team with a wiki of instructions, Goldie studied the laptop, *This piece of junk's not gonna replace anyone.*

The thought of addressing a roomful of higher-ups caused her to fidget. Yet, Patricia had assured Goldie that they were a sympathetic lot who had performed their share of presentations. At the moment, Goldie's self-esteem was buoyed exclusively by her manager's confidence in her abilities, so she was determined to meet the challenge and entrench her persona as a whiz kid. *It's a ten-minute prez. No biggie. Stay chill.*

Goldie turned on the laptop, groaning at the whirring sound it emitted every time it started up, and opened the applications she would need during the presentation. There were fifteen minutes left until Patricia picked up Goldie at her cubicle for the walk to the conference room in the second tower. Enough time for Goldie to run through her demonstration again.

During the previous two weeks, Goldie had watched dozens of tutorials on how to create a wiki. To her delight, she'd found a channel of how-to videos that were soundtracked with K-pop hits, making the channel her go-to resource for all things wiki-related. *Hardo! I slayed.*

Creating the skeleton of the wiki had been a complicated task, and populating it with instructions had been problematic. She had never been taught to use the database to generate reports, neither for her division nor for others. Running reports was Beth's responsibility, and she shared minimal information about how to perform this task and that too solely with Sandra. Aware of the possible ramifications of the wiki on Sandra's, Holly's, and Beth's jobs, Goldie rationalized, *They should've known something like this would happen. Seriously, it's not the 90s.*

At Patricia's subtle behest to remain discreet about the wiki, Goldie had resorted to clandestine measures to gather the necessary information. She had scoured the City of Toronto intranet and compiled a list of reports most frequently requested of the Transportation Services Division. Then, using readily available documentation online, she had composed instructions on how to generate those reports.

The wiki and those instructions — the information that Beth had guarded for ten years — was about to make its debut at a managerial meeting, and then made available to forty-two divisions via the City of Toronto intranet. *Beth's gonna lose her fucking mind. She didn't want me running reports, and I'm in her department! Soon, anyone can access her precious database. She's gonna freak out.*

The image of Beth's possible reaction to the wiki sent a shiver down Goldie's spine. She imagined thunderbolts and earthquakes, a raging hurricane, and a torrent of insults and accusations. The thought made her want to close down the antiquated laptop and seek shelter. She tried to remind herself of all the reasons for pursuing this death wish. Building the wiki demonstrated her research and tech skills, her aptitude for problem solving, and her drive to help others. Her efforts would improve efficiency in divisions throughout City Hall. *You're bad. You're one bad bitch.*

Only two weeks were left on Goldie's contract, and the internal postings to which she'd applied had not panned out. Developing the wiki was her chance to demonstrate her value to Patricia Addington, to persuade her manager to find a permanent position for her in the division. Goldie desperately wanted to continue to work at City Hall, even if that meant working in the same building as Beth. *They'll all probably get moved to some other department. Probably.*

"Ready?" Patricia asked cheerily, appearing in the opening of Goldie's cubicle, clutching a tanned leather briefcase.

"Yup," Goldie said as she shut the laptop, tucked it under her arm, and made to follow.

"Will you need those?" Patricia asked, pointing to the power cord and VGA cable on the desk.

"Oh," Goldie gasped. *Nice, real nice. You're slaying it, a'ight.*

She grabbed the cord and cable, jammed them into her blazer's shallow pockets, only to walk two steps and have both items fall out onto the floor. Patricia noticed, smiled, and stopped to give Goldie a chance to collect the items and tuck them between her forearm and laptop.

"Sorry," Goldie apologized. "I probably should have brought a bag."

They walked past Beth's empty cubicle, and Goldie felt grateful for her absence. Although working on a project secretly was not difficult, given Beth's predilection to ignore her, Goldie knew that being seen with Patricia and walking off with a laptop underarm would definitely give rise to suspicions. A junior database administrator performed work from a desk using an outmoded computer: no laptops, no meetings, and no trips to the second tower were called for.

For this reason alone, Goldie nearly jumped behind a potted palm tree when she spotted Holly approaching from the other end of the hall. Holly was carrying a hot drink in a mug and walking slowly so as to not spill the steaming contents. Goldie continued alongside Patricia, who had not broken her stride.

"Good morning, Holly," Patricia said confidently as they reached each other in the hallway.

"Morning," Holly replied to her manager, discreetly scanning Patricia and Goldie.

Goldie smiled at Holly, trying to appear friendly, possibly harmless. The corners of Holly's lips rose slightly as she walked past, the smile never reaching her eyes, and Goldie recognized the gesture as a performance for their manager, a demonstration of Holly's amiability. *So basic. Whatever.*

Goldie hugged the laptop closer to her chest and shrugged off the slight. She was more concerned about Holly relating the scene to Beth and about Beth's reaction. The image of a volcano violently spewing lava came to mind. *She ain't gonna spill the tea. Like, what's there to say?!*

As Goldie walked alongside Patricia, stopping several times for her manager to discuss a matter with a passing colleague, she thought about Holly's guardedness toward everyone in the office. Though Holly was the least hostile of the three administrators, at her warmest she was just cordial. Even her cubicle was sparse, the only personal item being a school photo of her preteen son.

From a chance conversation in the washroom, which started by Holly asking Goldie about the difference between a social science and a science degree, Goldie learned that Holly became a mother in her late teens and completed a diploma in her late twenties. Holly shared these facts plainly, without embellishment, but her demeanour became furtive the longer they discussed university degrees.

Goldie suspected that Holly was interested in an internal posting which required a degree. Being uncomfortable discussing her application with her longtime colleagues, Holly chose to ask the new girl, the one on her way out. When Goldie offered to read through the job requirements, Holly withdrew and rushed off without a word of gratitude. Since that exchange, Goldie wondered whether Holly also feared reprisals for wanting to climb the corporate ladder. *They hate me for trying but they be doing the same … no cap yahurrd.*

As they exited the elevator on the fourth floor of the West Tower, Goldie became consumed by the fear that when she returned to her desk Beth would be waiting for her, raging with questions about her accompanying Patricia to a meeting. How would she explain her treachery? She had invaded Beth's professional territory and now she was going to invite everyone else to do the same.

Patricia interrupted her fretting, "This is the first time a member of my team has presented at the directors' meeting."

Goldie smiled and nodded, willing her feet to continue forward and take the final steps into the conference room. She was no longer worried about the presentation going badly. Now, she feared that it would go well and the wiki would go live. How would Beth punish her? What else could she do to make Goldie's life miserable? *She's gonna be big mad. Least there's only two weeks on my contract.*

"Here we are," Patricia said brightly as they stepped into the conference room.

For a moment, they stood at the entrance and Goldie registered the refreshments table along the left wall, the horseshoe ring of tables and chairs in the centre, and the speaker's table at the front under a hanging projector screen. In small clusters around the room, people dressed in formal business attire chatted. A few of them were already seated, typing furiously on their laptops, as if they were submitting work at the last minute.

Goldie imagined that she looked pathetic and out of place in her blazer, leggings, and flats, like a child in a pinafore at a cocktail party. She had felt considerably more confident that morning when she had dressed. In the full length mirror of her bedroom closet, her outfit had appeared stylish and serious, but she had had no point of comparison. Now, with every adult in the conference room looking like they were dressed for court, she felt frumpy and amateurish. *Least my hair's nicer.*

"Alright, you can set up …" Patricia said distractedly, pointing to the front but cutting herself off to greet a cluster in the far left corner with a casual yoo-hoo.

"Okay," Goldie replied with waning confidence as the front of the room — which was a stone's throw away — seemed to ebb farther away from her.

All the excitement and pride she had felt as she created the wiki and prepared her presentation had curdled into anxiety and fear. She now expected Beth to retaliate for her infringement into Beth's sphere regardless of whether the presentation went well, and, trapped in her cubicle, Goldie would be the perfect target for her cruel remarks and dirty looks. When the presentation did fail miserably, as she expected it would based on her nausea and ringing ears, Goldie would also lose Patricia's backing and ruin her chance to be hired by any of the directors present. *This shit's extra. I gotta blast outta here.*

Before Goldie could excuse herself from presenting, Patricia had skipped over to her colleagues and their huddle closed for a private conversation. Goldie stood alone, clutching her equipment to her chest. A sudden stream of attendees flowed in and around her, forcing Goldie to move farther into the space to avoid the accompanying cloud of fragrance. *Drench much? Sheesh.*

She weaved between groups and walked along the outer ring

of tables and chairs to reach the speaker's table at the front. There, she placed her equipment and knelt under the table to examine the plane of outlets embedded in the carpeted floor. Hidden from the room of directors, she experienced a moment of respite. Instead of resurfacing when she plugged in her cord cable, she gave herself a pep talk. *Stay up. This prez is valid and you know it. You're gonna slay this, no cap. Just breathe, and don't hurl.*

When Goldie rose from under the table, the seats around the ring were filled with directors, most of them preoccupied with their own screens. She spotted Patricia a few seats to her left, flanked on each side by other attendees. One seat remained unoccupied; the one immediately before her, at the front of the room. Goldie slid into the chair and lowered the seat fully, shielding herself with the laptop screen.

"Looks like most everyone is here," said the woman next to Goldie. "Howard won't be making it this week but he sends his regards."

Goldie heard the woman's familiar accent, and she dared to glance at her. She had never encountered an Iranian woman in a management role. At once, Goldie was delighted and distressed. She felt concern for this woman, in the same way she worried for her mother. Would they treat her respectfully? Would they recognize her intellect and skill? Would they defer to her expertise? Would they profile her based on her accent and colour?

"Can someone please close the door? Thank you, Derek," the woman continued. "The minutes of the last meeting were posted by Greta in the ..."

While the woman spoke at length about items from the previous meeting, Goldie subtly glanced around the room to study the directors. Everyone's attention was divided, as they were all typing or scrolling on phones. Goldie wondered if their scattered attention bothered the woman. *Seems kinda rude.*

Then, it occurred to Goldie that they might behave similarly throughout her presentation. *Sheeet, they better not ignore me.* She thought of every university lecture that she had sat through and how she had barely raised her eyes from her own screen to examine the lecturer's. *Yeah, but theirs were meh, and mine jams.*

"I'll turn it over to Patricia," the woman concluded, taking a seat and immediately starting on her laptop.

Patricia rose and walked the outer ring to join Goldie at the front. She smiled confidently at her junior database administrator, and Goldie felt the butterflies in her stomach slow their fluttering. *Time to slay it!*

Goldie started the presentation on her computer and cranked her neck to check the hanging projector. On the big screen appeared her flashy slideshow and she smiled to herself with pride. Most of the directors remained preoccupied with their own screens but she noticed that her presentation had captured the undivided attention of a handful who smiled encouragingly at Goldie. This caused her anxiety to morph into excitement.

"Thank you, Faiza," Patricia said, holding court like a well-practised toastmaster. "Before I begin, I'd like to introduce the newest hire to my team, Golnuz Sheer."

Smiling into the middle distance, Goldie tried to not flinch at Patricia's use of her birth name. When Goldie began her contract, Patricia had called her Golnuz. Eventually, Goldie had asked Patricia to call her Goldie, her preferred name. Patricia had agreed but only after she remarked that Golnuz was the prettier and more authentic name.

"Golnuz completed her BA with honours at the University of Toronto," Patricia boasted. "Actually, she was born in Toronto. Her family moved here from Iran? Correct?"

Sis! What the fuck's this?

Patricia looked to Goldie for confirmation, and Goldie could only nod her response, dismayed as she was about the unexpected biography.

"That's where you're from, Faiza, am I right?" Patricia asked in an inspired tone, her forefingers pointing between Goldie and the woman who had started the meeting, Faiza.

Feeling trapped by the collective gaze of a roomful of people, Goldie smiled at Faiza who smiled back. She wished that she could return to a few minutes earlier when everyone was preoccupied with their work, too distracted to stare at her. She hid behind her laptop screen and tugged at the ends of her hair.

Patricia continued, "Small world. Anyhow, Golnuz has done some fantastic work for my team, and I think what we've brought you today is going to be a game-changer for many other teams. On that note, I will turn it over to Golnuz."

Goldie sat up and smiled at her manager who returned to her seat.

"Hi," Goldie said, smiling at no one in particular before resting her gaze on her screen. "This is a wiki that has all the steps to generate reports from the regional transit database."

Goldie presented her work as she had practised, navigating the wiki and drawing attention to common reports. As the minutes passed, she became more confident, speaking slower and louder. While she did not look at her audience, choosing to focus on the laptop and overhead screens, she did notice several people nodding as she spoke.

Adlibbing at the end of her presentation, she concluded by saying, "It's not that hard to run a report, once you have the steps."

Patricia returned to her place at the front of the room, "Thank you, Golnuz—"

"Goldie," Goldie chimed in, and then addressed the audience. "You can call me Goldie."

"Thank you," Patricia said, without turning away from the audience. "Any questions?"

This prompted a discussion among Patricia and a handful of directors about timelines and accessibility. The comments were coded with references to teams and processes about which Goldie was ignorant, so she remained respectfully quiet. Inwardly, she was preoccupied with competing emotions: exultation at having performed well and vexation at Patricia for fixating on her ethnicity. *What's everybody's fixation on that shiz? Issa too! It's just one part of a person. There's so much other stuff, like age, or the money you make, or … Besides, I'm here to talk about a wiki. A fucking wiki.*

As she took in the meeting room filled with directors discussing the wiki she had created, Goldie recognized the opportunity Patricia Addington had bestowed on her. Now every director in the building was familiar with Goldie Sheer and her work, and in spite of feeling overwhelmed by the concept of networking, she knew that the possibilities were tremendous and she had Patricia to thank for that. She decided that Patricia's fixation with ethnicity was benign, something she could ignore. *She did do me a solid. I'm finna ignore that shit.*

"Thank you all for your time and your feedback," Patricia concluded. "We will keep you updated on the wiki. Golnuz is with us for another two weeks before her contract ends. She's been an asset to our division and we'd like to keep her at City Hall. Someone to keep in mind."

Looking over her shoulder at Goldie, Patricia smiled and discreetly offered a thumbs-up. Goldie returned a smile while inwardly rolling her eyes and shaking her head. *Hella smh but a win for me.*

* * *

"Thank you, everyone. Another productive session," Faiza said, ending the directors' meeting late Friday afternoon. "See you all next month … and have a good weekend."

The room came alive with a burst of activity as the majority of the attendees collected their belongings and scuttled off to their next engagement. Several people milled about, chatting in pairs or groups, and some returned to the refreshments table to refill travel mugs with coffee and scavenge what remained of the trays of mini muffins and grape clusters.

Feeling light and satisfied with her performance, Faiza smiled as she surveyed the batch of messages that had come in during the two-hour meeting. Among the numerous messages from IT about server maintenance and from the Health and Safety Committee promoting lunch-and-learns, there were a few from attendees expressing their enthusiasm for the Inclusivity initiative.

While these encouraging messages pleased her, she also felt a current of unease grow as another day passed without word from Howard. On a typical day, she answered a series of messages from Howard, mostly progress checks on work assigned to him and delegated to her, interspersed with complaints and suggestions that were not actionable. As much as she disliked his proclivity for treating her like his personal assistant, their regular communications offered Faiza insight into his state of mind and improved her ability to guess his next move.

Now, she suspected that he might be vacationing at his Muskoka cottage though his assistant insisted otherwise. Usually, he kept tabs on high-profile projects even on holiday. She began to compose another message to the CM's assistant, Shirley, under the guise of sharing project information. *Is Howard sick? Maybe some kind of surgery? He wouldn't want anyone to know, that's for sure.*

As she was writing the email, Jeffery Stanton, director of Business Improvement Services, perched on the edge of the table, his leg flush with Faiza's open laptop. Sighing audibly, he crossed his arms and caused his collared shirt and suit jacket to bunch up like a ruffled plume. After five years of working together, Jeffery's posture was familiar, a signal that he was about to begin a monologue.

Predictably, Nick Becker, program manager and Jeffery's sidekick appeared. He assumed his usual stance: his hands deep in his pants pockets, his eyes lowered, and his expression on standby. Nick was the first, and often the only, person to react to Jeffery's remarks. He would grimace, chuckle, or whistle in astonishment at all the right moments.

In anticipation of a speech, Faiza rose from her seat and began to gather her things. She would permit Jeffery the opportunity to vent his opinions but she wouldn't engage him in debate. His observations consisted of poorly disguised self-promotion, and his management style was archaic with its feudal treatment of subordinates. Jeffery Stanton was not interested in collaboration or building on the ideas of others — he wanted to sermonize. Out of deference to his tenure and membership in the senior management team, Faiza allowed him to preach from his soapbox before she continued with her afternoon agenda.

"Listen, Fay-za," Jeffery began, incorrectly pronouncing her name in spite of her numerous corrections. "I just don't understand why we're pouring money into new projects when we're so cash strapped."

"Hmm," Faiza managed, offering a tight-lipped smile as she tucked her phone into her handbag and began piling up her note paper.

"I know this is your pet project," Jeffery said in a stage whisper. "I would even congratulate you on your … creativity, hmm. It's all very admirable, really."

"Hmm," Faiza repeated unfazed as she gathered the cord for her laptop.

Faiza's authorship of the Inclusivity initiative was an open secret among senior management. At some time or another, each of them had completed the CM's work on his behalf. Howard Crawley infamously delegated the grunt work of high-profile projects to directors, and then took credit on completion. Though he never promised favours in exchange, it was implied that he would advance the careers of those who made him look the best. The previous five promotions among the directors had gone to those who designed and spearheaded Howard's most popular and celebrated civic projects. As the CM's current go-to director to ghostwrite his projects, Faiza was likely the next to be promoted.

"I'm just not sure it'll see the light of day … you know, with the changes coming up," Jeffery mused, and at his shoulder Nick Becker nodded enthusiastically.

Before she could catch herself from becoming entangled in Jeffery's trap, Faiza asked, "This initiative has already been accepted by Council. And, the funds are allocated, too. What changes? What do you mean?"

With the dramatic flair of a theatrical villain, Jeffery smiled conspiratorially at Nick, who delighted in his director's attention. The drawn-out pause and exaggerated expressions exchanged between the men might have entertained Faiza, like the hammy performances in soap operas, but this was a real-life conversation among colleagues. She was uninterested in their mind games and she had hours of work ahead of her.

"I'm sorry, Jeffery. I have to be elsewhere," Faiza politely excused herself as she resumed packing up her equipment. "Maybe we could continue this conversation another time?"

"Oh sure," Jeffery replied with a smirk meant for Nick. "Another time."

The two men whispered as they made their way across the conference hall, and Faiza heard Nick snicker. She was disappointed in Nick Becker's behaviour. As part of the hiring team who selected him, she had expected his people skills to match his work ethic. As Jeffery's mentee, Nick had developed a nasty habit of undermining the status of female managers. While she could not address Jeffery's behaviour without damaging her career prospects by way of antagonizing Jeffery's network of higher-ups, which included the CM, she could expose Nick Becker to Human Resources. *It might help him in the long run. Maybe, he'll learn to distance himself from Jeffery.*

With her bags packed, Faiza headed toward the exit, stopping every few feet to acknowledge the recent work of an attendee. The smile on her face was worthy of a magazine cover for a stateswoman: elegant, confident, and composed. Though her stomach ached from hunger and a small headache was forming behind her eyes, she made sure to give her best to every person she passed on her way to her office.

She was thinking about the future, of serving as a Deputy City Manager, and the significance of individual relationships with directors at City Hall. Without their confidence and cooperation, it would be nearly impossible to succeed as a DCM. Howard Crawley's tactic to use favouritism to produce complacent directors would never satisfy Faiza. She wanted to be held in esteem, and she knew that Howard's lackeys, including herself, did not respect or admire him.

As she crossed the rotunda that connected the East and West Towers, she caught the aroma of food emanating from City Café, a bustling soup, salad, and sandwich eatery. When her stomach growled in response, Faiza was thankful to be standing alone at the elevator doors. Glancing back, she considered getting an undressed spring salad. Then, she decided against it and focused her attention on the elevator dial. Earlier that day, she had weighed herself at the gym and was delighted to have lost two and a half pounds. To celebrate and relax after a long week, she planned to spend the evening with Robert and a bottle of wine. This meant that she would have to conserve her caloric intake, so there was no allowance for food, not yet. *You'll have salad for dinner. Just another three hours to go.*

Faiza considered her ongoing inner dialogue about eating. She recognized its toxic nature, and she prayed that her daughters lived unfettered by her preoccupation. Her weight, the tautness of her skin, the glossiness of her hair, the firmness of her stomach, arms and legs, all of the work involved in looking like a sensual middle-aged model was equal to the time and effort she invested in her career. She was convinced that she wouldn't have advanced as a leader if she were unattractive. It was an unspoken truth that female directors were expected to be attractive and amiable, in addition to outperforming their male counterparts.

As she was making a list of potential careers for her daughters, ones that might place less emphasis on a woman's beauty, the elevator arrived and its occupants stepped out. She entered, pressed the button for the tenth floor, and as the doors began to close, she heard Voula calling her name. Promptly, Faiza jutted out her arm to activate the sensor which caused the doors to reopen, giving Voula enough time to slide in next to her.

"Hello," Faiza greeted her confidante and colleague cheerily. "I didn't see you at the meeting. Everything alright?"

Voula nodded but she did not smile or speak. Faiza wondered if she was catching her breath from the sprint across the rotunda, and then she considered inviting her to a Pilates class as a plus one, a benefit of her gym membership. She recalled that Voula was averse to exercise, even the gentle restorative yoga class that Faiza had once suggested. Voula had countered that a spa date would be much more restorative.

"Can we talk? In your office?" Voula asked, pursing her lips and knitting her brow.

"Yes, of course," Faiza replied, growing concerned. "Are you alright?"

Voula inhaled deeply and nodded but her severe expression did not change. The doors opened onto the tenth floor and Faiza led the way to her office. Worried about Voula and eager to learn more, Faiza passed others without offering more than a polite smile. Once they arrived, Faiza shut the door behind them. She asked Voula if she wanted a glass of water or tea, and when Voula declined, Faiza took the seat directly next to her friend.

"Can you tell me what's wrong?" Faiza asked patiently as she reached out for Voula's hand.

Voula inhaled again, seemingly composing herself and preparing her speech. She looked left and right but she refused to meet Faiza's eyes. Soon, tears streamed down, creating streaks of mascara that ran from her eyes to her chin. Still holding Voula's hand, Faiza leaned over and grabbed the box of tissues from her desk. She pulled out a couple and held the bundle out for her friend.

The tears stopped eventually and Voula patted her cheeks dry. "Sorry."

Faiza continued to hold her hand and squeeze it gently. "What's happened?"

Finally, Voula met Faiza's gaze, and Faiza sensed that Voula was as concerned about her as she was for Voula.

"I wasn't at the meeting because I was talking to Lisa Henley, in HR—" Voula said before she was interrupted by a knock at the door.

Faiza frowned at the interruption. "One sec," she said to Voula as she stepped out into the hallway to address the visitor. She returned a couple of minutes later, and explained apologetically, "Just Arman. A glitch with the Q3 spreadsheet … You were saying? About Lisa? I remember she used to be in accounting."

Voula nodded and swallowed. "Lisa and I … we're friends from … Doesn't matter." She seemed to be losing her nerve but she inhaled and pressed on. "She knows we're friends, you and me. She wanted to tell me about the shortlist … for the DCM interviews."

"Uh-huh," she said, perking up at the mention of the DCM position.

Suddenly, Voula was holding and squeezing Faiza's hands.

"You're not on the shortlist," Voula breathed, not breaking eye contact.

"I'm not on the shortlist," Faiza echoed. When she realized that Voula meant the interview list for the position of DCM, she pulled her hands away as if she had been scalded.

"That's what Lisa said … that you're not on the list," Voula fumed, shaking her head indignantly. "Faiza, this is bullshit. I am so sorry that they are such assholes."

Faiza stood and then sat, unable to respond. The possibility that she wouldn't be interviewed for the position, a position she was practically performing, had not occurred to her. She had been concerned about performing well during the interview, tying in her accomplishments into every response, and presenting as powerful and personable. It seemed implausible that she had not even made the interview list. *This doesn't make sense. No. Something's gone wrong.*

"This doesn't make sense," Faiza said with garnered confidence. "I talked to Howard. About endorsing me."

Voula pursed her lips and nodded in response, her expression a blend of sympathy and skepticism. Faiza supposed that Voula pitied her, as she herself had pitied others who failed in their attempts to climb the corporate ladder. Her confidence had led her to reveal her aspirations to Voula, and now their intimacy pained her like an open wound.

"Who is on the list?" Faiza asked through clenched teeth.

Voula shifted in her seat and straightened her skirt. After a pause, she spoke with eyes downcast, "I'm not supposed to know."

"But you do," Faiza replied in a tone that was supposed to be jocular but sounded vexed.

"There's only one internal candidate," Voula disclosed, nervously smoothing out her skirt.

"Only one!" Faiza exclaimed, her neck muscles contracting and her eyes narrowing. "It's Adaego."

Faiza considered Adaego Musa, director of Business Development Services, her closest rival for the position of DCM, however far behind she trailed. In spite of being an indomitable competitor with a network of connections and a proven track record, Adaego's career had been stalled by Howard Crawley's antagonism. He often complained that Adaego was unable to collaborate and exceed expectations — coded expressions that described Adaego's unwillingness to do Howard's work. Then, there was the unspoken truth — one which greatly displeased Faiza even while she felt some secret satisfaction. *She's as black as the night. They'd never choose someone that dark, not with me in the running. Compared to her, I am white.*

Voula shook her head in response, her curly black hair waggling on her shoulders.

"This doesn't make sense, Vee," Faiza said, adding a hint of shock to mask her lack of dismay. *Voula wouldn't understand, not with her creamy skin and small waist.* Resting her gaze in her palms, she spun her wedding ring and filled the silence with respectable lies. "Adaego is a shoe-in. She even went to Rotman's."

"You're the shoe-in, Faiza," Voula rebuked. "You've been his deputy all this time."

"It just doesn't make sense," Faiza repeated.

"I can't say I'm surprised," Voula muttered, shifting in her seat, and smoothing out her creaseless skirt. "Howard is a fucking asshole. This is just like him."

Another knock on the door interrupted their conversation. This time it was the ever-condescending manager of Corporate Services, questioning Faiza's changes to the fine print of their taxation and expenditure forms. As quickly as possible, Faiza answered his questions, which were in fact aspersions disguised as concerns.

Shutting the door behind her, she paced the small room. Finally, she settled in her high-backed leather chair and picked up where they had left off, "What does Howard have to do with this? This is a bureaucratic glitch. They work in a bubble. They don't know me, or Adaego, from the hundreds of applicants off the street."

Voula's silence alerted Faiza and she swivelled to gaze intensely at her friend.

"Who's the internal candidate?" asked Faiza, the muscles between her shoulder blades pulsating with pain.

Voula lowered her eyes as she said, "Jeffery."

"Jeffery," Faiza echoed as a montage of conversations played in her mind.

In her chair, she leaned back, closed her eyes, and pinched the bridge of her nose. Pain pulsed in her temples and coursed through her neck and back, before it returned with vigour to her throbbing head. She had a high threshold for discomfort, after decades of enduring hunger pains from dieting, mangled toes from high heels, and scalded skin from wax treatments.

It took a few moments to contain the pain and collect her thoughts. She would manage this pain like the others — she would take action.

"I'm going down there. I know a couple of people," Faiza declared, straightening objects on her desk in a nervous habit. When Voula remained silent, Faiza busied herself tidying papers. She hesitated but asked, "You don't think I should go down?"

"I didn't say that," Voula answered, shifting her seat again and keeping her eyes downcast.

"Okay," Faiza replied, pausing for more. When nothing came, she asked, "What would you do?"

Voula laid her hands delicately on her lap and paused for a few breaths. Then, she announced, "This is not about me. You need to do what's right for you."

Faiza frowned but she was pleased by her friend's sentiment. She moved the sheets of paper closer and farther from the edge of the desk, and when she was ready to smile genuinely, she lifted her gaze to Voula.

"Okay, thanks, Vee," Faiza said softly.

"Let me know how it goes," Voula replied with a small smile, rising and smoothing out her skirt before she left Faiza's office.

Once alone, Faiza navigated the directory on her phone, looking for her contact in Human Resources: Barb Fisher. A couple of years earlier, she and Barb had attended a week-long conference in Detroit. Barb was a conscientious manager without a sense of humour, which suited Faiza, who preferred to keep work relationships professional.

"Barb, this is Faiza Hosseini," Faiza introduced herself on the phone.

"Hi, Faiza. How are you doing?" Barb asked politely on the other end.

Faiza spun in her chair to face the window, hoping that the late-day sunshine might lighten her tone.

"Doing well, Barb. How about you? I haven't seen you since the DBP conference," Faiza said with a smile, trying harder to minimize the aggression and urgency she sensed in her tone.

"That's right. That was a couple of years ago. Things are going well. What can I do for you?" Barb asked, getting to the point as Faiza expected she would.

"Yes, Barb, I am …" Faiza hesitated.

Untypically, she had not thought through the conversation. Propelled by indignation at not having secured an interview for the position of Deputy City Manager, she had jumped on the phone. Lack of poise and preparation was not her style but she was driven by fear and resentment stronger than she had felt in years.

"Barb, I'm calling about the position of Deputy City Manager," Faiza restarted, slowing her pace to increase her self-confidence.

"Yes," Barb replied impassively.

Trying to remain unfazed by Barb's coolness, Faiza paused and plodded on, "Yes, I applied for the position, and I am following up … on it."

"Yes," Barb said. "Well, let me bring up the file."

"Thank you," Faiza replied.

While she heard Barb clicking on a keyboard, Faiza took a moment to breathe deeply and consider what she would say next. Suddenly, it occurred to her that this phone call was futile. Barb could not independently add Faiza to the interview list, even if she was willing. The only way to change the course of the hiring process was to involve upper management.

"Yes, I have the file," Barb said curtly.

"Barb, I …" Faiza started and paused, hearing the desperation in her voice.

Barb waited patiently, and Faiza considered how many times a week Barb received this kind of call. She felt foolish for having phoned.

To buy time while she sorted out her thoughts, Faiza asked a question to which she already knew the answer, "I wondered whether I made the interview list."

"Has someone called you?" Barb asked plainly.

"No, I …" Faiza admitted. "I'm just following up. You know."

"Okay, let me check," Barb said nonplussed, and Faiza heard more clicking on the keyboard.

"Unfortunately, you will not continue to the interview portion," Barb answered, a statement that sounded practised.

"Hmm, okay," Faiza stammered. "I … Can I know why? I mean, was there something lacking in my application?"

"Let me find out," Barb said to the sound of keys clicking.

Faiza had a comprehensive understanding of hiring practices in the public service. Hiring decisions were based on a matrix of points, which were assigned according to the candidate's skills, knowledge, and abilities. Making the first cut, being chosen for an interview, was not an arbitrary decision based on an individual's preference or that of a panel of individuals.

"Your application scored in the ninety-fifth percentile," Barb reported. "If the hiring panel chose to interview additional applicants, your application could be among them."

The news did not soothe her. She knew her worth, and she did not need an application tracking system to calculate it.

"I … My references. I included Howard. Crawley. Did you, I mean, do you know if HR reached out to him?"

Speaking calmly, Barb answered, "Typically, references are contacted once an applicant passes the interview portion."

"Yes, of course," Faiza conceded. "I assumed that an endorsement from the CM would go some way in this process."

Silence followed, and Faiza listened closely to confirm that Barb was still on the line.

"Faiza," Barb said gently, "the CM did endorse a candidate."

"Okay," Faiza replied. Though Barb's insinuation blared loudly through Faiza's psyche, she couldn't help but ask, "And?"

Barb answered kindly, "And, that candidate has continued onto the interview portion of the hiring process."

Faiza said nothing. She stared at the carpet, at one spot. There was nothing left to say, not to Barb.

"Well, good luck, Faiza. Have a good weekend," Barb said, ending their call.

"Yes, goodbye" Faiza replied.

The urgency, the anger — they were gone. She was numb, except for the headache festering behind her eyes. She continued to stare at the carpet, thinking over the course of events that had led to this point.

The strangeness of the previous days made sense. Howard's demands had lessened and his after-hours intrusions had stopped altogether. Mistakenly, Faiza had assumed that he was on vacation or distributing his work among others.

Howard was steering clear of her. He did not want to face her when she learned of his endorsing someone else for the position. He did not tell her directly about his plans, and he did not want to talk about it now.

Glancing out the window, Faiza noticed the gloriously blue sky, even as a dense fog enveloped her and disoriented her sense of place and time. Along with her mind, her body became fatigued from striving. Her hands lay in her lap and her shoulders sloped forward, a posture she had trained herself to avoid.

Her thoughts jerked between the past, present, and future, jostled by rising emotions. Mercilessly, she sifted through the weeks, months, and years for her missteps, the opportunities she had lost to prove herself. Every few moments, she returned to the present, to abject shame. Having invested wholly in securing the position only to fail, not even landing an interview, she concluded that her goal was unattainable; she had been overreaching, and she was not good enough for the job.

Unable to grapple with the enormity of her shame, her mind propelled her forward. She imagined new tactics and new pursuits, anything to avoid feeling the disappointment and loss of the present. Before long, she had returned to analyzing the past, desperate to understand the series of events that had led to her downfall.

Time passed while Faiza remained slumped in her chair, facing the window and mentally running laps. Soon, the fog lifted enough that she registered the ache between her shoulders. Languidly, she inhaled until her chest expanded and her shoulder blades descended down her back. She repeated the action several times, even wiggling her fingers in her lap to return her body to the present moment, however psychologically painful.

Having gained some momentum, Faiza placed her laptop in a desk drawer, keeping the drawer open and sweeping in her folders with one arm. She locked the drawer, collected her phone and handbag, and went home early.

* * *

Goldie was overjoyed after her presentation at the directors' meeting on Friday afternoon. On the way out of the conference room, Patricia and a bunch of other directors had congratulated her. Now, she was capering back to her cubicle in the East Tower. For the first time in weeks, she did not care about running into those bitches from her division. *Nothing can bring me down! I got this.*

Patricia had come through for her, as promised, having praised her mad skills and advertised her availability to a conference room of directors. Following that hype, she was sure that she'd find another contract — or a permanent position — once this one ended in two weeks.

While she waited for the elevator up to her cubicle on the ninth floor of the East Tower, Goldie pressed the bulky laptop, cords, and water bottle to her chest, freeing her hands to browse messages on her phone. She considered messaging Issa about her valid set. It was hard to judge what Issa's reaction would be. *She definitely doesn't like Patricia.* Since the incident at the beauty shop and the station, they had not discussed the event. They had restricted their messaging to making plans and bitching about parents. Bouncing on the spot in front of the elevator, Goldie could not recall Issa's big issue with Patricia, or her exact wording from two days earlier. She thought Issa was being extra when she accused Patricia of ignoring how bad things were. Goldie had grown attached to Patricia, and it was painful to think that Patricia did not care about her feelings. *She mostly feels what I'm putting down. She didn't have to pick me. There's probably a bunch of other people who can make this wiki.*

It occurred to Goldie that Issa might be salty about her landing a job at City Hall. Being jealous was not like her friend but Issa also hated her own basic job as a junior market analyst. For more than a year, Issa had bitched about the way managers assigned work. She'd said that they picked men for the important jobs and gave the basic work to women. One time, Issa had been told to clean up after a meeting, and when she had clapped back, her supervisor had said she was not acting like a team player. *She's just pissed about her own shit. All this rage's got nothin' to do with me.*

The elevator arrived and Goldie boarded, along with a few others she did not recognize. On the way up, she messaged Issa without mentioning the presentation. On arriving at her floor, Goldie rearranged the equipment under her arms and strolled to her cubicle. Friendly faces greeted her along the way, and she smiled back, still pleased from slaying her presentation. There was no sign of Beth but that was not unusual. It seemed like Beth spent a lot of time away from her desk. She did not know whether Beth had always worked this way or if Beth was distancing herself from Goldie. Either way, Goldie was fine keeping a distance for the last two weeks of her contract.

At her cubicle, she unloaded all the equipment into a corner and bid the clunky laptop farewell. Another box of paper records had been placed on her desk but Goldie delayed returning to work. It was Friday afternoon and she was thinking about the weekend. After killing it at the meeting, sitting in front of the screen to update database records seemed anticlimactic.

She browsed messages and feeds, adding to the threads which piqued her interest. Issa messaged about weekend plans and Goldie felt relieved to see the series of silly emojis she had included. Presently, she heard voices nearing and, panicking like a naughty child, she pocketed her phone and scrambled into her seat. Wiggling her mouse, she brought the computer to life and typed her password, twice incorrectly. By then, the voices had passed and Goldie chuckled to herself for being uncoordinated. *Might as well do some work.*

She pushed the newly arrived box of records away from the screen and keyboard — she had yet to complete the last box of files at her feet — and it revealed a yellow sticky note the size of her palm. It had been tacked onto her desk while she was away. The message on the note was written in a thick black marker, and the nondescript capital letters read, "YOU DON'T BELONG HERE."

Goldie reached out to pick it up but stopped herself, freezing in place. The message shocked her though it was a sentiment that had nagged at her since her arrival ten weeks earlier. Her eyes filled with tears and she sucked in her lower lip to keep from whimpering.

Why? Why? I haven't done anything. I've only been quiet and nice. Why are they doing this to me?

For a long time, she stared at the yellow note, unsure of how to proceed. Through her blurred vision, she raised her phone to the missive and snapped a photo. It felt like the right thing to do, a smart move to document the experience without having to touch the offending note. As soon as she heard voices approaching, she took flight. She did not want to be trapped in her cubicle if Beth was returning to her desk or if any of her three co-workers were preparing to corner her. Without looking around, she jetted away from her cubicle and down a couple of corridors. At first, she considered hiding in the washroom but she feared being caught alone with Beth, Sandra, or Holly.

When she came upon the enclosed stairwell, she thought it might offer her some privacy. She pushed open the heavy door and slumped on the first set of concrete steps. There was no comfort in the cold stairwell with its unpainted walls and stark lighting, and her whimpering soon turned to sobs. Folding in on herself, Goldie cried into her lap — until she heard a door open. Then, there were voices and footsteps coming up from a lower floor. Desperate to avoid other people, she scurried up the stairs to the tenth floor and slipped out of the stairwell. The hallway was empty, and when she spotted the women's washroom a few steps away, she ran in and rushed directly into a stall.

Within moments, her fear of being discovered crying was replaced by her agony. Pulling out her phone, she looked more closely at the photo of the yellow note. She mouthed the words to herself and wondered why they were attacking her, especially with the end date of her contract nearing. Goldie did not expect them to like her — though she did not understand why they hated her — but she did not get their rage mode.

By habit, she started to message Issa, seeking support and sympathy. Then, it occurred to her that Issa might press her to quit on the spot. After writing and rewriting a few words, she gave up and sent a line of upset emojis. She would explain later when she did not feel so raw. For the moment, she needed to figure out her next step. She had every intention of leaving for the day but she thought about stopping by Patricia's first. Possibly, she could get to her office without walking past the others. The last thing she wanted to do was see any of them. Still, her bus pass and wallet remained at her desk. How could she get her things without risking a run-in with Beth? Maybe Patricia could collect her belongings. Maybe she could message Patricia now to meet at her office, all without being seen by the others.

Goldie typed, *Meet?* She waited a minute for a reply, thinking that older people took forever to respond to messages.

In meetings until 5, Patricia messaged back.

Goldie checked the time, nearly two hours before Patricia became available. She did not want to demand attention like a petulant child but she felt overwhelmed, in need of compassion and some soothing. Certain that Patricia would hasten to meet were she informed about the urgency of the matter, Goldie sent the photo of the yellow sticky note along with a message.

Found this on my desk, she typed.

To Goldie, it seemed like a lifetime passed while she waited for a reply, smoothing out her hair compulsively. She presumed that Patricia was carefully composing her message, words to express her sympathy and outrage. Wiping away tears that had restarted, she imagined Patricia typing while she abruptly excused herself from her meeting and walked briskly back in search of Goldie. *Would she try to hug me? Can we hug? I'm okay with hugging her.*

The thought of Patricia coming to her rescue nearly brought a smile to her face. She felt a connection to Patricia that echoed the close relationship she enjoyed with her high school French teacher, Madame Chastain. For four years, Goldie relied on Madame for praise and perspective, and Madame never failed in her support.

During her years at the University of Toronto, as one of 60,000 faceless students who was distanced from her professors by rigid office hours and teaching assistants, Goldie missed Madame acutely. Now, at her first serious job, she was lucky to have Patricia, a mentor who advocated for her success.

When Patricia's response arrived, Goldie had no words, no thoughts, only the feeling of the floor falling away.

And? Patricia's message read.

Goldie's brows knitted and she fought back tears that fell in spite of her. She chastised herself for reacting emotionally, told herself to grow up and reply. *She's just asking a follow-up question. That's allowed.*

I'm not sure what to do, Goldie typed.

This was a statement of fact, a truth without any emotional embellishment. She did not know how to proceed. She wanted help from her manager, from someone she trusted. Goldie wanted to elaborate, to express her fear and sadness, to admit hiding in the tenth-floor washroom but she held back. The tone of the conversation, as set by Patricia, was cooler that she had expected, and out of deference to her superior Goldie wanted to follow suit.

Presently, her phone rang. It was Patricia calling, and Goldie's spirits rose at the possibility that Patricia intended to comfort her.

"Hi," Goldie answered, her soft voice resonating in the tiled washroom.

"Hello, Goldie. I thought this might be easier if we talk instead," her manager said plainly.

"Okay," Goldie replied gratefully, misinterpreting Patricia's comment as an invitation to meet.

"So, what's going on?" Patricia asked.

"Uh, oh …" Goldie stammered. "Um, well. I found that note on my desk …" Goldie paused, waiting for a sympathetic response. When none came, she shrugged off her uneasiness and continued, "Um, well, I don't really know what to do now."

"Hmm, yes. This note, you believe it's about you?" Patricia asked flatly.

Surprised by the question, Goldie was slow and hesitant in her response. "Yes?"

"Hmm, I see. Are you at your desk now?"

"Now? No," Goldie said, looking about the toilet stall which she'd occupied for a quarter-hour. "I'm on the tenth floor, in the washroom."

"Hmm, alright ..." Patricia replied coolly, seeming unfazed by Goldie's need to take refuge. "Well, if you feel it is necessary, you have my permission to take the rest of the day off."

Goldie tried to respond but words failed her. She had expected Patricia to express concern and outrage. Instead, her manager was downplaying the incident. She wondered whether she had over-reacted to the note, whether she was behaving like an immature twenty-something, overly dramatic and unprofessional.

"Thank you." Goldie managed to sound appreciative. "Uh, there's ... I need my wallet and bus pass. They're at my desk."

"Yes," Patricia said, not grasping Goldie's intimation that she felt unsafe returning to her desk.

"They're at my desk ..." Goldie repeated, unsure how to elicit help without revealing her fear and offending Patricia's cool sensibility.

"Yes," Patricia answered, sounding distracted by her surroundings.

"I don't feel ... safe, returning to my desk," Goldie blurted, worried that Patricia might end the call any moment.

"Why? What ..." Patricia started but paused, giving Goldie hope that her manager was finally cluing in to the gravity of the moment. "Goldie, I think you might be ... having a disproportionate reaction to this note. You are perfectly safe to return to your desk."

Stunned, Goldie made only the slightest sound, a muffled signal to acknowledge that she had heard her manager. Any remaining strength drained from her. She slumped in her seat on the toilet.

"Alright, then. Have a good weekend. I will see you on Monday," Patricia said in a rush as she hung up.

Goldie stared at the phone, its screen returning to a wallpaper photo of her and Issa and a backdrop of anime cosplayers outside the Metro Toronto Convention Centre. *A disproportionate reaction? Like, making a big deal about nothing? She thinks I'm overreacting?* Dropping her phone into her lap, Goldie began rubbing her face vigorously, not caring about the layers of makeup she smeared into a kaleidoscope of colour. She squeezed shut her eyes and wished to be anywhere else. It seemed impossible that less than an hour ago she had walked the halls feeling self-assured. Now, she was hiding in a stall overwhelmed by the prospect of leaving the washroom. *Am I overreacting? Why can't I just get my wallet and pass?*

She replayed her conversation with Patricia, verifying that she had thoroughly described the events. Then again, she had sent Patricia a photo of the note. They had both read the same message but Patricia was undisturbed by its tone and implication. Goldie scrolled through her phone for the photo, and she examined it, re-reading the lines in search of a harmless message. *Maybe* you *doesn't mean* me*? Maybe someone wrote the message about the box of files? Like, "You, box, don't belong here." Maybe it's not about me … but who calls a box* you*?!*

Then, she wondered whether she had not conveyed her fear and anxiety clearly. Could it be that Patricia didn't realize the gravity of the situation because Goldie had downplayed her reaction? If she had admitted to hiding in the washroom for fear of reprisals from Beth, Sandra, or Holly, might their conversation have taken a different turn?

Goldie shook her head in disappointment. She had created drama when that was the last thing she wanted to do, and she had involved her manager, the one person who was advocating on her behalf for a permanent position. There would be consequences for her behaviour, Goldie was certain. Her reputation as a reasonable and reliable employee was tarnished by her overreacting to an inoffensive note. She had to remedy this situation, to counteract Patricia's negative opinions. *I'll send her an apology for overreacting, and say I'm working till end of day. Just a misunderstanding.*

Desperate to restore her earlier glory and confidence, she straightened up, smoothed her clothes and hair, and stepped out of the stall. Washing her hands at the row of sinks was a woman, younger than her own mother but older than herself. In the reflection of the mirror, the woman smiled briefly at Goldie before she rinsed her hands, shook off the excess water, and ran her wet fingers through her large mane of wavy black hair. Her hair flattened for a moment and then bounced back to its full voluminous glory.

"Hi," the woman said, leaning closer toward the mirror to examine her makeup-less face.

"Hi," Goldie said softly as she soaped her hands and scrubbed at the smeared makeup on her palms.

"Are you new? I mean, I haven't seen you on this floor before. Then again, I'm new so …" the woman rambled, her eyes fixed on her reflection, her hands wrestling her hair. "Anyways, hi. I'm Sameera."

Goldie did not mind Sameera's rambling because it served as a distraction from her worries. Also, Sameera's unruly hair put her at ease. With her own makeup sullied, she was glad to share the washroom with someone who was not perfectly put together.

"Hi, I'm new, too. Ninth floor. Transportation Services," Goldie replied, collecting a handful of tissues from a box on the counter and leaning in to wipe the black and brown streaks on her face.

"Nice," Sameera said, pleased. She wet her hands again and tried to flatten her locks but they sprung up instantly. Goldie chuckled at the familiar experience.

"I know, I know," Sameera replied with a grin, still wrangling her wavy hair. "It's my wild Persian hair. Refuses to be tamed."

"Mine, too," Goldie said as she finished cleaning her face, leaving it streaked with reddened skin. "If I don't blow-dry and use treatment, I look like a sheepdog."

Sameera's brows knitted as she examined her reflection, and then it occurred to Goldie that she might have offended Sameera.

"Not that you look like a dog," Goldie backpedalled, her palms facing out in surrender. "I just mean that my hair is wild and it's … it's a lot worse than yours." Another pause followed as Goldie heard herself, and she rushed forward, "Not that there's anything wrong with your hair. I mean, it's totally cool. Natural is the new … Lots of people like it natural. I think it looks really good on you."

Sameera faced Goldie with a bemused expression and hands on hips. She nodded slowly without breaking eye contact, and with every nod, Goldie cringed further. She tallied all the insults that she had dealt in one five-minute exchange with a stranger, and she imagined how this stranger might retaliate. Goldie braced herself for a tongue lashing. Presently, Sameera crossed her arms but her expression contorted into a wide grin as she failed to hold the perturbed pose she had feigned.

"So, you're Persian, too?" Sameera asked in a congenial tone, dropping her warrior stance to lean against the counter, thus pivoting the mood. "What's your name?"

"Goldie," she said shyly, surprised and relieved by the shift.

"Nice to meet you, Goldie," Sameera said, offering her hand. "What brings you to the tenth floor?"

Goldie took her hand, feeling the warmth and respect in Sameera's firm grip. Inside, she lost her hold on the fear and anxiety she had reined in for weeks. All the criticism hurled by Beth and ignored by Goldie because she did not want to seem disruptive to Patricia. All the honest conversations Goldie had not started with

Issa because she worried about being judged for staying on. All the cutting remarks made by Dariush, attempting to undermine her confidence but fortifying her resolve to endure this ordeal no matter the cost.

It was too much pain to manage every day. She needed to confide in someone, and presently this stranger was the safest option.

* * *

"You did what?!" exclaimed Shannon, appearing in the bathroom doorway where Sameera was styling the errant hairs framing her face.

Shannon's brow was furrowed and her pale lips were pursed but Sameera did not react to the expression or to the indignation in her girlfriend's voice. Moments earlier, they had been bantering about their Friday night double-date — dinner at the brewery with a friend and her new lover. After weeks of cold exchanges, Sameera had sensed the fire of intimacy relighting, and the heat felt good, too good to lose again. Nothing was going to extinguish the fragile sparks of their romance and rapport. Sameera needed to feel loved and adored by Shannon, even if they disagreed about the best response to a distraught young woman panicking in a City Hall washroom.

"I did what I'd want done for me," Sameera answered tactfully, examining her hairdo at every angle to avoid meeting Shannon's narrowed eyes.

Show me what solidarity looks like! This is what solidarity looks like! From within, she heard the chants of the thousands of protestors among whom she had walked. Her impulse to soothe and support Goldie by offering encouragement and practical information was integral to her expression of solidarity for women of colour. Listening, validating, and offering her skills and knowledge was her way of changing the world for the better, her way of contributing to social justice. Given a second chance, she couldn't, wouldn't, have responded differently in her exchange with Goldie — but that was beside the point. But placating Shannon was her current objective, so she tried changing the topic by changing tactics. She posed coquettishly in her cut-off denim overalls and skimpy tank top, her twin braids pulled forward and her kissable lips pouted invitingly.

"Hot?" Sameera asked in a sultry voice as she moved to press into Shannon's body.

Shannon nodded curtly and pulled back into the bedroom, undeterred. "You don't know her. You don't know what she wants."

Sameera remained in the bathroom, taking a moment to recover from the slight. It was tempting to respond with anger, to accuse Shannon of speaking out of turn and behaving arrogantly. Intellectually, Sameera recognized Shannon's discomfort as a manifestation of white fragility, the reluctance to accept evidence of racial injustice. Again. Emotionally, Sameera needed the love and affection of her girlfriend. She ached for tenderness in Shannon's voice, her touch, her gaze, the tenderness that bonded them as a couple. *We've just hit a bump in the road. Arguments happen in every relationship.*

While the sustained antagonism at work was wearing her down, it was the severe undercurrent of her home life that threatened to ruin her. She needed to balance the discomfort with comfort to remind her of the joy she was capable of feeling. Spending time with their friends over greasy food and overpriced beer, chatting about the newest art exhibits and the most anticipated festivals, was going to be the balm to their relationship pains, not intellectual discourse about white fragility.

"You're right," she started, sidling up to Shannon, who sat on the edge of their cold and unmade bed. "I just met her. But I was only trying to help."

Shannon spun and knocked knees with Sameera, not stopping to apologize before snapping, "Did she ask for help? Or did you just assume? Is this another crusade?"

Sameera understood the implications, and it stung her deeply to think that Shannon considered her a fanatic, a radical with tunnel-vision who mangled circumstances and forced them to fit into a rigid paradigm. As much as Sameera feared becoming such a person unwittingly, she was certain that this was not the case. Goldie had described a series of incidents that exemplified covert racism: the use of her name to distinguish her as Other, the insinuation that her poor work performance was attributable to ethnicity, the repeated attempts by her teammates to ostracize her, the white saviour performance of her manager, all topped off by a racist note on her desk. These were classic examples of microaggressions, behaviours that Sameera had experienced and read about. She felt confident in this assessment but she realized that any statement to this effect would be read by Shannon as self-assured paranoia. *She doesn't have context or experience. It's not her fault. Don't punish her. Don't destroy your relationship.*

"She was crying and scared," Sameera said softly, trying to absorb Shannon's vitriol and ease the tension. "I told her that she hadn't done anything wrong, that she should talk to HR. I fetched her wallet. Basic stuff."

"No, not basic," Shannon snapped though her tone had softened, and when she turned away from Sameera, she made an effort to avoid knocking their knees. "You don't know her situation, Sam. What if she is really bad at her job and she's just making it sound like … I don't know. She's a kid. It's not a big deal if she gets fired for being bad at her job. That's how they learn about the real world. You don't have to interfere."

Again, Sameera chose to ignore the implication that she was inserting herself needlessly in a trivial matter. *It's okay. Shannon didn't see Goldie crying.* She counselled herself to return to this conversation at a much later time, when their relationship had recovered and Shannon was no longer angry, more willing to listen to reason. *She needs time to come around, to understand. Be patient, don't push her.*

On the bed, she slid closer to Shannon and placed a hand on her girlfriend's thigh, rubbing small circles with her forefinger. The end of their argument seemed near, and Sameera was ready to bring it to a close, ready to transition into happier times. The hard work of non-resistance, of receiving Shannon's opinions without opposition, was about to pay off, and Sameera felt proud of herself for remaining calm and loving.

For a brief time, they sat in silence, Sameera gently rubbing her girlfriend's thigh. Soon, Shannon was leaning into her while Sameera rubbed her lower back and kissed the top of her head. Satisfaction coursed through her, a sense of victory over the reigning gloom of the last few weeks. She imagined their upcoming weekend: waking up tangled in each other's arms, morning sex and late brunch, followed by browsing bookstores, cooing at other people's dogs at the park, maybe more sex before grabbing dinner.

"Seriously though, Sam," Shannon moaned, her head now resting in Sameera's lap, her girlfriend combing her fingers through her hair, lifting it up and away from her neck in rhythmic strokes. "Things aren't as bad as you think."

"Hmm," Sameera replied, deflecting Shannon's remark by envisioning a change in their bedroom décor — anything to subdue her inner voice, the advocate with a megaphone who was screaming for her to rebuke Shannon.

In a grave tone, Shannon continued, "You wouldn't believe the shit I went through in Pactonville. I mean, you know some. Man, they'd throw stuff at me … dump trash in my locker … Once, they cornered me in the halls … scary shit." Shannon turned her head to lock eyes with Sameera, who nodded sympathetically. "Really fucked up shit, Sammy. Undeniably fucked up, you know."

Sameera nodded, and then she kissed her own two fingertips and rested them on Shannon's cheek. Shannon offered a small smile and turned away, wordlessly prompting Sameera to continue stroking her hair.

"The world is full of monsters … you know, men who hate women, like want-us-dead hate, even the straight ones," Shannon continued her lecture. "We've gotta be united. We can't be fighting with each other. It just makes them more powerful."

We could paint the room, Sameera scanned the room for ideas while her fingers stroked absentmindedly. *Maybe rose or caramel.*

"Fighting each other is just stupid. We're all women. Period. We have enough bullshit to deal with just being female. We don't need to confuse everything with special interests."

We could put in a small bookshelf, or mount a shelf, Sameera thought about the far wall, forcing down the counterarguments that threatened to burst forth.

"Hmm, babe, that feels nice," Shannon said with a contended sigh, rolling over on her back and facing Sameera.

"Good," Sameera cooed and pinched Shannon's freckled cheek. "Ready for dinner?"

"Oh yeah!" Shannon exclaimed, sitting up and rubbing her belly. "I could eat a platter of nachos by myself. When are we meeting Maisy?"

Sameera checked her phone, "In fifteen. We've got time."

"I still need to take a shower," said Shannon as she hurriedly undressed on her way to the bathroom. "I stink from work, stuck between two boilers for ten hours. I smell worse than the guys."

"Not possible," Sameera said, lingering in the doorway to admire Shannon's silhouette behind the curtain. "Besides, Maisy never shows up on time."

"Yeah, especially when she's got someone new," Shannon agreed. Then poking out her sudsy head from behind the shower curtain, she quipped, "I'm surprised they're leaving the bed at all."

Sameera performed her amusement with a loud chortle, diligently nurturing the cheerful mood.

"Do we know her?" asked Shannon, her voice garbled as she rinsed.

"The ladylove? I don't know. I don't think so but Maisy says we're gonna love her. Actually, her exact words were ..." Sameera paused, checking her phone for the message, "... She a snack."

"A snack? What does that even mean?" Shannon replied, turning off the shower and pulling back the curtains to receive the towel Sameera offered lovingly. "Thanks, babe."

"You know, like yummy," Sameera said with a knowing look, eyeing her girlfriend's wet and naked curves.

Shannon smirked and said, "Yeah, yeah. I get it. Just weird that she talks like a twenty-something but she's older than us."

They carried the conversation into the bedroom where Shannon dressed in a clean T-shirt and jeans while Sameera filled her handbag with necessities.

"She's a bit of a chameleon, no? Like, she changes to fit," Sameera described Maisy, not unkindly.

"Yeah, I guess," Shannon answered distractedly as she tucked in her grey tee and examined herself in the full length mirror. "Sometimes, it's just weird. You know? It's like, she's without ... like, she's not ... I don't know, defined? Or, something like that." Pivoting to face Sameera, she asked, "Do I look okay?"

Coupling her compliment with a passionate kiss, Sameera grinned and replied, "Like a snack."

Falling onto the bed, the women fondled each other like new lovers. Sameera could not get enough of Shannon's scent, breathing in her musk like it was essential to her existence. At her core, there was a vessel that had nearly emptied of joy and pleasure, and now it was overflowing with an elixir, a life force that coursed through her limbs. She pressed her body into Shannon's and laid her open mouth on every inch of exposed skin. She did not want to have sex so much as she wanted to consume Shannon, to absorb her essence and her affection. *I want to spend forever with you.*

While Sameera nibbled on her neck, Shannon moaned, "Shouldn't be we going?"

"No," Sameera said unequivocally, making Shannon laugh out loud.

Moments later, they were out the door and on the way to the brewery in the heart of the Queer Village. Sameera slipped herself under Shannon's arm and tucked her hand into Shannon's back pocket, signalling to the world her claim on this woman. This act did not put a full stop to the parade of white women who ignored Sameera and ogled Shannon, but it did lessen the number of incidents.

The sun had set and the street lights offered an electric quality to the thickening crowds on Church Street. Scantily dressed queers lounged on sidewalk patios enjoying cold drinks on a warm night. Some bodies were chiselled, tanned, and hairless, while others were curvaceous and pouring out of their seductive wrappers. Piled on the crowded steps of the all-night café were the teenagers, studying the landscape for a taste of their future, boisterous with each other but timid in their exchanges with the surrounding adults.

Sameera remembered being one of them, lying to her parents about going to the movies when she was attending youth groups at the Village community centre, a stone's throw from her current residence. Sitting in those circles, she knew she was one of the lucky ones: not a foster kid, not a street kid, and increasingly confident that her parents wouldn't disown her when she came out of the closet. Glancing at the youthful faces nursing their syrupy drinks and trading earbuds, Sameera hoped that they all survived this difficult stage less traumatized than preceding generations.

"Babe," Shannon said, pulling them out of the stream of pedestrians and into the fenced-in patio of the brewery. "There's Maisy."

Under a red canvas umbrella adorned with a string of vintage style bulbs, Maisy and her date sat at a wrought-iron table for four, tucked away between the brewery and the brick wall of the adjoining building. Along the sidewalk, a dozen other tables were linked by the daisy chain of overhead lights, the narrow patio packed with an assortment of patrons, young and old, some moneyed and some spending their last student-loan dollars on beer and sliders.

As Shannon led the way to the private nook, Sameera recognized Maisy's date as Tina, the grocery store clerk from The Organic Village. The very hot grocery store clerk. *So, she's the snack!*

Sameera chuckled inwardly at Maisy having summed up Tina with this one word. From her handful of chance conversations with Tina — nearly always discussions on race and gender — she'd have described her as subversive or audacious. Then again, Maisy perceived the world through an erotic lens of desire and conquest.

"Women, I'd like you to meet Ta-yang," Maisy said proudly, introducing Tina with a flourish of her ivory hands.

"Hi," Tina greeted Sameera and Shannon with a winning smile that reached the upper folds of her eyes, "you can call me Tina."

"No, no. That's not cool," Maisy pouted, replacing her drink on the table to present her practised lines. "Your name is Ta-yang, so we call you by your name. Right, women?"

"Sure, no big deal. Nice to meet you," Shannon said, returning Tina's smile, and settling in between Maisy and Sameera to study the drinks menu.

"Hi," Sameera addressed Tina, ignoring the off-putting debate about Tina's name which she was certain Maisy was mispronouncing. "It's been a while."

At this comment, Maisy leaned in closer with a curious expression, "Does everyone know each other in this city of millions?"

She chuckled at her own joke but Sameera sensed the undercurrent of unease. Maisy could just as easily be accused of knowing everyone in the Village, at least all the ones with money or sculpted physiques. Her job as a realtor in one of the country's hottest markets meant that she associated with the wealthiest queers downtown. Her frequent sessions at the local gym placed her in a stream of young, attractive women, including Shannon. The two had dated briefly a few years earlier before they settled into their casual friendship.

"Oh, we met at the grocery store," replied Sameera casually, eager to avoid any misunderstandings about her familiarity with Tina.

Maisy's diametric traits — being fickle about her lovers while demanding their undivided attention — were the running joke among her friends. She bristled at the possibility that a companion of hers might be a known commodity, so she dated the newest and youngest arrivals in the Village.

"The grocery store, oh," Maisy said as she balanced her chin on one manicured finger and eyed Tina hungrily. "With that gorgeous figure of yours, I didn't know you ate anything."

"I work there," Tina said, smirking at Maisy like an imp. "I'm a juice master."

"Well, that explains everything …" Maisy purred, pulling into Tina and initiating an opened mouth kiss that caused Sameera to turn away.

Shannon rolled her eyes from behind the menu, causing Sameera to snicker.

"Hi, ladies. How's everyone tonight?" The young, pale server asked cheerily, placing glasses of ice water before Sameera and Shannon.

Leaning in to read the server's name tag, Maisy answered for everyone, "Fabulous … Gracie!"

"Great, so—" the server started, only to be cut off by Maisy.

"But first, let's not call us ladies, hmm?" Maisy lectured. "After all, we are strong women, not demure ladies. Yes?" She searched the faces around the table for confirmation.

Sameera kept her eyes on the menu, displeased by Maisy's putting an overworked and underpaid woman on the spot. At another time, she might have censured Maisy but she was fatigued from her earlier conversation with Shannon. *Two white women can sort out what to call each other. They don't need my help.*

"Well, this woman-lady," Shannon started, grinning and pointing at her chest with her thumb, "would like a pint of stout, please. Thank you."

"Yes, of course," the server smiled, seemingly unfazed by the rocky start. "How about you?"

"Um, yeah. I'll take the … a pint of the raspberry ale," Sameera decided. "Thank you."

"Great," the server continued cheerily, turning to Tina and Maisy. "And can I refresh your drinks?"

Maisy grabbed Tina's forearm and answered for both of them, "This time, two orange-ginger ciders." Turning to Tina, she added, "They're delicious. You'll love it."

"I'll be right back with your drinks and to take your orders," the server said, maintaining her pleasant smile as she slipped away.

Grateful for the server's composure but still agitated by the close call with conflict, Sameera breathed deeply to force calmness upon herself. She admired the nighttime sky that never completely darkened in the city, and she considered booking a weekend cottage where she and Shannon could nestle under the stars.

As the brewery filled to capacity, the mellow and subversive soundtrack of Clario's "Pretty Girl" transitioned into the upbeat rhythms of Big Freedia and the funky dance beats of Janelle Monae. The music reminded Sameera of late nights at dance clubs, necking in doorways, and heartfelt talks that climaxed with sunrises. She missed those days and promised herself to get out more often with Shannon.

The conversation turned to real estate, and Maisy described a revitalization plan on the eastern borders of the Village, a highly lucrative project sought out by prominent developers. While they debated the merits of multi-use buildings and the decreasing percentage of affordable units, the server returned with drinks and took their food orders. The four were viewing development mockups on Maisy's phone when the food arrived, momentarily halting all talk as they dug into their meals.

As she filled up on gourmet macaroni and cheese, Sameera felt her shoulders relax. Pasta was her ideal comfort food and at the moment she craved comfort, keto diet be damned. She leaned back to chew her mouthful and caught Tina doing the same.

"It's good, right?" Tina asked from the corner of her overstuffed mouth. "Bacon in mac and cheese makes so much sense."

Sameera nodded vigorously and mumbled, "Salty and creamy. So good."

"I don't know how you two can eat that," Maisy scoffed, nibbling daintily on her kale salad, then putting down her fork to explain in earnest. "I mean, Ta-yang, you're trim naturally but, Sameera, the rate of heart disease in South Asians is stupendous. I read this article about how the North American diet does five times more damage to South Asians."

"Sammy's not South Asian," Shannon interjected, chewing around her words. "She's from the Middle East," she added before drinking heartily from her glass and returning to slathering her fries with the house mayonnaise.

Sameera devoured another spoonful for an excuse to remain silent, to avoid calling out Maisy's bad behaviour — her body shaming and unsolicited counselling. It pleased her that Shannon corrected Maisy's error, however dispassionately, but Sameera was in the habit of advocating for herself. Keeping quiet for the sake of a harmonious relationship required the use of physical measures.

Indeed, this was not the first time Sameera had encountered Maisy's ignorance. As a couple, they had dined with Maisy on a dozen occasions in as many months, and each time Sameera had addressed her misconceptions and missteps. With an air of amusement, Maisy would accuse Sameera of being idealistic or naïve but she would relent and change topics.

Since an admission of wrongdoing or an apology never

followed, Sameera had concluded that Maisy liked to maintain a public persona that was charitable, but rarely brought that persona to her relationships. Sameera wondered sometimes whether Maisy maintained their relationship in the hopes of a future condo sale.

"South Asian, Middle Eastern. Last I checked the world map, it's all Asian, right?" Maisy said, and without awaiting an answer, she pointed to the bowl of pasta and declared, "That stuff'll kill you."

"Let the woman enjoy her meal," Tina said in Sameera's defence, taking her first sip of the orange-ginger cider and exclaiming in disgust, "Now, this, this will kill you. Ugh."

Tina placed her glass at arm's length and gulped water as she waved theatrically for the server.

"What are you talking about?" Maisy huffed and took a long drink. "This is so refreshing. Ginger is so good for you. Of all people, you should know that."

Sameera glanced at Shannon, checking whether her girlfriend had registered Maisy's comment as racial stereotyping. Shannon was grinning at Tina who was jokingly signing the cross to ward off the glass of cider. By the time the server appeared to take Tina's drink order, Sameera had decided to let Maisy's comment go unchallenged. The four of them seemed to be having a nice time, and Sameera did not want to be accused of being a fanatic, or to cement Shannon's perceptions of her apparent single-mindedness.

After they finished their meal, they stayed for a last round of drinks. Maisy continued to dominate the conversation, moving unfettered from one topic to another. Shannon drank steadily, enjoying the company of friends but happily distracted by passersby. Tina and Maisy pulled their seats closer, tangling their arms and legs together. Their long whispers and roaming hands inspired Sameera to turn her seat so she could join Shannon in people watching.

"Oh, don't forget, you have to dress up for my Pride party. No rainbow leis or overalls," Maisy instructed lazily, tilting her head to allow Tina to nibble her neck.

"Umm, yeah," Sameera started, looking over at Shannon. "That's next week … so, I think we'll be there?"

Shannon, who smiled like a happy drunk, shrugged at Sameera, signalling that she could take the lead.

"And you have to come to the Dyke March," Maisy insisted, lightly kicking the back of Shannon's chair.

"Sure, I'm a dyke," Shannon quipped before surprising herself with a question. "Wait, that's like really early isn't it? It's too early. Babe?"

Chuckling at her girlfriend's childlike complaints, Sameera confirmed, "Yeah, it starts at one." Then, turning to the others, she explained, "Shannon doesn't wake up before noon on Saturdays."

"Well, this year you're gonna have to," Maisy insisted with a modicum of severity, enough to cause Sameera to turn around. "We head out from my place at quarter to one. Don't be late."

"I'm up for it," Sameera confirmed. "I love the Dyke March."

"And you too, Ta-yang," Maisy stated instead of asking. "We need a strong female presence at this year's parade."

Tina, who had been nuzzling Maisy's neck, raised her head slightly and demurred, "I'm pan."

"As long as you're a woman, you're on the list," Maisy said as she leaned over and cupped Tina's breast.

"You know I'm all woman," Tina bantered, taking hold of Maisy's earlobe with her teeth.

Sameera joined Shannon in watching passersby, not wanting to gawk at the couple's groping and grateful that they were tucked into a dark corner. She and Shannon did not overtly display affection in public. They might wind and grind to the music on a packed dance floor but they did not kiss and cuddle outdoors. Even in the Village, Shannon remained withdrawn, and Sameera saw in that withdrawal the small-town girl who hid her identity to protect herself from bigots and hate crimes.

"I'm having signs made," Maisy continued, her speech now slightly slurred. "So you'll need to come by early to pick 'em up."

"Nice," Sameera replied, keeping her eyes straight ahead as she heard Tina emit a quiet moan.

"Oh, I have a good one for a sign," Shannon cheered languidly. "Okay, it's a photo. Of a cat, but like with a shocked face. On top, like above the cat's head, it says 'Lesbians eat what?!' Get it?"

Shannon folded over laughing at her own description, her right hand flailing at Sameera for affirmation who burst out laughing.

After a long exhale and a final chuckle, Shannon wiped the corner of her eyes and said, "It's hilarious. Seriously. I'd carry that sign."

"I think someone's had her fill," Maisy joked in a sing-song voice, nudging Shannon's chair with her foot and draining the dregs of her glass. "Don't worry about the signs. The signs are done and paid for, and they are awesome."

"That's great," Sameera replied politely, knowing that Maisy expected some praise for her efforts. "What do the signs say?"

Counting them off on her fingers, Maisy listed, "Women don't have penises. Drop the T. Stand up for women and girls. And … oh, there was another one … um, oh, yes. No wrong bodies ever."

Sameera whipped around to stare at Maisy who was distracted by her manicured nails.

Before Sameera could express her shock at the transphobic messaging, Tina exclaimed, "Serious, Em?! What the fuck?!"

Distancing herself from Maisy, Tina pushed back her metal chair that let out a jarring noise that attracted the attention of everyone nearby. All three women were gaping at Maisy, and she returned their stares indignantly.

"Don't you what-the-fuck me!" Maisy snapped at Tina, looking down her nose. "It takes a strong person to take a stand, and I won't be intimidated by anyone."

"But Maisy, this is … I don't understand," Sameera said in exasperation, finding comfort in the horrified expression on Shannon's face. "Why are you attacking trans women?"

"I am not attacking anyone. They're the ones attacking," Maisy hissed as she rifled through her designer purse. "Don't be so naïve, Sameera. They're trying to take away our rights."

"Just calm down," Shannon mediated, her speech slightly slurred. "Maisy, can you … can you just explain … um, like?"

"Here," Maisy announced as she pulled a glossy brochure from her purse and placed it on the table between soiled napkins and damp coasters. "You three need to get educated."

Tina swiped the brochure, nearly knocking over their glasses. After a brief glance, she let out a wail and crumpled the paper, throwing it back on the table. Maisy sneered at Tina in disgust, and then she turned to Sameera and Shannon.

"Are you just as small-minded?" Maisy accused the couple.

"You know who they are, right?" Tina asked of Sameera and Shannon, referring to the pamphlet. "The same bigots who tried to steal the march last year."

This pronouncement received considerable attention from the other patrons. Several heads turned their way, intrigued by the prospect of political gossip. Shannon scratched her temple in a gesture Sameera recognized as embarrassment.

"Listen, you," Maisy chastised Tina, pointing a slender finger in her direction. "They are smart women. They understand much more than you do. You have no idea how these … people … are undermining our rights as women."

"I know hate when I see it," Tina snapped as she shot to her feet and searched her pockets. "I can't believe I slept with you."

Infuriated, Maisy snarled under her breath, "I can't believe I slept with *you*! Uncultured peasant!"

"Forget you, fucking bully!" Tina thundered at Maisy, throwing cash on the table and collecting her belongings. "You're disgusting!"

Maisy did not acknowledge Tina's words or her departure. She rooted through her purse for her wallet while Sameera and Shannon shared a disturbed look, too stunned to speak.

From the sidewalk, Tina yelled back at their corner table, "And it's Taeyang! Taeyang! You transphobe!"

Shannon slunk lower in her seat, hiding her face from the patrons and passersby gawking at them, while Sameera stared wide-eyed as Tina crossed the street with middle fingers raised over her head. Though shaken by the intensity of the exchange, Sameera felt electrified by Tina's urgency, her immediate response to Maisy's inhumanity. She recognized Tina's unabashed morality, the practice of advocating for others without thought to potential reprisal for self.

Even after she lost sight of Tina among the pedestrians, Sameera continued to stare off, relishing the glorious feelings that had been stirred by this incident. Strangely, she felt the urge to chant as she did during protests and marches, and she wondered whether her elation was induced by alcohol.

At the table, Shannon flattened the brochure and held it open for her and Sameera to read. The pamphlet promoted a women's organization that opposed trans rights, a group who claimed that trans gender identity threatened to erase the rights of women and girls. Sameera was familiar with the group's tenets from online reports and local gossip, and she agreed with Tina in her assessment: they were frightened, and they targeted trans people based on misguided notions.

"Maisy, this group is …" Sameera started, speaking softly to appease Maisy but struggling to be heard over the piped-in music. "It's divisive. I mean, I don't want to lose my rights. But I don't want to take any away from trans people."

"Are you gonna make a scene, too?" Maisy snapped, tipping her glass to her lips only to realize it was empty. "Go ahead, embarrass yourself."

Maisy waved at the server, signalling for the bill. From her purse, she produced a compact and set about checking her immaculate makeup. Sameera tried to respond but came up short. She did not want to aggravate the situation but she was determined to defend her beliefs. Before she spoke, Sameera glanced at Shannon for a cue, a sign that Maisy's behaviour provided reasonable grounds for her to pursue an uncomfortable conversation.

Fumbling through her well-worn wallet for a credit card, Shannon did not notice her gaze but she did raise her head momentarily to chide Maisy, "Don't be mean. Sammy's cool."

Maisy rolled her eyes and sighed, clicking shut the compact and sitting slightly taller.

"No, no," Sameera managed uneasily, directing her words to both women. "This is not okay, Maisy. And it's not about making a scene."

Maisy moaned in frustration just as the server appeared with the bill and a handful of wrapped mints. The trio maintained silence as they paid. While Maisy entered her banking information, Shannon flashed Sameera a pleading, or possibly irritated, look.

"What?!" Sameera mouthed, frustrated by Shannon's desire to avoid confrontation.

"Five more minutes," Shannon whispered with matching frustration.

"I'll see you at home," Sameera said aloud, rising from her seat. "'Bye, Maisy."

Maisy did not look up, seemingly captivated by the console as she waited for her transaction to be approved. Sameera registered being snubbed but refused to respond. Instead, she thanked the server and without another look at Shannon, she weaved her way around the patio tables and out onto the bustling sidewalk.

Fuck y'all, she thought as she headed in the direction of home, her tears streaming.

* * *

"Are you sure you don't want me to stay home?" Robert asked, his concern reaching Faiza through the bathroom door. "We don't have to go. The observatory puts this show on every Friday."

Inside the master bathroom, Faiza stared at her tired reflection. The layers of makeup hid the dark circles under her eyes but she needed something else to conceal her dejected mood. She'd driven home in a stupor and blurted the news to Robert as soon as she saw him. Now, he waited in the wings, intent on soothing her, and she wanted to avoid talking about it altogether. *I don't need advice. I know City Hall better than anyone and I will figure this out myself.*

Looking into the mirror, she attempted a neutral expression, one she could use as a shield to protect herself from her husband's probing questions. But even indifference was a state too arduous to feign. It occurred to her to use a mud mask to disguise her downcast visage. In her best impression of a woman unscathed, Faiza repeated, "No, go. I'll be fine."

"Really, Faiza," Robert insisted. "I can take Pari another time."

Faiza closed her eyes to gather the strength to lie, "Really, Rob. Go ahead. I'm fine."

"Sweetheart," Robert pleaded. "Can you please come out and talk to me?"

Again closing her eyes to direct all her energy into a peaceful tone, Faiza managed, "Yes, of course. I'll be out in a minute."

Rooting through some clothes on hooks, Faiza spotted a tracksuit which was clean though wrinkled. Turning away from the mirror to avoid seeing the body she barely tolerated, she changed out of her tailored work clothes and freed herself from her underwire bra and shapewear. Mechanically, she wiped away her makeup and applied a mud mask's creamy brown layer to her face. The coolness of the mask brought temporary distraction from her inner distress, her emotions a hot mass fuelled by self-denigration and desperate scheming. *I know I can fix this. I just need to talk to Howard, convince him that I'm the best person for the job.*

When she opened the bathroom door, she found Robert sitting on the edge of their king-sized bed, dressed in a T-shirt and shorts for an evening with Pari, spent exploring stars at the Observatory. His expression was soft-hearted, making Faiza wish she had not opened the door. She did not want sympathy. She wanted success, the satisfaction of her goal accomplished, her status elevated.

He rose to comfort her with kisses, and it was more than she could endure. Trying, but failing, to sound frivolous, she warned, "Be careful, my mask!"

Without a hint of acrimony, Robert lowered his outstretched arms and offered a compassionate smile instead. Faiza forced a smile of her own, a peace offering for being curt in response to his kindness.

"I just need an evening to myself," she said gently, crossing over to her bedside table and sitting with her back to him. "Mina's at Ali's. Bibi's probably going to watch her show. I'll read."

Faiza lifted the first book from a stack she had not touched in months, a hardcover book about the interconnectedness of subterranean mushrooms. She could not remember how it'd come into her possession and she did not know whether it was any good, but that did not matter; she had no intention of reading it. She needed to devise a strategy to get an interview for the job which was going to require all her time and effort.

"Can we talk later?" Robert asked, generously not commenting on her choice of books.

"Sure, whatever you like," Faiza replied as graciously as she could manage. "Really, I'm fine. Just tired."

Robert rose and walked around to her side, kneeling by her feet to catch her gaze. With one hand squeezing her knee, he assured her, "We'll figure this out. You're not in this alone."

Faiza offered a pursed smile and nodded, desperate to be rid of her husband and his opinions about her career. Work was her domain, even when she failed miserably.

Minutes later, she heard Pari shout goodbye as she rushed out the door, then the sound of Robert's car pulling out of the driveway. The empty hours ahead offered some consolation, and Faiza dragged herself back into the bathroom to remove the mud from her face so she could settle into an evening of strategizing a new game plan.

Back on the bed, she eyed the remote control, tempted to lose herself in a movie or a show. When her stomach groaned, she considered scavenging leftovers from the fridge. But she did not want to run into her mother, who had remained on the periphery since Faiza had arrived home an hour earlier. Then again, Faiza had been longing for wine, and the bottles were nestled in the upper kitchen cabinet; fetching a plate of food could serve as a cover for sneaking a bottle back to her room. She felt foolish for devising a plan to drink wine in her own house but she did not want Bibi to judge her for drinking alone.

There was no sign of Bibi as Faiza walked the long hall of the bungalow to the dimly lit kitchen. She wondered if Bibi was holed up in the basement with a box of sweets and episodes of *Shahrazad.* Faiza made fast work of filling a plate with a very small serving of roasted chicken and a larger serving of salad. *My career might be over but the diet never ends.*

From the kitchen window, Faiza caught sight of the persimmon sun as it edged the horizon and created long shadows of the trees in the backyard. She paused, gripped by the thought that shadows exist only in the presence of light, and the greater the intensity of the light, the sharper the shadows. Faiza wondered whether she was light or shadow. Was she a source of cosmic light and energy, a celestial body on an inexorable course, creating shadows of everyone in her presence? Or, was her existence fleeting, a shadow produced by an indifferent sun?

"*Salaam*," Bibi interrupted her daughter's musings. "Did you find the chicken in the fridge?"

Faiza froze, irked at herself for being discovered by her mother. She'd planned to grab some food and the unopened bottle of wine and retreat to her bedroom. Trapped by decades of conditioning, Faiza could not take leave of her mother, especially not with a plate of food cooked by her and definitely not to eat in a bedroom alone. Custom dictated that Bibi dote on her daughter by preparing a follow-up course, most likely a small plate of cut fruit, while Faiza ate at the dining table, repeatedly voicing her gratitude.

"*Bale*, yes, Bibi. *Merci*, thank you," Faiza conceded, hoping that the momentary pause had not alerted her mother to the turmoil brewing within her. "It smells delicious. Can I get you a plate? Have you had dinner?"

As if on cue, mother and daughter performed a practised exchange that led them to the dining table where Bibi expertly sliced an orange, an apple, and a pear while Faiza ate her dinner sans wine. They talked about Pari's teeth and Mina's volunteering prospects. Bibi shared gossip about the personal and professional pursuits of relations in Iran and Germany, people with whom Faiza infrequently spoke by phone and had not seen for two decades. As they speculated on the cause and consequence of family matters, Faiza grew irritated at having to consider others when she only wanted to focus on herself.

"What's that?" Bibi leaned in to wipe a smear of mud from below Faiza's earlobe.

Knowing better than to dodge her mother's approaching hand, which would be construed as an affront to Bibi's thoughtfulness, Faiza allowed her to rub away the smear.

"A mud mask. I must have missed a spot," Faiza explained, handing Bibi a napkin to wipe off her finger.

"Hmm, mud mask. Maybe I should try that," Bibi wondered, sniffing at the smear on the white napkin.

Faiza took the opportunity to break away from their conversation. She collected their dishes and beelined for the kitchen. As she filled the dishwasher, she thought about the bottle of wine in the overhead cupboard. Ideally, she would get to spend the rest of the evening in her bedroom, drinking wine and plotting how to win over Howard Crawley.

"Maybe you and I could go to the spa sometime?" Bibi asked, approaching the island that separated the kitchen and dining room. "Hengameh recommended Gae-low. They have a two-for-one special."

"Glow, *Maman-jaan*, mother dear," Faiza corrected Bibi's pronunciation, buying time to consider her request. "It's Glow."

"Yes, Gae-low," Bibi repeated, not hearing the difference in their pronunciations. "What do you think? You and me. We could go this weekend."

Faiza wiped her hands dry for a moment too long, prompting Bibi to add, "We don't have to go to that one. You could probably find something even better."

"Moshkel neest, it's not a problem," Faiza recovered though she remained preoccupied by her plan to return to her bedroom with the bottle of wine. "I've heard good things about Glow."

"So you'll make an appointment for us?" Bibi petitioned, her delight evident in the clasping of her hands atop her breasts. "How about this weekend? Do you think Mina would want to come? We can book a session during the week, after school. *Chi fehk meknonee?* What do you think?"

"Hmm," Faiza stalled, pretending to consider the options.

She did not want to disappoint her mother but she was in no shape to make leisure plans for the near future. Her only plans were to compose a much more persuasive narrative to convince Howard that he needed her as his deputy, that she must be interviewed for the position.

Visiting a spa that weekend, even for a series of rejuvenating treatments, seemed like too much stimulation. Her head still spun from Howard's betrayal and her failure to advance her career, and her psyche felt bruised by the pessimism and self-doubt that flooded her thoughts. She had no capacity for hours of stilted conversation with Bibi and spa attendants.

"I can look at my schedule," Faiza negotiated, playing the part of an enthusiastic daughter eager to spend time with her mother. "Probably not this weekend but soon. *Hatman*, of course."

Bibi saw through Faiza's assurances. Her face fell, as did her clasped hands. Faiza looked away from the subtle body language that marked her mother's disappointment, clues which were indiscernible to others except to Faiza and Bibi's sisters.

"*Hatman*, of course," Bibi echoed amicably as she rose to take leave, smoothing out her cotton blouse and linen pants.

Faiza looked out the window at the night sky that had blanketed the Scarborough Bluffs, darkness that deepened over the distant expanse of Lake Ontario. The bluish sheen of moonlight glimmered on their patio stones and made new shadows of the pine trees. Faiza fantasized about escaping into the grove to be alone with her thoughts, if only for an evening.

"If you need me, I'll be downstairs," Bibi interrupted her reverie.

"*Beseyar khoob*, alright," Faiza replied, so thoroughly relieved by the imminence of solitude that she leaned against the counter to remain upright.

At the doorway leading out of the dining room and toward the basement door, Bibi turned to add, "You are welcome to join me. We can watch one of your shows."

"*Merci*, thank you, Maman," Faiza said, observing social graces even as she went on to lie to Bibi. "I think I'll read a little. Go to sleep early."

"Yes, of course. It's been a long day," Bibi said with a series of slow nods.

Faiza knew better than to respond to that comment if she wanted to have any time alone. Her mother might have overheard her conversation with Robert about her missing out on the Deputy CM position, or she might be fishing for information based on intuition. Either way, Faiza refused to engage Bibi. She was moments away from whisking the wine to her bedroom for a solitary night of wallowing in her misery and working out new tactics.

When Faiza responded with a small nod and silence, Bibi did not press the matter. She bid her daughter a good night's sleep and then disappeared around the corner.

Immediately, Faiza leapt into action. The bottle was at the back of the cupboard and just out of arm's reach, forcing her to lift herself onto the island counter. Without a sound, she descended with the bottle and placed it on the counter to collect a corkscrew and an oversized coffee mug to conceal her drinking.

"I think I'll make myself a cup of hot water," Bibi's said from the doorway, looking past the bottle and directly at her daughter. "Would you like one?"

Faiza nearly dropped the mug, startled by her mother's reappearance. To her surprise, she did not feel ashamed at having been caught secretly drinking. By this time, she'd lost patience and did not want to postpone her craving. Rather, she was angry with Bibi for interrupting her, for complicating her plans.

"*Nah, merci.* No, thank you," Faiza answered brusquely as she retrieved the bottle, pocketed the corkscrew, and abandoned the mug.

"*Shab-bekhair*, goodnight," she added as she headed down the hall, away from Bibi and toward the sanctum of her bedroom.

"Faiza-*jaan*," Bibi called out, still positioned at the doorway.

Faiza slowed but she continued down the hall, "*Bale*, yes?"

In and of itself, this was a bold act of defiance. Etiquette required Faiza to face her mother when they spoke. Her own daughters knew that such an act would prompt a lecture about respect and kindness. Faiza wondered whether her mother was engineering their interaction to lead up to an argument; it was an uncustomary tactic but one Bibi had previously employed in desperation.

"Faiza-*jaan*," Bibi repeated firmly, offering her daughter the chance to recover from her social misstep.

Faiza stopped in her tracks, uncertain how to proceed, how to avoid an argument, how to complete the remaining two metres to her bedroom. The weight of the bottle in her hand reminded her of the near certainty of an imminent drink. She coached herself to mitigate the problem, to apply a bandage, however temporary, and then pursue her ends.

She assumed a less perturbed expression, and then she faced her mother, though she remained in place, refusing to forfeit any of the distance she'd covered.

Using an impassive tone which she reserved for difficult conversations at work, Faiza asked, "*Bale, Maman?* Yes, Mother?"

"Faiza-*jaan*," Bibi said, followed by a sigh. "I know this is a difficult time. I'm not blind to your pain."

Her mother paused, searching Faiza's face for understanding. Faiza waited for the remainder of the speech, intuiting that the worst was yet to come.

Bibi glanced at the wine bottle covertly and continued, "Maybe, this is for the best. This could be your opportunity to reconsider your priorities."

Faiza closed her eyes and exhaled loudly through her nostrils as her knuckles whitened from gripping the wine bottle. This was an old war marked by petty strikes but in light of Faiza's present circumstance, Bibi's attack felt like a bombardment, a targeted assault timed for maximum devastation.

"Faghad baeman goosh-baedae, hear me out," Bibi pressed on, approaching Faiza. "I know this wasn't what you wanted but … it might be like bad-tasting medicine, something you need. It might make things better, especially for the girls."

Faiza shook her head, unable to open her eyes, aware that her mother was nearing. As Bibi peddled the primacy of motherhood and home life, Faiza closed her mind and heart to the propaganda. There had never been a happy ending to this conversation. Neither of them had ever walked away feeling heard. To be able to cross this minefield of unfulfilled desires and disapproval with their selves intact, however disturbed, was a best case scenario hardly ever achieved.

"Faiza-*jaan*, look at the state of this household," Bibi pleaded as if she were referring to a landfill. "Don't you want better for your family?"

Angry tears escaped from the edges of Faiza's closed lids but her pursed lips stayed her angry words. She wanted to run for her bedroom and shut the door on her mother's insistent voice but that was unlikely to end the blitz. Bibi would spend all her rounds to deliver her message, even if it meant speaking through a door. Faiza had to endure the onslaught if she wanted a quicker end to this battle.

"I mean, here we are," Bibi continued, undeterred from her mission, "Robert is taking care of Pari. Ali is taking care of Mina. And … well, you're here alone. You should be with your family, your beautiful girls. Not … well, not home alone like this."

More tears escaped and her lips trembled under the strain. Then, she felt Bibi's warm hand on her arm, and out of respect, Faiza opened her eyes and looked at her mother's lined face. She noticed that Bibi was also crying, and it shamed her to know that she had caused distress in her 79-year-old mother. Faiza's shoulders fell with the burden of remorse added to her baggage of resentment.

Bibi reached out for the wine bottle, gently taking it into her possession. Faiza did not resist, knowing she could not forgive herself for wrestling a bottle from her elderly mother's hands. Instead, she resigned herself to an early night, hoping that she would find a package of sleeping pills in her medicine cabinet. If she was not going to dull herself with drink, then she wanted to be unconsciousness, immediately. In the morning, she'd work on new ways to butter up Howard.

"I'm going to bed, Maman," Faiza whispered in capitulation. "*Shab-bekhair*, goodnight."

"*Rahhat basheed*, be comfortable," Bibi said, equally subdued. "Shall I prepare some herbal tea?"

"As you wish," Faiza answered reflexively, knowing that she lacked the will or energy to exert her own way and refuse.

In her bathroom, Faiza scoured the shelves of the medicine cabinet, feeling a desperate sort of relief wash over her on finding a bubble pack with two remaining pills. As she downed the pills and dressed in her pyjamas, she avoided her reflection. Underneath the spiritless surface of her fatigue and dejection, there was a riptide of indignation and loathing. Faiza feared the strength of this unruly current and the possibility of being pulled under, to suffocate on resentment; or worse yet, to seize upon those nearest to her and drown them too.

By the time she re-entered her bedroom, she was crying without restraint, tears blurring her vision. Bibi appeared at her side. Together, they walked to the bed where Bibi pulled back the covers and helped Faiza in. Presently, her mother turned off the overhead light and turned on the reading lamp, bathing them in a warm golden glow.

Faiza curled up, grasping her blanket to her chest. Her tears were unrelenting but her throbbing headache was dissipating as the sleeping aid took effect. The sudden drowsiness that forced her to close her eyes caused her to question whether she had taken one too many.

"The tea is here, on the table," Bibi said softly, indicating the steaming cup on the bedside table.

Tucked into Faiza's body, her mother sat at the edge of the bed and stroked her daughter's forehead. It was a reciprocal act of love which they had perfected long ago but had not performed for years, probably since Faiza's youth. Was it possible that they had stopped demonstrating their love for each other as they did for the rest of their kin? A longing to be mothered overwhelmed Faiza and she curled tighter around Bibi, abandoning her pillow for her mother's lap. Bibi accepted her wholly, even lifting Faiza's long hair as she settled in place.

"You are such a wonderful woman, *dokhtar-am,*" Bibi cooed, combing Faiza's lustrous locks with her fingers, from their roots to their ends. "You are intelligent … beautiful, so hardworking, so determined."

But a failure, an utter failure. Since youth, Faiza had striven for greatness, setting aside her studies only to perform social obligations dictated by her parents — a chore from which her brother was exempt. She outpaced Firouz academically but she never forgave her parents for the double standard. Then, the ministry hired her on graduation and Faiza invested herself wholly in her career and gained considerable traction. Her 25-year-old husband Ali was equally consumed by his career, negating the need for any discussion between the newlyweds about work-life balance.

When Mina was born, everyone's perspectives shifted. That is, everyone's except Faiza's. Suddenly, her parents criticized her ambitions, Ali questioned her judgement, and her superiors no longer considered her for high-profile projects. She thought they had all lost their minds. After all, she was still the same woman who had set out to command the ministry from its highest echelons.

Was she paranoid, or had they been waiting for the opportunity to dictate her priorities? It did not matter what they wanted because she intended to head the ministry within ten years. She never thought that their misgivings would overshadow her determination and that her career would remain in stasis for years to come. *None of them shed a tear. None of them stood up for me. Now, it's the same all over again.*

Faiza recalled the shame of being passed over for other

promotions she had merited, as well as the betrayal she experienced when her family appeared relieved by her crushing news. The memories intensified her pain, and she wept without reservation, gulping air and shuddering as waves of anguish crashed upon her. Bibi continued to stroke her hair and rub her back, soothing her with whispered words of comfort. As the minutes passed, the intensity of Faiza's crying diminished but Bibi continued her efforts.

"I am so proud of you," she said to Faiza. "You are so intelligent and beautiful, so loyal and caring."

"No," Faiza rebuked in a weak and gravelly voice, not lifting her head to face her mother. "You're not proud of me."

After a lifetime of biting her tongue, Faiza had refuted Bibi's alleged pride. How could her mother be proud of her when she disapproved of her choices? Was she pretending in an attempt to nurture Faiza, or did she imagine that speaking the words might evoke genuine feelings of pride?

"Of course, I am," Bibi insisted, sufficiently surprised to stop stroking Faiza's hair. "You are wonderful. How can you say that?"

Faiza turned to look up, too drowsy from the sleeping aids to sit up. Cool air touched her wet cheek and she wiped her face with the bedsheets, feeling childlike in the act.

"You think I'm selfish," Faiza weakly accused Bibi, who shrank with pain.

"Faiza-*jaan*, you're not thinking clearly," Bibi excused her daughter's cutting remark. "It's late and you're tired. Let me tuck you in."

Faiza allowed her mother to slide out from under her head but she remained curled up in place, refusing to surrender the tangled bedsheets in her grip. The thin scab that protected her raw emotions had been disturbed, and she felt the stinging pain of indignities past, wounds that needed tending. Were she to express her misery, she had faith that Bibi would listen respectfully. It was Bibi's delayed reaction that concerned Faiza, the likelihood that her mother would set off to live with Firouz in Boston, or return to Iran. The last thing Faiza wanted was to drive her mother away but she needed to be heard.

Into the balled up bedsheets, which she held to her chest, Faiza cried, "You think I'm a bad mother … that I only care about my job."

She heard her mother gasp, and the sound frightened her but she did not dare open her eyes. She needed to empty herself of anguish, to admit that she had always known of Bibi's disapproval and she had refused to concede to her mother's wishes.

"I know everything. I can see it all in your face, Maman. You want me home with the girls, like Nasim," whined Faiza, mentioning her sister-in-law. "But I'm not her. I want to work. I love my job … and I've worked so hard for it. You and Baba told me to work hard for it. Remember?"

There was no response from her mother. Faiza raised her lids just enough to see Bibi's housedress within arm's reach, to confirm that her mother was still listening. *Don't stop. Finish it.*

"I know you want me to work less but that's not going to happen," Faiza declared, failing every attempt to open her eyes again. "I can't even imagine it. I mean, imagine Firouz without his job. That's crazy, that'll never happen, and you accept that. You see that it makes him happy … okay, he's not happy … not exactly. But that's a different matter."

She knew she was slurring her words and rambling in parts, as fatigued and sedated as she was, but she tried to plow through.

"He gets to be … just, he gets to do what he wants, you know?" Faiza sniffled and wiped her face against the bundle of sheets, unable to even lift her head now. "But I'm supposed to give up everything, and I don't want to. I want to be … I want to keep going, you know?"

Bibi began stroking Faiza's head. She said nothing as Faiza cried and vented her frustration.

"The girls are fine, Maman. I mean, nothing's perfect but they're okay, and … that's okay, and … Robert isn't going to leave me, you know. He's okay, too. I know he is … Maman, he is," Faiza continued, pausing to take a deeper breath. "And he's not pretending … he wants me to work. He knows it makes me happy, well … it does make me happy … just … things are so hard right now, Maman," she sniffled, sighed, and squeezed the bundle of sheets against her chest. "You've no idea how hard it is at work for me. I have so much to do and … I have to do more than everyone else … just to prove I'm good enough, and even then … it's not fair … not fair but … I'm not giving up. I'm not …."

Faiza fell asleep without finishing her thought. Bibi tucked a pillow under her head, pulled the blanket over her shoulders, and turned off the reading lamp. Before she left the moonlit room, Bibi kissed her daughter's forehead and whispered, "*Shab-bekhair, azziz-am.*"

Chapter 5

Early Monday Morning, June 25, 2018

On Monday morning, Goldie woke up to the vibrations and melody of her 7:00 a.m. alarm. She could not remember falling asleep Sunday night but it had clearly happened, even if it happened after hours of tossing and turning in bed. The tension in her jaw told her that she'd been grinding her teeth. *I could call in sick.*

She ground her face into her pillow, wishing to go back in time. She wanted to go back to early Friday. She'd been so happy after her presentation to the directors. She had felt confident and optimistic about the future. *Then, I fucked it all up with one call to Patricia. Stupid, stupid, stupid.*

All weekend, Goldie had studied the last few text messages she had exchanged with Patricia, telling no one about her freak-out at work — not her mother with whom she spent most of Saturday shopping, not Issa who met her in the food court afterward, and not her father who took her to the grocery store on Sunday morning. She'd just sneak away to re-read the messages and fret about how to talk to Patricia come Monday morning. *I sound paranoid … about a sticky note. I sound stupid.*

She analyzed Patricia's messages — her word choice and the time lapse between replies — and reassured herself that Patricia had not registered her meltdown. Then, she recalled bits of her conversation with Sameera, and she became mortified at having involved someone else. *I got carried away … she's Persian, Iranian, whatever, and she was wearing super white Air Force Ones. I shared some stuff but I was just worked up. The woman is obviously … like, sensitive. Well, fuck going to the tenth floor. Add her to the avoid list.*

Tenting her blanket with her knees raised, Goldie scanned her notifications and re-read the two messages Sameera sent on Friday evening. The first included a cutesy clip of a kitten and an encouraging meme. The second message contained a link to the union's online presence and Sameera's suggestion to read the parts about workplace harassment. *Why didn't I … I could've lied, or just kept my mouth shut. Why'd I say all that stuff to her?*

She grimaced at the photo of the sticky note. Why had she gone off on this specific note? What did it say, really? *You don't belong here.* And, it had not even been stuck to her desk. *Stuck to the bottom of a box. So, everything was good, and then I got freaked out by a sticky note. Never. Mention. Again. Please.*

It had steamed up under the blanket tent and Goldie knew it was time to get out of bed. No one was going to nudge her along. Her father was on the road, Hussain and her mother had left for work, and the only people who remained in the house were Dariush and Goldie. There was just enough time to straighten her hair. In a half-hour, Goldie would be elbowing the main floor button on the elevator, catching the southbound bus for the 45-minute ride to Pape subway. *Dariush will still be flat on his face and drooling into the good sofa. He's already broken its shape.*

While on the toilet, she recalled the conversations she'd overheard that weekend, voices coming from her parents' bedroom into the bathroom.

"Your mother found this," her father could be heard saying to Dariush.

In the silence that had followed, Goldie made guesses about the contraband in question. *Smokes? Drugs?*

Her father had pressed, "Is this what we pay for?"

Again, silence had followed. Goldie had not dared move a muscle, only straining to hear. She did not want to miss a single word, especially not one of Dariush's excuses. He spent so much energy reminding Goldie she was naïve that it felt good to hear his faults listed.

Her mother had explained, "Dariush-*jaan*, your father and I work and save for everything you see here. Books, the beds, clothes. The money you waste on this is …"

"It doesn't cost that much," Dariush had whined.

Unimpressed, her father had snapped, "That's what you took away?!"

"Forget the money," her mother had negotiated.

"'Forget the money'?" her father had exclaimed. "Fereshteh, you know he needs—" He stopped abruptly, and Goldie imagined the look or touch from her mother that would have stopped her father mid-sentence.

Clearly speaking to Dariush, her mother had continued, "I speak for both of us when I say that we only want your health and happiness. We love you."

Some mumbled words had followed and it had become too hard to hear their conversation. Goldie had given up soon after that.

The following day, she was again in the bathroom when she overheard her father bemoan, "I should've been at the appointment, too."

"There wasn't room for another person," her mother had explained.

"I am not another person. I am his father." Silence had followed, and then he had asked, "What did the doctor say?"

"Same. Antidepressants," her mother had sighed. "Dariush wouldn't have anything to do with it."

"He's afraid of the drugs from the doctor but he's fine with the stuff in baggies."

"It's not in baggies, you know that," her mother had chided him. "He has a prescription. Besides, it'll all be legal soon enough."

When their conversation had turned to household finances, Goldie had slipped out of the bathroom, content to revel in the messiness of Dariush's life. *Loser. No apartment. No girlfriend. No job. Ha!*

In the unlit kitchen now, Goldie surveyed her breakfast options.

There was cut fruit and prepared sandwiches in the fridge but she settled on two cookie packets from the pantry. Minutes later, she was out the door and rushing to catch the bus, a cookie crammed into her cheek.

* * *

Monday morning couldn't have arrived sooner for Faiza. After her spaced-out monologue on Friday night, during which she had accused Bibi of being insincere, Faiza had been shamefaced all weekend. Saturday morning, she had awoken to news that Bibi had left early for an out-of-town trip to visit old friends and that she wouldn't return for several days. When Robert had asked Faiza about the sudden trip and what might have precipitated it, she had feigned ignorance.

"Did something happen last night?" Robert had asked sleepily from the doorway of their private bathroom.

At the bathroom sink, Faiza had fastened the knot on her housecoat and busied herself by rooting through drawers cluttered with jars and tubes of expensive creams.

"No, nothing happened," she had lied, too embarrassed to admit that she had railed against her elderly mother like an unruly adolescent. She had begun tidying the containers. "She's just … you know how she is. Always with her plans."

"Um, that doesn't sound like Bibi," Robert had said with a yawn and a stretch. "Are you sure something didn't happen?"

Perturbed by his insistence, she had dug in her heels, "Rob, she's my mother. I know how she is."

"I believe you," Robert had relented, "but aren't you just a little worried about … why she left all of a sudden?"

Faiza's fingers had landed in a shimmery puddle of toner that had oozed from a tube left uncapped. Instantly, she had lost her temper and called over Robert's shoulder, "Mina! Mina! You're banned from my bathroom."

"She's at Ali's," he had explained, looking even more concerned. "Faiza, what's going on? What's happened? Is this because of the deputy position?"

"Don't start, Robert," Faiza had lashed out. She'd pulled several tissues from an ornate box and wiped up the puddle. "It's human to forget things. I can't remember everyone's schedules off the top of my head. And, it's not my business when a grown woman goes off to see her friends. And, what does the deputy job have to do with anything? Do I blame your job every time you forget something?"

Robert had raised his hands in surrender and backed up into their bedroom. "Okay, first, can you please stop yelling at me?"

"No, I can speak as loudly as I feel like, and I feel like speaking very loudly," Faiza had raised her voice even more, flustered while searching about for a hair tie having abandoned the drawer clean-up.

"Faiza, I know you're stressed. I get it," he had tried, his features softening to reflect his compassion.

"No, you don't get it," she had snapped, giving up on her search and securing her hair in a sparkly butterfly clip that belonged to Pari. "You have no idea what it's like." *You get everything you want. The world is made for you.*

"Right, I don't get it," Robert conceded, slumping on the edge of the bed. "So, help me understand. What's going on?"

Her husband's sympathy and concern had riled her even more. Faiza had thrown up her hands, "Why?! Why do I have to explain this to you? Why can't you figure it out on your own? As if I don't have enough to do … why do I have to explain things to you?"

"Honey, I just want to help," Robert had pleaded, stacking his long arms in his lap.

She had not known how to respond to his outpouring of compassion. She had taken shallow breaths though she knew it only served to heighten her temper. She had felt frustrated but Robert was not the cause of her suffering. She had slumped onto the bed, then, and released all the air in her lungs toward the ceiling. Robert had turned toward her and laid one hand on her thigh, squeezing it gently to let her know that he was listening.

"You can't help," Faiza had said, choking on the words.

Robert had continued to rub her thigh but he had not moved any closer.

"This is my thing," she had continued, her voice trembling.

Gently, he'd asked, "What is your thing?"

Faiza had swallowed the lump in her throat but she had not been able to air her grievances. Besides, it was not news to Robert. On many occasions, they had discussed the pressures and challenges she faced at work. Robert knew all about Howard Crawley, and he was the first to label the man's behaviour sexist and self-serving. Yet, despite Robert's unwavering understanding and support, Faiza never felt good complaining about the slights and injustices she routinely suffered at work. There was no catharsis in sharing yet another sob story. *What's the point?! I might as well cry over war or famine. This is part of life. If I don't like it, I should just quit.*

"Forget about it," Faiza had dismissed the topic with a wave. "It's nothing."

Robert had inched closer and lain on his side, next to her, his head propped on his arm. "You can lean on me," he had encouraged softly.

Faiza had groaned and then shook her head, eyes squeezed shut. She felt like all she did was lean on him. Bibi's missives echoed in her thoughts, reminding her about the magnitude of Robert's contributions around the house and for their family.

"No," she'd protested, pinching the bridge of her nose to ward off an imminent headache. "You already do too much."

"What does that mean?" Robert had shot back, sounding hurt.

Faiza had turned away and sighed. As much as she'd regretted her hurtful tone, she had not been in the mood to soothe him. "This is not your fight, Rob," she'd tried to curtail his agitation.

He had not answered, at least, not with words. Instead, he sat up, his back to her, his large frame hunched. Faiza had perceived this gesture as an act of retaliation, and she'd curled her body away from him. *I ask for space and he takes it personally. Why can't I have some space? Why do I have to beg for what I deserve?*

"Faiza …" Robert had said quietly, "You … I … I think … no, it feels like … it's like you don't … I feel like you don't think I'm good enough."

Facing the wall, Faiza allowed herself the luxury of rolling her eyes and clenching her teeth. *Dear god! Is he seriously doing this to me? I will not dignify your childish response with an answer. I don't fucking care how you feel.*

Robert had turned and placed a hand on her hip. When she hadn't responded, he'd continued with greater resolve, "I am trying to support you … with the girls, and with stuff around the house, and …"

Thank you, thank you, thank you, my benevolent patron! How lucky am I to have a husband who does so much?!

"… but I … I don't know what I'm doing wrong. You're so unhappy."

In a flash, Faiza had gotten on her feet, staring down at Robert. With fists clenched and eyes narrowed, she'd yelled at him, "This is not about you. Do you understand?"

Robert had pulled back, his saddened expression transforming into disgust.

"Mama, what's wrong?" Pari had appeared in the doorway, clutching no fewer than seven stuffed animals. Sternly, she'd demanded to know, "Why are you yelling at Daddy?"

Faiza had narrowed her eyes and hissed, "Pari, this is a private conversation."

Pari had taken a step back but she'd continued to glare at her mother. "It's not okay to yell."

Faiza had huffed and stomped back into the bathroom,

slamming the door behind her. With her throbbing head in her hands, seated on the edge of the tub, she'd overheard Pari's whimpers and Robert's soothing words. It had felt awful to lash out at her loved ones and she was still distressed by how easily she was triggered. She'd wondered whether her moodiness and rage were symptoms of perimenopause. *I need to see a doctor. I can't even remember the last time I had a check-up.*

After a few minutes, she'd heard movement in the kitchen, the sounds of Robert's Saturday morning breakfast rituals. Over pancakes and smoothies, Faiza had sheepishly apologized to her husband and daughter for her outburst. They had forgiven her as easily as ever, which had caused her greater remorse over her bad behaviour. She'd spent the remainder of the weekend at the dining table, eyes fixed on her laptop as she'd prepared for her Monday morning offensive. Once her mother returned, she would deal with the fallout of having said too much. Until then, she needed to focus on her career, specifically getting an interview for the Deputy CM position.

By the time Voula knocked on her office door at nine o'clock on Monday morning, Faiza had already been at work for two hours. Her neck and shoulders were cramped from typing and her stomach ached with hunger but she had accomplished a lot and that lifted her spirits.

"Good morning," Voula said in greeting, clearly assessing Faiza's mood. "You seem quite pleased with yourself. Good weekend?"

"It was alright," Faiza lied, pivoting away from her screen and taking the opportunity to stretch her muscles. "You?"

"Same," Voula said as she settled into the chair across the desk from Faiza. "I wasn't sure what to expect this morning, from you. I thought you might be … less this." Voula motioned at her friend's smiling face. "So, what's up? Who'd you kill?"

Faiza sat up taller and smoothed out her silk blouse. She nudged a gleaming portfolio toward Voula. "I made a matching slideshow but I think this is flashier."

Bemused, Voula leaned in to examine the glossy pages. She read aloud from the cover, “Toronto for the People.”

Pleased with the results of her work, Faiza beamed proudly as Voula skimmed the executive summary and the candid shots of residents patronizing local businesses, all the customers and vendors people of colour.

“See, it’s my best ideas, all in one package,” Faiza explained, clasping her hands to her chest with excitement. “The photos are stock but you get the idea. It’s about meeting business owners where they are at, tapping into the talent and capital of newcomers — racialized proprietors.”

Through the frosty pane of glass that bordered her office door, Faiza perceived the interruption before she heard the knock. It was the manager of Corporate Services.

“Come in,” she called out, sounding light and confident. He had returned to restate his unwarranted concerns about their new forms. Faiza was accustomed to being underestimated by male managers, and she was practised at handling condescension. Patiently, she assured him that the legal team had reviewed and authorized their use of the new forms — he did not have to rely on her decades of expertise alone.

When he left, shutting the door behind him, she sighed, “Don’t they get tired of being so smart?”

Voula did not reply. She had reached the last page of the portfolio, and her earlier look of concern had deepened into an unsettling frown. Slowly, she raised her gaze to meet Faiza’s. “Is this for the Inclusivity initiative? For Howard?” Voula asked, leaning back and distancing herself from the portfolio.

“No! Of course not,” Faiza waved away the question, smiling broadly.

“Ah, thank god!” Voula exclaimed following an audible sigh of relief. “I thought you’d lost your mind, handing over your ideas to that wolf. Phew!”

"No," Faiza declared, shutting the portfolio and wiping the already clean cover. "This is all for me."

"What's it for?" Voula asked as she relaxed into her chair.

"I'm making a direct appeal to Jamieson, Gunder, and Linehan," Faiza revealed, naming three bureaucrats who had the ear of the mayor. These three had encouraged the mayor to appoint Howard as the CM. *They want Howard 'cuz he makes them look good. I can do that. I do that already.* "Once they see that I'm the brains behind the last proposal and that I have a vision for the future, they'll realize that I'm a shoe-in for deputy CM. They'll demand that I be added to the interview list. Brilliant, right?"

Voula's easy smile waned and her frown lines reappeared. She chewed the corner of her lip and inhaled deeply. Faiza waited a moment, expecting praise for her scheme. When silence ensued, she could not help but feel perturbed, even slightly angry.

"What? Is something wrong with the portfolio?" she challenged, seizing the portfolio and scanning its pages.

Voula smiled at her friend, a sympathetic smile that made the silence more difficult to endure. "There's nothing wrong with the portfolio. It's quite impressive," Voula dragged out her response. "I'm just worried about the reception you'll get."

"Oh," Faiza said with a dismissive wave. "Those three, they owe me one. Remember the Shaunessy debacle? I mean, after this many years of putting out their fires, I've got a few favours coming my way."

Voula looked away, her lips thinned with hesitation. "I'm not disagreeing with you. I think you've proven your mettle."

"But?" Faiza probed, slowly losing patience with the conversation. "Come on, Voula. Just say whatever you're thinking. I'm a grown woman. I can take criticism."

Voula rushed to correct her, "It's not criticism. It's not anything you've done." Then she returned to staring at the wall, contemplating her choice of words.

Faiza wanted to stomp her feet and demand a speedier response. She had conceived of an ingenious plan and developed a convincing portfolio and presentation to substantiate her cause. It irked her deeply that Voula did not appreciate the potential of her plan. Voula was Faiza's greatest supporter, second only to Robert, and now at the eleventh hour her support was waning. *Is she vying for the job? Did she make the list?*

"I'm just worried they won't respond the way you hope," Voula grimaced and swallowed audibly. "It's an old boys' club, you know. You've seen how close they are, and Howard is one of them. I'm just not sure how they'll react to this." She waved in the general direction of the portfolio.

Now Faiza was fuming but she did not want to lash out at Voula. She took several deep breaths and tidied the papers on her desk. There was truth in Voula's statement, and it was known to every woman in management in City Hall. The men might not admit to a social network based on club memberships and enrolment at elite academies but a brief background search would offer plenty of proof of its existence. A woman had to establish a close relationship with a man in power for her to rise through the ranks, like the relationship Faiza had fostered with Howard, and even that could only take a woman so far.

"I have tried everything else. I have to try this," Faiza muttered, nudging the edges of a sheet, tidying up an already perfect pile of papers destined for the recycling bin. "If they refuse, then … they refuse. I just can't not try."

Another knock on the door led to a short interruption by the manager of Court Services. Faiza advised the manager on how to approach a conflict of interest, wishing her luck on the matter. Once they were alone again, the two sat in silence, consumed by the injustice of Faiza's dilemma. Out of habit, Faiza lined up two pens parallel to the edges of the portfolio, finding little comfort in orderliness. The intensity of feelings, first excitement and then irritation, had dissipated and now she felt depleted. Her early starts and late nights, coupled with her shooting hunger pains, threatened to drain her of all energy.

"And Howard?" Voula asked quietly, uncrossing and crossing her legs, avoiding eye contact.

Faiza sighed and shrugged, "If they want me interviewed, he'll have to concede."

"Yes, but he'll know you went over his head."

"Right," Faiza agreed, offering another shrug. *Howard Crawley is a vindictive man, gets ahead by stealing ideas, cheating others. When he finds out about this meeting, he'll be furious. He'll probably freeze me out.* "I'll deal with that when the time comes. For now, just wish me luck at my meeting," Faiza said, donning a dazzling smile to coax one — even a little one — from her friend.

Voula managed a small smile but her eyes betrayed her concern. Rising, she asked, "When's your meeting?"

"In an hour," Faiza answered, also standing. She took the opportunity to change topics, "Oh, I found those infrastructure reports. I sent you a link this morning. I think they'll have the numbers you need."

"You did?" Voula asked, surprised but pleased. "After a month, I got tired of searching. Where were they?"

"They were five levels deep in the planners' site," Faiza said, shaking her head. "I don't think they realize anyone uses those reports."

Voula squeezed Faiza's arm and expressed her gratitude, "Thank you, Faiza. You've saved me a lot of grief."

"Of course," Faiza replied graciously as she followed Voula into the hall. "Now, I need protein. Any suggestions?"

"There's always Bellinos. They've got protein shakes."

"Uh, I'm thinking more bite-size. Just to tide me over."

"There's usually protein bars in the machines," Voula suggested as they reached the intersection of two hallways. "They're not good but they're protein."

Faiza thought that Voula was preparing to say more, to warn her again about Howard. Already, her confidence in the chief officers was ebbing, and she did not want to lose any more strength or momentum.

"Protein bars, it is!" Faiza said, a little too loudly, and then rushed to the kitchen. "Wish me luck!"

"Good luck," Voula replied weakly.

* * *

Just as it approached nine o'clock, Goldie entered City Hall. The rotunda was bustling with the usual people: lanyard-carrying technocrats, locals rushing with sheaves of paperwork in hand, and transients using the public restrooms. She felt relieved to see that everything was the same. *Everything is fine. See. Nobody cared about your freak-out on Friday.*

She hung her lanyard around her neck, smoothed her hair, and started toward the elevators.

A woman called, "Excuse me! Excuse me!"

It did not occur to Goldie that the person calling out was addressing her until she heard her name. She turned to see the front desk clerk rushing the hundred metres toward her. The elevator doors chimed opened and from over her shoulder Goldie watched it fill and depart.

"Goldie Sheer, right?" the clerk asked panting, her chest rising and falling in time with her breaths. "I didn't expect you from the south entrance."

"I'm …"Goldie was about to apologize but stopped short.

"You're supposed to go to conference room 17," the clerk said, pointing in the direction of the West Tower.

Having delivered her missive, the clerk started back to her booth where a line had formed.

"For what?" Goldie called out.

The clerk turned around long enough to shrug. *It's okay.*

Probably a meeting. A staff meeting. Or a HR training thing. These people love their meetings.

Goldie crossed the rotunda to catch an elevator up to the second floor of the West Tower. She tried to look confident as she turned corners searching for the right conference room. She expected to see some familiar faces en route, people from her division who would be attending the meeting or training, but the lanyard-carrying passersby were strangers. *Shit! I must be late. They've probably started it already.*

Conference room 17 was very small, not much larger than a walk-in closet, and a conference table took up much of the space. Patricia and two unfamiliar women sat around the table, each absorbed in their screens. Goldie paused in the doorway, willing herself to speak.

"Hi," she managed, keeping to her side of the threshold, one hand tugging the ends of her long hair.

Patricia and the two women came alive, setting aside their phones and locking eyes with Goldie.

"Good morning, Goldie. Thank you for joining us," Patricia said cheerfully as she directed Goldie to a seat. "You can close the door behind you."

No one else was attending this meeting, and the implications were bearing down on Goldie. She sucked in her lower lip and tried to stop her legs from shaking. Patricia smiled at her reassuringly and then shifted focus to the woman in the blazer.

"Hi Goldie," she said, offering a wide smile that didn't reach her eyes. "I'm Donna. I work in HR. Nice to meet you."

"Hi. Nice to meet you," Goldie replied, her voice quavering and her palms sweating.

The other woman looked up from her screen momentarily to introduce herself, "Hi, I'm Stacey. I represent CUPE Local 341…." She paused to glance at her screen, and then added, "I'm your union rep."

"Hi," Goldie whispered, shrinking in her seat.

"No need to look so concerned. No one is in trouble," Patricia assured her. "Actually, you're here because of the great work you've done."

Stacey remained distracted but Donna nodded in agreement. Still, Goldie detected misfortune ahead.

"The work you were hired to complete is … well, complete," Patricia explained. "You performed very well, very efficiently. You should be proud of yourself."

"Thank you," Goldie replied, recognizing these statements as falsehoods. Presently, two boxes of files sat in her cubicle, and she knew many more were in storage. Goldie was not about to contradict her manager, not that she could speak for any length of time for fear of tearing up.

"This happens sometimes," Donna from HR took the baton from Patricia. "We guestimate the length of contracts and sometimes we overshoot." Donna shrugged apologetically, and the other two women offered commiserating nods.

"No worries," Donna assured her. "You will be compensated for the weeks remaining in your contract. That's still another …." Donna paused to survey the papers before her while Patricia and Stacey watched her intently, their faces turned away from Goldie.

Two weeks. I still have two weeks.

"Oh, here," Donna said, thumbing a sheet. "Two weeks left."

Nausea threatened to overtake Goldie, spurred by the phony smiles of Donna and Patricia. She settled her gaze on Donna's papers and willed herself to speak, however timidly.

"I'm … I … I applied for jobs …." Goldie stammered, stopping to bite her lower lip to keep from crying.

"It's okay. Take your time," Patricia soothed, reaching out only to pat the table reassuringly.

Keeping her eyes on Donna's papers, Goldie nodded, swallowing hard to dislodge the lump in her throat, anything to avoid crying in front of these people.

"Do I … what happens to the … to my applications?" Goldie asked, rhythmically pressing a lock of hair against her sweater.

Stacey did not look up from her screen and Patricia turned to Donna with an insincere expression of intrigue.

"Oh, that doesn't change. And, you'll still have access to the job portal. For the two weeks," Donna said, leafing through papers only to settle with her hands clasped on the table.

Despite feeling stuck in place, Goldie's mind revved, producing a mess of questions. Were they letting her go because she freaked out about the sticky note? Was there any way she could redeem herself? What would it take to change their minds, to let her stay?

Of all her concerns, the one she voiced was the least sensitive, "What about the wiki?"

Donna blinked, puzzled by the question, and then turned to Patricia.

"Oh, you don't need to worry about that," assured Patricia while signalling to Donna, with a slight shake of her head, that the issue was irrelevant.

"Alright, seems like everything is settled," Donna concluded, leafing through her papers again. "I just need your initials at the top and your signature at the bottom line."

She pushed the papers toward Goldie, which roused Stacey's attention. Goldie looked to the union rep in the hopes of prompting an explanation but Stacey immediately returned to scrolling on her phone. The papers sat within reach but she did not dare touch them. She stared at the words which danced about the page, aggravating her nausea.

Patricia broke the spell, "You can use my pen."

"Thank you," Goldie mumbled, taking the pen.

With the pen hovering above the document, Goldie surveyed the others. She needed to know how this moment had been made possible. What had she done? Could she return to their good graces? If she apologized for freaking out, would they keep her on?

Patricia and Donna looked at her expectantly, and Goldie feared upsetting them with her questions. Would they think badly of her if she asked for more information? Would Patricia refuse to serve as her reference for internal postings? Would Donna put a note in her employee records, warning HR to never hire her again?

Instead of speaking up, Goldie signed the document, agreeing to the terms described by Donna. Instantly, Stacey rose and excused herself.

"Nice meeting you," she mumbled as she crossed the threshold.

Donna tidied her papers as Patricia retrieved her pen and collected her belongings. Both women seemed satisfied by the proceedings.

"Thanks, Donna," Patricia said, smoothing out her skirt.

"My pleasure," Donna replied, inching her way along the perimeter of the cramped room. As an afterthought, she turned and said, "Good luck, Goldie."

Alone, Goldie thought she could muster enough courage to ask her question but Patricia was halfway to the door.

"I can walk you out. I'm heading that way," Patricia offered, stepping into the hallway.

"Oh, okay," Goldie said, getting to her feet, relieved to escape the confined room.

"Your belongings are at the front desk," Patricia said, walking quickly toward the elevators.

"Okay," Goldie replied, hurrying to catch up to her manager who'd already pressed the button.

"Patricia, I'm really sorry about freaking out on Friday," Goldie entreated, her voice shaky. "I shouldn't have made a big deal about that. I really don't care about it. I swear it won't happen again."

Seemingly astonished, Patricia said, "Oh, that. All's forgotten."

The doors chimed open, and Patricia walked in to the empty elevator with Goldie trailing behind.

"Is that why you … why I'm …." Goldie tried to finish her question but the words eluded her.

"You did a great job. You should be proud of that," Patricia insisted, looking briefly at Goldie before returning her attention to her phone.

They arrived at the rotunda, and Patricia walked quickly to the front desk. Goldie tried to keep up but her legs felt leaden. She watched as Patricia said something to the desk clerk and pointed in Goldie's direction. The clerk looked her way and nodded.

As Goldie approached the front desk, Patricia jutted out her hand and said, "It's been a pleasure working with you. Good luck."

Goldie took Patricia's hand, immediately embarrassed by her clammy palms. Before she could respond, Patricia released her grip and rushed off to the elevators for the East Tower.

* * *

When Faiza entered the kitchen, it was hectic with foot traffic and conversation. At the refrigerator, a trio collaborated to cram their lunch bags into the densely packed shelves. By the microwave, a few people holding mugs and bowls chatted in a cluster as they waited for a turn. Along the counter, an animated crew of millennials sipped hot drinks as they shared weekend photos.

As Faiza crossed the floor to the vending machine, the hubbub lessened. In that room, and in nearly all rooms, Faiza was the most senior member present. There were other directors of her ranking but she was the closest aid to the city manager, and she knew that her position granted her prestige and power. It was not surprising that her juniors restrained themselves in her presence. When she had hung from the bottom rungs of the corporate ladder, she'd performed the same act, balancing spiritedness with subservience. *This is how it works. Everyone has to prove themselves.*

While she played the role of a benevolent director to put them at ease, she enjoyed the reverence attributed to her rank. Unlike them, she had already spent decades writing and reviewing reports, negotiating lucrative contracts, and collaborating with disgruntled stakeholders. She'd put in her time and she was no longer hanging from the bottom rungs. She was not one of them, and she enjoyed the distinction.

"Good morning, Faiza!" chirped a young and enterprising manager who had expressed an interest in transferring to Faiza's team.

"Good morning, Lindsey," Faiza replied, smiling at the manager and her peers, and returning her attention to the vending machine.

"Did you have a nice weekend?" Lindsey asked, sidling up to Faiza, a mug of steaming coffee in hand.

"Yes, thank you. And you?" Faiza said politely.

"Oh, yes," Lindsey's eyes sparkled at the opening, and she let loose. "I completed a predictive modelling course, that's part of my masters in business analytics, and it's such an interesting topic. I mean with the way big data runs the show, it's really an essential course for anyone in our field."

Sensing that Lindsey had prepared this speech, and recalling her own youthful attempts to present her accomplishments to her superiors, Faiza offered her best smile as a prize, "Certainly, and congratulations! You're an asset to the team."

Lindsey took the praise to heart, standing taller and straightening her suit jacket. Meanwhile, Faiza turned her attention back to the vending machine. If she did not eat something soon, her grumbling stomach might become audible to others.

Lindsey went on to describe the course, appreciative of Faiza's attention, even if it was divided, "There is a second predictive modelling course, that's next semester, but I think I can put the basic concepts to use already. I mean, there's always room for improvement, and if I was—"

"Good morning," Sameera Jahani interrupted, standing

next to Lindsey and taking inventory of the vending machine offerings.

In her oversized cream blouse, matching palazzos, and white high tops, Sameera's vogue outfit sharply contrasted Lindsey's navy blue skirt suit and delicate gold jewellery. Compared to the conventional look of everyone else in the room, Sameera's fashion sense and natural locks visibly set her apart. Inwardly, Faiza rolled her eyes at what she perceived to be an act of subversion. *And here comes trouble …*

Caught off guard, Lindsey paused. Her eyes darted from Sameera to Faiza, from a pariah to a pillar of the corporation. Ignoring Sameera altogether, she resettled her focus on Faiza but having lost her momentum, she stammered to restart, "I mean, uh … about improvements … um, there's room, always. There's always room for improvement—"

"That's for sure," Sameera huffed, leaning in to read the labels on a package of dried apple chips. "I mean, how long has that been in there?"

Bewildered by Sameera's response, Lindsey looked to Faiza for direction. Faiza looked past Lindsey and closely regarded Sameera, momentarily forgetting her hunger but remembering their last conversation, the previous Wednesday. She had advised Sameera to solicit champions and garner support for her ideas, to successfully execute one play at a time in order to win the long game — advice that Sameera had seemed to doubt. *She'll learn these lessons the hard way.*

Feeling confident, Faiza replied coolly, "From what I understand, the offerings are subject to change, and there are proper channels for seeking change."

Sameera nodded but she kept her eyes on the vending machine. "Yes, I have heard that. Though, I was thinking it might be beneficial to move away from vending machines altogether."

Lindsey was side-eying Sameera in an attempt to align herself with the director. Faiza sympathized with Lindsey's desire to distance herself professionally from the corporate outcast. The ardent manager was trying to protect her reputation, her career at City Hall. *Sameera Jahani could learn a thing or two from Lindsey. It might make her life easier.*

Still, forming cliques and shunning co-workers were unprincipled tactics, and Faiza discouraged such behaviour, especially among her female colleagues. She was painfully aware of the innumerable hurdles in a woman's career path, not to mention the traumatizing and debilitating nature of these obstacles. To reach the finish line, they had to support each other. *Like me and Voula. Like Howard and the old boys' club.*

Besides, Faiza considered Sameera's pursuit of justice to be an integral component of civil service. The well-being and productivity of the corporation necessitated a mélange of mindsets, including the sharp contrasts of Lindsey's acumen and Sameera's grit. *I'm not at war with her, and, with the approach she's taking, there'll be plenty of battles ahead.*

"The vending machines are presently the only option," Faiza countered, feeling her confidence soar, "and improving their offerings is the most reliable route to change."

Crossing her arms and looking right at Faiza, Sameera replied wistfully, "Interesting. I'm not sure how there can be real change with vending machines as the status quo."

Lindsey stood with mouth agape, unable to form a segue back to her speech. As Faiza paid for and retrieved a protein bar, Lindsey blinked furiously at Sameera, trying to will her out of existence. Sameera shrugged and offered an innocent smile.

"Personally, I like vending machines. Just so convenient," Faiza sallied, smiling broadly at both managers on her way out.

* * *

On her way back to her cubicle, Sameera crammed piece after

piece of dried fruit into her mouth, aggressively chewing on the leathery clump as she replayed her conversation with Faiza. *What a load of shit! She's a hypocrite, that's what she is.*

Sameera was now certain that Howard Crawley's inclusivity initiatives were Faiza's inventions. She had eavesdropped on enough office talk to learn about the CM's style, his poaching of ideas from directors in exchange for lucrative promotions. It seemed to be an open secret that Faiza Hosseini had designed and developed the run of progressive programs which were attributed to Howard Crawley. *Of course, she doesn't want to stir things up. It'd complicate her plans. Boss lady needs a bigger office, or fancy title, or whatever!*

A tickle in the base of her throat threatened to turn into a coughing fit, stopping her partway along a corridor, allowing others to pass by. She forced herself to swallow the sticky pool that had formed around the masticated ball of apples and pears, a mass that threatened to shoot out of her mouth at any moment. Slipping into an empty, unlit meeting room, she spit the pulpy clump into its crinkly package and dumped it all into the waste basket. As she wiped away the droplets on her lips with her thumb, a ping alerted her to a text message.

luv u. miss u. good luck at wrk, Shannon had written.

In the darkened room, Sameera slumped into the nearest chair. She typed a number of replies but deleted each one, unable to settle on the right words. Leaning back, she stared at the shadowy ceiling tiles of the windowless room, trying to find answers in the pockmarks. *Write something, Sameera! The longer you wait, the worse it gets.* All weekend, she had skirted a heart-to-heart talk with Shannon. On Friday night, she had feigned sleep when Shannon returned home from dinner with Maisy. On Saturday morning, while Shannon slept in, Sameera had packed an overnight bag and left to visit Masoumeh, her eldest sister. They had texted often, sticking to innocuous topics. Now, on Monday morning, her thumbs hovered over the keyboard, worried about triggering an argument.

me 2. work ok. u? She jabbed at her phone, resenting Shannon and hating herself for it. *Things aren't that bad. This is par for the course. Relationships take time, effort. I'm not giving up.*

Shannon then texted *brb*, and *bbl* in quick succession, effectively postponing their chat, and Sameera sighed with immense relief. The clenched muscles of her shoulders, knotted deeply from two nights spent on an inflatable bed, released their grip and allowed Sameera to sink deeper into the time-tested office chair. The windowless room offered considerable privacy from hallway traffic. The farthest corner of the narrow room was all in shadow, and Sameera rolled herself far enough into that corner to trigger the night setting on her screen. She stretched out on the sturdy office chair and browsed her favourite blogs.

Despite texting each other frequently, Sameera felt untethered each time she was away from Shannon. Late Saturday night, they'd had a heated phone conversation — Shannon at home and Sameera in the jam-packed den of her sister's condo. Moments into that conversation, Sameera had realized that the call was doomed. She had not wanted to talk, and Shannon had been sullen despite having insisted that they talk on the phone.

"I'm telling you I love you" Shannon had protested. "Why is that not good enough?"

Sombrely, Sameera had replied, "I know you love me—"

"I do!" Shannon had interrupted. "That's ju—"

"Please, let me—"

"Go ahead. Finish," Shannon had finally conceded, impatient and eager to make a point.

After a pause, Sameera had continued unhurriedly. "Shan, I know you love me. It's more like … I don't think you … you really … you really know me."

"I know you," Shannon had sounded shaken. "Seriously? Me? I

know you better than anyone else."

"I … you know, I … I don't … know about that," Sameera had finally confessed, certain that she had delivered a painful truth, a message that might bring harm to its messenger. "I think you like some parts of me … the parts that make sense to you, the things we have in common."

Sounding betrayed and hurt, definitely crying, Shannon had demanded, "Do you like everything about me? Are we supposed to like everything about each other?"

Summoning her remaining patience and drive, Sameera had explained, "I don't expect you to like everything about me. It's … I don't want to ignore our differences … and I don't want to pretend we're the same."

"If this is about Maisy, I've taken care of that," Shannon had offered, confident to a fault.

Sameera had grimaced. *Surprise, surprise. Her conversation with Maisy went well?! Of course, it did. It always goes well. They'll redraw every border to make it work out.*

While the memories of her exchanges with Maisy and Shannon still angered Sameera, Shannon seemed unconcerned by the incident, claiming that she'd resolved the matter. Sameera guessed that Shannon's friendship with Maisy would be unfazed by this ugliness. Knowing Maisy, Sameera expected her to claim that it was all harmless talk.

On Sunday morning, Masoumeh had weighed in on the relationship. Patting her wet brow with a hand towel as she stepped off the elliptical — one of several in her condo's fifth-floor gym — Masoumeh had proclaimed, "You've gotta chose your battles. You can't be fighting at work and at home."

Nearby, Sameera had been sitting on a yoga mat, having started a series of strenuous poses but ultimately resigning herself to the comfort of the child pose. She'd come to Masoumeh for comfort because her sister was the most open-minded member of her family but now she felt overwhelmed by the tone of their conversation.

"There're enough white people fighting for trans rights. They got their shit locked down," huffed Masoumeh as she continued with sets of lunges, the muscles of her broad thighs flexing impressively. "Your boss, that white asshole's racist. Plain and simple. That's where you gotta put your energy."

Sameera had grunted, unwilling to lift her forehead from the mat to acknowledge Masoumeh's advice to shelve her queerness in favour of her battle against racism — as if such an act were possible, or such a simplistic approach were pioneering. In the university's women's club, members were encouraged to identify as women first, irrespective of race. In her queer youth group, counsellors sidestepped discussions about race and gender that might reveal tensions. At that moment, Masoumeh was asking her to prioritize racial identity, to pretend that gender and sexual orientation did not shape her experience. *Why do I always have to choose?*

"Listen, I know you love Shannon. She loves you, too," Masoumeh had said plainly, ducking her head under the bar of a weightlifting machine and positioning herself on its narrow seat. "But it's not about love. It's about experience. She has no idea what it's like to be coloured—"

"A person of colour," Sameera had corrected reflexively, grateful that no one else was nearby.

"Right," Masoumeh had continued, barely registering the speed bump in the conversation as she pulled the weighted bar down to her chest. "She's from small-town white Canada. They think anti-racism's about tolerance. They're not interested in equity. They expect us to be grateful for equality."

"Yeah but we're talking about my girlfriend," Sameera had interjected, tired of hearing her own ideologies recited to her. Tears welled in her eyes as she spoke, "This is personal. I love her."

On hearing the tremor in her sister's voice, Masoumeh had

joined Sameera on the mat. Wiping away the tears with her arm, Sameera had explained, "I don't know what to do. She doesn't want to hurt me. I know that. But when she acts like I'm the problem, like I cause the problems, it hurts so bad."

Masoumeh had offered a sympathetic sigh and brushed away an errant hair from her sister's cheek. Sameera had stared off, out the expansive windows that sparkled with early morning light. The view could not distract her from her inner turmoil. *There's a way through all this. This is not an impossible situation.*

Presently, the overhead lights turned on in the empty meeting room, startling Sameera and making her shoot upright in her seat. A few familiar faces filed into the room, each person carrying a laptop and a notebook. Efficiently, Sameera murmured her apologies and excused herself.

In need of a distraction, she headed to Agatha to laugh about her comedic run-in with Lindsey Martin at the vending machines. In her retelling, she planned to minimize the tension between her and Faiza Hosseini — it seemed unwise and unprofessional for a manager to speak disparagingly of a director, in spite of Agatha's trustworthiness. Instead, she would dwell on Lindsey's sour disposition and her stark neediness. It wouldn't be the first time Agatha and Sameera had privately made sport of Lindsey.

"Hey," Sameera whispered, barely containing her grin as she tucked herself into Agatha's cubicle.

The office hummed with the ambient noise of keyboards clicking, printers chugging, and phones ringing. In every direction, cubicles were occupied and a steady flow of staff streamed by. It appeared like everyone was consumed by their work but Sameera did not want to take a chance at being overheard. She crouched, and Agatha's eyes widened in anticipation of gossip. *Maybe she's Mexican. She's definitely Latina.* Sameera realized she was profiling Agatha again. She reminded herself, *If you want to know about a person, get to know the person.*

"What?" Agatha whispered back, biting her lower lip and scooting closer with her chair.

"You're gonna love this. I just had a seriously hilarious conversation with—" Sameera was interrupted by a ping. "One sec," she said, raising a finger and checking her phone.

"Oh shit, oh shit," Sameera muttered as her smile faded.

* * *

"Thank you, Sheila," Faiza said, rising from her office chair to receive the stack of portfolios the receptionist carried. "I appreciate the last-minute print job, really. Lunch is my treat."

"You're welcome," Sheila accepted the thanks and rewards of a rush job done well. "Alright, gotta get back now." She waved over her shoulder, looking like she needed to be back at her desk immediately.

The portfolios were slim and sleek, ready to go, and so was Faiza. She tucked them into her oversized designer handbag and pulled out her compact, checking her smile after eating that protein bar. A sharp, attractive woman was reflected back, and Faiza grinned and tingled with anticipation. She was on the hunt, and it felt thrilling. *Perfect.*

As she gathered her laptop and bag, she wondered whether this turn of events — her omission from the interview list — had not been for the better. Howard did not want her as a deputy — certainly not anymore, if ever. The more staffers and councillors took notice of Faiza, the more Howard resented her. *He never meant to recommend me. He's gotten enough from me to coast on … maybe enough to take him into retirement.* Her absence from the list of interviewees forced her hand to network directly with the chief officers in charge. There was going to be no more routing her plans through Howard, the gatekeeper to the higher-ups.

With twenty minutes left, Faiza stopped by Voula's office, feeling the need to reconnect with her friend. They had parted on a strange note, with Voula concerned about Faiza's meeting, and Faiza imagined she might reassure her friend with a show of confidence. It seemed that Voula had been thinking about her, too.

"Why these three?" Voula started as she closed her office door behind Faiza. "I mean, why Jamieson and Gunder, and Linehan? Why not a more receptive set?"

Placing her laptop and weighty handbag on Voula's desk, Faiza struck a fierce pose — hands on hips, chin up, and eyes narrowed. Holding a brave expression, she asked with a hint of irony, "How do I look?"

"You look brilliant, Faiza but that's not the point," Voula said as she slumped into the nearest chair and chewed on her lower lip.

"Thank you," Faiza replied, trying her best to maintain her smile.

Voula offered a small nod, in a sombre and sisterly way. "You know it doesn't matter what they say. You're brilliant and it's obvious to everyone else."

"Thank you. Now, I need to convince Howard's buddies."

"Jamieson, Gunder, and Linehan."

"Yes. I know it's direct, or a little too direct for them … I'm not asking for the job outright. I'm bringing attention to … a timely matter, an error, an omission from the list of candidates. This presentation is only a gentle reminder of what I bring to the table."

Voula nodded her understanding but she seemed no more reassured than earlier. Faiza decided to cut her losses. *She'll come around once I land the interview.* Gently, she poked Voula's knee to get her smiling. "I have to go now. We're meeting in the West Tower, Jamieson's office mansion. I'll message later."

* * *

Nearing ten o'clock, Goldie walked out of City Hall and into Nathan Phillips Square, the 12-acre concrete plaza situated at the base of the two towers. In her arms, she carried a file box with her belongings. It was not heavy but carrying the box made it difficult to dodge the foot traffic coming from every direction. Some people rushed past her into the municipal building, and others cut her off as they crossed the plaza, on their way elsewhere. Some moved purposefully, and others loitered. Goldie blinked at the bright sunlight, feeling exposed, under examination. It occurred to her that her former co-workers might be watching her from the ninth floor. *Probably laughing, throwing a party.*

Goldie chose the path of least resistance, the one through the pigeons and seagulls fighting for crumbs, raised her chin and walked across the plaza toward Queen Street West. If anyone was watching from the ninth floor, she hoped they noticed her strut. *Fuck you bitches! Fuck you all!*

As she continued across the plaza, she convinced herself that she was being watched. It was inconceivable to her that such a tragic moment in her life would go unobserved, without witnesses. *No way. They're definitely watching me. They've been waiting for this. They wouldn't miss it.*

Determined to make a bold exit, she stood taller and walked vigorously. Her exaggerated movements caused something in the cardboard box, something clunky, to shift about. She decided to rid herself of the burden, feeling that the box undermined her performance. Presently, an unoccupied bench called to Goldie. It was close to the food trucks that edged the plaza and was out of view of the towers. There, she examined the contents — a ceramic mug with the City Hall emblem which she had received as a new hire and her infinity scarf. *Seems about right.* She wondered who had cleared her desk. *Was it Holly? Not Beth, I'm sure of that.*

She stashed the scarf in her handbag, replaced the box's lid, and left it next to an adjacent garbage can. Turning back toward Queen Street, she thought about going home and then contemplated the long subway ride and the even longer bus ride, but she was not prepared to go, not with Dariush permanently installed on the couch and ready to pepper her with questions about her early return. *He won't be able to help himself. He loves it when I get fucked over.*

Instead, Goldie sat in the sun and soothed herself with Pokémon. She did not know what else to do with herself. She was supposed to be at work. She imagined telling her mother the story she was told — *we ran out of work, so they sent me home. I still get paid for the two weeks* — but it brought tears to her eyes, threatening to disturb her mascara art. She blinked away the tears and returned to catching Pokémon.

Minutes passed while she battled online, seemingly lost in the game. Then, a surge of emotion rose through her and she heard herself exclaim aloud, "What about the wiki?!"

Immediately, she curled in on herself to avoid the stares of passersby, though most were desensitized to people yelling into the air. *Dear fucking god, Goldie! Keep it together.* She was mortified, that much she knew, but she realized that she was also very angry. With every passing minute, more questions rose to the surface, questions she could not answer with the flimsy explanation she had received from Patricia. *I wasn't perfect but I wasn't that bad at updating their fucking records. Besides, there was loads of work to do on the wiki. I could've done so much in two weeks.*

This time, she could not keep her tears at bay. She sheltered herself by leaning forward and allowing a curtain of hair to conceal her face. Her movements disturbed a few nearby birds and the flock flew away in a rush. She did not look up. She let the tears stream down her cheeks and drip off her chin, ruining the face she'd put on that morning. More angry thoughts pestered her. *Was it about the note?* She'd apologized to Patricia for overreacting. *Was it my updates? Had Beth found some massive mistake?*

The more she speculated, the angrier she became and the more she needed to talk it out. She did what came naturally: she texted Issa, *hi.*

Issa replied, *hi. wrk?*

kinda, Goldie answered with a cryptic response, fishing for concern, or at the very least, curiosity.

Issa returned three emojis — a memo, a fireball, and an extinguisher — to express her own frustrations at work and signed off with *ttyl.*

Goldie replied with a collection of sympathetic emojis, and for a short while worded and reworded another text, an attempt to describe her circumstances, but could not find the right words. So she abandoned the effort. It felt like her omission was in fact a lie, her attempt to hide the truth from her friend. Angry at herself for creating a chasm between herself and Issa, she swiped furiously in search of a sympathetic ear. *Not Mama. Not Baba. Not Hussain. Not Fatima. Not Anne.* Then, she spotted her conversation history with Sameera. *She was okay*, Goldie tried to convince herself.

Despite Sameera's supportiveness, Goldie didn't think much of her. Sameera was extra, putting in too much effort at everything. Goldie wanted to tell her to relax, to stop trying so hard to impress. Still, of all the people in her life, Sameera was the one person who knew the awful truth about work and, most importantly, she sympathized. *At least she'll be on my side.*

* * *

Crouched in Agatha's cubicle and eager to gossip about Lindsey Martin, Sameera paused to check a new text message. *It probably makes me a bad girlfriend just for thinking it but please don't let it be Shannon.*

The message was from Goldie, causing Sameera to feel both relieved and surprised. Toward the end of their conversation on Friday, after Goldie had dried her tears and reapplied her makeup, the young woman had seemed reticent, cool even to Sameera's warmth and concern. Sameera suspected that she'd come on too strong, spoken too long about employment standards and expressed too much zeal about worker's rights. Sometimes, she lost the reins on her enthusiasm, forgetting that other people weren't interested in fighting battles or addressing injustices. *They just want their problem solved. They want to go back to normal, back to life uninterrupted. They don't wanna hear about laws or rights or systemic factors.*

Even though Sameera had gone as far as to reference the Employment Standards Act, she had also provided the sympathy and reassurances that Goldie sought. *Good enough. She'll message if she needs more*, Sameera had thought, certain that Goldie would never message her again.

Except, the young woman had just messaged, *got laid off. don't know what to do. in nathan phillips.*

"What? What?" Agatha leaned in, her curiosity piqued.

Distressed and overcome with a sense of urgency, Sameera made to leave the cubicle.

"What's going on?" Agatha asked with concern, no longer amused by the mystery.

"Uh," Sameera paused mid-step to offer an explanation, but all she managed was, "Come on."

Agatha was locking her laptop and pocketing her phone even before she inquired, "Where to?"

"I'll tell you on the way down," she whispered, and they navigated the maze of cubicles leading to the elevators.

Sameera jabbed the button to go down. Following a few furtive glances to ensure they were alone, she asked gravely, "Remember the new hire? The one I met crying in the bathroom? On Friday."

"Yeah, the one in … from the ninth floor, right?" Agatha answered as they walked into an empty elevator. "What floor?" Her hand lingered over the buttons.

Reaching across, Sameera hit the button for the Main Floor. "She just texted me. They laid her off."

"Aw, that's too bad," Agatha replied, genuinely sympathetic but confused all the same. "But, where are we going?"

"Downstairs. She's in the plaza," Sameera said, her brows furrowed, repeatedly checking her phone.

The elevator doors opened to the rotunda, and the heavy aroma of coffee from the City Café greeted them. It was a typical Monday morning at Toronto City Hall. The sunlit atrium was bustling with foot traffic. Members of the public crossed between the revolving front doors and the municipal offices at the far end. Several people dressed in worn-out clothes and carrying overstuffed backpacks lingered. Civil servants with laptops and lanyards streamed from one set of elevators to the other. Sameera thought she saw Faiza Hosseini walking to the West Tower elevators.

"But why are we rushing?" Agatha asked in pursuit of Sameera who weaved between passersby as she zipped toward the revolving doors.

Outside, the morning sun cast long shadows on Nathan Phillips Square. Sameera stopped at the edge of the plaza and scanned the dozens of benches for Goldie Sheer. When Agatha caught up, Sameera pointed at a young woman hunched over her phone on a distant bench.

"There. Come on," she urged, walking hurriedly to Goldie.

As Sameera approached the near stranger, who looked defeated and defenceless, she immediately regretted bringing Agatha along, worried that she might be infringing on Goldie's privacy.

Speaking softly, for fear of scaring away Goldie, Sameera breathed, "Hi."

"Hi," Goldie repeated, offering a thin smile on a round face smeared with mascara.

"This is Agatha," Sameera said, by way of breaking the ice. "We work together."

Agatha greeted Goldie in a voice so gentle that Sameera turned to her. Without hesitation, Agatha sat next to Goldie and wrapped an arm around the shoulders of the young woman. Goldie leaned into the embrace, and soon she was sobbing.

Chapter 6

Late Monday Morning, June 25, 2018

On the elevator, Faiza ran into Claire Brigman, a corporate lawyer with the city. They had previously collaborated on real estate and vendor contracts, spending nights and weekends at the office, sorting out details of legal agreements linked to billions in revenue. And they had much more in common. Claire's husband, Thomas, like Faiza's, was ten years older than her, and the couple had two daughters, though Claire's girls were soon to graduate high school.

Over the years, they had met as families, visited each other's homes. Faiza and Robert had first met Claire and Thomas at a fete at the private school that their daughters all attended. Years later, when Claire became the city lawyer, she referred Faiza for a manager's position that happened to open up; it became her first job at City Hall. Since then, there had been numerous evenings spent barbecuing at Claire and Thomas's, next to their infinity pool, which was always occupied by the girls, their bodies glowing from underwater lights. Faiza and Robert had reciprocated with resplendent dinners, fine wines and ports, and cosmopolitan conversation into the night. Their talks felt good, safe, life-affirming, even if they were also shallow.

"Very nice suit," Faiza admired Claire's tailored attire as she set her phone's notification status to Priority Only, restricting alerts to incoming calls from Robert, Mina, Voula, and Howard. She did not want the usual stream of online chatter to interrupt her meeting with the higher-ups. "How was your weekend? You went to Princeton, New Jersey?"

"We went to New York, my alma mater, Columbia. You might be thinking about Thomas. He attended Princeton," Claire answered without a hint of self-consciousness. They walked out of the elevator and began striding across the rotunda to the West Tower elevators. "We toured campus and the residences, caught a show. Molly seemed to like Columbia but Jenna not so much." She sighed and shook her head. "Even New York cannot please my 17-year-old."

"Hmm, you know how they can be," Fauzia remarked while they waited for the elevator up. "One minute they hate a thing, next they love it."

"I wish she'd be more grateful for the opportunity," Claire sighed. "They're legacy, and with her grades ...." Again, she shook her head at the thought of her youngest not appreciating the gravity of the matter.

In a show of sympathy, Faiza nodded but she felt more envy than understanding. Neither Mina nor Pari had ready access to an Ivy League education. Faiza and her ex-husband had graduated university in Iran, and Robert was an alumnus of the University of Toronto — all renowned schools but none Ivy League. To give her daughters a leg up, Faiza had enrolled them in Toronto's prominent all-girls private school, alongside the daughters of other affluent bureaucrats, but she knew that they could not compete with legacy students, even the ones with lacklustre grades, like Jenna. Enrolment at the private school was meant to enhance their social network. Possibly better than anyone else, Faiza grasped the significance of joining social networks very early on — a lesson learned through experience. Without acceptance into affluent society, Mina's access to power, status, and influence would be limited. *She hasn't figured out how to make connections. She needs to learn this.*

"I'm sure she'll come around," Faiza assured her with a confident smile. When they boarded the West Tower elevator, she pressed the button for the nineteenth floor, and with her finger hovering over the dials, she asked, "Which floor?"

"Same," Claire answered, momentarily bemused. "Jamieson's."

Faiza's brows furrowed — one of the top brass had invited Claire Brigman without informing or consulting her. It was her meeting, after all. Her certitude of a positive outcome to the meeting soured, transforming into panic and outrage. *What the fuck?! What're they playing at?*

"Are you attending as counsel?" Faiza asked, her tone direct if not a little brusque.

Claire blinked and offered a conciliatory smile, "Matthew will explain everything. There's nothing to worry about, Faiza."

Faiza doubted that very much but she nodded and turned away. She was not interested in pressing Claire for details. Begging for information was beneath her, unlike her. The remainder of the elevator ride was spent in silence, and when the doors opened to the nineteenth floor, Faiza charged ahead, her heels announcing her imminent arrival at Matthew Jamieson's office.

* * *

Goldie sniffled and wiped her runny nose, folding and refolding the overused napkin. "This … was … supposed to be my in … you know," she stammered, and then paused to wipe again. "I've … been … looking for … an office job … for so long. It's been so hard."

She took ragged breaths, smoothed her hair, and sniffled some more. On any other day, she'd rather die than cry in public, but she was past the point of caring about the smokers, the meandering tourists, and the people living on the street. *As long as no one gets this on video.* The thought caused her to snap out of her slump and quickly scan the area for gawkers.

"It's really hard, getting your first job. I remember," Agatha commiserated, offering Goldie a fresh restaurant napkin from her jacket pocket.

Goldie sniffed, accepted the napkin, and blew her nose noisily. "Sorry. I probably look nasty," she apologized to Agatha who was sitting on her right, but took no notice of Sameera who was squatting within arm's reach.

"You look like someone going through a hard time." Agatha squeezed her shoulder and smiled.

"Thanks," Goldie said softly, returning a sad smile. *She even smiles like Effie.* The list of similarities between Agatha and Issa's older sister was growing. *They're both smart and good looking, and they've got their shit in order. Why can't I be like that?!*

"It's okay to cry, to get it out of your system," Sameera chimed in, tilting her head to catch Goldie's eye.

Goldie nodded but offered little else, fearful any encouragement on her part might incite a lecture about employment laws. *Sameera's nice but she tries too hard. Agatha's chill, though.* If it were up to Goldie, Sameera would go back inside, leave her and Agatha alone. She was desperate to tell someone about her morning.

"Do you want to talk about it?" Agatha asked patiently.

Not with hardo around, Goldie thought, though she did want to talk. She wanted to hear Agatha's interpretation of what had happened that morning. She could not explain it to herself, and she knew she would be asked about it by her parents, Issa, maybe even her brothers. Maybe Agatha could explain why she had been laid off when there was still work to do. She needed an explanation that did not make her sound incompetent.

"They said there was no more work," Goldie spoke into her lap, glancing briefly at Agatha. "But I know there's still work. Like, the boxes are still on my desk. I was supposed to work on them today. And there's a thing I was working on that was still … it wasn't finished."

"Did they mention that note you found, the one from Friday?" Sameera probed as she rose from squatting and took a seat on Goldie's left.

Goldie shook her head and chewed on her lower lip. Turning to Agatha, she continued, "I know I wasn't great at the record updates. Maybe they didn't want to tell me, like so they didn't hurt my feelings?"

Agatha frowned and shook her head sympathetically. "I don't think so. I mean, it's not impossible but it's not how unions work. When there's a problem like that, incompetence, there's rules about handling it. Did you get a verbal and written warning?"

"A verbal one, I guess," Goldie replied softly. *But maybe I sucked so hard they made an exception.*

"This is all fishy," Sameera interjected. "You're entitled to a union rep. They can't just meet with you without a rep."

Goldie stopped herself from rolling her eyes but her tone was brusque when she replied, "There was a union rep."

"There was?" Sameera asked incredulously. She got to her feet and began pacing. "What did the rep say?"

"Nothing," Goldie answered with a shrug. "She just sat there." Turning to Agatha, Goldie added, "I was really trying hard, I swear. I even made this wiki thing that my manager thought was really cool. I showed it to a bunch of directors. That was on Friday. And I thought she was trying to help me get another contract. But like today, she was ice cold. Like, she didn't even care. I don't get it. What did I do?"

Pursing her lips, Agatha took a deep breath before speaking. "From what you've told me, Goldie, it doesn't sound like you did anything wrong."

"But what am I gonna tell my mom?" Goldie shook her head in disbelief. "I know it sounds dumb, like I'm a kid but I don't know what to tell her. She's gonna wanna know what happened."

Agatha nodded. "Just tell her the truth. I think she'll understand."

"I don't even understand," Goldie admitted, tears welling in her eyes. "How did I fuck this up?"

"You didn't," Agatha assured her, blinking away her own tears. "You didn't cause this. This was done to you."

* * *

The executive offices on the upper floors of the West Tower were designed to impress guests, and they did. Unlike the offices of directors with their fibreglass walls and grey palettes, these offices were beautifully decorated with tasteful touches of glass, stained wood, brushed metal, and ornate rugs. Natural light permeated every corner, and if Faiza was not on a mission, she might have taken a moment to admire the view of Lake Ontario, a great blue expanse that began at the southern edges of downtown Toronto. Instead, she marched past the leather armchairs and majestic palms to address the receptionist. Claire arrived a moment later.

"Hello, Ms. Hosseini, Ms. Brigman. Mr. Jamieson is waiting for you," the receptionist said politely, tilting her head toward Jamieson's open office door.

Faiza proceeded, taking a moment put on her game face before stepping into the doorway. Sitting around one end of an elegant live edge wooden conference table were Jamieson, Gunder, and Linehan. Jamieson, a lean man with wavy silver hair and wire-rimmed glasses, motioned with a nod for her to enter.

This was not the first time she had attended a meeting with these influential bureaucrats, though it was the first time she had attended one unaccompanied by Howard. More often than not, he invited her to join them at the table, to listen in on their discussions and debates. No one ever commented on her presence or asked her to contribute, and she was not certain why Howard invited her along. She suspected that he liked parading her, an attractive bauble to amuse his contemporaries — all male, all white. Having Faiza attend meetings also spared Howard the effort of relaying key information when he invariably delegated his assignments to her. For her part, Faiza attended eagerly, hungry for the chance to network, contribute, and prove herself — no matter how often they ignored or patronized her. *It's better to have a seat at the table, even with all their bullshit, than to have no seat at all.*

Sitting through those meetings had fortified her for this one, or so she hoped. Typically, such gatherings were jovial, complete with good-natured teasing, humble bragging, and catered plates of fruit and cheese on the sideboard. On this day, the room was lifeless. In tailored suits, the three heavyweights wore matching expressions — sombre, severe, resolute. Faiza immediately realized that this was no longer her meeting. She might have requested the audience but now they set the agenda. With every step forward, she fortified herself. *You can do this. Don't let them get to you. Stay on track.* By the time she reached the table, she had even managed a gracious smile.

"Hello," Jamieson said coolly.

"Good morning, Matthew. Hello John, Paul," Faiza replied pleasantly, determined to overcome the icy atmosphere, and moved to take the proffered seat.

Placing the portfolios and her laptop on the bare table, Faiza took a seat next to John Gunder, who did not meet her gaze. Quietly, Claire greeted the men and sat across from Faiza, next to Paul Linehan. Faiza opened her mouth to speak, prepared to break the ice with some light conversation — asking after Jamieson's catamaran, Gunder's riding horses, and Linehan's cottage renovations — when Jamieson took the lead.

"It's unfortunate we are meeting under these circumstances," he declared, holding Faiza's gaze, his displeasure emanating across the table.

Faiza's heart sank but she maintained her composure. She needed to regain control over this meeting, to change the tenor, to get them onside. *You can do this. You've done it before.*

In an upbeat tone, she began, "First off, thank you for meeting with me on such short notice. I understand—"

"Faiza," Jamieson cut in. Then, waving a finger at the portfolios she had placed on the table in front of her, "I assure you, this is not the way forward."

She opened her mouth to speak, to ask him to clarify his meaning. Jamieson narrowed his eyes, as if daring her to defy him. The hairs on the back of her neck stood on end, and Faiza wondered how it had all gone wrong. *It's not over yet. You can get them on side. Play to your strengths.*

Adjusting her tone to convey deference to their status, Faiza tried again. "Gentlemen, I see that my ardour has … caused acrimony, and for that I apologize sincerely. I'm sorry." She looked from Linehan, to Gunder, to Jamieson. The latter was the only man to meet her gaze, but with a stony expression that sent shivers down her back.

Modulating her voice to free the quiver that threatened to undermine her composure, she continued, "The truth is that I have dedicated my career to the people of Toronto—"

At that moment, Gunder cleared his throat loudly, forcing Faiza to pause. He did not acknowledge his interruption or excuse himself. Faiza recognized his attempt to unnerve her, one that was having its desired effect. She folded one hand into the other to settle a developing tremor but maintained her façade, even smiling sympathetically at Gunder before proceeding.

"I strive to contribute to their quality of life, to follow in the footsteps of prominent leaders like yourselves." She used a delicate gesture in their general direction but her compliment was disregarded. Across the table, she caught Claire subtly nodding, encouraging her but she did not let their eyes meet. This discussion was difficult enough without the presence of a witness. "These portfolios," she said, daring to touch the corner of one, "are a testament to my dedication to the people of Toronto, to City Hall. They contain—"

Jamieson raised a palm to stop her. "Alright," he rebuffed. "This meeting is not an opportunity to promote yourself. We have agreed to meet out of respect for Howard, because of his faith in you."

Howard?! Fuck me! Faiza clenched her teeth but she maintained eye contact with Jamieson, titling her head slightly to convey concern.

Jamieson pursed his lips and leaned forward on his elbows. "Frankly, I didn't expect this from you. This attempt — circumventing your superior, undermining corporate protocol — is beneath you. Acting like a maverick. It disappoints me."

Shaming me?! He's fucking shaming me?! Dismayed, Faiza eyes flitted to Claire, to catch her reaction. Was she as shocked as her? Or, had she advised them to use this tactic? Sitting upright with eyes on Jamieson, Claire was no longer cheering her on from the sidelines, even subtly.

Jamieson continued, though in a slightly more compassionate tone. "Apart from this incident, you are an upstanding member of our management team. In fact, you've been a mentor to several of the younger members of the team. That is why it pains me to learn that you have failed to observe our corporate conventions, failed to respect the chain of command." He shook his head, disappointed.

Of all the scenarios for which Faiza had prepared — including outright refusal to assist her — she had not imagined that they might scorn her for requesting an audience, for asking to be heard. She had not imagined that they would shame her for advocating on her own behalf, for politicking like leagues of directors before her, for networking as they did. Faiza was flabbergasted, rendered speechless. She stared at Jamieson, her eyes wide open and lips slightly parted.

"Lucky for you," Jamieson began, splaying his fingers with incredulity, "Howard has been very understanding about all this."

Across the table, Linehan gave a nod of admiration, a knot between his brows and his lower lip protruding. He did not lift his eyes from the table to look at Faiza, nor did Gunder or Claire. Had they done so, they would have seen her face flush with colour, her eyes bulge, and her nostrils flare. *Of course, they talked to Howard! What the fuck is this bullshit?!*

After a deep exhale to communicate his weariness with their conversation, Jamieson continued, "He spoke very highly of you, said he understood your error in judgement. Said you could be trusted to learn from this mistake."

That fucking snake! That piece of shit! Her heart was racing, beating so hard that she could feel it in her fingertips. Staying silent was not helping but she needed to calm down before she spoke, before she added fuel to the fire that was threatening to engulf her. She swallowed, dropped her shoulders, and attempted a neutral expression.

"Matthew, Paul, John," Faiza said reverently, looking at each man as she uttered his name, "with all due respect to Howard, I believe there has been some misunderstanding."

All three men stared at her and Faiza sat up taller to demonstrate her fortitude in the face of such hostility. *I'm not scared of you, fuckers. I never was. I never will be.* She maintained a veneer of serenity, an act of defiance in the face of those who were intent on bullying her into submission.

"While it is true that I have circumvented the chain of command, I did not intend to breach protocol," Faiza explained in her defence.

"Huh!" Gunder huffed, sending Jamieson a meaningful look, no longer bothering to hide his contempt.

Faiza bit her lip to avoid reacting to his bad manners. Across from her, Claire stared at the middle of the table, her expression blank. To keep calm, she pretended that Claire was not present. Pedar sag, *asshole! I can't believe I ever trusted you. Two-faced scoundrel! Forget you.*

With iron will, she continued, "I have no intention of disrespecting this institution or its conventions. My sole intention is to express my commitment to this corporation and to request an interview to—"

Raising a finger, Gunder snapped, "Well, we aren't HR." He glanced at his watch and then at Jamieson and Linehan.

"My understanding is that an offer letter is to be sent out this afternoon," Linehan said to no one in particular.

Faiza fell back in her seat, feeling punched in the gut. It became difficult to breathe. Her chest muscles constricted, preventing her from taking a full breath. *How can that be? When did they interview? Who did they interview?* Her lips moved but she did not speak — her thoughts were scattered, skidding in her mind, unable to gain traction, to compose a response.

"We hope this conversation has been edifying," Jamieson said, moving to conclude the meeting, leaning back and crossing his arms. "And don't be discouraged, Faiza. Succession takes time." With that, he flashed a disquieting smile, an ugly expression that made Faiza reel.

"Now, if you'll excuse us, we're expected in Council chambers." Jamieson rose, buttoning his suit jacket and striding to the office door. Gunder and Linehan said nothing, did nothing, other than stare severely at their folded hands. Claire stood, buttoned her suit jacket and pushed in her chair deliberately, waiting for Faiza, who remained seated, rigid, eyes downcast.

Softly, Claire prompted, "Faiza."

The gentleness of her tone was enough to break Faiza's trance. *How dare you?! Don't fucking look at me.* She sneered at Claire as she rose, collected her laptop and handbag, leaving behind the portfolios. On her way out the door, she shook Jamieson's outreached hand silently, refusing to reciprocate his cordial smile. *To hell with all of you!*

* * *

Tired of looking at the back of Goldie's head, Sameera was growing distracted. For the last quarter-hour, Goldie had faced Agatha, asked questions of Agatha, and directed all her replies to Agatha. Initially, Sameera had felt snubbed by the friendship burgeoning before her eyes. After all, she had met Goldie first, and it was she whom Goldie had texted that morning, not Agatha. Yet, there they were: Goldie crying into Agatha's shoulder while Sameera's gaze flitted from pigeons to pedestrians back to the pair on the bench.

But when Goldie began to rehash her experience for a third time, and with the same degree of incredulity as the first telling, Sameera was grateful that the young woman could not see her roll her eyes. She was even more grateful for Agatha's patience and compassion.

"I hear you think you did something wrong but it also sounds like you've been doing your best," Agatha soothed with a confidence that caused Sameera's attention to snap back. "This wasn't your doing."

Agatha's approach to this situation — to Goldie's distress, to management's dubious decision, to the union's disinterest — was significantly different from her own. Where Sameera yearned to empower Goldie with facts about her rights as an employee, Agatha paraphrased Goldie's fears and buoyed her with reassurances, repeatedly. Listening patiently was not one of Sameera's strengths, especially listening to others express dismay at having been wronged. *Why is anyone surprised when it happens to them?!*

Sameera was eager to take action. They had learned the crucial details and she had identified the legal issues; there was nothing left to talk about. Goldie had been subjected to workplace harassment — persistent behaviour meant to frighten and intimidate her — and when she had brought it to the attention of her immediate supervisor, the issue had been ignored and she had been laid off. Clearly, the next step was to file an application with the Human Rights Commission. They could rehash the unpleasantness of her experience all day but it wouldn't change the necessary course of action.

As soon as she heard a pause in the conversation, Sameera interjected, "It sucks. I get it. It's not fair, and that's where your human rights come in. You can—"

"I told you," Goldie snapped, barely turning her head to speak to Sameera. "The union rep just sat there. She didn't do anything."

"Yeah, not the union but the—" Sameera started, and then stopped when she noticed the discouraging look on Agatha's face. Quietly, she apologized, "Sorry. That sucks."

Goldie shrugged, sniffled, and wiped her nose. "It's okay." Then, she turned back to Agatha.

"We are here for you," Agatha assured her with a sad smile. "Whatever you decide to do next, we are here to support you."

Argh! No, not whatever you decide. You need to file an application with the HRC! Sameera sucked in her lower lip and clasped her hands. When her phone pinged, she leaped at the much-needed distraction, taking the call without checking the caller. It was Shannon.

"Hey, one sec," Sameera said to Shannon, and then looking to Agatha, she mouthed "Gotta take this."

She walked toward the centre of the square, steadying her nerves with every step. "Hey, what's up?"

Shannon's voice wavered, uncertain and unlike her usual confident self. "Nothing, just calling to say hi … Hi."

"Hi." A pause followed and Sameera rushed to fill it, babbling at a comedic pace. "How's work? Are you at the Lancaster site? No, it's Downsview, right? I can never remember … you guys move around so much. It's Downsview, right? The thing with the older transformers and the … umm … umm, the … ." She stammered, forgetting the term and wishing her phone would die.

Shannon did not rush to complete the sentence. "Regulators. It's maintenance, the usual." A deep sigh followed, and Sameera envisioned Shannon chewing on her lip, as was her habit when she gathered her thoughts. "Yeah, we just got here … at Downsview. I had a minute … I … How're you doing?"

"Good, good." Sameera answered mechanically as she paced the square in the ensuing silence. Repeatedly, she glanced at Agatha and Goldie who were engrossed in their conversation. She wished they would summon her and she could end the call, and this thought made her groan inwardly. *What is fucking wrong with you?! You're supposed to be in love. Not ditching your girlfriend for a whiner who couldn't care less about you. Geesh, Sameera. Get a grip.*

"Cool … You're working on … a web thing, right? I wanna say … something like optimization."

"Yup, that's it. Just making things less crappy." Sameera forced a chuckle. A series of car horns blared from nearby Queen Street West, and Shannon asked, "Are you outside?"

"Yup, out in the square." A quick response followed by another long pause.

"How come?" Shannon latched on to the topic, most likely seeking relief from the awkward silences. "You on break?"

"Yes. No … well, yes." Instantly, Sameera regretted flip flopping.

"What do you mean?" Shannon's curiosity had been piqued. "Whatchya up to?"

"Aw … it's nothing. Just some personnel stuff." Sameera downplayed the situation, concerned that Shannon would disapprove of her becoming involved in Goldie's affairs. *Am I going to be hiding like this forever?*

"Sounds juicy." Her tone lightened, briefly. "I mean, if everyone's okay and all … Is everything okay?"

"Oh yeah, everything's fine." Sameera caught herself chewing on her nails but she did not stop.

"Oh, okay … so, you're taking a break … or something?" Shannon asked with less fascination and greater concern.

Sameera searched for a viable response, not a lie but not the complete truth. "I'm out with Agatha." As soon as the words passed her lips, Sameera heard the implication. Though Shannon took a dim view of jealousy, Sameera still rushed to correct any misconceptions. "With Goldie. The clerk. The one crying in the bathroom. On Friday."

There was a brief pause before Shannon asked coolly, "How come?"

Fuck! Fuck! Fuck! Now what?! We argue all over again. Fuck! Sameera said nothing but she shook her head vigorously.

"What's going on?" Shannon probed. Sameera remained silent, chewing her nails, unable to form an honest response that wouldn't trigger another argument.

"Come on, Sammy. You can talk to me." Shannon pleaded. "We can't hide things from each other. That's not good."

"Uh-huh." Sameera grunted softly, dragging her feet as she walked in a large circle, eyes downcast. *I wouldn't want to hide anything if you'd take my side, stop telling me I'm imagining bad behaviour.*

"So, what's going on?"

Sameera sighed, exhausted by the effort of forming a response that was not provocative. "Goldie got laid off. She messaged me. We're helping her sort things out."

"Oh, okay." Shannon said, sounding restrained but not displeased. "That's nice of you."

Nice of me? Now, it's nice of me?! Despite having bypassed an argument, Sameera did not feel relieved. Even though she was generally compassionate, Shannon only volunteered to help others when the circumstances were apolitical — a flat tire, a leaky faucet, a drive to the airport, or the search for a lost dog. When she heard a racial slur, she did not speak up. When a trusted coworker seeking permanent residency asked for a character reference, she refused. She thought of herself as a neutral entity, unblemished by politics, and blameless for the world's ills — as long as she did not take sides. *If I can save myself from a homophobic death trap of a small town, then anyone can save themselves from their problems*, Shannon had philosophized far too often.

Sameera shook away the angry thoughts and chastised herself. *Don't be so cynical. People can change. This is what growth looks like.*

"Thanks," Sameera managed graciously, spitting out the nail she had torn off. She wanted to believe that Shannon had changed her attitude, that Sameera could share her thoughts more freely. It could be a new chapter in their relationship, a closeness she craved. *Changing is a process. I need to learn to recognize baby steps.* Still, she had to understand the cause before she could trust its effect. *If I know what caused the change, then I can build on it. Honestly, what does it mean if I don't ask questions? Is that another attempt to avoid a fight? I need to understand the difference.* Silence stretched as Sameera fretted about her choice of words, managing only to agitate herself. "Why? Why is it nice of me? Last week, you said I was meddling, and now it's nice of me. Why?"

Waiting in the absence of a response, Sameera chewed off another nail. She pressed, "Why do I have to worry about what I say, Shan? I mean, we're supposed to be kind, respectful, but why am I worrying about what to tell you?"

"You can tell me anything, Sammy. Anything," Shannon shot back, sounding hurt and defensive.

Sameera shook her head, frowning in response. "See, that's not true. I can't tell you I'm trying to help this girl 'cuz you get so weird." She was distraught and walking in a tight circle. A mountainous knot of emotions threatened to bury her; she was unable to experience each feeling distinctly. There was no disgust without sorrow, and no desperation without resentment. Peripherally, memories surfaced of the upsetting moments, the incidents that had slowly wedged them apart. "And, what about Elewa?"

"Who?" Shannon's question caused deeper creases in Sameera's brow.

"Elewa, the server at Friendly Bean," Sameera snipped. "I helped him get his vacation pay and you freaked out on me."

"You're still mad about that? Sammy, seriously. That was months ago."

"What's wrong with me helping other people?" Sameera demanded. Over the phone, she heard Shannon's sigh of exasperation, which infuriated her, but Sameera made every effort not to speak, not to fill the silence with her own voice. *I have to understand. I need to know why you react like you do. You can't just say nothing; that's not fair.*

"Nothing. Nothing's wrong with that," Shannon muttered.

This time, Sameera leaped into the silence. "So, what then? Why'd you freak-out when I helped Elewa? Or, with Goldie? Why does it bother you?"

"It doesn't," Shannon protested. "I don't care. Do what you want to. And for the record, this argument was your doing. I was trying to avoid a fight."

Sameera stomped her foot, not caring how she might appear to others. "Ugh, Shannon, I'm trying to understand you. I'm not looking for a fight. I just want to know why it bothers you so much."

"I don't know," Shannon admitted. "I don't know. Why do you do it?"

"I've told you: it feels right. It feels important."

"That sounds selfish, like it's all about you — you trying to feel good."

Sameera recoiled from the accusation, pulling the phone from her ear to distance herself from Shannon. *How does she not understand this, understand me?*

"Sammy? Sammy?" Shannon pleaded, her voice ringing with remorse.

"Yes," Sameera replied, wounded and saddened. *Rich white dudes help each other with banks full of money. How's it excessive for me to help a friend, or a coworker?* Shannon had accused her of virtue signalling and evading her own problems. Sameera could have laughed at the ignorance of these claims. *I am virtue signalling?! I do it so people catch on, so people start behaving better — so I can deal with my own shit and not all the fucking crap kicked around by the Courtneys and the Maisys of the world.*

"I'm sorry, babe. I shouldn't have said that." Shannon apologized, and then waited for an acknowledgement. When none came, she added, "I just think … maybe, it's not necessary to get … um, involved in other people's stuff." She paused but Sameera did not respond. "I mean, we all have things to deal with, right? Why take on other people's stuff?"

"Shan, we don't all have the same things to deal with." Sameera contended, her temperature rising with each assertion. "Some of us have it way harder. Some of us need more help 'cuz some of us are going against the current."

"Right. You do and I don't." Shannon said flatly.

"We all do. We all have hurdles but some people are forced to run the race with their legs bound." Sameera hoped the use of an analogy did not diminish her message; she could not compose her thoughts any more clearly.

"Uh-huh. And you're doing what? Saving the world?" Shannon asked cynically. "Maybe, people need to sort out their own shit, without your help. Maybe, you're not actually helping them. Did you ever think of that?"

"Seriously, is that what you really think?" Sameera snapped, regretting it instantly. *She's just upset, and now she's being mean. Don't latch on to this. She's just upset.* She pinched the bridge of her nose to dispel the looming headache.

"I don't know," Shannon admitted with a drawn-out sigh. "I don't know, babe. I just don't understand this chip on your shoulder, this crusader complex. No one expects you to solve the world's problems. There've always been problems. You can just live your life. You don't need to get involved in every sob story."

"Uh-huh," Sameera replied. *Sob story. She thinks these are sob stories.* The tangled knot of feelings was unravelling. Heartache, loneliness, distress, and misery threatened to overwhelm her, to provoke her to retaliate. She needed time to consider Shannon's words before she could respond without malice. "Okay, I have to go. I'll call later."

"Sammy, I love you."

"Me, too. Okay, bye." Sameera ended the call.

* * *

"Faiza," Claire called as Faiza marched away from Jamieson's office toward the elevators. "Faiza. Please wait."

She bashed the elevator button with the base of her fist and stared at the overhead dial, waiting with clenched teeth. Soon, Claire appeared by her side.

"Faiza," she pleaded, trying to catch her eye. "Faiza."

She spun on her heels and hissed, "You knew, and you didn't warn me."

"Faiza, I'm not the enemy," Claire whispered, looking behind her, down the hall.

"Hmm," Faiza huffed, disbelieving. She returned to staring at the elevator panel above the doors.

"Listen," Claire tried. She reached out to console Faiza but her hand hovered between them before retreating. "You heard Jamieson. There'll be other opportunities."

The elevator doors chimed open, and to Faiza's relief, it was empty. She stepped in and pivoted, and as Claire proceeded to follow, she pointed her index finger at Claire's chest, causing her to stop in her tracks.

"Please," Faiza snarled as the doors began to shut. "Take the next one."

Claire did not step forward, nor did she retreat. With one arm, she triggered the sensor so the doors would reopen. "Faiza, this doesn't have to be … a battle. These positions are … complicated. You must understand."

"Complicated? How?" Faiza shot back.

"It's complicated … there's some manoeuvring required. They're looking for a win … assurances that the candidate will work out."

Faiza punctuated her words, "I've been doing this job for three years, Claire. I can assure you that it would work out."

Once again, the doors began to close and Claire waived a hand to trigger the sensor. "Well, yes … and no. It's not just about the work. The position comes with a lot of power. The right person has to be able to … handle that power."

Faiza's eyes widened with disbelief. She stepped into the doorway, causing Claire to take a step back. "Claire, I negotiate multimillion dollar contracts. I liaise with the boards of the biggest banks. The last three initiatives — all award-winners — were designed by me. You know all this. You know it all and you said nothing."

With brows knitted and lips thinned, Claire met Faiza's gaze. She spoke softly, to avoid being overheard, to dampen the impact of her words, or both. "It's a matter of trust."

The doors attempted to close but Faiza smacked the metal doorjamb, her gaze locked on Claire. Incredulous, she hissed, "They don't trust me?"

"They just don't know you as well as they know the other candidate," Claire explained, her tone charitable.

"The other candidate? Jeffery Stanton?!" Faiza glared.

For a moment, Claire seemed taken aback by Faiza's insight. She regained composure, pressed her lips into a thin line, and confirmed Faiza's conjecture with a nod. Faiza was stunned. When Voula had mentioned that Jeffery was the only internal candidate, Faiza had presumed that he had secured an interview with Howard's help. After all, Jeffery was adequate on every level — not a contender when compared with the myriad of other potential candidates Faiza could have listed — but with Jeffery as the only internal candidate, it had seemed certain that they would hire externally. She had spat out Jeffery's name to get more information from Claire about the real candidate, the external hire. She had not expected them to actually hire Jeffery Stanton.

The elevator began to emit a dull buzzing sound, finally signalling the obstruction in the doorway, Faiza's trembling hand on the jamb. Claire's mouth was pinched to one side. She looked prepared to end the conversation, shifting her weight from one heel to the other.

Leaning in, Faiza narrowed her eyes at Claire. "You let them choose Jeffery over me?"

"I didn't let them do anything. I don't have that kind of power." Her voice rising uncharacteristically, Claire took another step back.

"But you didn't challenge them either," Faiza accused, standing taller as she made her point.

"You don't understand, Faiza." Claire crossed her arms and stared back, petulant. "I don't have the pull you think I have. If I object every time I disagree, I'll never get heard."

"Right, and this time?" Faiza grimaced. "This time, it wasn't worth objecting."

Claire was shaking her head before Faiza finished her thought. She rushed in, "No. This time, there was no room to object. If you'd got an interview, then I might—"

Faiza interrupted, her eyes narrowing to slits, "You didn't question why I didn't get an interview? I'm the best person for this job — the person currently doing it — and you didn't think to ask why I didn't get shortlisted?"

The buzzing of the elevator filled the silence as Faiza watched Claire become rigid with indignation, her face contorting into a pinched grimace. Lifting her chin and raising her brows in condescension, Claire replied, "I am not responsible for your career, Faiza. You will have to put in the time and effort, like all of us."

"Like Jeffery?" Faiza retorted with a derisive chuckle.

"I am not on the hiring committee, Faiza." Claire jerked, her crossed arms tightening against her chest. "Jeffery topped the list. He passed the test. Accept that. Learn from the experience. There'll be other—"

"Please, stop." Faiza raised her free hand. "Whatever test Jeffery passed, it's designed to weed me out."

With a pitying look, Claire rolled her eyes, but Faiza continued, "You're afraid of them. I understand. But I'm not."

"Oh, come on, Faiza," Claire complained. "Can we stop with the melodrama?"

"Yes," Faiza answered with two confident steps backwards. "End of conversation." The two women stared coolly at each other as the buzzing stopped and the elevator doors finally closed.

* * *

Goldie accepted another restaurant napkin from Agatha and wiped her sore nose, glancing at Sameera who stood a little ways away, her back turned to them. She was tired of crying, and she'd become aware that she was repeating herself. Still, Agatha was gentle and attentive, listening to her complaints and assuring her that it was not her fault. She did not know whether she believed Agatha's interpretation of the events leading to her lay-off but it was a kinder explanation than the one Goldie had arrived at on her own. *They laid me off 'cuz I suck.*

"It's tempting to blame yourself," Agatha started. "I understand that. You sound like someone who tries hard to go a good job." She looked at Goldie, who nodded back with a sad smile. "Now, don't get me wrong, it's important to know your problem areas — I'm not saying you should fool yourself."

Goldie sat up and chimed in, "I tried really hard to do the updates without mistakes. I know the first couple of boxes weren't great but I did way better later, like way better." She wiped her nose, smoothed her hair, and slumped in place.

"I can see. You're honest with yourself." Agatha affirmed, leaning to catch her eye. "And part of being honest is to admit that some things aren't in your control, like you couldn't have caused them, even when it feels like you did."

This last statement confused Goldie and she tried to think of what was beyond her control. *Baba being away all the time. Dariush living on the couch. Beth being a basic bitch.* When she'd gotten this job, she'd felt more in control of her life than ever. She could save money and plan to move out with Issa. She could change her reputation from unemployed kid to working adult. She could beef up her resume and qualify for less shitty jobs. She could pay down some of her student loans and stress less.

Agatha continued, "I think this is one of those things, something that happened that you didn't cause." She waited for Goldie's response.

Bewildered, Goldie chewed the inside of her cheek, causing her face to pucker. "What do you mean?"

"From your honest account," Agatha smiled and paused, waiting for Goldie to look up, "you did a good job. You also had work left to do. And, you were working on a new project, and that wasn't finished either." Again, she paused, waiting for Goldie to acknowledge her statements.

Goldie nodded hesitantly, trying to see where Agatha was leading her. *Even if I wasn't perfect, I got it mostly right. And the wiki was a hit; Patricia said so. And it wasn't even populated yet. There was still a bunch of data to enter. Why lay me off when there's so much left to do?*

"It's possible that you were ..." Agatha narrowed her eyes and glanced away to think of the right words. "... laid off for reasons that didn't have to do with work." She looked at Goldie knowingly but the younger woman shook her head in response.

"Like what? Money?" Goldie guessed. She sat upright and

turned to Agatha, trying hard to understand what she was getting at. *But they're still paying me. How can they save money by laying me off? How can this be about money?*

"Not money, but people," Agatha explained, pausing for acknowledgement, if not understanding. Goldie grimaced to herself and shrugged slowly, a tentative signal to proceed. Agatha inhaled and chose her next words carefully, worried about scaring off Goldie. "Sometimes, when there is conflict at work, someone is scapegoated to avoid dealing with the conflict."

Beth! She got me fired because of the wiki. That fucking bitch! Goldie's breathing sped up as she envisioned Beth glowering over Patricia, bullying their manager into firing her. She leapt to her feet and decried, "Totally, yes. That bitch Beth was so salty, always trying to get me in trouble. She made Patricia—" Goldie stopped mid-sentence, rethinking the notion as she heard herself.

Patiently, Agatha observed Goldie as she processed her thoughts. She remained silent as Goldie deflated and slumped in her seat. After a moment, Agatha placed a hand on Goldie's arm and squeezed. "This is not your fault. These kinds of things happen to people all the time."

Goldie sighed, exhausted from grasping for answers that weren't forthcoming. "What happens?"

Agatha shrugged apologetically, "Scapegoating."

Shaking her head, confused and tired, Goldie muttered, "But that doesn't make sense. How can Beth make Patricia do that? Patricia's the manager. Beth's just another clerk."

Agatha nodded. She turned toward Goldie and interlaced her fingers in a manner that signalled the imminent arrival of bad news. "It sounds like your team members treated you badly, and not just *Mean Girls* bad but like *Get Out* bad." She paused and studied Goldie's expression.

Get Out *bad? Like, racism?* The implications began to dawn on Goldie. She glanced at Agatha, who nodded, as if reading her thoughts. *They let me go because … what? I'm not white? She saw I wasn't white when she hired me.* "I don't understand. Patricia hired me herself, and she saw I'm not white. Besides, she was really nice to me, like the whole time. Why lay me off now?"

Unhurriedly, Agatha replied, "It sounds like your team members were excluding you, even attempting to upset you, and your manager didn't address their behaviour. It sounds like she tried to solve the conflict by removing you from the situation."

"Oh," Goldie replied distractedly, tugging on a strand. *So, she laid me off because she didn't want to deal with … with what? I never made a stink. I didn't even say shit about Beth, or them other bitches. I said sorry for even calling about that note.* "No, that doesn't make sense. I mean, like I didn't complain or nothing. I kept my mouth shut even when Beth was being a right twat. The only time I said shit was about that stupid note, and I apologized today." Tears had started to stream down her cheeks as her words caught and her voice quavered with emotion.

Agatha handed her another napkin. She squeezed her shoulder while Goldie dried her tears and spoke in jagged bursts. "For fuck's sake … that's so crazy … like, batshit crazy. I … didn't even say anything … about Beth … not Holly … not Sandra … I just did my work … you know."

"This is not on you, Goldie," Agatha assured her.

"So, why am I … the one … being punished … laid off? I didn't do anything wrong," Goldie pleaded, wiping the tip of her nose aggressively.

"It's easy to scapegoat someone young, new, the one with the least privilege."

"But I was doing my job, and I was doing the wiki stuff that Patricia asked me to." *She said I was doing a really good job. She was so excited about the wiki. What the fuck?!*

"That's right. You were doing everything right. This is not on you. Your manager, HR, and even the union rep did this. They have power. They made this decision."

Goldie blew her nose and exhaled. *Bullshit. Nothing but bullshit.* "That's fucking unfair."

"Yes," Agatha affirmed her indignation. "Completely unfair. You didn't cause this, and you deserve better."

"Hmm, okay," Goldie agreed weakly. Then meeting Agatha's gaze, she ventured to ask, "So, that's it?"

Agatha raised her brows and shook her head. "You can stand up for yourself. Ask questions, get answers, and you don't have to do that alone. You have me, Sameera—"

"You mean like go back in there?" Goldie looked horrified by the thought. *That's not fucking happening.* "Oh, no. No, no. You don't know what they were like. Like, totally nice to my face but like stabbing me in the back the whole time. Nuh-uh, no way." Shaking her head, she leaned away from Agatha, as if further distancing herself from the very idea.

At that moment, Sameera approached. "How's it going here?" She glanced at Goldie who refused to meet her gaze, and then questioned Agatha with her eyes.

"It's going okay," Agatha replied, offering a pinched smile that betrayed her assured tone. "We were talking about some next steps."

"Great!" Sameera exclaimed, getting ahead of them. "I can contact the Human Rights Commission and start the application process. That'll take at least—"

"No, no, no," Goldie resisted, speaking into her lap. *So fucking extra all the time. Don't you ever stop?!* "I'm not doing that. I won't go back in there. You don't know what it's like to—"

"Yes, we do," Sameera countered, now standing with her arms crossed and her eyes narrowed. "What you're going through, we've all been there. You're not the first, and if you don't do—"

Agatha interrupted her, "Let's just … just take a breath." Then, turning to Goldie, she added, "We're here to support you, whatever you decide. We're not going to pressure you to do anything. That's not what this is about. Okay?" Agatha reassured Goldie, who eyed Sameera before nodding in response.

"Good," Agatha said, presenting a compassionate smile that went some ways to soothe Goldie's agitation. "We're gonna give you some space." Agatha went on, nodding vigorously at Sameera until Sameera nodded along, clearly resistant to the suggestion. "So, we'll be right there. Okay?"

Goldie watched as the pair walked into the centre of the square. She browsed her phone for messages, posts, anything to distract herself from the terrifying thought of approaching Patricia. *They're fucking loco if they think I'm ever going back in there.*

Chapter 7

Monday Afternoon, June 25, 2018

On the ride down, Faiza's mind reeled, creating a tangled mess of memories: Jamieson's loathsome expression, Linehan's unconcerned tone, the contemptuous mutterings of Gunder, and Claire's underhandedness, her unexpected betrayal. *A band of fiends. Swine.* Bisharaf-ha, *wretches!*

With fists and jaw clenched, she restrained her tears. She refused to allow anyone to see her breakdown, and she knew a breakdown was imminent. The tremor in her throat was spreading through her body, causing spasms interspersed with uncontrollable shaking. Wrath, raw and volatile, detonated in her core, creating fissures where white hot anger escaped. *Stupid, stupid, stupid. I'm a fucking idiot. What the hell was I thinking? Why didn't I see this coming?*

The elevator stopped midway to the atrium, and a pair of suited men entered. Pretending to check her phone, Faiza kept her eyes lowered. She contemplated simply taking the elevator past the lobby and down to the carpark, going home, working remotely. Returning to her office was the last thing she wanted to do. Even with her door closed, there was no peace or privacy as a stream of managers dropped in. Still, commuting for 45 minutes in her present state seemed imprudent — she could barely keep her limbs from shaking. *I need a minute. I have to figure this out.*

Recalling Voula's recent trip to the observation deck, she decided to find a quiet space on the twenty-seventh floor of the East Tower. After a twenty-five story ascent by elevator and a walk up two flights of stairs, she arrived on the deck, relieved to find it vacant. The cool breeze lifted her hair from her shoulders and she stopped to breathe deeply. The deck was a walkway in the sky, an airy promenade that followed the gentle curve of the building. Open to the elements but closed to the public, for safety concerns, the deck offered scenic views of Toronto in every direction. Concrete and metal railings edged the lengths of the curved walkway, and along its spine, wide concrete pillars rose to support the roof and a series of skylights. Benches, placed between pillars, created private alcoves from which to gape at the skyscrapers multiplying, glimpse the shimmering waters of Lake Ontario, and gaze down on dozens of pigeons as they circled Nathan Philips Square.

Faiza walked the length of the deck and found a concrete bench, out of view of the stairway door overlooking the city's west end. She slipped off her heels and exhaled deeply, her hands resting limply on her skirt as her hair blew in all directions. The view of the city was clear. It would have been captivating on any other occasion but Faiza could not keep her eyes open. A quiver in her chest signalled the tears threatening to pour out, now that she could cry, freely and unguarded. She wanted to cry, she wanted to release the virulent emotions that were poisoning her, so she let lose. Through unrestrained sobs and wails, she expelled all the anger and resentment that had been festering. *All these years … and nothing. They still think I'm not good enough … after all these years.*

When her phone pinged, alerting her to a message, she picked it up habitually. Through the tears that blurred her vision and the locks of hair that whipped her face, she read Voula's message, *where r u.*

She attempted a reply but her running eye makeup stung her eyes. She paused to dab her eyes in broad strokes, unconcerned about her complexion but knowing that she must look like a raccoon.

Obs deck, she texted.

Instantly, Voula replied, *On my way.*

Faiza put the phone down and stared ahead. To the southwest were the rippling blue waters of Lake Ontario dotted with rainbow-striped parasailers and gleaming white sailboats. To the northwest was a patchwork of green parks, glass buildings, and grey bands of highways, as far as she could see. What she could not see of Toronto from her seat, she knew intimately from meetings with councillors, boards of directors, trustees, planners, developers, NGOs, and chambers of commerce. As Howard's right hand, she had reached out in every direction to make connections, to make City Hall relevant. It had taken years to foster new relationships, to secure the trust of people whose concerns had been marginalized since before Toronto was known as York. She'd envisioned a lifelong career at City Hall, doing good work, meaningful work. *Now, that's over.*

* * *

As Sameera walked alongside Agatha to the fountain in the centre of the square, she chewed on her lower lip to avoid saying something she might regret. She glanced back at Goldie, seeing only the top of her head, her body curled over her screen. *Goldie's a kid and Agatha's doing her best. This's gonna be complicated no matter what. Just relax. Stop pushing.*

"You okay?" Agatha asked, stopping at the edge of the shallow square pond that served as an ice rink in the winter. Its waters rippled, offering a distorted reflection of the skyscrapers encircling them.

Without taking a breath, Sameera unleased her inner thoughts, "I just want her to do the right thing, and I know, I know, there is no right thing. I get that. Everyone has their own path and all that, but the right thing here is to file a human rights complaint. There's no doubt in my mind. Management fucked up, the union, too. She has to file an application with the Commission."

Agatha looked at the water, then at the sky. "Hmm," she started, a curious smile at the corners of her mouth. "Yeah. I was asking about you. The call you got. It looked intense."

Sameera had to laugh at herself for misunderstanding a simple question. "Sorry. I was just …." She took a breath and looked about the square, taking a moment to gather her thoughts. *Am I okay? Uh … no.*

"That, uh, was my girlfriend, Shannon." She didn't know where to go from there. She had not discussed her private life with her co-workers, unlike others who went on about their first dates and upcoming trips. The intrepid woman of a few months earlier, the one who had resolved to live authentically, had ended up flattening her identity, minimizing her existence to avoid scrutiny. The CM's scornful treatment and the subsequent shunning had unnerved her, and Sameera had resorted to an old habit of presenting herself as a two dimensional woman, the professional without the personal. *There's more to it than that — Shannon's attitude has made it all worse.*

If there were anyone she would confide in, it was Agatha. Yet, Sameera was hesitant to open up at a time when she was struggling. It seemed like the unveiling of a grotesque science experiment — Sameera's life in a petri dish with its edges oozing and decaying. Besides, she feared she might vilify Shannon. *Am I supposed to spin this so Shannon doesn't sound ignorant, callous?*

"Is she okay?" Agatha asked softly, gazing into the water, standing with her hands buried in her jacket pockets in an endearing pose.

"Oh, yeah. Well, no, not exactly. She's okay but … we're not." Sameera allowed her gaze to drift, first settling on a group of well-heeled tourists taking selfies, and then on an elderly woman in a long but torn puffer jacket pulling a rickety cart jammed with overstuffed shopping bags. *Nothing's fair. Nothing evens out.*

"I'm sorry." Agatha looked her way but Sameera stared into the distance, avoiding eye contact. Her feelings were too close to the surface, threatening her composure. Revealing any more might undermine the reputation she was struggling to establish.

"So, about Goldie," Sameera changed the topic, spinning on her heels to face the young woman who remained on the bench, engrossed by her screen. "It looks like you have a real connection with her."

"Yeah, she's nice." From over her shoulder, Agatha glanced worriedly at Goldie, but she made no movement toward the bench. Instead, she checked her phone, and then tucked her hands back into her deep pockets.

"What do you want to do?" Sameera prompted, eager to determine a viable tactic, some way to convince Goldie to file an application.

Agatha thinned her lips in contemplation. "I think I've done all I want to. I mean, I don't think there is anything else to do."

What the fuck?! What am I missing here? Sameera blinked repeatedly, trying to soften the grimace on her face. "And, what about filing an application?"

"Yeah?" Agatha asked earnestly.

"Don't you think she should file an application? I mean, isn't that the right thing to do?" Sameera shot back, hearing her voice rise and her speech quicken. "How else does anything change if we don't make a point of speaking out?"

Agatha nodded but she did not answer. She glanced at Goldie and back at the rippling waters. "Did you talk to HR?"

Sameera spun about to face her, taken aback. "Me?"

"For what happened, at the ADM," Agatha replied evenly.

"Me? Uh," Sameera stumbled, surprised by the turn their conversation had taken. "I … uh, I hadn't thought of it. I mean, I guess I could have but … that was different. I, uh …."

It had not occurred to her to talk to HR, or take any action other than to repair her reputation and pass her probationary period. *A year ago, I'd have marched down to HR straight from the ADM. I wouldn't take that shit from anyone. Now? I don't know.*

"Honestly, it didn't occur to me," Sameera admitted, running her jagged nails along her palm.

"Hmm, okay." Agatha toed the rim of the pond and pulled back, leaving wet crescent-shaped prints on the concrete. She repeated the act, creating a delicate pattern at their feet. "And now? Would you go to HR now?"

Sameera turned to face the fountain. She glimpsed the fleeting reflection of a flock of seagulls flying west. *Would I? I don't know. I guess I could but … why? What's the point?*

"I don't mean to put you on the spot," Agatha said, working at the pattern of wet prints. "And, I'm not saying you should. I'm just thinking about what it takes, you know, to take that step."

Robotically, Sameera recited, "It takes support. When we feel supported, then we feel strong enough to take risks." These were phrases from her feeds, wisdom for her thousands of followers. *When you feel supported, you feel confident to be yourself.*

Agatha nodded. "Sure. When we feel less vulnerable, we are prepared to demand more." She dipped the toe of her sneaker again but water rose unexpectedly, wetting its canvas edges. She pulled back and shook drops off her shoe, producing a constellation of stars about the crescent moon prints.

Sameera stared into the pool of water and watched the reflection of billowy clouds hurried along by a slight breeze. *Be honest. Speak openly. Stop living like a statue.*

"Right, and I guess, I felt … feel, vulnerable. I'm worried I don't have support …." Sameera thought about Shannon's discouraging reaction following the ADM. *How can I feel supported when Shannon's tearing me down?* She nodded to herself. "Yeah, that's why I didn't."

"And now?" Agatha asked, keeping her gaze on the starry scene she had produced. "Why not go now?"

Sameera scoffed, "Uh 'cuz nothing's changed. I basically have no one on my side."

"Well, that might not be accurate." Agatha's diplomatic tone softened the subtext. "You have several allies. Actually, you're much more popular than you might think."

"No, that's not true." Sameera waved her hand, banishing the suggestion.

"Have you asked?" Agatha countered. "I mean, from the things I've heard, you got people talking about Crawley, about his attitude. He's done this to other people before. And no one's against you. It's not like that. I mean, I know Courtney and Lindsey aren't fans but there're a lot of people who get it."

They get it?! Sameera shook her head in disbelief. She'd isolated herself to such an extent that she'd missed this sea change. *Crawley's the one who fucked up, not me. I'm not paranoid. Other people see it.* If Shannon's accusations of paranoia had not been overshadowing her feelings, she might have smiled at Agatha's revelation that her peers supported her.

Changing the subject to keep composure, Sameera asked, "So, you think Goldie should file?"

Agatha looked in Goldie's direction, who was tapping rapidly on her phone. "I think she'll figure it out. Right now, it's too raw."

Sameera glanced at Goldie, too. "Right. Okay. So, what do we do now?"

Shrugging, Agatha smiled at her. "Good question. 'What do we do now, Nick?'"

Shaking her head at the movie quote, Sameera played along. "'Fuck like minks, raise rugrats and live happily ever after.'"

"'Hate rugrats.'" Agatha recited.

"'Fuck like minks, forget the rugrats, and live happily ever after.'"

Together, they pronounced, "*Basic Instinct.*" The two chuckled, and Sameera felt a step closer to presenting her genuine self.

* * *

"Here, it's herbal, wild raspberry and something." Voula handed Faiza a paper cup, the tag of the tea bag blowing in the wind. She nudged Faiza's handbag and laptop to the centre of the bench and took a seat at the other end, facing the cityscape. In one hand, she held a takeaway cup of coffee, and with the other she brushed back her airborne bangs, her long hair secured tightly in a bun.

"Thanks." Faiza accepted the cup but placed it on the floor by her feet. Her hair was dancing about her head and she needed both hands to tie it back into a ponytail. For a few minutes, they sat together quietly as Faiza tended to her hair and tidied the smeared makeup around her eyes and cheeks. Her appearance was not as refined as she liked but she still looked elegant and attractive. *Okay, good to go.*

"Thanks, Vee. I needed this," Faiza said, raising her cup of tea and sipping gingerly to minimize contact with the fresh coat of lipstick she'd applied.

"Anytime," Voula replied with a sympathetic smile.

Faiza slipped on her heels and rose to collect her belongings, eager to return to work, but Voula did not budge. With brows raised and head tilted, Voula stared at her expectantly, "Well? How did it go?"

Pulling the strap of her handbag higher up her shoulder, Faiza spoke plainly, "The meeting was a disaster. That's all." With a dismissive shrug, she signalled the uselessness of rehashing the experience. "Shall we?" She motioned toward the stairwell at the opposite end of the walkway.

"Can we sit for a minute?" Voula requested, pretending not to notice Faiza's reluctance to discuss the meeting. "The view is so nice."

Faiza nodded, "Sure. Okay." She set down her belongings and settled back on the hidden bench overlooking downtown on the beautiful summer's day. A minute passed in silence, and then a couple more. Voula sipped her coffee and stared out at the lake, seemingly mesmerized by its sparkling surface. Faiza tried to calm her mind and experience the beauty and peacefulness that surrounded them but she failed every attempt. For brief moments, she was present and aware of her surroundings — the pleasant breeze on her cheeks, seagulls flying on the wind, the heat of the cup between her palms — but every attempt was cut short by an upsetting memory or an unsettling realization. She could not sit still any longer; she needed to distract herself from the resentment within, to forge ahead with her plans.

Jumping to her feet, she announced, "I've got to go. I'll meet you back at the office."

As if she hadn't heard Faiza, Voula took a sip of her coffee and inquired, "What happened at the meeting?"

Faiza continued to collect her belongings, buying time as she prepared a response. She did not want to talk about the meeting. There was nothing left to talk about, nothing left to do. She had positioned herself as the ideal candidate and they had rejected her. *Why rehash it like a soap opera?* Still, Voula was her friend, and after her continued support, it seemed unkind to freeze her out.

"They've already picked someone for the job," Faiza said, skipping over the painful details. "Jeffery."

Voula looked up at Faiza for confirmation. Her expression was severe but not surprised. Faiza gave a nod, and then she turned away, feeling the stinging sensation in her nostrils that preceded tears. *No, no, no. We're not doing this again. No more tears.*

In a chilly tone, Voula probed, "Did they say why you weren't interviewed?"

Faiza turned back to her, using a thin smile and a soft tone to conceal her exasperation. "Vee, what does it matter? It's done. Lesson learned."

Voula nodded, her eyes not meeting Faiza's, choosing to stare at the horizon. "Hmm. What about—"

"Nothing," Faiza snipped, pressing her laptop closer to her chest. "This is a dead end. It's over."

"Over?" Voula repeated, head tilted and brows knitted, her bangs flying.

Eyeing the stairwell, Faiza considered making a run for it, simply to shut down the conversation. *Do we have to do this? Why?* She was desperate to explain her rationale without appearing victimized but it seemed hopeless. Petitioning for an interview was self-promotion — common practice in corporate settings, part of running a race in which first place is the only standing that matters. She was proud of her substantive effort, her hustle. She had not lost the race; she'd been denied the opportunity to run. No matter how she presented the events of the day, Voula would also recognize this fact. *They didn't give me a chance.*

After shifting on her feet for a time, she gave up on an escape, put down her belongings, and took a seat. Softly, she explained, "They accused me of insubordination, of going over Howard's head." She inhaled deeply, and as she exhaled, her torso slumped further, her arms limp in her lap and her gaze on the concrete floor. "They don't want me, Vee. They don't." One shoulder raised in a weak shrug as tears fell onto her skirt.

Voula inched closer and placed her hand on Faiza's arched back, rubbing soothing circles. They did not speak while Faiza cried, and Voula stopped only once to procure a package of tissues from Faiza's handbag. When Faiza's tears subsided, Voula offered her the cup of warm tea.

"I think you should speak to Adaego," Voula suggested, referring to the director of Business Development Services, someone she had considered Faiza's competition for the position of Deputy City Manager.

Faiza pulled back and eyed Voula. "So we can cry together?! No, thank you." She shook her head and rolled her eyes at the suggestion. *Besides, Adaego never had a real shot. If the bastards can't bring themselves to hire an Iranian, a Nigerian doesn't stand a chance.*

"You're both facing the same problem, a bigger problem," Voula explained plainly. "It's systemic."

Scoffing, Faiza retorted, "You think I should sue?"

Voula uncrossed and crossed her legs. "I think it's time to draw a line, to assert your rights."

"I'm not a receptionist, Vee. I can't work for the city while I sue them." Throwing her hands in the air, Faiza turned to Voula. "I'm expected to represent them, not take them to court." Voula nodded sympathetically but said nothing.

"It's too messy, and even if it panned out, who's going to want to work with me? I mean, really. Imagine the reputation I'd have. No," Faiza insisted, shaking her head, assured in her assessment. "I need to end this while my reputation is still intact."

"You're quitting?" Voula asked, now visibly alarmed and confounded, her mouth slightly agape.

"Moving on," Faiza clarified, sitting up taller to exude confidence. "I know better than to bang my head against a brick wall." Flashing a smile, she gestured to the city, "I can sell myself. With all the contacts I have here, I'm a hot commodity out there. Hell, I could start my own consulting firm tomorrow. You could join me." Faiza nudged Voula with her elbow, soliciting a smile.

Instead, Voula looked away, frowning deeply.

* * *

"No cap, I'm not feeling this," Goldie admitted, slowing her pace as they neared the revolving front doors of City Hall.

Agatha wrapped an arm around her shoulder, smiling reassuringly as she nudged Goldie ahead. "No worries. You can go in, like anybody. Like pulling up at the mall."

When Agatha had suggested a change of scenery, Goldie had

agreed, imagining they were heading to one of the nearby cafés. There was still so much she wanted to talk about, to ask about. The woman's chill vibe attracted Goldie — she appeared to be natural, transparent — and since Agatha had saved her from Sameera's campaign rant about making a human rights complaint, her confidence in Agatha had bloomed. She seemed to know how things were supposed to work, and Goldie was still desperate for an explanation, a version of events that did not make her sound and feel like a failure. She hoped for a little more time together, to chat and sort things out, to help her form a perspective to take home. Now, Agatha was leading them back to City Hall, and Goldie was panicking. *This is not good. So not good.*

Desperate for an escape, Goldie glanced back at Sameera who was walking a step behind. She caught a glimpse of hesitation before Sameera flashed a sympathetic smile, nodding encouragingly. *Oh, now you're chill?! Now? You were pressed twenty minutes ago.* Without returning the smile, Goldie looked ahead. *Argh! I can't go in there.*

"Uh, how about bubble tea … or something, instead?" Goldie negotiated, steps away from joining the stream of people entering the revolving door.

Agatha pivoted in front of Goldie and held her shoulders; her present touch was as firm and gentle as her words earlier. Unlike Sameera, who ranted about discrimination and bossed her around, Agatha had listened patiently to Goldie and offered sympathy, not advice. *Just like Effie,* Goldie thought as she recalled Issa's sister consoling her about a failed exam, assuring her that it was a common occurrence during first year. *Wish I had a big sister — instead of two basic bros.*

Leaning in, her expression as kind as ever, Agatha said, "I know what it's like to feel like an outsider. It breaks you." She waited for a sign from Goldie, who replied with a small nod. "Salty bitches gonna trigger you. They wanna shut you down. Hmm?" Goldie nodded again, sucking in her lower lip and blinking away her tears. "So, clap back. They don't own this place; they just work here."

"I'm not talking to anyone," Goldie insisted, her forehead creasing deeply at the thought of confronting her ex–co-workers.

"No, of course not. It's not about them," Agatha assured her, squeezing Goldie's shoulders lightly.

"'A'ight … but where're we going?" She smoothed her hair, preparing herself for re-entry.

"Top floor, observation deck. It's iconic. You see everything." Agatha looked up at the East Tower.

Goldie glanced up, less than impressed. She dragged one foot after another toward the doors, propelled by her trust in Agatha. *She's got my back.* More than anything, she wanted more time with Agatha. She had questions about things Agatha had said earlier — about Patricia's responsibility toward her, what Patricia was supposed to do about Beth. When Goldie described the wiki project, Agatha had cringed, calling it "typical spineless exploitation. Worthy of complaint." She wanted to know what all of it meant. *You do the work your boss gives you, right? I mean, the wiki isn't mine. Is it?*

Until that morning, Goldie had revered Patricia — she had appeared composed and competent, enthusiastic about Goldie's ideas and excited to help her land a full-time job. She could not find fault in Patricia's optimism and championship, and at times she felt underserving and overwhelmed in Patricia's spotlight. Before Goldie had performed a single task, Patricia had showered her with approval. It had been unsettling but not unpleasant, and Goldie felt embarrassed to admit that she had not questioned Patricia's behaviour — not until that morning, and that too at Agatha's prompting. *First, she was all fam. Then, all fake. Sus.*

* * *

They stared at the lake in silence as the minutes passed. Faiza drank the last of her now cold tea and wished that she had a bottle of water. She was ready to head back to her office and get lost in her work. That night, she would tell Rob about her plan to resign from City Hall, and then she could get the ball rolling — set up lunch dates with contacts, generate buzz about her projects, prepare the narrative about her departure. *I've done it all before. I can do it all again.*

"You're meeting with the infrastructure committee, no?" Faiza asked, hinting at her desire to get going. Voula kept her eyes on the horizon and her hands in her lap as she shook her head. Faiza turned away and sighed. *What am I supposed to do? I can't stay here. They don't want me.*

"Listen, Vee," Faiza started, shifting in her seat to face Voula. "I know you want what's best for me."

Voula replied with a fleeting glance and a small nod. She appeared disappointed by the turn of events, not angry. Faiza wondered, *Is she grieving?* Their close friendship was enviable, given the competitiveness among executive-types, and Faiza knew that she would be lucky to find another such friendship at her next job.

"We'll still be friends," she reasoned, placing her hand on Voula's and squeezing lightly.

Instantly, Voula turned toward Faiza, her face pinched with irritation. "Of course!" She huffed and shook her head at Faiza, disapprovingly. With nostrils flaring and hands gesticulating, she berated Faiza. "This is not about us. This is about all of us. You're just walking away. You didn't get what you wanted and now you're giving up."

Shocked by the outburst, Faiza's hands clasped together and her limbs pulled closer to her centre. She was accustomed to Voula being upset at others but Faiza had never been on the receiving end of her temper. *Just listen to her. She deserves that much from you.* Faiza softened her body language — loosening her tightened face and neck muscles, releasing her tense shoulders, and laying her hands loosely on her lap. Listening to others air grievances was part of her job, and she knew when to remain silent.

"What do you think is going to happen at the next place? You think it'll be any different?" Voula narrowed her eyes, daring Faiza to answer. She spoke rapidly, and Faiza could hear the quiver in her voice. "You know it'll just follow you, like it follows all of us. It doesn't matter where you go. There'll always be someone to keep you down."

Faiza nodded once and slowly, to acknowledge that she had heard Voula. This tongue lashing was not going to change her mind, and she had no intention to engage Voula when she was in such a charged state. *Don't say a thing. Don't say one single thing. Let her get it out. Just listen.*

"You are such a smart woman." Voula had changed her tone, sounding less antagonistic but no less flustered. She brushed away her fringe of fluttering hair but strands returned to whip at her face. "Why don't you see this? There's no getting away. We need to fight this, and this is the ideal setting." She took Faiza's hands in her own. "If we can make a stand here, in City Hall, it sets the bar for every other fight everywhere else. We can't keep playing their game. We have to throw it all out, start from scratch."

Once again, Faiza nodded slowly, biding time until Voula stopped spouting her angry agenda. Except that this time Voula crossed her arms and glared back, forcing an awkward silence. *Don't say a thing. It'll only feed her fire. You know there is no reason to stay here. They don't want you and there's no point fighting them on this. End of story. Voula will get over it. Just stay quiet and let her wind down.*

The sound of a door slamming, closed by the high winds, alerted Faiza and Voula to new arrivals on the observation deck. The newcomers cursed for effect as they admired the view, evidently unaware of the two executives seated between concrete pillars at the end of the walkway. Faiza lifted her shoulders and raised an eyebrow, looking at Voula for direction. After all, it was Voula who was in the process of dressing her down; Faiza had been content to end the conversation some time ago. Shrugging in response, Voula sat bemused by this peculiar development.

"Fucking iconic, right?" One woman exclaimed over the wind.

"On fleek! I have to get this up on Insta," another woman squealed.

Voula brushed hair out of her eyes as she tapped on her phone. A second later, Faiza grabbed her vibrating phone from her handbag. Voula's message read, *go?*

Faiza nodded, reaching for her bag and laptop. Presently, they heard footsteps approaching; the newcomers stopped on the other side of the pillar that concealed Faiza and Voula. She looked at Voula, whose puckish expression nearly caused her to laugh out loud. Voula shrugged and smiled playfully, prepared to step out into the open. *At least she's not lecturing me anymore!*

"What's the plan? Are we just up here for selfies?" asked one of the newcomers. Instantly, Faiza recognized Sameera Jahani's voice, and she touched Voula's arm to keep her from rising. She needed a minute to check her appearance before they stepped out into the open and faced her subordinates, to make sure she did not look as awful as she felt. As she examined her makeup and hair in her compact, she listened closely to the heated exchange.

"There's no plan. We can't make her do anything. This is Goldie's choice." Another woman whispered; a familiar voice but not one that Faiza recognized. *Goldie … Goldie, I remember. A new hire. Young. Really young. Presented her project last Friday.*

"She doesn't know what to do. She can barely tell what's happened to her," Sameera insisted. Faiza noticed that these remarks caught Voula's attention as her eyes widened, her hands fell into her lap, and she leaned in to listen closely, too. *Voula, forever a guardian. Always looking out for others, even strangers.*

"All we can offer her is support. We can't pressure her to file an application with the Commission." Upon hearing these words, Faiza turned to Voula. *We should go. We should not be here right now.*

"It's not pressure. It's guidance. She doesn't even get how wrong this is. Her white co-workers harass her, and when she says something, her white manager lays her off. Did you know she was tasked with making a wiki that'd make her whole team redundant? It's fucking crazy wrong. We've gotta do something."

Faiza's phone vibrated in her hand. She read Voula's message, *im going in,* and her eyes leaped from her screen to Voula. Faiza shook her head and raised a finger to buy time. A moment later, she typed her reply to Voula, *no no can't get involved. union business.*

Voula's expression of incredulity prompted Faiza to add to her reply, *conflict of interest. we're execs.*

Voula rolled her eyes and replied, *you're leaving. remember?*

Other than returning a reproachful gaze, Faiza did not respond to the message.

"You know I can hear you," the third woman called out. "I heard everything you said." Faiza recognized that voice. *Goldie, Patricia Addington's new hire.*

"Goldie, listen. This is serious." Sameera Jahani's tone was a blend of fear, disapproval, and concern. Faiza could not see any of them but she could imagine Sameera's stance as she reproved Goldie — her hands would be on her hips and her face would be leaning in for added effect. "If you don't complain, they'll get away with it. Don't you care about justice?"

Faiza caught Voula glaring at her knowingly through her fluttering fringe. For a conceited moment, she wondered whether the conversation was an act performed for her benefit, to persuade her to file a lawsuit. *It wouldn't work anyways. I'm not throwing away my reputation to get a job working with people who resent me.*

"I'm tired of you raging at me. I'm not stupid. I get it: they fucked up—"

Sameera interrupted. "So you get that you gotta fight back? Like, not go home and pretend nothing happened?"

"I'm not going to!" Goldie hollered, her anger overtaking the howling wind. "You act like you know me. Just back off."

"Fair, totally fair," declared the mediator over the duelling voices of Goldie and Sameera. "Sameera, I think our sense of urgency is creating bad vibes." A long pause followed, and Faiza imagined Sameera rolling her eyes and shaking her head, refusing to admit the obvious: she was not making any headway by haranguing Goldie. The mediator continued, "Goldie, you're right. We need to back off. We have no right to pressure you into anything."

Following another pause, Faiza thought she heard Goldie express her gratitude but the muttered words were swallowed by the wind. In her seat, Voula was consumed by the conversation, uncaring about the strands dancing about her face.

The mediator explained, "Besides, that's not why we brought you up here. I mean, we just wanted to give you a chance to …." She chuckled before continuing, "Okay, don't laugh — I know this sounds really Oprah — but we thought this might help you to … reclaim this place. I mean, a lot of bad shit happened to you here — and that's not your fault — but it doesn't mean you don't belong here. The people who fucked up — they don't belong here. They done fucked up, and it wouldn't be fair for you to walk away thinking you don't fit in here. You totally fit here. City Hall is lucky to have someone like you."

Faiza heard the mediator's tone shift from encouraging to conciliatory, as Goldie's sought reassurance, pressing for answers to the same questions Faiza had been asking herself that morning. *Don't they see my worth, what I'm capable of? How can they be so blind, so biased? Why didn't they take my side?*

The mediator soothed, "It's not fair, Goldie. I know. We both know. We've been through this shit, too. A few of the times, I didn't realize what had happened until years later, and then it was too late to do anything."

"Right, 'cept you have a job, and I don't." Goldie shot back. "I need this reference. How do you think they're gonna be if I complain?"

"I'm filing a complaint with HR, today," Sameera announced. "Against the CM."

Faiza and Voula eyed each other at the unexpected news. They had been as disgusted by the CM's dismissive attitude and derogatory response to Sameera as they were nonplussed by Sameera's subsequent passivity. To pass the probationary period, a new hire required management approval, and filing a complaint against management was a surefire way to be branded unsuitable — a bad fit for the corporation — and then dismissed. At any point, a formal complaint against management could tarnish Sameera's chances for either passing probation or getting a promotion. Like Faiza herself, most people either endured misbehaviour or attempted to resolve issues off the record. *Whatever good that does!*

"You are? For what?" Goldie asked incredulously.

"He belittled me." Sameera's shaky confidence could be heard despite the blowing wind. "He implied that I was … that I wanted to … I asked about a policy and he treated me like I was asking him for a favour. He made some stupid racist joke. He made it sound like I wanted him to hire my relatives. I never said anything like that. I was asking about his policy. I was asking a legitimate question. He did not even have to answer the question. He didn't have to be an asshole."

Voula frowned deeply and chewed on her lower lip. Faiza felt her heart breaking, hearing these young women relating their hateful experiences. The difficulty of their circumstances seemed relentless, without resolution. In their place, Faiza had bit her tongue and borne down. For the entirety of her academic and professional career, she had endured injustice and humiliation to rise through the ranks. She was indestructible — a powerhouse of intellect, drive, and charm — but success had always been bittersweet. Faiza had survived hardships systematically designed to disrupt her progress; there had been no alternative road to success, and it seemed that these women faced the same conditions. *Nothing's changed. It's all the same bullshit. What are they supposed to do? And Mina? She's going to come up against this, too.*

Faiza recalled her indifference at Patricia spotlighting Goldie's ethnicity during the Friday meeting. *To what extent is Mina's career going to be shaped by stupid questions and silent bystanders?* She had worked relentlessly to establish Mina in prestigious networks, to ensure that her daughter was a member of the establishment, not one of the many vying to get in. Considering the generous donations to the school, ski trips to Whistler, summer camps at Lake Tahoe, tennis and riding lessons, piano classes, Farsi and Mandarin tutors, her daughter was set to take on the world. *I can only control so much. She'll have to be ready for challenges. She'll have to work the system, take advantage where she can. She'll have to be faster and smarter, the fastest and smartest. And then she might still just be tired and angry, like me.*

The phone vibrated in Faiza's hand, and the message from Voula read, *heard enough?*

Faiza nodded gravely and rose.

* * *

Sameera's decision to file a complaint against the CM took everyone by surprise — even herself. She was stunned by how relieved she felt at having said it out loud. While Agatha smiled encouragingly and Goldie stared in disbelief, Sameera shook in place, rattled by her own words. *Why did I say that?! Am I trying to impress some kid who doesn't even realize she's been jerked around? For fuck's sake, I'm still on probation! What's the point of busting my ass and keeping my mouth shut if I'm gonna throw it all away now?! Two more weeks, that's all I have to get through. Two weeks to keep it together, to pass probation, and seal the fucking deal! Not fuck it up royally. Not throw it all away to prove a point to an ignorant twerp who hates me!*

"Won't you get in trouble?" Goldie asked with childlike concern, crossing her arms to keep her shirt from flapping in the wind.

Fine lines formed between Goldie's knitted brows, softening Sameera's brittle impression of her. At twenty-five, Goldie's awareness of humanity and human history was still developing. For her, context was limited, defined by the actions and reactions of those around her, and when Goldie suffered, she turned to others to validate her feelings to corroborate her perceptions. She had failed to recognize her mistreatment because no one acknowledged it as harassment and discrimination. In comparison, Sameera had fields of context in which to ground her experience. *She's afraid. She's never gone through this before. I know better. I should know better.*

"Maybe," Sameera admitted, offering Goldie a brave smile. "I'm going to have to figure it out." She glanced at Agatha who nodded in agreement. "I still have two weeks on my probation—"

"Hello." A voice came from behind Sameera, and she turned to see Faiza Hosseini and Voula Stavros step out from around a cement pillar. The directors stood side by side, dignified in their tailored suits and immaculate makeup. The wind tugged at their shirt collars and tousled loose strands of their hair, making their entrance startling, cinematic.

What the fuck?! Sameera looked at Agatha who offered a bemused smile. *Is this some kind of ambush? I am so confused. What the hell is going on?* Just as Sameera opened her mouth to accuse the directors of eavesdropping, Voula Stavros stepped forward with a brilliant smile and an outstretched hand.

"Hi Sameera. I'm Voula Stavros, director of the Customer Services team," she smiled warmly, shaking Sameera's hand and squeezing it gently before releasing her grip. "We haven't met formally but I've heard about the great work you've done with the Web and Digital Comm team."

"Thanks." Sameera plunged her hands into her pockets, embarrassed by her chewed nails.

Voula shook hands with Agatha and Goldie, offering the same genuine smile. "Agatha, nice to see you again. And, Goldie, right? I heard about your wiki from a couple of directors. I hear it's going to make it a lot easier to find reports. Personally, I needed that." Voula chuckled at her own joke, and when Sameera caught Agatha and Goldie laughing along she rolled her eyes and frowned. *Have you lost your minds, people?!*

"Thanks," Goldie murmured, gathering her wind-whipped hair and glancing at Agatha for direction.

"It's a beautiful view, isn't it?" Faiza asked, looking over her shoulder at the lake. "We came up for some air."

Sameera's heart raced, feeling cornered, her body ready to fight, as she considered her next steps. *They must have heard everything. About Goldie, about me. Fuck! Fuck! Fuck! But what can they do? Warn HR. Warn Crawley. Get me fired today. But on what grounds? I haven't done anything wrong. Does that even matter?!* Her eyes flitted from director to director, surveilling expressions and gathering intel. She tried to lock eyes with Agatha, desperate for reassurance that she was not alone in this trap.

"Yeah, it is really nice." Agatha agreed with Faiza, smiling and turning to face the lake. Sameera scowled, staring intensely at the back of Agatha's head. *What the fuck?! Why are we talking about the view?! Jesus, Agatha!*

"I think I can see the other shore," Voula joined in. "Is that the States? Or, is it still Canada?"

"Hmm. Good question." Agatha headed toward the railing without a glance backward.

Voula followed, thinking aloud, "Would it be Niagara-on-the-Lake?"

Don't go! What the fuck?! Come back. Come back! At a loss for how to conduct herself in the company of Faiza Hosseini after that messed up conversation about the vending machines, she cycled through aspersions and reproofs, unable to settle on a statement that positioned her on the moral high ground.

"Goldie," said Faiza as she stepped closer to the young woman, setting off alarms for Sameera. "I overheard that your job situation has changed. Is that right?"

Oh, sneaky, sneaky. Sameera clenched her jaw and narrowed her gaze. At this point, she might be frustrated and fatigued by Goldie's ignorance but she remained protective of the young woman. She feared Faiza's charisma, her underhanded way of upholding the conformist agenda. *Goldie is no match for her. She probably doesn't even know who Hosseini is.*

Goldie nodded slowly in response, securing her hair with one hand and smoothing it out with the other. She murmured, "Yeah, I got laid off." Sameera winced, willing Goldie to stop revealing any information to Faiza. *Don't say anything else. You can't trust her. Please, stop talking. Please.*

"I'm surprised to hear that," said Faiza, without taking her eyes off Goldie. "I thought there was still a deal of work required on the wiki."

To Sameera's horror, Goldie's face lit up. For a time, the young woman nodded with eyes wide and mouth agape, her words slow to gain traction. Once she started, she sped ahead, "Yeah, there is. There's a lot of work still to do. I mean, I didn't even fill it in. I filled it, yeah, but only enough for the presentation. You know, for it to look real. There's all this other data that needs to be added and organized. I think it needs lots of time. The articles I read — about information architecture — said that it's more of a team project because you need buy-in from people. I think that makes sense, 'cuz people know what they want where, you know. Still, there's lots to do just to make the protocols for adding files and reports and ...." Goldie continued to explain herself at length while Sameera watched Faiza's expression. *What the fuck are you up to? Oh, Goldie, just shut up!*

Suddenly, Faiza was leading Goldie to a nearby bench. Sameera rushed to Agatha who was discussing architecture with Voula, their forearms perched on the stone ledge and their hair fluttering in the breeze. Nothing seemed right. One minute they were talking about filing complaints, and the next they were chatting about the weather and the view. Regardless of the directors' intentions, they had divided and conquered their trio. *Not me!*

Sidling up to Agatha, Sameera hissed in her ear, "Hosseini is squeezing Goldie for information."

Picking up on Sameera's hostility, Voula excused herself to check her phone.

"Goldie has no information," Agatha reminded her, pulling an errant hair from the corner of her own mouth. "She got laid off, and that's not a secret."

"Yeah, but if she plans to file an application with the Commission, then—"

"Can we dial it back?" Agatha requested, a kind smile encouraging Sameera to accept her advice. "Goldie's an adult, right? She decides what happens. We're just here to help, when she asks for it."

Sameera paced in a tight circle and shook her head, incredulous. "This isn't about her independence. She just doesn't understand these things. She doesn't know who she's dealing with." Sameera nodded in the direction of Faiza. On the bench and out of earshot, the older woman was sitting upright, her eyes smiling, her gaze locked on Goldie who talked with her hands dancing in the air, her hair whipping about her head. The scene reminded Sameera of the wicked queen, disguised as a peddler, approaching Snow White with a bright red apple. *She'll poison her.*

"I think you're reading this all wrong," Agatha tried to talk her down. "Faiza's all about empowering women."

"No, that's not true," Sameera insisted. She felt invisible, unseen, and unheard. Shoulder to shoulder, facing opposite directions, Sameera whispered her pleas into Agatha's ear. "You don't know her. She only cares about herself. She doesn't care about helping anyone else. Do you know the inclusivity initiatives are hers? She'd do anything for a promotion. She doesn't care about Goldie. She's probably spying for Goldie's manager, Patricia. You can't trust her. I know." Waiting for acknowledgement — a sign that Agatha recognized the imminent danger to Goldie — Sameera stared at the concrete floor, unwilling to see the blue sky.

"I'm not so sure." Agatha admitted, exuding sympathy for Sameera, not uncertainty about the director. She touched Sameera's shoulder without resting her hand. "I think she might be trying to help."

Sameera scoffed and shrugged. *This is pointless.* "I've gotta get back," Sameera announced as she turned to the stairway. The wind swallowed her words but she didn't bother to repeat herself. *I've lost enough time today.*

Chapter 8

Monday Afternoon, June 25, 2018

Goldie walked alongside Faiza Hosseini as they toured the tenth floor. She was enamoured by the posh director who seemed to own the floor, encountering smiles and greetings at every turn. This woman and Goldie's mother belonged to the same generation of Iranian women, but they shared little else. Shoulders squared, the director walked with a degree of confidence rarely exhibited by Fereshteh Sheer, a woman who stooped under the weight of her worries. Goldie had attributed her mother's worry lines and hunched back to her generation and ancestry — physical traits shared among her mother's friends, all middle-aged Iranian women. Now realizing that she had stereotyped a generation of women, she felt foolish. It was an act she would have decried were it perpetuated against her. *She's just another person.*

The tour was the director's idea, a generous offer to familiarize Goldie with the marketing, promotions, and strategic planning teams at City Hall.

"Networking is key to career success," the director had advised, and Goldie had glanced at Agatha who nodded reassuringly. Sameera had disappeared but Goldie had not cared. From the observation deck, they descended to the tenth floor, where Agatha and the other director branched off, leaving Goldie in Faiza Hosseini's care. Since then, she'd zigzagged and met a half-dozen sharply dressed people whose titles both impressed and puzzled her. At a busy smartboard and cluttered conference table, the director paused again. Now, they were surrounded by a constellation of cubicles and moving bodies.

"This is where my team collaborates on active projects," she said proudly. "It sounds cliché but teamwork is essential to getting the results we want."

Goldie nodded, eager to make a good impression. She racked her brain for an intelligent question but nothing occurred to her. Desperate to signal her interest, she stood taller and lifted her lids. Three women at the smartboard engaged Faiza Hosseini, creating a cluster that tightened as the director entered the conversation. These women were in their element. They understood the labels, charts, and figures that covered the smartboard. Goldie felt like a child visiting a grown up at work. *This's crazy. This whole day's been crazy. What am I even doing here? What's networking, anyway?*

Smiling warmly, the director extended her arm to Goldie and broke her dispirited spell. "I'd like to introduce you to Goldie Sheer. She created the wiki that'll open up access to the transit database."

"Excellent," one woman remarked, evoking agreement from the others. "It makes so much sense."

As Goldie shook hands with the trio, the director offered an overview of the project presented on the smartboard. "It's currently being deployed, which can be a shaky time. Things can look good on paper but projects need adjusting, to make them work out there." At this sentiment, the group chuckled knowingly, and Goldie smiled along, feeling grateful to have grasped the gist of the comment.

"We'll leave you to it," the director said, pulling away from the group. Goldie offered a small and silent wave to the friendly faces. The two walked a short distance before they arrived at a prominent corner office, bearing Faiza Hosseini's name plate — an office that was significantly more distinguished than Patricia's. It was at this time when Goldie realized that a director was senior in rank to a manager. *Faiza Hosseini's a bigger boss than Patricia.*

"Please, make yourself comfortable." The director motioned to the chairs across from her desk as she unloaded her phone and handbag. "Would you like something to drink? There's coffee, tea, and cold drinks in the kitchen. I also have some bottled water here. Room temperature."

Goldie declined politely and took a seat, placing her bag on her lap and making sure to not hug it for comfort. For the last half-hour, the director had introduced her to a series of random people who outlined their work upon prompting. She did not know what she was supposed to take away from these encounters but each interaction was friendly and authentic. While she had already forgotten names and facts, an impression of a fellowship remained with her — a distinct difference from the hostility she experienced on the ninth floor.

"So, what do you think?" The director asked, leaning back in her chair, and smoothing out her skirt.

"Your office is really nice," Goldie answered, looking about approvingly.

The director smiled, amused. "Thank you. And, about the team? Can you see yourself contributing to their work?"

Um-mana. Um-mana. What?! Goldie swallowed and clutched her handbag to herself. She opened her mouth, and then closed. She looked from one corner to another. *Am I supposed to know what you're talking about? Did I miss something?* Squinting, she managed, "Pardon?"

The director leaned forward and crossed her arms on the desk. She smiled pleasantly, patiently. "From your presentation on Friday, I understood that you'd like to continue on at City Hall. Is that right?"

"Yes." Goldie felt her mind taking leaps to catch up with Faiza Hosseini. *OMG. OMG. O. M. G. She wants to hire me. She wants to hire me. Ah!*

"I'd like to hear your ideas on how you imagine contributing to this team." The director gestured with her eyes to the people beyond her closed office door.

"Right. Right." Goldie bought time trying to recall the projects people had mentioned. For a moment, she nodded without speaking. Her mind stalled, unable to formulate an idea, but her mouth sputtered ahead. "There's a lot I think I can do for the team. I can help. I can organize … stuff. I'm good with computers. I can do a lot on computers." *Stupid, stupid, stupid.*

Repulsed by her own blathering, Goldie tugged nervously at the ends of her hair. She wanted to impress Faiza Hosseini, to land her next job. Her internal engine revved, fuelled by the persistent fear that each job offer might be her last. The momentum that propelled her forward blurred her field of vision, and she careened headlong toward an unknown destination, a job without a title or a description.

The director seemed unfazed by Goldie's scattered response. She nodded along and smiled kindly. "What type of experience do you have with databases?"

There was a knock on the door. The director raised a finger, instructing Goldie to hold her thought, and called out, "Come in."

A suited man drenched in cologne opened the door and chatted with the director from the doorway. He requested her attendance at a last-minute conference call. While she asked him follow-up questions and browsed her calendar, Goldie searched for an intelligent answer about her work experience. She came across an unfamiliar voice, that of a reluctant young woman who wanted answers to her own questions. *What is this job? What does she want me to do? What's in it for me?* Goldie silenced this voice, *Losers can't be choosers.* She persisted, and memories surfaced and fused into a coherent story about her work at the university.

Once they were alone, the director gestured for Goldie to continue. This time, she replied with greater confidence. "I've worked with databases a lot. I did a bunch of work for my department chair. Actually, it became a thing all the profs used — the ones in my department. It was a database. I didn't code or anything. It's a free program, open source. It stored research contacts but with a lot of search parameters. It connected with the file system, too. They could see the docs for each contact. I sorted the data and the tags, and a bunch of other stuff. They still use it." She paused, unable to think of any other details, and the director waited patiently. "Yup, that's it." Goldie offered a half-smile and a shrug.

"That sounds relevant." The director leaned back in her chair, crossed her arms and glanced at the ceiling. "I think you'd do well with Gemi and Ahmya. They could use help with sorting their field data."

Goldie nodded in response but she did not know to what she was agreeing. All she wanted to do was please this woman, this powerful person who could set things right. Questions stacked upon concerns as she digested this turn of events. *What's happening? Am I hired? I don't code. Does she think I code? What's field data? Don't I have to fill out an application, or something? Why is she hiring me?*

"I need a day to get everyone caught up," the director concluded. She came around the desk, perched on its edge, and interlaced her fingers.

I did it. I got the job. She had reached a destination but she was lost. The reluctant voice grew louder. *Stop agreeing to everything! You're not her bitch.* With a modicum of courage, Goldie raised her eyes to meet the director's and asked softly, "Thank you, but why are you hiring me?"

For an instant, Faiza Hosseini frowned and Goldie feared she'd upset the director. Then, her brows relaxed and the worry lines faded. The director exhaled and swallowed, gazing at her own hands and nodding to herself as she arrived at her answer.

"Your presentation on Friday, it impressed me. You spotted a break in the system. You came up with a viable fix. You went above and beyond to help your team members."

Goldie chortled inadvertently, and then blushed with

embarrassment. "Sorry. I wasn't laughing at you. I just. Sorry. Forget about it."

The director seemed amused. Tilting her head to one side, a smile at the corner of her lips, she insisted, "Please, go on. Why is it so hard to believe I want to hire you?"

Slightly panicked, Goldie stammered, "No. No. Not like that. I just … When you said I went above and beyond to help my co-workers, I thought … Well, I don't think they would see it that way." *Definitely not.* Goldie imagined Beth's disdainful reaction to the wiki.

The director nodded, signalling Goldie to continue. She did not know what to say. She feared she might say something self-incriminating, something that might cause the director to reconsider her job offer. Yet, more than she wanted to secure a full time job and prove herself, Goldie wanted to be free of drama. She did not want to be treated like a prize or a pariah. She wanted to work with people who saw her as a person, not a problem or a pet project. Faiza Hosseini's abrupt job offer reminded Goldie of Patricia's overly generous compliments. *No fucking way I'm going through that again.*

Hugging her bag to her chest, Goldie took the plunge. "I wasn't perfect at my job. I make a bunch of mistakes. I fixed them but I still made mistakes. And the other admins didn't like me. At. All. They barely talked to me. The one who trained me was …." She realized she was crying when the director held out a box of tissues for her. "Thanks." She wiped her face and nose. "She was really mean. From the first day. And, she was not happy about the wiki. She was pis — She was really mad. Anyways, no one liked me there." Goldie deflated in her seat, gripping her bag and preparing to be escorted out. She glanced at the director, who was leaning forward and staring at the floor, a spot midway between their shoes. *There goes the job.*

"Patricia seemed to think highly of you. On Friday, she made quite the case for your staying on here."

If Goldie's nose weren't stuffed-up, she would have snorted at that comment. Instead, she shrugged and shook her head. "I thought so."

"Well, she convinced me. I think you'd be an asset to this team." From the nearby counter, the director offered Goldie a bottle of water. "They need someone with fresh ideas about sharing data. You've got the right mindset for breaking down barriers. We can teach you the business concepts and anything you need about the programs. That's easy enough, over time. What matters is that you have the right attitude."

Goldie drank heartily, grateful for the opportunity to close her eyes as she tipped back her head. *She still wants to hire me. No cap.* It could have been hunger that was making her combative but she wanted to fire her last round. "What happens with my old job?"

The director considered her question but revealed nothing. When the silence became unbearable, Goldie rephrased her question, "Agatha said that … I'm thinking of … making a complaint."

"Okay," said the director, unfazed. She took the seat beside Goldie's, pivoting the chair to face her. Goldie wondered whether Faiza Hosseini was tricking her in some way. Suddenly, the conversation felt dangerous and she wished Agatha were here — even Sameera would do. She felt trapped by her words, unsure how to continue the conversation safely.

This time, the director broke the silence. "I presume there are people you trust, people who can advise you about the process."

Goldie nodded, thinking of Issa and Effie, her parents, Agatha, Sameera.

"Good. They can help you with the next steps." The director paused to smile at Goldie. When Goldie returned a small smile, the director continued. "My objective is to build a strong team. I've worked very hard to bring together people who are creative and intelligent, open-minded. When I meet someone who fits, I seize the opportunity."

More questions stacked up in Goldie's mind. She set aside the practical ones, about start dates and hourly pay, and considered the ones which were emotionally fraught, the ones spoken by the reluctant voice. *How can I trust you? At first, Patricia was nice, too.* Foremost in her thoughts were Agatha's cues about Patricia — her inaction in the face of harassment, her scapegoating Goldie to appease the others. *Some assholes don't even realize they're assholes.* She had overlooked the self-serving nature of Patricia's benevolence, repeatedly. Every time Patricia buried her under praise or disinterred her ethnicity, Goldie had brushed it off. It was not enough to focus on her goals like her mother had advised; she needed to assert herself and keep other people in check.

"I really appreciate the offer. It sounds really good but if it's alright with you, I'd like some time to think about it."

"Of course," the director agreed. "I'll have HR send over a contract. We can talk in a few days."

Seriously?! That's all it takes. Goldie was stunned by the simplicity of buying time. Simultaneously, she felt mature and pompous. Making every effort to sound humble, she replied. "Okay, thanks. I appreciate it. I just need a little time. Thank you."

As she rode the elevator and walked out of City Hall, Goldie thought about Issa. She'd warned Goldie about her blind spot, her reluctance to talk about race. Goldie had rejected Issa's warning because her message had been infuriating. Goldie identified as just Canadian, even in a family of self-proclaimed Iranian Canadians. No matter how she dressed, what she ate, or where she shopped, she was firstly Canadian. But there were always people who wanted to classify her another way — whether it was as an Iranian Canadian, Canadian Iranian, or Iranian immigrant. *What do I care what other people think of me?* For a long time, she'd managed to not think about her race. She'd hoped the world would catch up to her sensibilities. She was practised at ignoring slights and slurs.

She could choose to ignore what others think, and she did. *Till I worked for them. Till they tried to take me down.*

Outside, observing the differences among the stream of pedestrians for the first time, Goldie realized that Issa's insistence on addressing race and colour was not that off the mark, but she still was not ready to think about it. *Why? Why do I have to think about that? Does Patricia do that? Does Beth? So, why do I have to? Why do I always have to say I'm Iranian?! They get to be Canadian — I'm Canadian!* The last thing she wanted was to talk about race — not her own, not other people's. *People say stupid shit — racist shit — when they don't have to say anything at all.* There were so many conversations she'd endured; well-intentioned people who asked small-minded questions which they expected her to answer. The answers were rote for Goldie. As necessary, she recited them with detachment for the well-intentioned person. *Nope, I'm not a refugee; I was born at North York General. Yup, English is my first language. Nope, I don't speak Arabic; Iranians speak Farsi, and no, I don't read or write Farsi. I can speak Farsi but less than fluently.* Now, Issa had challenged her to acknowledge race, and Goldie wanted to do anything but.

She marched away from City Hall, clenching her jaw to keep from crying in public again. Soon she had joined the stream of people: she was just another person. *Just another person desperate to get home.* At the clogged and crooked intersection of Queen and Bay streets, people swarmed about an eastbound streetcar's double doors. Goldie joined them. Aboard, she settled against the small strip of window and wall across from the exit. Despite the uncomfortable closeness of others, the music blasting in her ears, and the streetscape, Goldie's mind returned to the one thought: *Issa understood weeks ago. She saw Patricia even without meeting her. She got it before me. Fuck, I still don't get it really.* The thought of Patricia triggered such resentment at her helplessness that she could not stop herself from crying again, blinking rapidly in a feeble attempt to stem the tears. She chided herself, *Patricia is a fucking vampire! She stole my wiki — and instead of getting me a job, she laid me off.* She still wondered, earnestly, *Why me?! I was so good.*

Issa's words surfaced, "… you don't want to admit that you're not white, or, that white people treat you badly because you're not white." *Yes, I don't want to admit that; who'd want to?!* With the cuff of her sleeve, Goldie caught a stray tear, blurring her view of Queen Street life. *Is that what Patricia did? Did she fire me 'cuz it's easier than firing the white people?* Shame gripped her tighter as she considered how she had spent weeks admiring a woman who used her. In her chest, a muscle tugged painfully. A sob threatened to escape. She tried to think other thoughts, anything to stop from crying on transit. She scrolled through cat pictures and bird videos. Out of habit, she shared her favourites with Issa.

The tightness began to loosen but her mind was still reeling. *Maybe Issa's not telling me to label myself. Maybe, she wants me to read the labels people stick to me; to know what it says about those people, their prejudices.* Goldie straightened up as she caught hold of the tail end of a new understanding: Patricia uplifted Goldie to diminish her own guilt. *Wait, what?* And as it threatened to slip out of her grasp, she redoubled her efforts, causing her to say aloud, "She cared until it was inconvenient!"

Goldie recoiled in embarrassment at her public outburst, pulling herself even closer to the window. The faces of Beth, Patricia, Sandra, and Holly haunted her thoughts. *I never want to see any of them again.* And, she did not have to see any of them because she was not returning to that office or to that team. *I'm working for Faiza Hosseini, boss.* Once she did return to work, Goldie would start over with a new boss. *No more keeping quiet when things are that bad. No more putting people on pedestals — keep it real. It's gonna be fucking awesome!*

With this thought, the tightness dissipated. Her muscles ached from overuse but she could breathe more easily. She had stopped crying, and realized that she was very hungry. Her phone pinged. It was Issa. *Lunch?* In quick succession, Issa added: *near city hall; at least 15min; sushi? burgs?*

Goldie answered in a series of replies: *on streetcar; going east. almost at church.*

Issa sent an array of happy emojis, followed by *good. im at jarvis. sushi wins!*

ok but no more vomiting! Goldie snickered, and she did not care who caught her laughing to herself as she disembarked the streetcar.

ODG. I puked once. once. that's normal.

normal??? we. need. to. talk. Goldie piled on the goofy emojis but she did want to talk to Issa. She just had not sorted out what she wanted to say.

Turning eastward onto Queen, Goldie slowed her gait. She could see Issa standing steps from the doors of the compact sushi bar — *she can't bear sitting alone.* Her intimate knowledge of Issa's quirks caused Goldie to smile. *Issa's boss. Fucking boss. She loves me. We're a fucking boss team.* On the front steps, the friends hugged. Together, they entered the eatery.

* * *

Hunched over her keyboard, Sameera picked at her large salad with a plastic fork. In a half-hour, she was due at a managers' meeting, followed by her own team meeting, and then a jog over to the West Tower where she was to attend software training. This gap in her schedule was her last chance to eat lunch, and she was determined to perform this small act of self-care, as the first step toward reconnecting with her body. *I need to get back to normal. I can't pretend I don't need sleep or proper meals or exercise.*

She'd grabbed the pre-packaged salad from City Café, deciding against the more alluring choice, a grilled cheese sandwich and fries. At the time, the bed of dark greens with bits of red and orange toppings had looked healthy, even attractive. Now, she raked limp leaves in search of cranberries and cashews, the only ingredients that seemed edible. *I should've bought the grilled cheese, or the fries. I could have salad and fries. After this morning, I deserve the fries.*

It had been a morning to remember. The conversations on the deck had disturbed her inordinately — a clear signal that she was out of touch with the present moment and responding to past trauma. Goldie reminded Sameera of her younger self when she had been exploited by co-workers and employers, used to further an agenda that did not involve her interests. She had learned from the experiences but she had never seen justice. There had been no truth-telling, no reconciliations, and no reparations. The wounds to her spirit remained, and they required constant care on her part — her acknowledgement of the trauma, her unconditional compassion toward herself, and the absolute primacy of her needs. To sustain good mental health — to live a life worth living — she had to prioritize her needs. Otherwise, the wound might develop into sepsis and poison her.

For months now, she'd ignored the signals that an infection had developed. Anxiety, anger, isolation, and inadequacy were poisoning her mind, body, and spirit. She had the sensation of slipping out of herself and disconnecting from her humanity. She remembered a conversation with Masoumeh from the previous year when she had declared, *I feel so grounded. I can hear myself really clearly. You know, I used to hear other people's voices better than I could hear my own. I was consumed by their … problems. It'd always felt more … urgent, to be there for other people.* How long had it been since she had heard her own voice, prioritized her own needs?

She recalled her decision to file a complaint against Crawley. This voice was her own, clearly demanding acknowledgement, compassion, and primacy. To advocate on her own behalf, to prioritize her experience and her needs, to pay much-needed attention to her infected wound. Agatha had assured Sameera that she had allies at City Hall, co-workers who shared Sameera's opinion of the CM's behaviour. Although she had been reluctant to accept this news, she recognized that it had affected her already — the air had been easier to breathe as she passed others, en route to her cubicle. *I need distance, to listen to myself. Figure out what's good for me. Take care of me first.*

With renewed effort, she plunged the fork into the salad. *Like a grown woman who knows what's good for her.* When she lifted a forkful to her mouth, the precarious pile of berries and nuts fell back into the bowl, and all that remained was a few speared leaves. Grimacing, Sameera dropped the fork back into the container and banished the salad to the far edges of her desk. *Like a grown woman who knows when to cut her losses.* From her bag, she grabbed the opened bag of dried fruit and chewed one at a time.

In a new light, she considered the morning's conversations. If it weren't tragic, Goldie's incredulity at being the target of racism might have been laughable. *She tried so hard to figure out why they hated her. She was certain she'd done something, something she could fix. She couldn't accept they'd hated her before they even knew her. They hated the idea of her, and when she was present, they hated her in person.* Sameera did not begrudge Goldie's drive to identify a transgression, some misdeed on her own part that might explain the hostility of her co-workers. *She'll come to her own conclusions.*

She remembered Agatha's counsel, *When we feel less vulnerable, we're ready to demand more.* Sameera thought that it had been a long time since she was in Goldie's predicament, unable to recognize and address injustice. Hadn't she overcome the psychological leg traps with their false dichotomies — dignity versus power, dissent versus harmony? Now, she suspected that she had been trapped again for some time. *Why didn't I go to HR? I know better than Goldie. I should've ....*

Shannon's framed picture, placed at the corner of her desk, caught her eye, answering her question. Sameera recalled the anxiety that had debilitated her after their ghastly fight. That night, it had seemed possible that Shannon might not return to their apartment, that their relationship was over. For hours, Sameera had cried in the dark, haunted by the angry words she had hurled at Shannon. Only recently had these words ceased echoing in the caverns of her psyche and reverberating panic at the thought of losing Shannon. These past weeks, she had lived in suspense, in search of signs, proof that their relationship was healing and it would endure. *When we feel vulnerable, we don't make demands.*

Sameera wiped away the tears that had collected at her chin. *I love Shannon. We love each other. But Shannon doesn't respect me. She tolerates me.* Shannon's rebukes played back, revealing the depth of her mistrust. *It's the world against Sam. Everything is a personal attack against you. Why would people attack you? You're fucking paranoid. Not everything is about race. You're nuts!* In their relationship, Shannon defined the terms of injustice and determined individual liability. In Shannon's opinion, she was an impartial judge, a blank slate. *And I'm too close to the issue, too brown, to think clearly, judge fairly. She doesn't trust my take. She thinks I'm unreliable. How am I supposed to count on her? How do I feel less vulnerable when Shannon doesn't have my back? How am I supposed to be strong enough to make demands when Shannon thinks I'm overreacting, paranoid?* Shannon's picture caught her eye. Sameera lunged for the framed portrait, knocking it over and into the salad bowl, scattering bits about her desk and keyboard.

"Oh, fuck!" Sameera muttered to herself. As she shook her keyboard over the trash bin to dislodge the grains and seeds trapped in its nooks, Agatha appeared.

"Clean up in aisle one?" She joked in the entryway of the cubicle. In one hand, she spun her phone, and in the other, she held a tall pink smoothie from City Café.

Sameera did not make an effort to smile as she brushed the debris from her desktop into the bin. Suddenly, she felt very tired, too tired for banter. Agatha picked up on her mood and asked, "Everything okay? Should I go?"

"No, no. Come in." Sameera waved her in, gesturing toward the spare chair. She picked off a couple of specks from her cream palazzos, grateful that she had not topped the salad with dressing, and then slumped in her chair, swivelling to face Agatha. "Sorry, I … I just … ." Her words quavered, and soon she had to bite her lip to keep from crying.

Agatha untucked her feet and leaned forward. She pressed Sameera's knee with her fingertips, and only for a moment. They sat in silence until Sameera caught her breath and wiped her nose.

"I'm sorry," Sameera said, gesturing at herself, her emotionality. "Long day." After her tantrum on the deck, she wanted to balance her agitation with composure. *Agatha deserves a good boss, a grown-up boss.* "I have a meeting in fifteen but I'm free right now. Did you need something?"

"No. Just saying hi." Agatha proffered the smoothie. When Sameera hesitated, she insisted. "I got it for you. I remember you said you like the Strawberry Shortcake blend."

"Thanks." She accepted the cup and took a long pull. The flavour was heavenly, the perfect blend of sweet and tangy. "It's good. Thanks." Sameera smiled but she felt unsettled. "Agatha, I wasn't behaving … very well … I behaved badly, upstairs, and out front. I was pushy, and I wasn't listening. I want to apologize. I'm sorry about that." She paused to glance at Agatha, to gauge her reaction and grant room for a response.

Agatha sat with feet tucked under herself and hands stacked in her lap. "Okay, thanks. It's all good."

"Yeah?" Sameera probed gently.

"Yeah. You were worried. I get that."

Sameera leaned back, grateful for Agatha's generous take. "Everything okay with Goldie?"

Agatha nodded and smiled. "Yup. She's good. Getting a tour with Faiza."

At the director's name, Sameera shuddered. Agatha laughed. "She's not that bad. You two have a lot in common."

"Oh, come on!" Sameera rebuked, rolling her eyes as she began gathering her belongings for the managers' meeting.

"Seriously," insisted Agatha, swivelling her chair in a semi-circle. "Her tactics are more mainstream than yours but she pushes the same left-of-centre ideas. Equity. Inclusivity. Distributive justice."

"Okay, now you're just throwing about jargon," Sameera teased. She drank most of the smoothie, checked her messages, and then packed her phone.

Gazing upward and counting on her fingers, Agatha listed more terms. "Normative economics, poverty measurement, practical idealism, Tickle Me Elmo, kale chips—"

Sameera laughed out loud, and raised her hands in surrender. "I get it. You know words."

After a moment, Agatha's smile faded. She squinted at Sameera, then announced theatrically, "Awkward question time."

Sameera squirmed under her gaze. She glanced at her smartwatch, looking for an out, but she conceded. "Okay. Shoot."

Agatha sat upright and asked plainly, "Are we … friends?"

"Uh, yeah, sure. We're friends." Sameera tried to sound confident though the same question had occurred to her. "I think we're friends."

"Okay, me too." Agatha nodded vigorously.

"Okay." Sameera nodded along. "Good."

"'Cuz you can talk to me about … stuff. I mean, I'm more than a beautiful face." Agatha grinned. "Yes, I'm highly intelligent, and incredibly humble, but I'm also a Grade-A listener, if you feel like talking."

Sameera chuckled and took another long pull from the smoothie. "Thanks. That sounds really good. Maybe we can grab a coffee, after work sometime? Maybe you can tell me about your incredibly humble existence?"

"Sounds good." Agatha smiled and resumed swivelling her chair.

Agatha's friendship had alleviated the pain of her social problems at work and her messy emotional life at home. Just thinking about some of their running jokes had Sameera chuckling. She envisioned Agatha joining her and her friends at Sunday brunch or Trivia Night. *She's so easy to talk to. I feel like we can share ideas really easily.*

Giddy about their blossoming friendship, Sameera blurted, "Where are you from?" She cringed at her own question even before she'd finished asking it. Chewing on her lower lip, she apologized, "Shit, that was so wrong. Sorry, Agatha. That was a racism in the workplace for sure."

Agatha nodded and shrugged, and then she admitted, "I guessed you're Iranian. Or is it Persian?" She paused her swivelling and offered her friend a sympathetic smile. "So, I guess I did a racism in the workplace, too."

The friends locked eyes and delivered lines at once.

Agatha gasped, her mouth open unnaturally, "'The horror, the horror ….'"

Sameera played a hokey accent, "'Nobody's perfect.'"

A pause followed as the women considered each other's quotes.

"*The Thing*? Or, *The Blob*?" Sameera wagered. "I don't know."

"*Apocalypse Now*."

Sameera leaned back. "Ah. Never seen it … don't judge!"

"I would never," Agatha raised a hand to swear her oath. "I haven't seen it either. 'I know it the same way we know anything.'"

"*The Simpsons*!" Sameera guessed, just as Agatha said, "Wikipedia."

"Cool, cool. Mine's from *Some Like It Hot*. I did see—" Suddenly recalling her itinerary, Sameera checked her phone. "Oh, time to go. Managers' meeting."

Agatha hopped to her feet. "With the dynamic duo?" she asked, referring to Courtney Moore and Lindsey Martin.

"Yup," Sameera answered, undocking her laptop.

"That all feels … okay?" Agatha lingered at the entryway, rocking on the spot.

Sameera straightened up and smiled with confidence. "What's there to worry about? Word has it, everybody loves me. Apparently, I'm a superstar. A managerial goddess. Brilliant, beautiful, and oh, the humblest, too."

"Fo' sho," agreed Agatha as she turned to go. "See you at the team meeting."

"See ya there."

Sameera drank the last of the smoothie and tucked her laptop under her arm. As she walked the halls, smiling and nodding at passersby, she reconsidered signing up for the Women in Tech conference.

* * *

Faiza stared at the rear lights of the cars ahead, a procession that travelled in spurts along the distinctly suburban Kingston Road. At this rate, she would arrive home in time to join the others at the dinner table. *There might even be time for a shower first.* The events of the day had exhausted her thoroughly. She wanted to rub her eyes with her fists, the way Pari did when she was tired. Instead, she rubbed her temple to keep from smudging her makeup. *A long shower and stretchy pants.*

Traffic moved ahead in spurts and Faiza's thoughts returned to work. The meeting with the bigwigs was the greatest disappointment of her career. Still, she felt more powerful knowing the truth about their attitudes and intentions. She could work with the truth, and presently, the truth precipitated change.

Initially, she'd wanted to resign, start afresh. Voula had warned her that she would face the same hurdles elsewhere but she did not plan to run the same race again. This time, she would apply exclusively for the top jobs. If she failed to secure a chief executive position, she would start her own venture. Indeed, the thought of getting out from under Howard's thumb had been very appealing, and by the end of her conversation with Voula, she had been set to resign from City Hall.

Then, Goldie came along. Lost in thought, Faiza nearly rear-ended the car in front of her. She swore at herself for driving distractedly but a moment later she had returned to thinking about her encounter with the young administrator. Goldie might as well have been Mina because her daughter was all Faiza could think about as Goldie described her experience working with Patricia and her team. Their career paths were not alike. *I should think so, considering I expect Mina to start her own practice after getting her doctorate. Still, it's their drive — their determination to prove themselves — that's the same!* Mina planned to change the world. Goldie planned to be indispensable. *They deserve a chance. They won't get far without help.*

Until today, Faiza had slept soundly believing that she had paved the way for Mina's progress toward power, status, and wealth. After the meeting with the top brass and the conversation with Goldie, she feared that she had underestimated the obstructions to her daughter's success. Goldie's experience reminded Faiza that white women subjugated women of colour, too. Privilege was a commodity that white men dispensed drop by drop, and it did not trickle down to women of colour, who stood beneath men and white women. *How's Mina supposed to make it to the top in a system set to keep her down?* It seemed very likely that Mina would hit a glass ceiling, as Faiza had. *Then, what? Is she going to go at it alone? What if she becomes a head surgeon or a diplomat?*

After her meeting with Goldie, Faiza attempted to create a plan of action, present-day tactics to circumvent future injustices against Mina. One calculating idea stacked atop another as she considered how to bribe and coerce the heads of corporations and secure Mina's ascent. *If we pick her field now, I can join the right boards of directors, maybe create a foundation.* She had been confident of her plan until she thought about Pari and the impracticality of influencing leaders of two disparate fields. *I can't save them both.*

At a loss, she had stared out her office window, searching the clear blue sky for insight. The answers came from within as Faiza recalled Voula's warnings. *There's no getting away. We need to fight this. We can't keep playing their game.* Voula had sounded severe, almost radical. Yet, Faiza trusted her friend's judgement, and the more she considered Voula's missives, the more she questioned her own conviction in manipulating the system. *If I'm so good at playing the game, why am I losing to a halfwit like Jeffery?*

That afternoon, she had left a message on Adaego's voicemail. "I thought we could have lunch this week. I think we have a lot in common." She had some ideas about how to approach the inequities they had faced but mostly she wanted to hear from another likeminded woman of colour. She wanted to hear Adaego's take on recent events.

On the dashboard mount, her phone rang. It was Robert. *He probably thinks I'm still at work.*

"Hi love, I'm twenty minutes away," she answered smugly. Then, added with greater modesty, "Traffic's moving along."

"Great." He sounded pleased, unsurprised. "Dinner's pasta Bolognese with asparagus — from the farmers' mall." He paused, she oohed generously, and they chuckled at their inside joke. In the background, she heard Pari protest. Robert explained, more for Pari's benefit than Faiza's, "There's also buttered peas — for anyone who doesn't want to branch out."

"And Mina's good?"

"Yup, right here, doing … I want to say … safety checking the dining chairs?" Robert's smile could be heard in his voice.

"Probably playing on her phone when she said she would help with dinner. Here, your mom's on the phone!"

A moment later, Mina murmured, "Hey mum."

"Hi, sweetheart. How was your day?"

"Good."

"Good." Faiza stalled, unsure whether she wanted to know more. *I do, just not on the phone and stuck in traffic.* "Mina, you wanna watch *Tangled* tonight? After dinner?"

"Uh, no."

"We used to—"

"Mauuum," Mina whined. "Please don't."

In an about-face, Faiza was glad they weren't talking in person. *Robert's not a saint but he's got a whole lot more patience talking with Mina.* She let the yellow light catch her, giving her an opportunity to close her eyes and shake out the tension in her neck.

"I just want to spend time with you. Do you want to do something else?"

"No."

"Okay ... so no movie ... no other activities. Hey, how about—"

Mina butted in, "I didn't say I don't want a movie."

"Oh, okay." *This is progress.* "I'm good with a different movie. What were you thinking?"

As if Mina had cupped the phone, her voice came through garbled, "I heard the new Disney movie's good."

Disney? Did she say Disney?! Faiza knew better than to press buttons unnecessarily. She cooed her approval as they agreed to find something that Pari might like.

After a pause, Mina asked, "So, what? You're coming home now?" Faiza could sense Mina's feigned indifference. She actually sounded excited to see her mother.

Faiza smiled to herself, "Yes, just another ten minutes, maybe fifteen."

"Who is this?" Mina's voice boomed. "Who are you, and what have you done with my mother?"

Faiza paused to breathe deeply, to feel lightheartedness once more. She wanted to be light, unburdened by guilt or shame. She managed a comedic groan, and added, "Ha ha! I do try to make time."

"You do," Mina affirmed kindly, sounding very much like the mature woman Faiza imagined her daughter would become. "I know, Mom. Just pulling your leg."

She didn't need to say that but she did, Faiza smiled widely at the thought.

"You want Dad?" Mina asked, and without waiting for an answer continued, "Bye, Mom. Love you."

"Hey," Robert said over the sounds of cutlery hitting the floor, followed by orders and instructions. After a moment, he explained, "Pari is helping set the table."

"Okay. Sounds … good. Does this mean Bibi's not back?" Other than a brief response to Faiza's text message on Saturday — confirming Bibi's safe arrival at her friend's home — Faiza had not heard a word from her mother.

Robert whispered, "She got back this afternoon, and … she let me make dinner all by myself."

Faiza was speechless at this news. Bibi insisted on preparing dinner for the family, every night. It was unlike her to allow Robert or Faiza to cook the evening meal without her presence and instructions. Car horns honked, returning Faiza to the present. The light had turned green and other cars had crossed the intersection. She accelerated to fill the gap.

"Hello?" Robert called.

"Is she mad?" Faiza imagined Bibi confining herself to her bedroom, indignant and inconsolable.

Robert returned to whispering, "No, she's actually really … happy, fine. Just … not bothered. She played with Pari after school.

We had tea on the deck. She says she wants us to go camping — something her friend mentioned. Then I started dinner and she went for a quick walk. Maybe I'm just not picking up on something but I think she's just fine."

Faiza nodded, uncertain about how to interpret Bibi's behaviour. "Okay. Guess we'll see." *She might be fine. Or she might be setting a subdued tone for her departure.* The thought of Bibi leaving sent a shiver through Faiza. She needed her mother to stay with them, to witness her triumphs and learn to trust her choices. *She has to stay. She can't leave like this. She needs to see Robert's not going to leave me, and the girls are fine, better than fine.* Where Bibi feared that Faiza neglected Robert and the girls, Faiza realized that it was their mother-daughter relationship that needed her attention. *I need her to see me.*

"I'm sure it'll be fine." Robert interrupted her thoughts. "How'd your meeting go?"

"I'll tell you all about it." Faiza shook herself free of concern. "Did you need anything from the store?"

"Nah, we don't need anything from the store. I think we have everyth—" Robert was cut off by Pari who began yelling a list of snack foods. Faiza imagined her youngest climbing Robert limb by limb to transmit her message into the receiver.

Addressing Pari, he said, "Okay, okay, please stop shouting. I'm putting it on speaker." The phone clicked, and Faiza heard father and daughter negotiate its placement on the island counter connecting the kitchen and dining room. She envisioned Pari perched on the counter, her face inches away from the phone, and Robert leaning close by, with one arm extended to serve as a railing, safeguarding Pari.

"Okay. It's on speaker … Mama can hear you. It's fine where it is … just leave it on the counter." To Faiza, he joked, "That was cheesies, gummies, licorice, and ice cream sandwiches. You got all that?"

"Sure thing. A bushel of asparagus, coming right up," Faiza quipped as she steered into the right lane and prepared to enter a shopping centre with a supermarket. "Or was that two bushels?"

"No!" Pari objected earnestly, oblivious to the teasing.

"Three bushels," Bibi chimed, her voice distant but clear and playful, "of chips and chocolates!" Her mother's casual tone dulled some of Faiza's apprehensions about their reunion. *She's not upset. She doesn't sound upset.*

"Yes! Yes!" Pari sang. "But not the mint kind. I don't like mint, Mama. I don't want mint."

"*Salaam*, Bibi-*jaan*," Faiza called, listening closely for a change in tone.

"*Salaam, azziz-am,*" Bibi's voice grew louder as she approached the phone.

"Mama, I don't want any mint," Pari repeated with urgency.

"Yes, I understand. No mint," Faiza confirmed, knowing that Pari would persist otherwise. In a softer tone, she addressed her mother, "Bibi, how was your trip? How's Hengameh and Nasser?"

"*Khoob ast-an, khalee khoob.* They're good, very good." The line clicked and the ambient sounds ceased as Faiza was taken off speakerphone. Bibi's voice came through clearly. "They send their regards. Hengameh invited all of you to visit."

"*Hatman.*" Faiza navigated a hectic parking lot, distracted by her own tone. She needed to engage in small talk long enough to convey her humility and affection, her desire to reconcile. "How're Shireen and Sarah? Shireen's eldest just graduated, right? UofT, or was it York? Hengameh must be so proud."

"Everyone's very good. Nasser worries about money but I think they're fine. That's just his way. Always planning two generations ahead."

"That sounds like Nasser. I'm glad you had a nice trip. We missed you." Faiza's voice caught, surprising herself.

"I missed you, too," Bibi replied promptly, evincing her mutual need to reconcile. "It's nice to get away for a bit but honestly, there's no place better than home."

Faiza sighed with relief. "*Khalee bahet mohafegham*, I couldn't agree with you more." She turned off the ignition and released the brake. *She's staying. She's staying.* "Maman-*jaan*, I'm at the store now. Did you need anything?"

"*Nah, merci.*"

"Okay, I won't be long."

"*Naegharan nabasht, azziz-am*. Don't worry, dear. Do what you need to."

Faiza felt the words as they came to rest on her heart. "*Merci, Maman-jaan*. See you soon."

Acknowledgements

Enough consumed me for many hours and for days at a time. When I was present with others, I was lost in thought. At times, I sulked in a sour mood — fretting over the lives of fictional people. The support of my family and friends kept me writing. They helped me progress — and if you can believe, they don't even want accolades! Well, they had better not read the rest of this page.

Andrew, thank you for nudging me forward. On those cloudy days when I barely peeked out from under the blankets, it was your confidence that helped me persevere. Thank you for believing in me, for prioritizing my work, and for cheering me on from the back of the room. I love you, dearly, and I like you a lot.

Mazzy, *meow*. You're my number one fan and I am thrilled. Your enthusiasm and praise remind me to be gentler with myself. Thank you for being the best publicist a mother could ever ask for! I love you more.

Katti, you sure did raise a troublemaker. *Where do I get all my opinions?!* My voice is loud and insistent because of the foundations you laid. Thank you for holding space for me to speak up. I love you with every breath.

Angelina, Jim and Mary, and Ian and Kerri, thank you for asking about my work, for attending readings, and for liking me on Instagram. Your confidence in me goes a long way on bad days. Tell you what, as a thank you gift, I will write all of you into the next novel; any strong objections to being lizards, in a murder mystery? We can talk more over Mary's biscotti. I love the lot of you, darlings.

Meghan and Linda, are you pleased with yourselves?! Now, I've gone and written a third book! All that encouragement, and see what you caused. Thank you for taking my side even when I am standing in shit. You've got open minds and great big hearts, and you teach me how to care for myself like a grown-ass woman. I love you both. Let's go for a walk?

Lisa and Joanne, for the record, I don't know where that key is? If Trish blames me, that's because she's jealous of my rock hard abs. Y'all have been in my corner since the start, even though I act like a hangry teen most days. Thank you for being available and present. Y'all show up! Respect!

Jerry and Marietta, the two most wonderful people in the world. When I learned this manuscript was accepted, I ran directly to your place to share my news. You received me with beautiful encouraging smiles. Thank you for your positivity and friendship. I am blessed.

Mark, thank you for being my buddy, and for letting me run my mouth. It's really nice. You're really nice. Love.

Michele, thanks for listening — hugs.

Misha, tell your lovely people — Navneet, Deeba, and John — thanks, a big wet thanks.

Kristine, seeing you in the audience was a treat — thanks!

Ella and Luke, can you please let Carcar know that your photos wallpaper the happiest place in my heart?

Beverley Rach, thank you for taking another chance on me. It has been a pleasure to work with Roseway and every member of staff. Best. Team. Ever. Thank you.

Anumeha Gokhale and Sanna Wani, thank you for getting this novel out into the world. You create waves of interest for my novel, and I appreciate that very much. I see the work you perform to get my novels seen — my deepest gratitude. Also, thank you simply for being smart and funny women. AG and SW rock!

Fazeela Jiwa, remember the convo about *virtue signalling*? I'm still thinking about it — that's how much I treasured the exchange. It's also a testament to your brilliant editing. Thank you for being such a fabulous editor!

Brenda Conroy and Amber Riaz, thank you for dedicating yourselves to putting out the very best version of the manuscript. I appreciate your thoroughness and attention to detail.

Discussion Questions

1) When Sameera is mistaken for the caterer, she experiences a microaggression. Microaggressions can be verbal, behavioural, environmental, or a combination. What stands out about the receptionist's response? How does Sameera navigate this moment to meet her needs? Did you notice other microaggressions throughout the book?
2) Early on in her time at City Hall, Goldie is questioned about her name. How does her reaction differ from that of other characters, and why do you think that is?
3) How does misogyny impact Goldie's relationship with her brothers? Is gender equality a concern for men? How do societal norms, conceptions of masculinity, and expectations of men shape their behaviour?
4) Goldie's boss Patricia ignores Beth's racism and hostility toward her new employee. Does this affect how Goldie sees Patricia? Does it affect Beth? How does apathy advance white supremacy? On the other hand, why does Patricia acknowledge Goldie's ethnicity before she presents her wiki to the managers?
5) Sameera plans to change City Hall from within, and she disagrees with Faiza's tactics. What do you make of Sameera's reaction to Faiza's advice? How does Sameera's behaviour at work reflect her needs and concerns? Can Sameera "burn it to the ground" from her position within Toronto City Hall?
6) Both Sameera and Shannon have experienced oppression, and both have experienced privilege. Why are they struggling to communicate about oppression and privilege? Why might

Shannon be reluctant to validate Sameera's experience at work?

7) Sameera's sister Masoumeh distinguishes equity from equality. What is the difference between equality and equity? Use examples from the book or your life.
8) Faiza often feels guilt about balancing work, parenting, and other relationships. How does she deal with this throughout the book?